THICKER THAN WATER

AVERY TIMMONS

WILD INK PUBLISHING

Wild Ink Publishing

A Wild Ink Publishing Original

Cover Design by Ria Designs

This is a work of fiction. Names, characters, places, and incidents are either the product of the author's imagination or used fictitiously. Any resemblance to actual events, locales, or persons, living or dead, is purely coincidental.

*For my family—for supporting my love of writing.
And for my Chicago friends—had I not found my place with
you, Lydia couldn't have found her place, either.*

CHAPTER ONE

ONE THING they don't cover in freshman orientation is how to hide you're a vampire when you have a vampire-obsessed roommate.

Yet, here I am.

Well, okay, let me rephrase.

I'm only *half* vampire. I don't burn to death in the sunlight or get stuck outside houses without an invitation or whatever "real" vampires do. I still have blood that runs through my veins and a reflection and a need for food and water to survive. So, unless someone is specifically looking for a vampire—which isn't likely because your average person doesn't believe they even exist—I like to think it's hard, if not impossible, to tell I'm not totally human.

But I do have the traditional vampire *thirst*, which sucks.

No pun intended.

And I still need to be careful, considering my roommate is vampire-mega-fan Imani Davis.

She's the personified version of all the exclamation points and smiley faces she used in her initial Instagram DMs to me, back when she sought me out over the summer to introduce herself as my roommate after we were randomly assigned to each other. She made it known in the very first message that she's a Libra, from California, and there are few things she loves more than her boyfriend, except for vampire media—but "he knows, so it's totally okay."

And despite being slightly terrified she's going to figure me out, I like her so far.

Now, as my dad and I move the last of my boxes into the room, she's sitting crisscross on the floor in the middle of her fluffy, pale-pink rug on her side, rifling through one of her boxes as she tells him about what it's like where she's from. Dad listens attentively, leaning back against the wall next to my open closet door with his arms crossed over his chest. He nods along as if he knows what she's talking about, even though I know for a fact he hasn't left the state for at least twenty years.

Because twenty years ago, he married my mom only a week after their high school graduation. Nineteen years ago, she got knocked up by a stranger, letting Dad believe I was his, until eighteen years ago, when she died giving birth to me.

At least, that's what we've pieced together.

And for the last eighteen years, Dad has been preoccupied by raising his non-biological daughter, who quickly proved to be more troublesome than a normal, human child. So, even though I know he's stressed out of his mind by the idea of sending me off into downtown Chicago for college, I'm really doing both him and myself a favor.

"What's your Zodiac sign, Mr. Ross?" I hear Imani ask.

I purse my lips together tightly, trying to suppress a smile. One of my favorite things about my dad is that he's been forced to believe vampires exist, but astrology is where he draws the line.

He starts to say that he doesn't know, but that his birthday is in June. I just interrupt him and tell her he's a Gemini, to which she exclaims that she *loves* Geminis and how her brothers are Geminis.

After another minute of her rattling on about her brothers and how much she misses them, despite having just moved in herself earlier this morning, Dad smiles somewhat apologetically and tells her he has to go because he wants to beat the rush hour traffic home. Which I'm sure is true, but I'm also sure he's realized the same thing I have: if he gets her started on another topic, he'll never get out of here.

"I'll walk you down, Dad," I say, even though I don't really want to. I know the minute that Imani—or anyone else, for that matter—is out of earshot, he's going to (once again) ask me if I'm sure about this, and that I can always go to community college so I can stay home and avoid being a menace to society.

Even if he doesn't word it exactly like that.

"So nice meeting you, Mr. Ross! I'll see you in a bit, Lydia. Don't forget your ID so you can get back in." She points to my brand new ID card, which is sitting on top of my bookshelf. As I grab it, I grimace: it displays my full name, *Lydia May Ross*, right next to a horrific picture of me offering an obviously forced, tight-lipped smile. I offer Imani a more genuine smile over my shoulder before ushering Dad out of my room and down the hall, back to the elevators.

After the elevator doors slide shut and we descend a few floors, a *ding* accompanying each floor we pass, Dad says, right on cue, "Are you sure about this, Lydia? If you change your mind, there's always JJC. The drive isn't bad—"

"Dad."

The one word makes him go silent, but I don't continue when the elevator doors slide open to the first floor. A short, tanned boy with circular glasses is waiting to get on, clutching the handle of a suitcase. His curly black hair covers his eyes when he lowers his head, avoiding eye contact, and I can't help but notice how distractingly good his blood smells. Standing next to him is a short, curvy woman who is unmistakably his mother. They wait until Dad and I step out, and from the corner of my eye, I watch the woman practically push her son into the elevator. It doesn't seem like he's exactly happy to be here, or that *she's* happy to be here with *him*.

Once they're gone, I stop with Dad by the open double doors that lead back to the parking lot. It's packed, filled with cars and vans with trunks and doors open as other families begin to unpack and pile their students' belongings into the big, rolling cardboard boxes they supplied for us. I turn back to Dad, his stress clear in his lowered brows and set jaw.

"I'll be fine, really," I reassure him, lowering my voice, even though no one else is around, except for the security guards around the corner. I figure we should speed through this conversation, though, before the parking lot families start to make their way into the doors beside us. "I want to do this. And I know what I need and when I need it. I'll be fine, I swear."

That painfully conflicted look remains on his face as he sighs, shoving his hands in the pockets of his jeans. I hadn't noticed when we left that he wore his paint jeans, faded splotches of color still on the knees from when we repainted the house almost ten years ago. The colors that he admitted, years later, reminded him too much of Mom, so he said *forget it* and decided to redo the whole house.

And that's why I think he should be *glad* to finally be getting rid of me, considering I've seen the pictures. I look exactly like her when she was my age, when she married Dad. He should be relieved to be getting rid of the daily reminder of her. Of her betrayal.

And of what killed her.

"I worry about you, Lydia."

"I know," I say, trying to hide my exasperation, but it

bleeds into my tone. "But, I mean, we've talked about this. I haven't had a slip in over ten years, and I don't *want* to have a slip. I'm here because I wanna be... normal."

The word hangs in the air between us, and I know by the barely noticeable purse of Dad's lips that he's thinking the same thing I'm thinking: I'll never *be* normal—I'll just have to get really good at faking it—which is difficult when I have to find means to stock up on blood every week or so, or when I cringe at too-loud sounds other people can't hear, or when my heightened senses make large gatherings way too over-whelming way too soon. Even now, the sounds of the city roar in my ears: sirens, horns, car doors being slammed, laughter from the parking lot. And heartbeats. So many heartbeats.

But this is my chance to fake it. To ignore it, as much as possible.

"If it makes you feel better, I'll—"

I pause before I finish my sentence. I'll *what*? Keep him updated? Send him daily texts that say, *Hey, Dad, didn't kill anyone today! Are you proud?*

I cross my arms over my chest, letting out a deep breath. Dad just looks at me, waiting for me to finish my sentence, his hazel eyes searching my face. I know what *I* see, but I can't help but wonder what exactly he sees when he looks at me, besides the carbon copy of his dead wife—with her chocolate brown hair, wide blue eyes, and small, slightly curved nose— but with the added bonus of the slightly too-pale skin, sharp planes of my face, and the need for blood that reminds him of her infidelity.

But this is going to be good for both of us.

And I need him to see that.

"If there's an emergency I really can't handle on my own, I'll call. But I'll be fine. I promise."

He doesn't believe me. I can tell by the way he nods only once, somewhat stiffly, before pulling me into a hug, and by his deep exhale once I'm in his arms. I breathe in the comforting, earthy scent of his cologne, which helps mask the just-as-familiar-but-less-comforting scent of his blood.

"The plan is to see you at Thanksgiving, then?" he asks casually once we pull back from each other, but he keeps his hands on my forearms, holding me firmly at arms-length, as if he's scared to release me into the world.

If I *really* try and get into his perspective, I suppose it's only fair. While I don't remember the incidents myself, he's reminded me plenty of times over the years how before we figured out what I was, between doctors' appointments and hospital stays, he found me with my fangs in my own arm, so desperate for blood my vampire half took over my senses.

And another time, with my fangs in our dog.

Granted, I was young. I wasn't even school age yet. At that point, he just thought I was severely troubled to the point where I'd try to eat a dog.

But, we haven't had a pet since.

Now, I crack a smile. A real one, with teeth, which only Dad has ever gotten to see, thanks to my pointed, slightly-longer-than-normal canines I prefer to keep hidden.

In fact, about ten years ago, he was the one who first pointed out they were visible when I smiled, and the one to suggest that maybe I shouldn't smile with my teeth anymore.

"If I last that long," I say, in a weak attempt to lighten the mood.

Dad doesn't try to hide his scowl as he finally drops his hands from my arms. "Lydia—"

"It was a *joke*," I insist. He still doesn't look amused. "But I really should go. Lots of unpacking and totally human stuff to do. Like talking about Zodiac signs and *Twilight* and about how none of that stuff is real at all with Imani. Okay?"

He sighs—*again*—and shakes his head, running a hand

through his thinning hair. As much as I try to joke about it all, I really just wish he'd trust me.

"Okay," he says, not even bothering to sound like he's *actually* okay with it.

"Have a safe drive home." I'm already backing toward the elevator, taking one slow step at a time. I peek around him, out the back doors, to see one of the families—a short blonde girl with her tall, skinny brunette dad—starting to push their rolling box toward us. Perfect timing.

"I will," he replies, and *finally*, after looking like the epitome of stress all day, he lets the corner of his mouth quirk up in a small, barely-there smile that doesn't quite reach his eyes. But I'll take it. "Be safe, kid."

"I will." I wait until he turns around and walks out of the double doors before turning toward the elevators myself, hoping to get on one alone before I have to squeeze in with the girl, her dad, and their enormous box of stuff. But as I turn, a weird feeling settles over me at the idea that I *am* alone. Not *alone* alone, obviously, considering I have Imani—who will no doubt make me feel not extremely-not-alone—and a building full of God knows however many other people to worry about, but there's no Dad. Nobody here knows what I am. Nobody in this entire *city* knows what I am.

And it feels good. For once, *I* feel good.

I notice with surprise that somebody's holding open one of the elevators—I can't see who, but I see a large, masculine-looking hand splayed across the open door, and considering the others haven't gotten into the building yet and there's nobody else waiting by the front doors, he's clearly waiting for me.

I do an awkward, half-jog into the elevator, feeling guilty he was waiting for at *least* a minute or longer. I must have been so occupied with trying to shoo Dad away I didn't sense him enter through the set of doors behind us or hear the elevator arrive.

Once I'm inside, I mutter a quiet, embarrassed "thank you" as I reach forward to press the little silver button that says *eight*, but it's already pressed.

It's only then, as I let my hand drop awkwardly back to my side, that I risk a glance up at my companion.

The boy is already looking at me, but I fight the urge to instinctively tear my eyes away from him as we make eye contact. His eyes are brown—a light brown that any author would probably describe as caramel-colored, framed by unfairly long eyelashes. His hair is also brown, but darker, and on the shaggier side, sticking up in places as if he just rolled out of bed or ran his hands through it. And he's tall—probably around six feet or six feet one. Muscular, which I can tell, thanks to the t-shirt that hugs his biceps: an athlete, probably. He smells good, too, both cologne-wise and blood-wise.

In short, he's good-looking.

"Let me guess," he says, his voice not too low or too high, but somewhere right in the middle, and it suits him well. A smile plays on his full lips. "You're a freshman?"

"What makes you think that?" I ask. I can't remember the last time I held eye contact with someone this long who wasn't Dad. I fiddle with a string on the hem of my t-shirt as we slowly rise, passing floors four, five, and six.

He smiles fully now, displaying a mouthful of perfectly straight teeth, including perfectly normal canines.

"Not that I was watching you or anything, but your dad seemed a little stressed at the idea of leaving you. Which makes me think that maybe you're the first one in your family to go to college, too."

I raise my eyebrows at him. He continues to grin as we pass the seventh floor, never once breaking eye contact.

"Interesting analysis," I say, hoping deep down that if he

continues to further analyze me, he doesn't come to the conclusion that Dad was stressed to leave me not because I'm the first (and only) one in my family to go to college, but that I'm part-vampire, and that he's scared I'll neglect my needs and attack someone.

I suppose I'll let this boy believe he's completely right and that there's definitely not anything weird going on.

"And you'd be correct," I add, finally allowing myself to look away just as the elevator *dings* at the eighth floor, the doors sliding open with a groan. The boy holds out his hand toward the door, gesturing for me to leave first. I step out, looking down the cream-colored hallway with its gray carpets, not remembering which way I went when I first got here. There's a sign directly in front of me on the wall, indicating which apartment numbers are which way, but I hesitate just a little too long, because he asks:

"Which room number are you?"

I turn around to see he's still standing right behind me, smiling ever so slightly, even though I had been expecting him to abandon me by this point. He's closer now than he was in the elevator, too, and he seems even taller now that he's closer, and I'm even more nervous. Especially since I can hear his heartbeat, still nice and steady as it was in the elevator, unlike the erratic thumping of my own.

"First, you watch me and try and figure out my life, and now you want my room number?" I ask.

Oh God, should I have said that? I'm not sure where this confidence is coming from, considering I barely spoke to anyone in high school—especially not cute boys. I never got close enough to *anyone* in case they were able to figure me out, which was, admittedly, mostly due to Dad's insistence. Hell, he would've homeschooled me had he not *had* to work over forty hours a week to keep us afloat.

But as nervous as this new experience makes me, as

nervous as this new *boy* makes me, there's something kind of welcoming about him. Like a dog.

One I won't put my fangs in.

"I don't even know your name yet," I remind him.

He laughs, and my heart swells a little. When was the last time I was able to make someone laugh? When was the last time I had the courage to make a *joke* to someone who wasn't Dad? I smile up at this boy, making sure to keep my lips pressed together. Maybe Chicago-Lydia really *is* a brand-new Lydia.

"Touché," he says, holding out his right hand. "I'm Jake Hampton. Room eight-twenty-nine."

I reach out, taking his significantly larger and much warmer hand, and shake it firmly.

"Lydia Ross. Room eight-twenty-eight."

Jake pulls his hand away from mine, shoving it back into the front pocket of his jeans. He grins, tilting his head to his right, indicating that's the way to my room. Well, *our* rooms, I suppose, considering he's eight-twenty-nine. Does that mean this good-looking stranger will be either right next door or right across the hall?

Oh, shit. I hope the first cute boy I meet in college isn't Imani's boyfriend, who she told me is going to be living across the hall.

But if he recognizes my room number, he doesn't make any indication of it. He just steps closer to me to make sure he's out of the way as one of the elevators opens and a group of three girls step out. They glance at us, eyes lingering on Jake, before walking the other way down the hallway, away from the direction of our rooms. Their quick heartbeats and giggles and whispers of "He's *cute*" still ring loud in my ears even after they're long out of my sight.

"Nice to meet you, Lydia Ross," is all Jake says, a contagious ease lighting up his eyes. "Looks like we're gonna be neighbors."

CHAPTER TWO

I LEARN three more things about Jake Hampton in the next five minutes:

1. He knows Imani.
2. He knows I'm rooming with Imani.
3. He's not Imani's boyfriend.

I feel an odd sense of relief upon learning that last fact, though I push it away almost as soon as it surfaces. Why should I care about that? I shouldn't care about that. I'm here to act like a normal human and to take a shot at a normal, human life and make normal, human friends. A *boyfriend* is definitely crossing the line.

And I don't even know him. He could be a serial killer for all I know. A nice, good-looking serial killer. Why am I suddenly fantasizing about him anyway? Because he *smiled* at me?

Yep, that's exactly why.

But I'd never be able to hide what I am from a boyfriend. Which is why I've never had one. Or friends, for that matter.

If I really do make friends, how will I hide it from them? How will I hide it from Imani, who I'm *living* with?

My stomach churns, but I don't have time to focus on it. I need to be present, in the moment, because Jake has stopped us in front of his now-open door, right across the hall from mine, where Imani is also standing, her arms wrapped around the torso of—

Wow.

He looks like the mysterious, bad boy who would be the main love interest in almost any teen romance, and while that's not really my type, anyone could see he's ridiculously attractive.

He's a few inches shorter than Jake, which still looks tall next to Imani, and dressed in a black t-shirt and dark blue jeans, a rip in one knee. His hair is thick and dark and messy but in an attractive way, falling just above his shoulders. And as he leans against the doorframe, his arm slung around Imani's shoulders, I catch the scent of his shampoo, the strong sting of freshly sprayed cologne, and—as always—the underlying smell of blood.

We make eye contact as Imani handles the introductions, and as I learn his name is Tripp, I see his eyes are a dark, rich brown. The corner of his mouth tugs upward in a smirk, stubble covering his jaw and above his lips, as he greets me in a low voice with a "Hey, Lydia."

He's intimidating with the way he's looking at me, making it feel as if he's staring into my soul and trying to figure out my deepest, darkest secrets.

I might have to watch out for this one.

"What are the odds *you* two met already out of everyone in this building?" Imani says, still clutching on to Tripp as if she hasn't seen him in months. He presses an absentminded kiss to the top of her head as Jake and I watch and stand an awkward several inches apart. "And how'd you already find out she's my roommate?"

Before Jake can say anything, I pipe up, speaking for the first time, so all three of them immediately look at me. I feel myself flushing from the attention, but continue, "He asked me my room number before my name."

Tripp lets out a loud, abrupt laugh, and as Imani and Jake both laugh, too, I feel a little sense of pride. I'm on a roll, and I haven't even unpacked yet. I mean, if they think I'm funny, who cares that I'm a vampire?

"I can't deny that," Jake admits, and when he grins over at me, I'm surprised to see his cheeks are slightly pink, too.

"Keep it up, Jake, and you won't be invited to dinner," Imani mockingly warns, pointing a finger at him.

At that moment, the dark, curly-haired boy I saw earlier by the elevators passes us to my left, walking down the hall away from us, and without his mom this time. He must live on our floor; I can't help but watch the slight hunch in his shoulders as he walks, as if he's trying to become smaller than himself, trying not to be noticed. The scent of his blood floods my senses, and I feel my body almost involuntarily stiffen.

I watch him until he turns the corner to the left a little ways down the hall, and I can't see him anymore, all the while only half-listening to Imani making plans to go to dinner to celebrate moving in—and apparently, I'm invited, which feels nice.

I feel the strange urge to pull my phone out of my pocket and text my dad:

> Hey, Dad, guess what? I haven't killed anyone, I've spoken to a member of the male species that isn't you, AND I've been invited out to dinner with potential friends. See? You can trust me. I made the right choice.

Right?

"Sure," I reply to Imani when she asks me if I want to come.

"Good," she says, finally letting go of Tripp but continuing to hover close to his side. "I was gonna drag you along anyway. Babe—" she turns to Tripp, "—need help unpacking?"

Jake shakes his head, his hair flopping around.

"We *just* moved in, and you're already gonna steal him from me?"

Imani crosses her arms over her chest, her eyebrows furrowing as she looks at Jake.

"*You* had him all summer, and you're already trying to steal him from *me*?"

Tripp just grins, leaning back against the doorframe, and crossing his own arms over his chest as if this is a normal occurrence; despite the fact this, apparently, is the first time Jake and Imani have ever met in person. I caught—during Imani's quick explanation to catch me up—that Tripp and Imani have been long-distance for the last school year. Tripp was here as a freshman, and Imani was still a senior in high school, so Jake and Imani had met over FaceTime, but not face-to-face, until this moment. And honestly, I never would've guessed. It seems like they've been friends for years.

As Imani grabs Tripp's hand, she flashes a smile at me and tells me she'll see me later before disappearing through the doorway. Tripp offers me a small wave before disappearing behind her. And then, it was just me and Jake.

"I should unpack," I say, pointing awkwardly to the door of my room. When I allow myself to focus entirely on his presence, all the other sounds and smells from the accompanying rooms, all the heartbeats and blood and packing tape ripping and suitcases being unzipped are a little easier to push to the back of my mind.

I got good at tuning things out in high school. But there, even on the most overwhelming days, I got to escape home every night where I really only had the sounds and scents of Dad to worry about, since we lived in the most rural part of town. No neighbors for at least half a mile on all sides. All peace and quiet.

Here, I'll have to majorly adjust, and I have a feeling it's gonna take a while.

But I'm here. And I *want* to be here. I made the right choice.

"Same here. Sounds like I'll see you tonight, though. It was really nice meeting you, Lydia Ross."

I can't help but smile up at him. Is this an inside joke, to be called by my full name? Do I already have an inside joke with someone?

See, Dad? I already have an inside joke with the cute boy who lives across the hall from me. And I haven't even fantasized about drinking his blood once.

I can do this.

"Sounds like you will." I cross the hall, glancing over my shoulder one last time at him before scanning my ID card and pulling open the heavy door to mine and Imani's room. I pause, adding, "Jake Hampton," as an afterthought.

He disappears into his own room, but not before I catch his smile.

CHAPTER THREE

I DIDN'T REALLY REALIZE how sad my life has been until about two hours later, standing and staring at a now-fully-decorated room and realizing that, unlike Imani, I have zero pictures with friends.

I spin around, eyeing her side of the room—the pale pink comforter, the pristinely white, wrinkle-free pillowcases, the tapestry that hangs over her bed and displays the zodiac signs in a circle surrounded by little pink stars. Everything is matching, down to the pink-handled scissors in the pencil cup on her desk and the white stars on her laptop cover. Even the pictures of her on the wall above her desk are arranged in a collage-style, featuring pictures of her with girls, *lots* of pictures of her with Tripp, and pictures of her with two younger boys and a girl who share her dark skin and wide smile—her siblings, I assume.

Oh, and there's the stack of very-clearly-loved *Twilight* books sitting on the top of her bookshelf, the first book in particular looking as if it's on its last life with a nearly torn-off cover and a very, very broken-in spine. I can't begin to imagine how many times she's read it. The series is accompanied by a small stack of poetry books and other—presumably vampire—fiction.

On the other hand, my half looks like a teenage boy pointed at the first few things he saw in the store and called it a day. There's my mismatched black-and-gray comforter with my red pillowcases, the silver mini fridge next to my bed that's going to hold my supply of blood throughout the year, and the stark lack of any wall decorations or pictures, putting the depressingly hospital-white walls on display, which does nothing but remind me of my childhood.

I take one last look at Imani's side of the room. She came back after about a half hour across the hall to get unpacked herself, and is now sitting on her bed, hunched over and shuffling through a stack of *more* pictures. If she's aware I'm staring, she gives me the benefit of the doubt and doesn't call me out for it, which I appreciate.

But I have to admit, I'm jealous. Her aesthetic is clear on her side of the room, and mine...

The only thing that really even feels like *me* in the entire room is the bookshelf that's already almost full. I realize now I probably went a little overboard with the book-packing, but it's comforting even just looking at them in my otherwise disappointing room, even if I don't read them.

And *that's* something I'm never going to admit out loud.

Four short raps on our door startle me out of my thoughts. I glance at Imani, but because I'm the one already standing and my side of the room is closest to the door, I take it upon myself to answer it, even though it's probably for her.

I peek through the little peephole and see Jake on the other side. Which makes sense, considering we are getting dinner tonight, but he's also—I pull my phone out of my pocket to check the time—an hour and a half early.

He grins when I pull open the door, and I can't help but offer him a close-lipped smile in return—his smile is contagious and lights up his whole face.

"Hey, Lydia," he says, running a hand through his already mussed-up hair. "I know I'm way early. I just wanted to check out your guys' room, if that's cool with you?"

Of course he comes *now*, before I have the chance to go to some of the various stores downtown and splurge on decorations to try and fill the void. But I can't tell him no, that I'm embarrassed, so I step aside, holding the door for him. I follow him down the little hallway that separates our actual room from the door, and stop when he pauses to look around. I cringe inwardly, wishing he'd look away from my side of the room. It looks even worse compared to Imani's now that I have a minute away and came back.

"So, you complain about me being over at your place only to come bother me in my room?" Imani asks, but the smile on her face makes it clear she's teasing. She's abandoned her pictures and is now lying back on her bed, her phone on her stomach, her blue t-shirt rising up a little to show a sliver of skin between the hem and her jean shorts.

Jake walks further into the room, looking to his right at our bookshelves, and the small stand that sits between them holding the TV Imani brought for us to share since our room didn't come with one. As his gaze swings around, I mentally beg him not to open my mini fridge. I don't know why he *would*, but some people are nosey, I guess. Jake doesn't seem like that type of person, though, and the blood Dad stocked for me from the butcher is purposefully disguised in water bottles for:

1. Easier consumption and

2. Just in case someone opens my mini fridge

I'd rather not have to address it at all or use Dad's lie and say it's made specially for medical reasons or something or other. I'd rather completely ignore it. Thankfully, Jake turns back to my bookshelf, and the tightness in my chest eases a bit.

"I didn't come to bother you," he replies to Imani, picking up one of the books off the top of my bookshelf I hadn't put away yet, turning it over in his hands. "I came to bother Lydia." He smiles at me over his shoulder, and I smile back, unsure of what to do with this attention. He's just teasing, too, of course. We know nothing about each other.

Though it would be a nice feeling if he came here for me.

I'll take friends in any way I can get them. But it'd feel nice to be Lydia and be wanted as Lydia, instead of, *oh, here's Imani and her roommate Lydia.*

There's something sly and mischievous in the smile Imani gives me as Jake lays the book back where it was.

"You have a lot of books," he says, oblivious to the look Imani is giving me, and runs his fingers over the spines of the books on the shelf. "What's your major, anyway? I didn't get a chance to ask earlier."

He continues to look at my books as I answer, English, which was a no-brainer. I watch as the corner of his mouth tugs upward, and he looks over at me, his head cocked slightly.

"I see it," he says. "Makes sense. I'm in business. So's Tripp. But I'm really just here to play football."

Football. I recognized he has an athlete's body, and while I know next to nothing about football, it makes sense as I look at his wide shoulders and muscular frame, that makes it clear he works out.

"That means, get ready to go to football games, Lydia," Imani calls from her bed, not looking up from her phone.

"Sure," I respond, looking at Jake. "I can't promise I'll understand anything that's going on, though."

Jake's smile only grows. "That'll put you 'n Aiden in the

same boat. Just cheer when Imani and Tripp do, and you'll be fine. He may not look it, but Tripp's a football fanatic, and I've heard Imani's the same."

Out of the corner of my eye, I see Imani sit up so quickly her phone flies from her hands and onto the floor, missing her fuzzy, pale-pink rug by an inch and landing facedown on the hardwood floor. After letting loose a string of curses—which I can't say I was expecting from her—while she leans over the side of her bed to pick it up, she asks Jake, "Aiden! I can't *wait* to meet him in person. When's he coming?"

Aiden?

He's clearly pretty special if just a mention of his name causes Imani to practically throw her phone to the floor.

As if hearing my internal questioning, Jake explains, "He's our third roommate. I think the two of you will get along. You guys seem really alike."

Imani and Jake get sidetracked in conversation as Imani goes back to Jake's comment about football and asks him about the season; I think about this unknown Aiden character. I suppose it's reassuring if they clearly like him so much and think we're alike.

But things almost seem too good to be true. It's not *this* easy to make friends, is it? Is this what I've been missing out on all these years because of Dad's helicopter parenting?

Not that I'm blaming Dad.

Well, okay, I'm kind of blaming Dad.

Then again, I haven't even been here for a full day yet. What if, when they actually get to know me, they don't like me? What if I become the pity friend? What if I do just become *ugh, here's Imani's roommate again*. What if—

"That sound okay with you, Lydia?"

I turn toward Imani, lifting my eyebrows. "Hm?"

Great. I'm getting too much in my head already and

missing things that they're saying, and now they're going to think I'm spacey and weird and—

"We're talking about leaving now, goin' to Devil Dawgs. It's down the street, and they've got good milkshakes," Jake says. "It's one of our favorite places to go. Is that cool with you?"

"Oh, yeah," I say, drumming my fingers on the sides of my thighs. "That sounds good."

Jake's lips part in a smile. "Awesome. I'll go get Tripp and then we'll head out."

The second that he leaves, the heavy door closing with a thud behind him, Imani hops off her bed, smiling wide.

"He's so into you."

"What?"

She grins even wider, grabbing a small black purse off the floor at the end of her bed and tucking her phone and ID into the biggest pocket.

"I know I just met him in person for the first time today, technically, but listen, I *saw* the way he looks at you. He clearly thinks you're pretty, and he obviously *did* only come over here as an excuse to see you. He doesn't like me *that* much." She puts the purse strap over her shoulder before clapping her hands together excitedly. "It's so cute. What do *you* think of him?"

I pause. I have a feeling if I admit that, sure, he's cute, and from what I've seen in the not-even-twenty-four hours I've been here, he seems like a nice guy, that Imani will try her hardest to set us up. I'm sure she's thinking it'd be perfect: her roommate with her boyfriend's roommate/best friend. But at the same time, I mean, I can't really say, *well, I can't because even though he's nice and attractive, I have an incredibly huge secret about my existence I would have to hide from him, and you, for that matter, so just forget I said anything. I'm just not looking for a relationship right now.*

But Imani's waiting for an answer, so I say, "He's cute," and she squeals.

She hooks her arm through mine and, as she drags me over to the door to leave, she tells me how cute we'd be together and how he's really sweet, and I start to wonder what I just got myself into.

CHAPTER FOUR

DEVIL DAWGS IS tiny and crowded, but we find a table after getting our food. Me and Jake are on one side while Tripp and Imani sit as close as their chairs will allow them, his arm resting on the back of hers.

I settle on the chicken tenders with fries and a strawberry milkshake. I mostly stay quiet while the others start to talk about what classes they're taking, Tripp and Jake throwing out names of buildings and professors so fast I have trouble following along. And the noise isn't helping: people talking over one another and thumping hearts and the heavy smell of fries and grease and, of course, blood. This is way more than the small mom-and-pop place Dad and I used to go to when neither of us felt like making dinner.

"I'm taking geology," Jake says, "for my science gen ed. It was the only one that sounded kinda interesting that wasn't full."

"What time?" I ask. I'm taking geology, too. It was one of the few sciences available I thought wouldn't make me want to bash my head against a wall, cry, or both at the same time.

"Oh, uh, Mondays and Wednesdays at like, eleven, I think."

I feel a little spark of relief; at least I'll have a familiar face in one of my classes.

"Me too," I say, and Jake's face splits into a grin. I can feel Imani's eyes on us, and I know she's probably mentally cheering.

"I'm not ready for classes," Tripp sighs. "Or work. Any of it. I just wanna be rich and run around the city with no responsibilities."

"I don't know if I'm gonna get a job right away, so that I can focus on classes," Imani adds, absentmindedly circling her straw in her own strawberry milkshake. "I have enough in savings to last for a little while, at least."

I pick at my fries. To be honest, I hadn't thought about a job, which I realize now is stupid of me because I can't ask Dad for money forever, and getting a job wasn't something I did in high school—because Dad. He wasn't super keen on me being out of the house—or, I guess, out of his *sight*—more often than absolutely necessary.

Dear God, he didn't let me do anything.

I feel bad as soon as I think it, but it's true, and it's only further confirmed as I listen to Tripp and Jake and Imani talk about things like jobs or sports or eventually, the beach, which they suggest we go to when their friend Aiden gets here. I've never had a job, I've never played a sport, and I've never even been to the beach. I've never been to a sleepover (which, *technically*, I guess I get to cross off the list tonight, so hooray for me), I've never been to a birthday party, I've never even had someone to call a friend, unless you count my own father or the dog I killed when I was a toddler.

Do I lie about these things, so they think I'm normal?

Or do I tell them the truth, since technically, it wasn't my fault, since I wasn't allowed to?

No—they'd ask why.

I was in and out of hospitals a lot when I was younger, I could tell them, because that part is true. But, again, I'm sure they'd ask why. And I can't exactly say I was so sickly and weak like I was malnourished, despite a perfectly rounded, healthy, human diet. Because then I'd have to say the idea that maybe I wasn't completely human was sparked through books, since all I had the energy for those days was reading, and Dad was so desperate for a cure that he decided to humor me and buy me blood so I'd stop trying to tear into my own skin.

It was to keep me safe, I could say.

No—Dad kept me isolated to keep *others* safe.

From me.

That sense of dread fills me, twisting my stomach into knots as my chest tightens, squeezing around my heart. Maybe he was right. What was I thinking coming here, trying to make friends, letting myself entertain the idea even for a *second* that a boy *might* be interested in me? What if something does happen, and I do hurt someone? What if I hurt one of *them*, these people who have already been so nice and welcoming?

I take a bite of my last chicken tender, chewing slowly as I stare at the white-and-red-checkered paper that lines Tripp's basket of fries. And what if they get bored with me? What if I have nothing to offer? Imani and Jake each bring an excited sort of chatterbox energy that lightens the mood, and Tripp balances that out with his sarcastic, somewhat moody energy, but I've barely spoken. Should I be talking more? But what should I say? I don't know what to say. What do people say? What are they talking about? I—

"What about you, Lydia? Any brothers or sisters?" Jake asks.

I take a sip of my milkshake to wash down the chicken tender, desperately wishing I had water, before answering, trying to alternate my gaze between all three of them.

"Uh, no," I say. "Um, my, uh, mom died when I was born, and my dad hasn't remarried or anything."

There's a beat of silence, and I worry I made things awkward, until Tripp says, "Damn. That sucks."

"Tripp," Imani scolds him, but I can't help but smile hesitantly, even as she turns to me and says, "I'm sorry about him, Lydia. And about your mom. I had no idea."

I shrug, honestly preferring Tripp's response. "It's okay. I never knew her."

Besides the fact that if she'd never cheated, maybe her and Dad would be happy with some normal daughter. Instead of Dad being stuck with me, likely never to remarry because who in their right mind would take on the burden of, well, me? Not that he'll have to worry about that anymore, now that I'm an adult and plan to start living my own life. He's still young, after all; he can start over, have another, normal kid.

"I know how you feel," Tripp pipes up again, swirling one of his fries around in his ketchup until there's far more ketchup than fry. "My parents are dead to *me*, so."

"*Tripp.*"

I look over at Jake, who offers me a sheepish smile and a shrug, and I just smile back. I'd rather have whatever this is than sympathy for the death of someone who I never met and don't particularly care about.

Imani asks Tripp to move so she can go to the bathroom, and despite Tripp's grin as he adjusts back into his seat, there's something in his eyes that tells me that whatever is going on in his life, it actually hurts him beyond the jokes.

Which I understand more than he'll ever know.

"She hates when I do that," he explains, eyes locked on mine. "We have very different senses of humor."

I shrug at him, feeling Jake's eyes still on me from next to me.

"Sometimes joking about it makes things easier," I say.

The corners of Tripp's mouth turn up in a smile that seems to be considerably more genuine, and even though he doesn't say anything, mostly because Imani arrives back at the table and asks him to move again so she can sit, the look in his eyes tells me we're thinking the same thing. That maybe, we're more alike than we think.

CHAPTER FIVE

Dinner goes a little better after that, surprisingly. They ask me more questions about myself. Most I have to dance around, offering partial truths, but some I can tell the truth. Like, when they ask me when my birthday is, and I can confidently tell them February seventeenth.

Imani gets excited about that and tells me she *loves* Aquariuses.

She seems to love a lot of things, and honestly, I appreciate that. It's refreshing.

But now, it's hours later, and I don't know if she would ever talk to me again if she opened her eyes right now and caught me watching her sleep, but I can't help it.

Nights at home were, yes, filled with Dad's coughs and groans and steady heartbeats from down the hallway, but also crickets and branches creaking in the wind and occasionally the clicking of claws on the driveway when an animal decides to visit—sounds that were more white noise than anything.

But here, there's Imani. Right across the room from me. And there're the people on the other side of the wall by my head. And the people on the other side of the wall. And the city beyond the windows. Heartbeats upon heartbeats, some slow and steady, like Imani, some fast—*too* fast for two in the morning. And there's blood and breathing and creaking and laughter and sirens and honking and so.

Much.

Noise.

I have to remind myself that school hasn't even started, and not everyone has even moved in yet, so it's not even as bad as it's going to be. But I'll tune it out. I'll learn how to tune it out, like I did throughout high school, when I had to worry about sweaty boys with excessive amounts of Axe body spray and overly-perfumed girls who would text under their desks during classes, their acrylic nails tapping against the screen.

It's just twenty-four-seven now, instead of only eight hours a day.

I roll over onto my stomach, shoving my face into my silk pillowcase. I try to focus inward, which usually helps. I focus on my own heartbeat, my own breaths, and I count them, curling my hands into loose fists at my sides just to feel the sensation of my short, bitten nails scraping against my palms. I try to think about today, about hugging Dad, Jake smiling at me in the elevator, Tripp staring me down as if he could see into my soul, and how they've pretty much already decided they're adopting me into their friend group, which was the last thing I expected of my first day. I try focusing on *anything* other than *everything* else.

But it doesn't work.

I've given up hope when I see it's 3:07.

It's not like this hasn't happened before, even back home. It's happened plenty. In all the old lore and even modern stories, vampires don't sleep, so I can only wonder if my frequent insomnia is something more biological than I think.

But I guess I'll never know for sure, unless I happen to stumble upon a vampire, which doesn't seem likely.

I get out of bed, padding quietly across the room to where my shoes sit at the end of my bed. I don't know if Imani is a light sleeper or not, but the last thing I want is to wake her up the first night we're here and have her wonder why I'm leaving at three in the morning. I suppose insomnia is a solid enough excuse, but I'd rather avoid that chat altogether, or at least avoid it for as long as possible. So, as quietly as I can, grabbing my phone and key card on the way out so that I don't have to wake her to let me back into the room, I sneak out of the room, closing the door gently behind me so it doesn't slam.

I walk down the hall, unsure of where I'm going, past door after door after door, until I reach a room that appears to be some sort of hangout lounge. The lights flicker on automatically as soon as I take a few steps into the room. There're awkwardly-shaped stools and chairs, all either bright orange or lime green. It's a pretty big room, too, and the wall directly across from me is all window, putting the city lights on full display.

I walk over to the windows, sitting down sideways on the ledge that juts out—just enough room to sit on. I stretch my right leg out on the ledge as I lean back on my hands, looking at all the different colored lights coming from windows: blue and green and red and white and yellow, stretching on further than I can see, despite my night vision being better than most. It's beautiful, really. But then I hear it, over the rest of the noise: one heartbeat, louder than all the others, growing closer and closer. I start to push myself up from the ledge, not wanting to sit in here with some stranger—especially not at three in the morning. I stand, turn around, and find myself face-to-face with Tripp, who stops abruptly in the doorway, the corner of his mouth pulling up in a somewhat sheepish smirk. He's dressed in navy blue sweatpants and a black t-shirt, his feet covered by nothing except for black socks.

"Couldn't sleep either?"

I shake my head as he walks into the room, straddling one of the orange stools, and I take that as my cue to lower myself back down to the ledge. While Tripp *is* still a stranger, and while he makes me a little nervous, I don't want to just bolt from the room.

Last thing I need is him telling Imani or Jake I'm a weirdo.

"No," I admit, deciding to be partially truthful with my excuse. "It's noisier here than it is back home. It'll be an adjustment."

Tripp nods slowly like he understands, eyes fixed on me as if he's trying to stare into my soul.

"Imani said you come from a small town, right?"

I nod, rubbing my hands over my arms.

"Makes sense then. Me too." He leans forward, resting his forearms on his knees.

"Did you and Imani grow up in the same town, then?" I ask, trying to remember all the information about how everyone knows each other that Imani dumped on me today —or yesterday, technically, after dinner, when she also apologized about ten more times for Tripp's comments, even though I told her I don't care and that I get it, each of those ten times.

"Nah," Tripp says, sitting up and running a hand through his hair, only for it to fall back in place. "My town just didn't have a high school, so we all went to the nearest, and that just happened to be Imani's. We met in art class. We both just happened to choose it as an elective that same semester, and —" He chuckles, shaking his head to himself as he gazes past me out the window, a small smile on his face, "—it was pretty much instant. I was an idiot and didn't ask her to be my girlfriend until February, though, so it'll be four years then."

I can't help but smile at the way he talks about Imani. Earlier, around me and Jake, he seemed so laid back with her, but I can tell just how much he cares about her. It's sweet.

"Cool," I say. "That's a long time."

He nods, and I catch his smile fading slightly, even as he looks down at his hands, picking at something under one of his nails.

"Yeah," he confirms, not looking up, his dark hair slipping from behind his ears to cover either side of his face. "So what's your deal? What made you wanna come here? Besides getting a degree, obviously."

A chance at living a normal, human life even though I'm not a human.

A chance to make friends for the first time in my life with people who don't already have preconceived notions of me.

A chance to find a Lydia that's separate from the Lydia that my dad has been coddling for the last eighteen years.

"Uh," I say, picking at my nails now, too. It takes me an embarrassingly long amount of time to get the words out: "Well, I don't know. I didn't want to be *too* far from home, I guess, but far enough away where I can live without my dad breathing over my shoulder. He wanted me to go to the community college by us, and I know it was because he just wanted to watch over me. I love him, but..."

Tripp has an odd, somewhat pained expression on his face.

"I get it," he confirms, saving me from having to find the words to continue about my complicated feelings towards Dad. "Kind of. I wanted to get away, too, but for vastly different reasons. I'm sure you probably gathered that earlier." He sort of laughs, looking away after he says it, but there's also a weird kind of finality in his tone that gives me the hint he doesn't want to go into any further detail.

"Jake really likes you already, you know," he says a moment later, and I accept the subject change, perking up at the thought that someone already "really likes" me, even though I haven't even been here twenty-four hours yet.

I can practically hear my dad's voice, a warning in the back of my mind:

Don't get too close, Lydia.

But I can handle it. I need to prove to him—and myself—that I can handle this. I need this badly.

"Does he?"

Tripp nods, smiling a little. "He does. Makes sense, too, since you and Aiden seem to be really alike, and he's, like, obsessed with Aiden. He thinks you're prettier, though."

Tripp grins, and I can't help but smile back, feeling my cheeks warm at the possibility that Jake thinks I'm pretty, if Tripp is telling the truth. To think I've already caught someone's eye excites me, even if Tripp *did* just compare me to another one of their friends: the mysterious *Aiden* who everyone keeps bringing up.

"When will I get to meet this Aiden, anyway?" I ask, and after a second, I decide to add, "I need to make sure for myself I'm prettier."

I get a chuckle out of Tripp. "Two days. Well, I guess tomorrow, if we're being technical. But," he adds, "if you were Imani, you would have already searched him up on Instagram and stalked his tagged posts or whatever it is she does. She can find someone even if she doesn't know their name. It's kind of scary how good she is."

I smile, taking a slightly deeper breath and catching a stronger whiff of his blood, rich and inviting, the vein on his neck that becomes prominent whenever he smiles, coaxing me in.

I can't help but imagine how much different—how much *better*—blood would taste, coming from someone fully human, someone who wasn't me.

No.

Enough.

It's late. I'm delirious. I've been around more people for

longer than I've ever been without a break. I need to go to sleep.

"But," Tripp continues, as if he can't tell I've had a sudden spike of internal panic at letting myself fantasize about what his blood would taste like. "Picture tall, skinny, blond curls, green eyes, swoon-worthy, and that's Aiden."

A laugh escapes me, but it sounds more nervous than anything. I desperately hope Tripp can't tell my demeanor has changed as I try to get my mind off Tripp's scent and try, instead, to picture someone tall, skinny, and swoon-worthy with blond curls and green eyes.

"Sounds like you might think he's pretty, too," I say.

Tripp's grin is crooked, though it doesn't quite reach his eyes, so I force myself to look at his face instead of his veins, force myself to not inhale too deeply. It's just the new environment that's finally hitting me; after all, I was *fine* earlier.

I'm just adjusting, and maybe I'll have to feed more for the first few weeks, now that I'm going to constantly be surrounded by so many humans. That's fine. I'm fine. I'll be fine. I wanted this. I *want* this.

"Just don't tell Imani," he replies, that strange note in his voice again as he stands from the stool, and I follow his lead. I need to get back to my room and break into my blood stash, even though I didn't want to have to tonight. Because the sooner I go through it, the sooner I'm going to have to go on my own to replenish it, and that's not an errand I'm looking forward to. But I *do* need it tonight, I can tell.

It starts with the craving, building low in the pit of my stomach, and it only gets worse and more dangerous from there. Not that I've had an incident since I was young, but still. I remember the warning signs well enough. Sometimes they'd come during high school assemblies, when I was jam-packed, shoulder to shoulder with classmates in our gym. I'd have to dart away for a quick swig of blood during the next passing period, and I could just *feel* the looks I was getting: *there goes weirdo Lydia again.*

"I'm gonna head back, I think," Tripp says, and when I agree, we leave the lounge together. Our arms brush, my cold, pale skin against his warm, tanned skin, and I pray he doesn't notice when I jerk away, abruptly crossing my arms over my chest. I also pray he doesn't notice I'm practically holding my breath the entire walk.

"Good luck getting to sleep," I say when we reach our doors, because it seems like an appropriate thing to say.

"You, too, Lydia," he says, his eyes lingering on me for a moment longer before scanning his ID card and letting himself back into his room, softly shutting the door behind him. Only then do I release a deep breath, letting myself into my own room and making a beeline for my mini fridge, stubbing my toe on the corner of my bed along the way. I kneel down in front of the fridge, gritting my teeth against the pain as I open the door, light flooding my path. Imani is still sound asleep, and I thank the lord for that as I unscrew one of my bottles, tip my head back, and drink.

I down the bottle, the blood thick and cold as it slides down my throat and coats my tongue. I rinse the bottle in the bathroom when I'm done—making sure there's no trace of anything left—wipe my mouth and climb back into bed, already feeling that side of me calming. Satisfied—for now.

I flip onto my stomach, burying my face in my pillow, reminding myself this is what I want, and I'm going to be fine, before letting myself drift off.

CHAPTER SIX

OVER BREAKFAST THE NEXT MORNING—EVEN though it takes a while and Tripp and Jake veer off subject multiple times—we make plans to spend the day exploring the city.

To start off the tour, we visit the Bean. As we walk, I can't help but stare in awe at the buildings, letting the sights and sounds of the city wash over me, no matter how much of a headache they cause.

The Bean itself is interesting enough, but there's only so long I can stare at my warped reflection before I'm ready to move on to the next thing; I can't fathom why it's such a talked-about attraction. I think Jake notices this because, as I'm looking at myself, he sidles up to me.

"How is it?" he asks. "Does it live up to all of its glory?"

The corner of my mouth twitches, fighting back a smile. "Eh. It's okay."

Imani and Tripp are huddled together as Imani takes pictures of them in the reflection. There's something about their casual intimacy—and even just the way they look at each other—that only people who have been together for quite some time could have, and I find myself blushing as I tear my eyes away from them. Obviously, I've always had way too many problems to really think about having a boyfriend, but as a romance book lover, I'd like the opportunity to, one day, have a love like that.

But, will I? *Can* someone love someone like me when they aren't forced to, like Dad?

"What's something *you* wanna see?" Jake asks, and I'm so caught up in myself that it takes me a second to register his question. But, he continues, "If you could go anywhere right now, where would you go? Where's your go-to place?"

I shrug again, knowing my answer and knowing it's not as interesting or unique as the Bean or Navy Pier. But of course, just my luck, Jake doesn't take my shrug as an answer. I can't help but admire his persistence. And there's something in the way he looks at me that makes me admit, "A bookstore. Any bookstore, I guess."

He smiles at me. "I shoulda guessed. That's easy enough. There's a bunch in the city. Aiden works at one, too. Maybe when he gets here and starts up at work again—" There's a slight pause in his sentence, and I swear his cheeks redden and his heartbeat picks up— "I can show you."

"Sure," I say. "I'd like that."

He grins in that boyish way of his. I wonder if maybe Imani's right about his interest in me, but then again, what else do I have to base things off of? The only other two people I've seen him interact with are his best friend and his best friend's girlfriend. What about when classes start? When other girls start coming into the picture?

Even so, it's extremely tempting to sit here and think about what it'd be like if he reached over a few inches and held my hand. I've never held anyone's hand besides Dad's, let alone in a romantic sense.

Speaking of Dad—I should text him. He's probably lost

half his head of hair worrying about whether or not I've attacked someone already—myself included.

But then again, I'm here to be independent, aren't I? To *not* have him breathing down my neck, waiting for an update every five minutes about how I'm feeling, despite me having a feeding schedule for the last decade or so?

My hand lingers on my back pocket where my phone rests, but as Jake and I walk over to Imani and Tripp, I pull my hand away. I'm here. I'm fine. He doesn't need to worry about me anymore.

Things will be better for him once he realizes that.

After we decide we're done with the Bean, Jake leads the way east, toward the lake. As we walk, all in a line, Imani says,

"Did you guys know Chicago was actually ranked the second-best city for vampires?"

I stiffen, my heart climbing to my throat.

"So, *that's* why you came here, huh?" Tripp asks, his tone teasing.

"No, babe. It was all *you*, of course," Imani teases right back, nudging his shoulder. I try to force some sort of smile, but I probably just look like I'm in pain. "But, yeah. So, hey, whenever we decide to go out at night, just keep that in mind. You never know who you might be talking to. Isn't that *so* cool?"

Tripp snorts. "You really think if I run into a vampire it's gonna strike up a conversation with me instead of just sinking its teeth into my neck?"

"You act like they're uncivilized."

"No," Tripp says without missing a beat, "I'm acting like they're not real. Because they're not."

Imani tsks. And next thing I know, she's snaking her arm through mine, pulling me close. I feel my cheeks heating up. *Please, please don't bring me into this.*

"You're a reader, Lydia. What do you think? Do you *really* think humans are the only beings that exist?"

Any sort of answer gets caught in my throat and burns. *Yes. No. I don't know.*

"I believe in aliens," Jake chimes in, "if that counts. You know, my mom had this really weird experience once that she *swears* was aliens. She was out driving—"

Jake rattles on about his mom's alleged experience with aliens, and I can feel the tension leaving my shoulders. He doesn't have any idea he saved me—at least, for now.

CHAPTER SEVEN

ALL TALK of vampires and aliens soon ends, and I couldn't be more grateful. We end up walking all the way over to the lake and down to the museum campus until Tripp whines he's thirsty, so we find a Starbucks nearby—which I *do* admit I've never had before.

Imani and Tripp convince me to try a pink, strawberry drink that actually turns out to be pretty good, while Jake settles on an iced caramel drink of some sort. By the time we get back to our dorm, they're all sweaty—me less so, which Imani comments she's jealous about, but I can't exactly say that I think it's my vampire side helping me out, so I just laugh it off awkwardly.

Imani goes to Tripp's for the rest of the day after showering, so I have the room to myself. I finally cave and text Dad:

> me: everything's going good, i went sight-seeing with Imani, her boyfriend, and his roommate. they're all really nice. hope you're not worrying too much over there

He texts back a little too quickly, within two minutes, and

I feel a stab of guilt. He was probably waiting to hear from me but didn't want to text me first so he wouldn't seem overbearing.

Maybe I've been a little unfair to him.

> dad: Glad you're having a good time. Just make sure you're staying safe.

I reply,

> me: i am

I head to bed early, giving up reading the book I was working on after reading the same page about five times without processing anything. Maybe from my lack of sleep the night before, or all the walking today, I pass out pretty much as soon as my head hits the pillow.

I WAKE UP TO MY PHONE VIBRATING LIKE CRAZY ON my desk. I roll over and pick it up, thinking I'm getting a call or something, but no. It's just Jake and Tripp, and this mystery Aiden, completely blowing up a new group chat they've made. I open my messaging app, trying to catch up as well as I can, which is difficult considering they continue to send texts as I'm trying to read the older ones.

> jake hampton: ETA, Aiden? Close? We're up and waiting for you

> tripp daniel: Tell Papa Swanson to drive faster

> tripp daniel: Aiden

jake hampton: Aiden

tripp daniel: Don't do this to us A. We've
got coffee and your favorite creamer
up here

aiden swanson: The caramel macchiato
one?

tripp daniel: HE'S ALIVE!!

jake hampton: ETA?? AIDEN??

"They're idiots."

I look over at Imani after she speaks. Her bleary, half-lidded eyes make me suspect she was woken up by the flurry of texts too, her braids still hidden by her bonnet, and I return her smile.

Another minute later, Aiden finally responds again.

aiden swanson: We're pulling into a parking
spot. Be up in a few. Xoxo

jake hampton: Lydia and Imani if you're
reading this come over RIGHT NOW

imani davis: am i allowed to shower first??

tripp daniel: Absolutely not. This is a
monumental occasion

tripp daniel: Resident english major, did I
use that right?

me: yes tripp

I finally set my phone back on my desk and drag myself

out of bed, deciding I might as well go over and meet Aiden before Jake and Tripp inevitably break our door down to make sure we do.

I decide on a simple black t-shirt and a pair of ripped jeans before walking into the bathroom to change. Part of me is nervous because while I knew I'd be meeting Imani my first day and had time to be nervous about that, Jake and Tripp happened so suddenly I didn't have time to be nervous about them. Aiden, on the other hand, has been brought up so many times over the last two days, and I've heard *so* many times how well we're apparently going to get along, but what if we don't? What if he hates me? What if I get kicked out of the friend group because he hates me and they love him and they choose him over me, of course, and then I don't have any friends anymore?

No. That's stupid. Stop it. Act normal.

I hear noises coming from the hall as I step out of the bathroom, dressed and hair brushed and mascara on, trying to look as if I'm not overthinking every step I take. There's Tripp's voice, and Jake's, followed by a woman's voice, a loud, low, male voice, and a quieter, barely audible male voice. I hear heartbeats, and I smell new, unfamiliar blood, which I swear has an odd twinge to it, but then again, I can't really tell— especially with Imani in the room, sitting cross-legged on her bed doing her makeup, her small, circular mirror sitting in front of her.

Someone knocks on our door; I already recognize Jake's scent before I even open it. He grins at me eagerly, tilting his head, indicating to follow him. I look past him, at his open door, one of the big, rolling, moving boxes propping it open. My stomach flutters with nerves.

"C'mon, he's here with his mom and dad."

I follow Jake across the hall, squeezing through the little space between the door frame and the box, and I realize this is the first time I'm seeing the inside of their apartment. As soon as we come into sight of the living room—a small room, the far wall taken up by a huge window, a gray couch and two matching armchairs, a small, light wood coffee table, and against the opposite wall, a large TV on a light wood TV stand —three unfamiliar heads turn toward us, their eyes landing directly on me.

I assess the parents first, seeing as they're in my direct line of sight. His mother is tall, probably around five-ten or five-eleven, and she's absolutely stunning. From her wavy blonde hair and golden skin, and wide green eyes, she looks like she could easily be a model. His father is a few inches shorter than her and is the sort of handsome you'd suspect to see on a movie star, not your acquaintance's dad, with a sharp jawline, arched eyebrows, and blonde curls a few shades darker than his son's. Honestly, they're both unreal.

And their *son*. I object to anyone saying I'm prettier than Aiden, because he is, like his parents, on a different level, and I can't not stare. He's insanely tall, a good few inches taller than Jake, who I thought was tall. His skin is slightly paler than his mother's, but his blonde curls are the same shade as her hair, and his shockingly green eyes are the same as opposed to his father's brown ones.

We make eye contact, and I hear Jake introducing us, but I'm too focused on the way the corners of Aiden's full lips pull upward in a small, somewhat shy smile that's directed at me, something gentle and welcoming in his eyes that has me on the verge of melting into a puddle on the floor.

All three of them feel familiar, almost, like I should know them from somewhere, even though I know for a fact I don't.

That's when I look back at his parents, preparing to offer them a polite smile, but instead, my heart stops when I see the looks on their faces. And then everyone's suddenly distracted by Imani walking into the room, announcing her presence from behind me. Maybe I imagined it, because it was gone a second later, but I don't think I did. Because they looked confused and shocked, and I swear—I *swear*—there was disgust on Aiden's dad's face.

As if they can see right through me.

I hope nobody else can hear my heart, which is pounding as if I had just run a marathon. As Imani crosses the room to Tripp, as Jake talks to Aiden's parents about football season, as there's the overwhelming flurry of new blood and heartbeats and anxiety weighing down on me, I want to slip out of the apartment before anyone notices I'm gone.

But then I look at Aiden, whose gaze is locked on me. I brace myself, for what, I don't know. Shock? Disgust? Whatever I *thought* I saw on his parents' faces?

But we make eye contact, and I swear, as he offers me another small smile, everything becomes lighter.

CHAPTER EIGHT

Aiden's parents don't stay long, much to my relief, because the entire time they're here, they're cold and stand-offish toward me in a way that they're not toward the others, and honestly, it hurts my feelings a little. Because even though I'm okay with not being noticed or questioned, the fact they smile at Imani and Jake, and Tripp and ask them questions and not me stings.

And makes me wonder *why*.

I mean, they can't know. There's no way.

Right? It's not like *they* were vampires. I know that. I watched them smile.

The minute they're gone, the mood lightens significantly. As Aiden goes downstairs to escort them out of the building, Jake gives me a little tour of the apartment. He shows me the kitchen, which is connected to the living room by an open doorway, and is relatively bare except for a used skillet sitting on the stove. He points back down the hall we came, toward the front door, and tells me the closed doors we passed are his room and his bathroom, and then points the other direction, past the kitchen and down another little hallway, where he says sits Tripp and Aiden's rooms and their bathroom.

At that point, we end up in the living room with Imani and Tripp, and when Aiden comes back, I'm abandoned as Jake practically tackles him into a hug and kisses him on not one, but both cheeks.

I realize there's something about Aiden I like, and we haven't even had a conversation yet. He's quiet, seeming to be more of an observer like I am, because he really only speaks up when one of the others asks him something or to make a joke. Maybe that's why he feels familiar—because we do seem to be similar, at least in that regard. And he brings what seems to be a calming, level-headed presence to the group, which I appreciate.

I don't get a chance to really interact with him besides us making eye contact a few times until I get up to go to the kitchen for a drink from the fridge. I hear him behind me, quiet as can be, his socked feet almost silent against the hardwood floor, so quiet that normal human ears probably wouldn't be able to pick it up.

"How has it been so far?" he asks. I turn to look at him, still holding the fridge door open, as I try to decide which kind of pop I want. It seems like Tripp and Jake went to the store and grabbed every possible option on the shelf, but other than that, just like the rest of the kitchen, the fridge seems to be pretty empty, apart from a carton of eggs. "I don't know Imani very well yet, but I know from first-hand experience Tripp and Jake can be a handful. Especially when they're together."

He smiles softly, and I smile back, amazed at how comfortable I feel in his presence, despite us having just met. There's almost none of that usual anxiety that I've gotten used to during conversations with people I don't or hardly know—

even my worry about his parents is pushed to the back of my mind.

"It's been good," I say earnestly. "I like everyone so far."

He smiles wider, and I can't help but notice how nice his smile is, how his green eyes seem to light up.

"That's great," he says. "They've been raving about you since you got here."

I finally grab a *Mountain Dew* from the fridge, holding it out to Aiden in silent question. He thanks me, taking it, our fingers brushing against each other in the process, and I feel a spark of nervous energy flutter through me. But the minute he pulls his hand away, it's gone.

I stare at him, watching as he pops open the can. There really is just something about him I can't quite place. I feel ridiculous, now, thinking his parents could possibly know what I am; there's no way to tell on the surface, and plus, nobody even knows vampires *exist*. Maybe I just reminded them of someone they know. Maybe—maybe they knew my mom. I mean, the odds aren't good, but we're all from the same state, and I look like her.

No. I'm overthinking it. Maybe they're just assholes.

"So, um," I say, listening to the oddly rapid beating of Aiden's heart under the laughter of the others in the living room, "I hear you're from Illinois, too?"

As he answers, telling me he's from somewhere I've never heard of called Decatur, I catch a whiff of his blood, and I hope the confusion doesn't show on my face. I was too over-whelmed by his parents and the flurry of everyone trying to help him unload and my other senses earlier to notice, but there's something different about it. Different blood types have slightly different scents, as I've come to learn, but I'd think that in my eighteen years of life, I'd come across every type at least once. And this smells like none of them.

I realize Aiden is looking at me expectantly, and I definitely missed a question or something. I feel myself flush deeply as I ask him to repeat himself.

Maybe I'm not doing as good at acting normal as I thought I was.

The corner of his mouth quirks up in an easy smile, and I relax a little. "Jake said you're an English major. What do you like to read?"

Thank God. I was hoping he wasn't going to ask me about where I'm from or my family or anything about my life, really. But I can do book-talk. Easy.

"Mostly fantasy and romance, but anything fiction, really. Except for classics," I admit, and Aiden clicks his tongue and shakes his head in fake disappointment.

"*Wow.* What kind of English major are you if you don't like classics?" He grins, and I can't help but smile back, catching myself before smiling with my teeth. "I'm just teasing you. I read classics, but I'm also kinda pretentious. I work at a bookstore, too, so I gotta be in the know, y'know?"

I laugh a little at that, and Aiden's grin grows.

"Oh, yeah, Jake mentioned that. Not the pretentious part," I add, and Aiden laughs, too. It's a nice sound—quiet, but obviously genuine. I kinda like that, because it feels private, like it's meant just for me.

He starts to say something but is interrupted by Tripp shouting our names from the other room, way too loudly for the minimal distance.

Aiden scrunches his nose at me. "You think they want us in there?"

I shake my head at him. "Nah, I don't think so."

I stop next to Aiden just inside the living room where Imani and Tripp are curled up on the couch together and Jake is sitting on the floor by the coffee table, despite there being two perfectly good chairs available.

"We're talking about going to the beach this weekend,"

Jake says, looking up at us as he snaps the tab off his *Dr. Pepper* can, turning it around between his fingers. "What do you guys think?"

I wait for Aiden to agree first for some reason before I do, despite how much I want to say no. Admittedly, I've never been to a beach before. Hell, I've never even *seen* a beach except for in movies. I've never been in a pool. And I can't swim. I don't even *own* a swimsuit.

Yes, I've been submerged in water before. In my bathtub, at home.

Dad and I never did anything when I was kid, because if I wasn't in the hospital, I was too weak to do anything. And then when I got my– "diagnosis," if you will, we *really* didn't do anything. The only way I was allowed to go to school was by sending him texts that said, *yes, i fed,* after I'd slip away to the bathroom during lunchtime to sip on a bottle of blood.

The others are clearly excited about planning the beach trip, because as Aiden and I settle down into the chairs, they start talking about when's the best time to go and what we should bring for lunch and if we should get dinner after, and which beach we should even go to, because apparently, there're a few.

I just nod and agree when needed, and I notice Aiden does the same thing. At one point, I look over at him to see he's already looking at me, and instead of immediately looking away like I would do if caught staring, he just gives me a somewhat sheepish smile.

I smile back, my heart stuttering as I turn back to the conversation. Between the other heartbeats and scents in this room—not to mention all the ones from the surrounding apartments—I can't place Aiden's, despite how curious I am about it still.

But for now, I have to worry about getting a swimsuit.

And how I'm going to act like I'm not terrified to go to the beach.

I don't say anything about it—the swimsuit part, that is—until after dinner that night when Imani and I are finally alone. I don't know why it feels so embarrassing, but I feel like if I admit it, she'll somehow be able to see right through me, as if swimsuits and being a vampire are related. I mean, maybe they are. Can vampires swim? It's fire that's bad for them, right?

But of course, she's Imani. And as I'm starting to learn, Imani isn't quick to judge.

"Oh, it's no big deal! I probably wouldn't have brought one either if Tripp hadn't brought it up to me before I finished packing. I can go with you to Target or something tomorrow if you want help picking one out."

She smiles brightly, and I can't refuse. I also don't refuse the next day when she holds up an olive green bikini in my size. I eye the black one-piece suit hanging next to it, thinking I'd feel considerably more comfortable the more I was covered, but again, I can't say no—especially when she looks so eager and so sincere when she says I'll look great in it.

I think about my deathly pale skin, my body that's more door-shaped than anything, about our boyfriends *seeing* my body, me seeing *their* bodies. I'm sure my face is beet red as I finally nod and take the hanger from Imani, who clutches her hands together excitedly and tells me our next stop is the shoe section.

Dear God.

CHAPTER NINE

Saturday morning, I'm already nervous before I even start changing.

The last few days, Jake has been at football practices pretty much all day every day, and while Imani and Tripp have invited me to hang out with them whenever they go out, I've refused more often than not, unless someone else goes, too. I don't think they *mean* to do it, but every time I'm alone with them it feels like I'm third wheeling to the point where I want to run and hide.

I've also been trying to figure out a feeding schedule, making sure I drink blood often enough to keep myself in check, but rationing it at the same time. And I have to do it when either Imani is out of the room or sleeping.

It was easier growing up: I'd feed at home every few days, at breakfast after Dad left for work, during lunch, and right after school before he got home. Because I didn't have any friends, there were no hangouts I had to work around, and because Dad knew what I needed, the rare times we *did* go out and do something, he always made sure to work around my schedule.

Now, I really am on my own.

The bus ride to the beach doesn't take long, but once we're there and have everything set up, Jake, Tripp, and Imani immediately strip off their clothes and run toward the water. I start to regret agreeing to this, my chest tightening with anxiety. I steal a glance at Aiden, who's tugging his shirt over his head slowly, somewhat reluctantly. He seems to sense me watching him, because he almost immediately looks over, the corner of his mouth quirking up in a small smile, but I look away, flushing. He's surprisingly lean, the muscle defined in his arms and chest.

"Tripp, Jake, and I came here last year, too," he tells me, reaching up to fix his hair. I just look at him, standing awkwardly with my arms crossed over my chest, not making any move to strip down to my own swimsuit. "They both love the water. I'm not the biggest fan, so I brought a book just in case."

He grins, nudging the backpack that sits on his towel with his foot.

I can't help but smile back, because not only does he have a contagious, comforting smile, but it was also a really good idea to bring a book. I wish I would've thought of that.

"I've never been to the beach before," I admit, because for whatever reason, I feel like that's information I can share with him and entrust in him not to tell anyone else, even though I've only known him for a few days. I'm going to pass on telling *anyone* I can't swim, though.

He shrugs one shoulder, looking toward the lake. I follow his gaze, watching the other three where they stand in the water, not too far from shore. Tripp wraps his arms around Imani's waist, picking her up and swinging her around before tossing her in. She shrieks his name before she disappears under the surface as Tripp and Jake both laugh. As he laughs,

Jake looks in our direction, waving us over, and Aiden gives him a thumbs-up in response. My eyes linger on Jake, his muscles even more prominent now that he's shirtless. He looks good with his messy, wet hair and the water droplets that glisten on his tanned chest under the sunlight.

I look back at Aiden, who's already looking at me, and he says, "You haven't been missing out on much. There's water that's never the right temperature and sand that gets stuck to every inch of you if you breathe wrong. Oh, and the sun that's burning you the entire time."

I let out a huff of laughter, and Aiden's smile grows. He's definitely right about that, though; it's not like I haven't been out in sunlight before, but something in me feels like if I do take off my clothes, my other side is going to act up and I'm going to disintegrate into ash right here and now.

"Something tells me you don't like the beach," I say, and when he chuckles, looking back out toward the water, I decide to just rip off the band-aid and start pulling my shirt over my head. Even though everyone here is dressed in either similar swimsuits or even less than I'm wearing, I still feel unbelievably exposed as I unbutton my jeans and step out of them, leaving me in my bikini. The top consists of two triangles that cover the barely existing curves of my breasts, but at least the bottoms are high-waisted, giving me a little more coverage.

I risk a glance over at Aiden. There's something almost vulnerably gentle in his expression that makes some, if not most, of my anxiety ease. He smiles at me, softly this time, and tilts his head towards the water.

"Wanna go grin and bear it together?" he asks.

"Sure," I reply, but before either of us can even take a step towards the water, we're greeted by a soaking wet and panting, but smiling, Imani.

"Don't you two take another step," she demands as she

kneels to rifle through her bag. I cast a sidelong glance at Aiden, who frowns and shrugs at me, as if to say, *What'd we do?*

I stifle a laugh as Imani straightens back up, holding an extra-large can of sunscreen.

"No offense, but both of you look like you'll burst into flames if you even *think* about stepping out into the sunlight, and I won't have that. Aiden, you first. Arms out."

"Yes, Mom," Aiden says before sticking his arms out to the side and turning so his back faces Imani. After she sprays every inch of him down and smears some across his face, she gives me the same treatment until I feel like I'm choking on it, the scent blocking out everything else, which I suppose isn't the worst thing in the world.

"Good," she says, dropping the can. "Now, c'mon, you two. Lydia, you look *amazing*, by the way. That color looks *so* good on you."

"Thanks," I murmur, letting her take my hand in her much warmer one and drag me after her toward the water where Tripp and Jake are splashing each other like little kids. *She's* the one who looks amazing in a royal blue bikini that looks absolutely gorgeous against her dark skin, and the way that Tripp looks up from the water at her as we approach suggests he's definitely thinking the same. It makes my heart ache a little.

Imani drops my hand and runs straight back into the water with no hesitation, but I stop at the edge. When the waves roll up every few seconds, the water sloshes over my feet, but nothing more. Aiden was right; the water is chilly. It's kind of beautiful, though, with the sun shining above us and the lake going out further than I can see and, when I turn around, the skyline of the city against the crystal-clear blue sky. It's probably peaceful here at night when the city has quieted some, and I can focus on the sound of the crashing waves and not everything else. But even now, it's not *horrible*. Sure, there's the usual sounds of traffic, but from down the beach, there's laughter and shrieks and splashes. The sounds of people. Totally normal, human life.

And I get to be a part of it.

Out of the corner of my eye, I see Aiden squat down, digging his fingers into the wet, slimy sand. When he stands up again, he holds out his hand, revealing a small white shell.

"This is the one good thing about the beach," he whispers, leaning down so I can hear him. "I used to collect shells. I'd take every single one I found."

I can't help but laugh, trying to picture a much shorter Aiden collecting handfuls of little shells. I carefully take it from him and turn it around in my hand, feeling the hard, ribbed texture. "You still have them?"

He shakes his head, and there's something almost mournful in his expression as he looks out at the water.

"Nah. My mom got kinda weird about it for whatever reason, so when she found my collection a few years back, she got rid of them all."

I don't know Aiden's parents as well as he does, obviously, but based off the vibes I got from them, I'm not surprised. Aiden shrugs as nonchalantly as possible, but I can tell those shells meant something to him, and that there's still a lingering disappointment they're gone. Because of that, I reach for his hand and place the shell on his palm, curling his long, slender fingers over it. I let my hands linger on his for what's probably a second too long as his gaze softens, and there's a look in his eyes that's so tender it makes my breath catch in my throat and makes me want to look away.

So, I do.

"There," I say, looking back out at the water, even though I can feel Aiden's eyes still on me. I find Tripp, Jake, and

Imani, who have ventured out even farther—way farther than I'll be comfortable going. "Start a new collection."

A slow smile spreads across Aiden's face as he tucks the shell into the left pocket of his swim trunks.

"Will do," he murmurs. When we make eye contact, a wave of calm washes over me. I take in the smell of the water and sunscreen and feel the heat of the sun beating on my shoulders—*not* turning me into ash—and it feels like we're the only two people here.

Until our names are called. Again.

"We should probably appease them and go out there for a little while, huh?" he says, not sounding too enthusiastic about it. I follow his gaze to see the others waving at us—still too far out.

"Um, yeah," I say, and when Aiden looks back at me, his eyebrows furrow ever so slightly as if he notices the hesitation in my voice. I guess I should tell him in case I drown, so somebody will know why.

But maybe I wouldn't die. Maybe the human half of me would be killed. Is that how that works? In all the lore, vampires don't breathe because they're dead, obviously, so can they drown? Guess we'll find out.

Now *that's* a joke Dad *definitely* wouldn't find funny.

"They're just pretty far out," I say, my voice lowering with every word as if they'll be able to hear me over the sounds of the waves and children screaming and traffic. "And I can't—I never—"

Aiden's gaze softens, the wrinkles between his brows smoothing. "It's nothing to be ashamed of," he says, offering me a small, reassuring smile. "We'll go out as far as you're comfortable, okay?"

I smile back, and Aiden and I begin our trek into the water. It's chilly, goosebumps forming on my skin, and the hair on my arms rising with every step. The water creeps up my legs, and my toes try to grip the slippery sand underneath. I can hear my heart above all, pounding in my ears, my chest tightening to the point where my breaths are more shallow. I feel pathetic.

I look around me, at the kids in floaties, held by their parents, handling it much better than I am, and stop abruptly once the water hits my belly button. I feel weird, near weightless, and I don't want to go any further. I feel a twinge of guilt once I look at Aiden and notice that, of course, the water is considerably lower on him, seeing how much taller than me he is.

"You can go on," I tell him. "I just—I think I'm gonna stay here."

He shakes his head, smiling softly.

"*We're* gonna stay here. I'm not gonna leave you alone." The sincerity in his tone makes my chest tighten even further, but then he pauses. "What if there're sharks? Who would save me from them if you're not around?"

I let out a laugh, the knot in my chest easing slightly.

"Sharks?" I do my best to match his sarcastic tone. "I thought it was piranhas that lived in lakes."

Aiden throws up his hand in mock exasperation.

"*Duh.* How could I forget?"

I laugh again, and he smiles at me, looking as if he's about to say something else, but then I hear three, somewhat erratic, heartbeats coming closer.

"Why're you stopping here?" Tripp calls as they near us, his hair slicked back. My eyes fly to the snake tattoo circling his right collarbone, which I didn't notice before. "The water keeps going, y'know!"

Jake grins at me as he pushes his wet hair back from his forehead, his biceps flexing. I feel my cheeks start to warm.

Aiden answers, "You guys *know* I'm not a huge fan of the beach. I don't wanna go out any farther."

I hope he's able to read the grateful look I shoot in his direction.

Tripp boos and dunks himself under the water, popping back up and shaking his hair out like a dog, making Imani hold up her hands and cringe away as she says his name in protest.

"You wanna go out farther with me, Lyds?" Jake asks.

Lyds.

A nickname? I've earned myself a *nickname*?

I shake my head, tucking my still-dry hair behind my ears.

"Um, no. I think I'm gonna head back to our stuff for now, actually."

Jake nods, and I swear there's a hint of disappointment on his face, but it's gone just as quick as I notice it.

"Sure, yeah, I think I will, too, actually. I'm starving."

"We'll meet you guys in a few," Imani says, wrapping her arms around Tripp's waist from behind. I smile a little, both at how cute they look together and at the thought of getting back to the shore. This was enough excitement for today. And plus—I realize, with a sharp pierce of panic as Jake's shoulder bumps against mine, his much-too-human scent wafting into my nose—I'm getting hungry, too.

But not for any of the food that we brought.

Why didn't I notice when I was with Aiden?

It's nothing unusual, and nothing I can't handle, seeing as we aren't going to be here for *too* much longer, but I wish I could be more consistent and figure out a set schedule already. Hopefully, everything will just fall into place once classes start.

I can't let Dad be right. I *can't.*

I stare toward the water as Jake asks Aiden about what classes he's taking this semester. I try and let their presence—their scents, more specifically—fade into the background as I focus on everything else: the crash of the waves, the birds overhead, the breeze that whips through my hair, blowing it away from face, some of the ache in my stomach easing as I close my eyes and tilt my head back, lifting my face toward the sun.

If I don't focus on my hunger, if I just think about the warmth of the sun on my skin and the voices of those around me—my *friends* —I feel normal. I feel *human*.

I just wish it could be this way all the time.

CHAPTER TEN

A FEW HOURS LATER, when we finally get back to the dorm, Imani goes over to the boys' apartment, but I tell them I'm tired and will probably spend the rest of the evening in my room. Which isn't entirely a lie. Being out in the sun, surrounded by people all day—human people, specifically— took a lot out of me.

The second the door shuts behind me, I'm jolted back to the reality I was able to lose sight of for just a few minutes while at the beach. I kneel in front of my fridge, quickly unscrewing the cap to one of my bottles—the last in the fridge. Once I've chugged its contents, wiping the back of my hand across my mouth, I open the small freezer door.

Shit.

I transfer one bottle to the fridge, leaving two in the freezer. I'll need to venture out soon to find the butcher Dad told me was in the city, the same butcher he called before he let me move here to make sure I could buy blood. But it's not a journey I'm particularly looking forward to.

I'll go next weekend. Three bottles should last me until Friday perfectly fine, since I don't have any classes on Fridays.

Classes.

Between exploring the city, getting to know the others, and just being able to (mostly) relax without Dad breathing down my neck, I've almost forgotten I start classes on Monday.

After washing my empty bottle, I change out of my clothes and swimsuit into a loose T-shirt and pajama shorts. As I head into the bathroom, I think about my schedule. To be honest, I'm excited about classes. High school, middle school, all of it was hell, but here, I get to choose my classes, and I get to start over fresh with classmates and teachers who don't know me or have any preexisting expectations.

Things are going well, for the most part. I think. I just need to get my ass in gear and get on a feeding schedule again.

As if he knows what I'm thinking, my phone vibrates on the bathroom vanity, lighting up with Dad's name, as I finish brushing through my tangled hair. I pick it up, swiping across the screen to answer before tucking my phone between my cheek and shoulder.

"Hi, Dad," I say, making my tone as pleasant as I can.

"Hi, honey," he replies, and the relief in his voice is clear. I pull my toothbrush and toothpaste out of my bathroom drawer, baring my teeth at myself in the mirror to see that yes, they are bloodstained, per usual.

"How's it going? I haven't heard a lot from you."

I can tell by the tone of his voice he wants to say and ask a lot more, but he's holding himself back. Which I appreciate, because I'm still deciding—as I pull my toothbrush out of my mouth, leaning over to spit before answering—how much I want to tell him.

It's not like I've done anything *wrong*. I just don't want to hear a lecture about being safe.

"Good," I say, rinsing my toothbrush off. "I've been hanging out with Imani and her boyfriend and his roommates. Today we went—" I pause. "—out. I really like them," I add, just to distract from my hesitation that *screams* I'm purposely omitting information.

Dad doesn't comment, much to my relief. I leave the bathroom and climb into bed, putting my phone on speaker and setting it next to me so I can comfortably curl up under my blanket.

"That's great," he says, but I can't tell if he really means it. "You ready for classes on Monday?"

"Yeah, I'm looking forward to it."

"Good, good. And you're being s—"

"Yes, Dad." The words come out more sharply than I'd intended.

I watch my phone screen as a few seconds of silence tick by before he says anything. "You know I can't help but worry, Lydia."

I realize, as I pull my blanket up to my chin, he's probably lonely without me. I bet he doesn't know what to do with himself.

A twinge of guilt squeezes my heart.

"I know. I'm sorry. But I'm doing good, okay? And I'm being safe. I promise."

He sighs, and I can picture him running his hands through his hair or over his face. I roll onto my back, staring up at the white popcorn ceiling.

"I trust you," he says slowly. "Remember, though, you can always call me if you need something. Even if you don't." He chuckles. "'Spose I should take a lesson from you and get out of the house a little more."

As much as I want to tell him he should finally get out and date, now that I'm not around to tie him down, I really can't see myself actually doing it. I feel like that's an odd conversation to have with your dad. So, instead, I force out a laugh and agree with him.

"But enough about me," he says a little louder, his voice rising above the competing noises of my dorm and the city. "Tell me about these new friends of yours. Are they astronomy fanatics, too?"

I laugh at that—genuinely this time.

"Well, it's astrology, but no." I tell him about Tripp, Jake, and then Aiden, about our trip to the Bean and the parks, and I finally cave and tell him about the beach. He's trying, after all, and it doesn't feel right lying to him.

"That's cool," he says, finally, though his voice sounds a little strained. I wish I could see his face, so I could tell what he's thinking. "That sounds fun. I—I'm glad you've found a place so fast. They sound like good kids."

"They are." I pause, rolling back over onto my side so that my face is closer to my phone, my cheek against the cool, soft silk of my pillowcase. "Maybe—maybe you could come visit me sometime and meet them. I could show you around."

There's a long pause, long enough where I think he's going to say no. And I know that if he does, I'll be disappointed—even though the thought of Dad meeting my—my friends? Can I call them friends after only a week? —scares me. I'm not even sure why.

"Yeah. Yeah, that'd be fun, honey. I've been swamped with work, you know that, but I'll see if there's a weekend I can drive up."

The conversation quickly drifts to a close, and after pressing the little red button to hang up the call, I pull my blanket over my head and close my eyes. Maybe it's the mixing of my two lives that terrifies me. There's Dad's Lydia and then there's this new Lydia that my friends—and *me*—are just starting to get to know. I have to figure out how to mix the two, but there's something about it that makes my chest constrict with anxiety. What if something happens and I slip up, or Dad slips up and makes them think there's something wrong with me? What if I lose the first friends I've ever had because of this? Because of *me*?

I squeeze my eyes shut tighter as if that will help block out the panic attack I'm seconds away from having. I breathe in and out slowly, focusing my attention on the beating of my *own* heart, on my *own* breathing, on the scent of sunscreen that lingers on my *own* skin.

Things that ground me, relax me, because they remind me of the one thing I've held on to all these years to keep me sane:

That I'm still human.

Monday comes faster than I expected. Sunday went by in the blink of an eye after I was dragged out to breakfast at 7:04 A.M. to this, apparently amazing, place downtown. I admit, the breakfast skillet I got was good, but I think it would have been equally as good a few hours later.

The rest of the day was spent doing absolutely nothing except watching movies in the boys' apartment. Imani had suggested *Twilight*, and I can't say I wasn't relieved when the boys all vetoed that, so we ended up watching the first three *Shrek* movies.

But now, I'm seated in a classroom at 7:48, waiting for my only 8 A.M. and very first college class to start. As nervous as I am, seated at one of four long tables that form a rectangle in the center of the room alone with one other girl who sits across from me, at least it's English, so I'm more in my element. I can do reading and writing. It's my math class I'm *really* anxious about.

But that's not til tonight. Focus on *now*, Lydia.

I also made sure to feed this morning, so I'm extra energized. But that energy is just turning into nervous energy; I drum my fingers on the table as my other classmates slowly filter in, fiddle with my birthstone necklace, and bounce my knee. Until finally, *finally*, my professor shows up at 7:56.

Something seems oddly familiar about him—almost like the feeling I got when I met Aiden. Or even Aiden's parents, though he definitely doesn't seem to be as asshole-ish as them. But again, I know I definitely haven't met him, so I can't understand why the feeling keeps nagging at me. He looks Dad's age, about mid-to-late thirties, but has a full beard, mustache, and head of thick, chocolate brown hair that curls at the nape of his neck and by his ears. Honestly, paired with his jeans and buttoned-up flannel shirt, he kind of reminds me of a lumberjack. Or at least someone who lives out in the woods and owns an axe.

Mostly everyone else in the room is still in quiet conversation, so almost as if he can feel me assessing him, he looks straight at me. His eyebrows lift slightly as if he recognizes me, too. I start, sitting up a little straighter. *Do* we know each other? But then again, I might have just imagined it, because it's gone in less than a second, replaced by a warm, close-lipped smile before he addresses the entire class.

"Alright, everyone, I'm here to break up your fun."

As the conversations die down, he continues:

"Nah, I'm just kidding. My goal is to be the most fun professor you have and make you not hate English, which I'm sure some of you do, and you're only here because it's required." There're a few scattered chuckles. "I'm not gonna make you do any icebreakers, either, because I'm sure you all hate those, too. But to introduce myself, I'm Roarke, and you can call me that. No need to be all formal or anything. Today, we're just gonna take attendance, go over the syllabus, and I'll send you on your way for the day. Cool?"

He holds out two thumbs up, glancing around the room.

There're a few "cools" and murmurs of agreement, to which he grins at, before jumping into calling attendance.

It's easy to pay attention, even just going over the syllabus —he makes it engaging, cracking jokes along the way. We make eye contact a few times during class, but I still can't pinpoint what it is about him that's so familiar.

When he dismisses us, everyone practically jumps and runs out of the room. I take longer packing my things up, to the point where Roarke and I are the only two people left in the room. I almost hope he doesn't say anything to me; as nice and as cool of a teacher as he is, I've never done well with one-on-ones with teachers. Or anyone, really, for that matter. But of course, as I start to zip up my backpack, I hear his voice to my right.

"Lydia, is it?"

I nod in confirmation before breaking eye contact, fiddling with my backpack zipper.

"I saw in my records that you're an English major. Always nice to meet a fellow English lover." I look up just in time to catch his smile. "I know this was your first class, but how're you liking things so far? The city treating you well?"

"Uh, yeah." I sling my backpack on, my cheeks betraying me and heating at the attention. "It's been nice. I really like it so far."

"Perfect." His grin seems to fade a little as he lifts the strap of his brown leather bag onto his shoulder, both of us starting to move towards the door. "I think I forgot to mention this in class, but seeing as I get mostly freshmen, I try to keep an open line of communication at all times as you guys adjust to the college life. I know how stressful things can get, especially when you're trying to balance school with your personal life. So, if you need anything, don't be afraid to reach out, yeah?"

He stops in front of the door, holding out his arm to indicate for me to go first. I murmur something along the lines of *yeah* and *thank you,* stopping just outside the classroom door and watching him walk away. Why did he single *me* out to tell me that?

No. He said it himself—he just forgot to tell the class. I'm letting myself overthink things too much, just like I did with Aiden's parents. Whatever this strange familiarity is, I'm sure it's nothing. Maybe they all just remind me of book characters.

As I follow the throng of people from my class to where I assume the elevators are, I hear my name. I turn to see Jake walking swiftly toward me, so I step off to the side to wait for him.

"Hey!" he all but exclaims when he reaches me. He looks good in his usual casual way, in a plain red T-shirt and jeans, hair tousled as it always is.

"Did you just get out of class?" he asks, and when I nod, he adds, "How'd we miss each other leaving this morning? I had an 8 A.M., too."

"I left early," I admit, as we start toward the elevators. As I tell him I'm terrified of being late, so I left twenty minutes early for a class that takes a five-minute walk to get to. A few tall, muscular guys pass, calling "Hampton!"

Jake nods at them briefly but immediately goes back to giving me his full attention. It makes me a little nervous, but I don't have to worry too long when we pile onto a nearly full elevator.

"Shit," he says, an easy smile tugging at the corner of his mouth as we stand at the front of the elevator, a few people behind us. I hate elevators this full, this many heartbeats and scents all packed into one too-tiny, inescapable space. I might have to start convincing Jake to take the stairs with me. "I might have to take a lesson from you. I leave at the last minute, but at least I'm better than Tripp. He considers it a win if he ends up going to class at all."

I force a little smile at him, mostly just so my discomfort

from the current elevator situation doesn't show. The second the doors slide open on the first floor, I make sure I'm the first one out.

"Do you wanna walk to our next class together?" Jake asks, catching up to me as I beeline as casually as possible out of the building, the fresh air a relief to my senses. Well, as much as a relief it can be when I get the fumes of cars and trash with it.

"Oh, yeah," I say, remembering we have geology together today. "Sure."

Much to my amusement, Jake shows up at my door at 10:40, twenty minutes before our class, all ready to go. It's pretty sweet, actually, and when Imani tells us to have fun at class, there's that suggestive, knowing tone in her sing-songy voice.

Jake and I sit together at one of the lab tables, at the high chairs with twisting seats. While our professor, an older man with an impressively long, white beard who smells distantly like grass, goes over the syllabus. Jake twists back and forth in his chair, gripping the table so he doesn't fall over. I can't help but stifle a laugh when his chair wobbles, threatening to tip him over, and he shoots me a sheepish grin in return.

"I'm pretty excited for that class, actually," Jake says when we're leaving, filing out the door behind most of the other students. "I like labs since they're so hands-on, and I actually feel like I'm *doing* something, y'know? There's not a lot of that in business. Part of the reason I'm not a fan." He pauses. "You have any more classes today?"

I sigh. "Yeah. My math class is tonight at 6."

Jake starts leading us toward the elevator, but when I see the line of people waiting for it, I take the opportunity to ask, "Wanna take the stairs?"

I'm relieved to hear him say, "Yeah, sure," before he looks

at me, the corner of his mouth quirking up. "You sound *thrilled* about math."

"I picked English as my major for a reason."

That makes Jake laugh as we start to descend the four flights of stairs to the first floor.

"Touche," he says. "Somedays I think I made a mistake in choosing business, but I dunno. I've already started it and everything, and I don't even know what I'd change it *to*, but."

In the stairwell, since it's just us, everything is a little louder; our footsteps echo loudly off the walls, Jake's heartbeat thunders in my ears, and his scent is a little stronger amongst the musty smell of the space.

"You still have time," I say, pausing before I add, "I mean, it's okay to change your mind. What's a few more years of school compared to being miserable your whole life?"

He looks over at me as we reach the doors that will take us out to the first floor, a small smile blossoming on his face.

"Yeah, I guess you're right. Thanks, Lyds."

There it is again. My chest tightens, and I smile.

"Of course," I say.

We talk the whole ten-minute walk back to our dorm— well, *Jake* mostly talks, but I reply or add my opinion when necessary—and I'm a little disappointed to have to say good-bye, but he has to go get ready for practice.

"Let me know how your math class goes," he tells me, lingering in the doorway of his apartment. "If you're completely miserable, text me and I'll call you with some sort of emergency to get you out of it."

I smile, finding it hard to keep my teeth hidden, but I manage.

"Sounds good. I appreciate your heroicness."

He grins at me, saying bye before disappearing into his apartment, the heavy door shutting behind him with a thud I feel all the way to my toes. I let myself into my room where Imani lies in her bed reading.

"Hey!" she exclaims, flipping her book over to keep her place. "How was class?"

"Good," I reply earnestly as I let my backpack slide down my arm to the floor. "I'm not a huge science person, but I think I'm gonna like it more having Jake there."

She smiles brightly. "I'm glad. It seems like the two of you are gettin' along."

I lower myself to sit on the edge of my bed, sitting back until my feet dangle slightly above the floor.

Yeah, we are. I like being around him.

He makes me feel like a normal girl.

I settle with a "Yeah, we are," and Imani seems excited about that. We can't talk for long, though, because Imani realizes she has a class she should be getting to. Once I have the room to myself, I lie back and close my eyes, only pulling myself up once I have to leave for math.

As I take my seat in the classroom, I feel dread building deep in the pit of my stomach. Unlike my first two classes, these desks are individual and not even really desks, but instead rolling chairs with little tables connected to them and spread throughout the classroom in haphazard rows. I pick one in the back, playing on my phone as my classmates start to enter the room, accompanied by various different scents.

One in particular grows considerably stronger. I glance up at the boy who takes the desk next to me, and I realize I recognize him. The curly black hair, the awkward way he moves. He's the kid I saw my first day here who lives on my floor. Only now he's wearing black-rimmed, rounded glasses that slide down the bridge of his nose when he leans over to pull his notebook from his backpack.

Once class starts, and our short professor calls our names off her computer, I find out his name is Xavier. I also soon find out he clearly knows what he's doing, because unlike my other classes so far, we jump into the first lesson, and his hand flies up almost every time the professor asks a question.

I make a mental note that if I need to cheat at any point during this class, which seems likely, I'll cheat off him.

Kidding.

At the end of class, as I'm shoving my notebook and pen back in my backpack, I hear him say, "Hey. Lydia, right?"

I whip my head up to see he's already standing, one hand in a front pocket of his jeans, the other clutching one of the straps of his backpack. He shifts from one foot to the other as I confirm my identity, surprised he remembered my name.

He cracks a small, almost shy smile. "Not to sound weird, but I feel like I've seen you in my dorm. Do you live in University Hall?"

I smile back, closing up my backpack and swinging it over my shoulder as I stand.

"I do, yeah. Eighth floor."

His smile grows a little. "Me too. I was wondering, since it's late, if you'd wanna walk back together?"

I'm a little relieved because I wasn't exactly excited about the prospect of walking back as it's growing dark. Granted, it's only about a ten-minute walk, but still. I'd rather walk back with someone, especially someone male—even if said male is a distractingly good-smelling human, and even if *I'm* potentially the most dangerous person we could come across.

"Yeah, yeah, that'd be great."

As we leave the building (via the elevator, unfortunately) and start to walk back, Xavier starts asking me all the basic questions about myself: my major, where I'm from, etc. He tells me he's a computer science major and explains it a little. We get on the topic of math, to which Xavier admits is one of his favorite subjects, and I confess I both hate it and suck at it. He smiles a little at that.

"I can get that. If you ever need help or anything, don't be afraid to ask. I'd be happy to help."

I hope my surprise at his offer doesn't completely show on my face. I hope I don't have to resort to being tutored by a classmate, but it's nice to have the option, and right away in the semester.

"Uh, sure, yeah. I'll let you know. Thanks."

When we get back to the dorm, he says bye to me when we reach my door and continues down the hall and around the corner. I watch him until I can't see him anymore. It feels kind of good to have at *least* an acquaintance in two of my three classes so far.

And speak of the devil, as I'm fumbling with my ID card to open my door, I hear the door behind me open. Jake stands in the doorway, his hair damp and sticking up in a few places, dressed in a plain black T-shirt that hugs his arm muscles, gray sweatpants, and a pair of circular glasses. I didn't know he had glasses, but he definitely looks cute in them.

"You survived," he notes, crossing his arms over his chest as he leans one shoulder against the doorframe.

"Barely. I might be needing your services in the near future."

He smiles crookedly. "Anytime, Lydia Ross."

By the time I end up in my room, I'm still smiling.

CHAPTER ELEVEN

THE WEEK PASSES QUICKLY, and by Saturday morning, I've finally convinced myself I really did make the right choice in coming here. I'm enjoying how it feels to be—well, *act*—normal.

Well, maybe not completely. Yesterday, I waited until Imani left for her 10:30 class before leaving to go find the butcher. It was about a twenty-minute bus ride, but I made it there, eventually. I tripped over my words and blushed the entire time when ordering the blood, as if they could see right through me, and made it even worse by laughing nervously when they made a comment about me cooking with it.

I practically sprinted out of there and vowed to find a different butcher for my next run.

And *today*, we're going to watch a football game of Jake's, and just because I'm adjusting to classes and a new, small group of friends doesn't mean I'm thrilled about sitting in a jam-packed stadium in the blistering heat for God knows how long. Not to mention, I don't know anything about football; Dad was never a sports guy. Like me, he's always preferred cracking into a book in his downtime. I can't remember the last time I even saw a game of any sort on TV.

I do my best to show my support by putting on an olive-green T-shirt, the closest I have to our school's actual colors, paired with my go-to dark-wash jeans. It's a cloudy day, and it's not supposed to be too hot, but Imani still makes sure I put sunscreen on before she lets me leave the room. She, on the other hand, is wearing a green shirt that says the name of our mascot, the *Lakers*, across the front in white, with white shorts, her braids piled in a bun on top of her head, and green sunglasses perched on the bridge of her nose so she can look at me over the top of them.

"It's fun, even if you don't really know much about football," she assures me, looking at herself in the mirror on the back of her closet door. "It's the energy that makes it fun. You ready to go?"

When I nod, she leads the way out of our room. I make sure the door is locked as she pounds her fist against the boys' door. It opens almost immediately, revealing Tripp, who I'm surprised to see is wearing none of his usual neutrals but is instead dressed in a green T-shirt, blue jeans, and a backward baseball hat that keeps his hair out of his face. He grins at Imani, stretching his arm out to pull her against him. After he kisses the top of her head, he lifts his chin in a greeting to me.

"Hey, Lydia," he says. "I heard you're not a huge fan of sports. Just cheer when a green player runs to the end and you'll be solid."

Imani rolls her eyes and purses her lips in an obvious attempt to hide a smile, pushing up on her tiptoes to kiss his cheek instead.

"Thanks, Tripp," I say. "I don't think I could've figured that out."

Tripp smiles crookedly just as I hear a quiet laugh come from somewhere within the apartment. I don't say anything, because I don't know if normal human ears would've been able to pick it up, but a few seconds later, Aiden peeks around the corner from behind Tripp. As expected, he's also dressed in green, and the color really makes his eyes stand out.

"C'mon, we gotta go," Imani says, a tad impatiently. "It's gonna take forever to get in."

"How do you know?" Tripp asks, following her as she starts to make her way down the hall without a glance back. "You've never been to a college game before."

"Um, ex*cuse* me?" I hear Imani shoot back as I stand and wait for Aiden. "You took me to a college game two years ago, Tripp Daniel. Or was that your other—"

I tune them out as they turn the corner, focusing on Aiden, who turns and gives me a soft smile as we start walking down the hall.

"You think they'd notice if we just stay here?" he asks.

"If they're still arguing, probably not."

"Five bucks says they are."

I grin, letting my teeth show before I even realize what I'm doing. "You're on."

Something in Aiden's expressions softens, his gaze flitting to my mouth just before I can clamp my lips shut. My heart stutters in fear—I hope he didn't notice my fangs, but he's already opening his mouth, saying, "You—"

"You guys comin'?" Tripp peeks around the corner from down the hall. "You'd think you'd walk a little faster with those giraffe legs of yours, Swanson."

I let out a laugh that's half-nervous, half-relieved, as Aiden takes off in a full sprint down the hall toward him. Though, of course, I can't help but wonder what was he going to say. *You* what? *You* have fangs? *You* have pointy teeth? *Youuu're* a vampire and I know it, and I've known it this whole time, and I've only been nice to you because I feel like I have to, and—

"Lydia!"

"Coming!" I quicken my pace to a light jog only to see they're already holding an elevator for me.

As soon as the doors close, I hear the pads of Aiden's fingers tapping against his phone screen. A few seconds later, my phone vibrates, and when I pull it out of my back pocket, the screen lights up with a text notification from Aiden. I glance at him to see that he's pursing his lips, just barely holding back a smile, before opening the notification.

aiden swanson: $5

I let out a small laugh and look over just in time to catch Aiden's grin. Tripp and Imani are talking with each other about something football-related, but I see Imani eyeing us out of my peripheral vision.

I quickly learn, once we're on the bus, that the ride to the football stadium is going to be over an hour since it's on the outskirts of the city. We settle into four seats near the back— Imani and Tripp sitting in front of us, and Aiden lets me take the window seat in our row.

"Where's the farthest from home you've ever been?" he asks me.

I hesitate before answering honestly. "Chicago."

His eyebrows fly upward. "Really?"

I nod, glancing down at my hands in my lap. "I mean, it was just me n my dad growing up, and he works all the time, so we never really got to go anywhere."

That's close enough to the truth.

Aiden nods. "Makes sense. Jake and Tripp *really* wanna do some sorta spring break trip one of these years, down to Florida or something. You and Imani have been included, now, of course, but..." He grins sheepishly. "Maybe we can find some other things to do while they have beach days."

The thought of going to Florida or somewhere with just

friends is exciting but also terrifying and something I thought I'd never get to do in my entire life. While I came here to distance myself from Dad, it's also a little reassuring to know he's still an hour away if I need him.

I have to remind myself, too, that I could never go away with friends if they didn't know what I was because I could never get away with buying or packing blood and them not finding out. And they never *can* know what I am, so...

I smile back at Aiden, despite the pang of disappointment in my chest. Maybe the extent of my normalcy can only go so far.

"Sounds good to me."

"I'll need to start saving more if that's the plan, though," he says.

I nod, sighing a little. "I need to get a job. My dad gives me a certain amount every week for necessities, but..."

His face lights up. "I could see if there's a spot open at the bookstore I work at. It's just down the street from our dorm and it pays decently."

As much as I want to tell him he doesn't have to do that, I really can't pass up the prospect of working with a friend *and* working at a bookstore.

"Really? You'd do that?"

"Yeah, of course. Let me talk to one of the owners when they're in next and I'll see if I can do anything."

I thank him, and time starts to pass way more quickly as we start talking about books, about the bookstore, about some of his other favorite bookstores. True to what he told me the first day we met, he tells me about some of his favorite classics, and I can't help but tease him a little for it. He gets me back right after by teasing me about my fantasy and romance books, and before long, Tripp is twisting in his seat and telling us it's time for our stop.

The stadium is huge, and the second we climb the stairs

and I spin around and can see just how many people are here, my stomach starts to churn, a familiar piercing in my head that tells me a headache is on the horizon. It's packed, and it's noisy, and honestly kind of a nightmare.

I follow Imani and Tripp single-file up the stairs, Aiden behind me. We end up nearly all the way at the top, and I realize we're in the student section, surrounded by people our own age in our school colors. When we sit, Tripp leans forward and starts talking to a girl he knows who's sitting in front of us, and Imani joins in from next to me.

I take a deep breath, focusing in. Aiden's presence doesn't seem to affect me as much for some reason, so it helps that he's my left.

I remind myself I can't bolt; I'm here for Jake, and plus, I fed recently—and more than enough—in preparation for this. I'll be fine. I might leave with the worst headache of my life and nail indentations in my palms, but I'll be fine.

As if he can feel something's wrong, Aiden leans over, his shoulder and arm pressing against mine, and says in a low voice, "You okay?"

I feel my pulse slow a little, just a little closer to normal speed.

"Yeah," I say back, quietly enough so only he can hear. I stare out at the sea of people dressed in green, and the people for the other team dressed in blue and white. I scan the long field, the white lines on it, just taking in all the details. "Just— Yeah. Crowds just aren't my favorite."

Aiden smiles sympathetically.

"They aren't mine, either. You wanna escape and go grab some food before the game starts?"

I nod enthusiastically, and he laughs before leading the way back down the bleachers, glancing over his shoulder every few steps to make sure I'm still behind him, smiling reassuringly each time.

Once we reach the concession stand, he insists on paying for my food, so I settle on nachos and a Coke. We walk back and forth under the bleachers for a while as Aiden does his best to explain to me what I'm about to see with his own football knowledge, which seems to be barely more than my own.

"Jake likes it, obviously, so I do my best," Aiden admits, pausing to take a sip from his own cup. "I always felt a little stupid last year because Tripp is a football fanatic, too, so he'd start cheering, but it wasn't because of a touchdown, so I'd be like, what happened?" He looks at me, and I catch a mischievous glint in his eye. "I feel a little better this year, because at least I know more than you," he adds.

The nacho I was trying to grab breaks off in my hand, and I mock-glare at him as he laughs, clearly pleased with himself —which is kind of endearing.

"I'm glad I'm only here to boost your self-esteem, Aiden," I tease back, and when we lock eyes, something passes over me —I can't tell what, but all I know is that it feels *right*.

Before Aiden can reply, there's noise—more than there's already been—from the stadium, and when he looks away, that feeling goes away.

What *is* it about him? Or is this just friendship, and I'm just so thrown off by something that literally almost every other person has experienced?

"They're starting," he says. "We should head back up there."

He steals a nacho before turning toward the nearest staircase, and I have to jog a little to catch up with his long strides. The stadium is somehow even more packed than before, but Tripp and Imani put their hat and purse down to save our seats. Before I'm even seated, Tripp reaches across Imani and steals a nacho from me.

"Thanks, Ross," he says, winking at me as he bites into it.

Imani rolls her eyes and asks if she can have one first, just as the crowd erupts in cheers, which seems to reverberate inside my skull.

This is gonna be a long day.

I slowly chew my nachos with Aiden, Imani, and Tripp stealing some from both sides as we watch the cheerleaders and the band, when finally, the football players run out, causing the crowd to go even crazier, the noise so loud it seems to pierce my brain.

As they get into position, Tripp leans over. "You see that one over there? 52? That's Jake. He's the center."

He turns just as Tripp points to him, so I'm able to see the 52 on his back. As the game begins and things start to happen all at once, and the crowd screams and cheers, I lose track of him more than once, and I can't really judge how he's doing since I don't know, but I have to give him props. It seems like a tough sport.

Both Imani and Tripp lean over to tell me what just happened at points where everyone cheers, but I'm not, because I'm confused—I would definitely be able to focus more if I were watching on a TV screen. I'm able to catch on a little, though, but before long, we win, thirty-seven to thirty-two. And by then, my head is pounding, and my skin feels like it's on fire, and I'm shaking to the point where I need to excuse myself to the bathroom.

I hurriedly lock myself into a stall, drop to my knees, and puke everything I've consumed all day out—including the blood I drank this morning. I tear off a few squares of toilet paper to wipe my mouth as I sit back and take deep, steadying breaths. My phone vibrates in my back pocket, and I pull it out, seeing I have a text from Aiden:

> aiden swanson: you okay? We're by
> concessions waiting for Jake

The bubble with the three dots is there to indicate he's typing, and a second later, I get another two texts:

> aiden swanson: you need us to send in troops? Imani's ready and willing

> aiden swanson: well okay maybe not totally willing but you get it

Despite the pounding in my head and the aching in my stomach, I laugh a little and text him back:

> me: nah i'm coming i just can't believe you wouldn't offer to come save me yourself

As I push myself up to my feet, making sure I'm steady before I start to venture out of my stall, Aiden sends:

> aiden swanson: I bought you a bottle of water and offered to send Imani in to save you. Is that not enough for you?

> aiden swanson: so needy Lydia

I feel myself blush, and I can see the proof of it in my red face when I go to wash my hands before leaving the bathroom. Sure enough, I find Tripp, Imani, and Aiden by the concession, and the second Aiden and I make eye contact, he holds a water bottle out to me with a smirk.

"Thanks," I murmur, chugging about three-quarters of it at once. It doesn't make me feel *much* better, but it helps a little, and I can't exactly explain the actual source of my discomfort. *Well,* I suppose I could, but not to the extent of it. So, I'm not going to.

Jake comes up to us a little while later, after the majority of people have, thankfully, cleared out of the stadium, making it a little easier to bear. He beams, the energy practically radiating off of him, his hair damp. He smells good, clean, like he just took a shower, and his heart pounds so rapidly I can't keep up.

Tripp goes in for a hug, and it's kind of a sweet moment to watch. Jake hugs Imani, Aiden, and then turns to me, holding out his arms in more of a question than anything. I step forward, and he pulls me into his embrace, and I almost lose it all over again at being this close to a human after everything being so overwhelming today. It definitely doesn't help that he smells as good as he does, and he's warm and envelopes me into his chest so easily, and it's actually kinda really nice.

It also makes me realize just how little hugs I've gotten in my life.

Wow, that's depressing.

"Hey," he says, addressing all of us once he lets me go, "I have some stuff to do, but I'll meet you guys back at the dorm, and I wanna take you out for dinner, okay? See you guys soon!"

I'm the last person he smiles at before he leaves. I feel the heat rushing back to my cheeks.

On the bus ride back, I sip the remainder of my water. I'm exhausted to the point I find myself almost drifting off, my head bumping against Aiden's shoulder as it lowers.

"Sorry," I murmur, straightening up.

He chuckles. "It's okay," he says, pausing before he adds, "Feel free to use me as a pillow if you want."

I don't hesitate—if today hadn't taken so much out of me, I'd probably be too embarrassed, but I'm too in pain and exhausted and tired of hiding it to refuse his offer. Within seconds of letting my head rest on his shoulder, a wave of calming energy passes through me, and I'm out like a light.

CHAPTER TWELVE

Between adjusting to classes, having *friends,* and working my feeding schedule around all of these things, time starts to fly. And in the blink of an eye, I've survived one full month of being in Chicago on my own.

In class that Monday, Roarke is still as enthusiastic as ever, if not more so. He asks everyone how their weekends were, taking a sip from the Starbucks cup that sits next to his pile of books. One girl immediately pipes up and says she's been feeling awful, and that it's probably because of the full moon coming up, which I heard Imani mention, too, because apparently, it's a thing. Roarke grins from behind his cup of coffee, the scent of it alone waking me up.

"I know exactly what you mean," he says. "I've been feeling it, too."

And I think he glances at me.

Class flies by as usual, and later during geology, I'm mostly zoning out while my professor lectures on minerals instead choosing to go on my favorite used-books website and adding several to my cart. I desperately need a job if I'm going to keep doing shit like this instead of using the money Dad gives me, which is supposed to be mostly for blood so I can, you know, *survive*. I also justify it by thinking that if I have to consume blood in order to survive, then I deserve to spend a little extra on something that's going to distract me from my own life for a little while, even if it's just reading about romances I'll never get to experience or beings that may or may not be real and live in rich, exciting fantasy worlds where they're accepted for what they are and don't have to hide it in fear of being ostracized by the people they care about. But, anyway. My savings are running low.

I'm snapped out of my daze by the sounds of zippers and shuffling as class ends. I close the lid of my own laptop, stretching my arms before I put it away. But then, Jake says my name.

"Hey, Lyds."

"Yeah?"

There's an odd look on his face, like he's... nervous? Which is definitely weird for Jake, who's not cocky, but always has a sort of easygoing confidence.

The chatter quiets as people leave the room, leaving us with our professor shuffling papers and the steady ticking of the clock on the wall.

Jake hesitates for a second longer.

"I, uh, was wondering if you'd like to hang out this weekend. But, like, as a date."

I swivel around in my seat to face him, trying to figure out if I just heard him correctly.

"A date?"

"Yeah," he confirms, a small, nervous smile appearing on his face. "But if not, it's totally cool."

Jake Hampton is asking me out on a date. I can't say that when I got here, I had expected the second person I ever met here, and a sweet, attractive *boy* at that, to become my friend, let alone ask me out a *date*. "Um, yeah," I say. "I'd love to."

Jake grins wide, his eyes crinkling at the corners. I smile back at him, keeping my lips clamped shut as a spark of anxiety flutters through me. I'm going on my first ever *date*.

It's exciting. And absolutely, utterly terrifying.

"By the way, I can give you the notes from today. I noticed you were shopping instead."

I smile sheepishly, shrugging my backpack on as I follow him out of the classroom. "Guilty," I say, even though my mind is reeling. "I need a job if I'm gonna keep doing that, though."

He asked me on a date.

A real, actual *date*.

He laughs, and we fall into step side-by-side as we walk to the elevators where there're a few people already standing. I see Xavier, and when he looks over, he offers me a small, shy smile, which I return.

"Has Aiden heard anything about the bookstore yet? He mentioned he was gonna ask about you."

"Yeah," I say as we pile onto the elevator, ending up at the front once the doors slide shut. I try not to stiffen *too* noticeably. "He said he brought me up to the owner or something. I haven't gotten my hopes up too much, though."

Jake grins crookedly. "I get it, but if anyone has sway there, it's him. He's a manager, after all."

I'm able to breathe a little better once the elevator doors open, and I hear the surprise in my own tone as I say, "Really? He didn't mention that."

Jake chuckles. "Typical. But yeah, he got promoted after like, only a few months of working there last year. He never brags about *any*thing, though, so Tripp 'n I have to do it for him."

Our walk back to our dorm doesn't take long, and Jake and I part ways, but not before he says, "I'll text you about the date?", which comes out more like a question, as if he's unsure if I've already changed my mind.

So, I smile at him as reassuringly as I can.

"Sounds good."

In my room, Imani's sitting on the floor, painting her toenails with her laptop open next to her, softly playing some pop music.

"Hey," she greets me, not looking up. "How was class?"

I hesitate, letting my backpack slide down my arm to the floor. How do I break the news that she's undoubtedly been waiting on for the last month?

"Good." I pause. "I, uh, I got asked on a date." Her head shoots up, just as I expected.

"Oh my God!" she exclaims. "*Lydia*! By Jake?"

I nod, letting myself smile and bask in her excitement for me as she waddles over, careful not to smudge her nails, to give me a hug. The hug feels nice—and it feels even nicer to have someone be genuinely excited for me.

To have a friend.

My throat tightens with the threat of tears as she steps back, grinning broadly, but I will it away.

"I'm so excited for you, girl! You have to tell me *exactly* how it happened," she says, her dark eyes lighting up with genuine excitement. "Want me to do your nails while we talk? I have every color you could possibly want."

I look down at my own bitten fingernails. One of many experiences I never had as a kid: a friend to paint my nails.

"Sure," I say, and there's something in her returning smile and her starting to rattle off what colors she thinks would look best on me that makes my heart swell and the realization settle in that maybe I can live my life like this, and that maybe, I've found exactly where I'm supposed to be.

CHAPTER THIRTEEN

Sunday comes faster than expected, and I'm both excited and nervous to the point where vomiting might be in my near future.

In the days since Jake asked me on a date, I've:

1. Gotten a shitload of homework for all of my classes

2. Landed an interview at the bookstore (Thank you, Aiden!)

3. Freaked out at least once a day about the date and questioned if maybe this is all one big joke.

But today, I look at myself in the mirror. Am I underdressed? I suppose if I am, it's only his fault for not telling me what we're doing or where we're going.

Or I can blame it on Imani, considering she helped me choose what to wear. Actually, I should rephrase. She *chose* an outfit for me to wear, reprimanding me for my limited choices and demanding we go shopping together soon, especially now that I'll—hopefully—have a job. I sat by and protested, but she didn't listen, and now, here I am.

I do look good, I will admit. She chose one of the shirts I brought that I wasn't ever really planning on wearing, but that

I brought just in case. It's cropped, showing a sliver of my stomach between my high-waisted jeans and where the hem of the shirt ends. It's also tight, clinging to my stomach and chest, and a v-neck, so while I don't have any cleavage to show off, it exposes far more of my abnormally pale skin than I usually put on display. The soft gray cardigan she paired with it makes me feel slightly less exposed.

But there's something about the whole thing that makes me feel almost normal, like I'm not the girl who has a stockpile of animal blood in her mini fridge. Instead, I'm just a college girl, going on her first ever date with her cute football-player friend who lives across the hall. And the thought makes me smile a little at my reflection—without showing my teeth.

But when I hear a knock on the door, my heart rate skyrockets, as if it wasn't already high enough.

"Have fun," Imani says from her perch on the edge of her bed, "And tell me *everything* when you get back. Pinkie promise."

I laugh a little, but wrap my pinkie around hers after she walks across the room to me. After saying bye to her, I make sure I have everything I need with me before walking over to answer the door.

Much to my relief, he's dressed somewhat casually, too, in dark jeans, a T-shirt, and nice jacket. I can't help but notice he also has a backpack on. He smiles, and his eyes quickly flit up and down, taking in my appearance.

"You look nice," he says, almost shyly. "You ready?"

There's something different about him: something unsure and hesitant and so not Jake at all, but it's endearing.

"I'm ready," I murmur. But just as I step out of the doorway, about to close the door behind me, Imani yells,

"Make a wrong move with her, Jacob Hampton, and I'll kill you!"

We both laugh as the door shuts. "I don't doubt it," Jake says.

"She *did* make me pinkie promise her to tell her everything, so if you do anything wrong, she'll be finding out," I tease, and he laughs, our hands bumping against each other. Part of me wonders if he'll hold my hand.

"I don't blame you," he replies as we reach the elevator. "Pinkie promises are serious. I can't begin to tell you how many times my little sister has made me pinkie promise her."

He steps forward to press the down button, and almost immediately, one of the elevators opens. He holds out his hand, letting me enter first.

"Have you ever broken any?" I ask as the elevator begins to descend.

Jake smiles proudly.

"Not one."

When we reach the first floor, Jake lets me out first again, but I hang back and let him take the lead out of the building, considering I have no clue what the plan is.

"Where are we going?" I ask. Considering it's a beautifully sunny morning, there are already plenty of people out and about, but it's not *as* overwhelming as it was when I first got here. Things are just turning out to be... so *right*.

"You'll see," he says. "I had half a mind to blindfold you so it could be a surprise, but something told me that'd be a little dangerous."

"Just a little," I agree.

We walk for a while until it finally dawns on me that he's bringing me toward one of the parks we walked through one of the first few days we were here. Once we enter the park, there are quite a few groups lounging on the grass, but there's still plenty of open space. I follow Jake to one of the open, sunny spaces, a good distance away from the other groups. Of course, I'm still highly aware of their presence and smells and can hear practically every word coming out of their mouths, but Jake doesn't need to know that. Instead, I keep quiet and close my eyes when he tells me to.

I hear the rustling of the backpack as he sets it on the grass, the zipper being unzipped, and after a few more minutes filled with more rustling and crinkling and swatting my hair away as the light breeze blows it into my face, he tells me to open my eyes.

I start to smile as he holds his arms out, proudly gesturing toward what he's set up: there's a light blue blanket spread out across the grass, the edges fluttering in the wind as it's held down in the center by the backpack and the various foods in containers, strawberries and raspberries and cookies, a jug of apple juice, two cups, and two sandwiches.

He brought me on a picnic.

A *picnic*.

My heart flutters. How sweet is that?

"I hope this is okay," he says. "I know it's a little windy, so if you'd rather go—"

"It's perfect," I interrupt, and his smile grows even bigger, if that's even possible at this point.

We sit on the blanket, both of us crossing our legs, and start to dig into the food. The sandwich is an Italian sandwich of some sort, and it's delicious. After a few bites, I set it back down and take a strawberry, which is just the perfect amount of sweet and juicy, some of the juice dripping onto my fingers.

"For the record," I say, as Jake pours us both a cup of apple juice, "Imani will be getting a very good report so far."

Jake laughs, handing me the cup, our fingers brushing as I take it from him. I hear his heart rate take a jump in response, and something swells inside of me, knowing I can illicit that kind of response from someone. From *Jake*, who's cute and sweet and so clearly adored by so many people.

He brings up classes first, but that quickly takes a turn,

and we start to talk about everything and nothing at the same time: how we decided to pursue our respective majors, his love for his family and football, my favorite books, me growing up an only child (which I have to tread carefully around). He keeps his gaze on me the entire time, eyes following my every move, listening attentively, hanging onto my every word.

Making me feel like I'm the only person in the world.

I'm nervous, to say the least.

I'm terrified.

If he had hearing like mine, he'd hear my heart threatening to pound straight out of my chest, feeling like if I say something wrong or weird or let anything about my past slip, this'll all come crashing down on me.

But as we continue to talk, as he makes little jokes and relaxes himself, I start to relax, too. I don't know how long we sit there, but it has to be for a few hours. It's only when the sun dips behind a cloud and goosebumps erupt on my arms from the breeze that we start to pack up, Jake stuffing everything back into his backpack. I feel a pang of disappointment squeezing my heart. I had a lot of fun today, and while we've technically already been out for a while, it feels like it's ending way too soon.

Until Jake tells me we have another stop.

He refuses to tell me, again, where we're going, walking straight down Michigan Avenue until we stop in front of a little shop, squished between two other buildings in the middle of one of the blocks. It's only when I read the little sign out front that I realize where he's taking me.

As we enter the building, walking up a flight of stairs and turning a corner down a long, narrow hallway, Jake lets me lead the way, and I hear him behind me. "Aiden suggested this one," he admits. "He said it always has a good selection."

I swing open the door to the bookstore, and am in awe of what my eyes land on. While it's tiny, the bookshelves reach the ceiling, and most of the shelves have those rolling ladders I've never actually seen in person but have always wanted to climb on since I saw them in *Beauty and the Beast*. I walk into the fiction section, not sure where to start, but just letting my fingers trail over the spines of the books. There's only one worker and one other customer in here, so I'm able to push away their humanness for a bit and focus on the scent of the store itself: there's no other way to describe it other than *clean*, but not clean in an uncomfortable hospital way—clean in a I-could-stay-in-here-forever-and-make-it-my-new-home way.

"Ooh," I say, mostly to myself, pulling a familiar cover off the shelf. "I've been wanting to read this one *forever*."

Before I really know what's happening, Jake is pulling the book out of my hands and tucking it under his arm, a mischievous smile on his face.

"What are you doing?" I ask, and he just continues to grin.

"Buying it for you. Which other ones do you want?"

I let my jaw go slack, and he just looks at me as if he didn't just win the way to my heart through a single sentence. Well, two sentences, I guess. And I suppose he's been winning the way to my heart all day, from planning out a *picnic* for us to making me feel like nobody else in the world mattered.

But *still*.

"I can't let you do that. Books are expensive," I protest, because as much as I adore the gesture, books *are* expensive, and I can't let him do that.

But he just shrugs. He *shrugs*.

"Would you rather I give you a limit?" he asks, totally nonchalantly. "I'll buy you three. Is that okay?"

I want to tell him that it's more than okay. And that it makes me want to kiss him, and I've never even *thought* about kissing anyone before. I mean, I have when reading about kissing in my stacks of romance novels, but not a specific person. Not a *real* person who took me on a *date*.

Does he want to kiss *me?*

Don't be an idiot, I tell myself. *He asked you on a date. That translates to wanting to kiss a person, right? I said yes to this date, and I've already thought about kissing him.*

Instead, I ask him about fifteen more times if he's sure, and after about fifteen times of him reassuring me that yes, he's sure, I pick out two more books. And when I choose the paperback because they're less expensive, even though I prefer hardcover, and even though I don't tell him that, he somehow sees right through me, yanks the paperbacks out of my hands, puts them back on the shelf, and grabs the hardcovers.

I have no words.

I cringe at the total when we check out, seeing as they happened to be new copies, but he doesn't even bat an eye. He just takes the bag from the cashier that holds my three books, hands it to me, thanks the cashier cheerily, and holds the door for me on the way out.

"Thank you," I say for the third time once we exit the bookstore. I move my bag to my left hand so it's not potentially bumping between us as we walk, and I soon feel his fingers brushing against mine. At first, I think it's an accident since we're just walking close together, but soon enough, his fingers slide through mine, and he's holding my hand, and I'm holding his hand, and *a boy is holding my hand.*

He asks me about the books I got, and when I'm done explaining what I know about them and why I want to read them, he just grins at me.

"If *three* books make you this happy," he says, "then I'd buy you the whole damn bookstore."

I can't control the blush that spreads over my entire face and probably every inch of my body. It's cheesy, and it's a sentence I'd *definitely* find in one of my romance novels, and I love it.

I've never felt so human.

I squeeze his hand back, stepping a little closer to him. When he pulls his hand away, I panic for a minute, thinking I did something wrong or my hand got too sweaty, but it's only to wrap his arm around me, pulling me even closer to his side.

I don't know if my face grows warm and my entire body tenses at the fact I'm this close to a cute, respectful, funny boy who clearly seems to like me and seems to care about my interests, or at the fact I'm this close to a living, breathing human with sweet, delicious-smelling blood running through his veins.

I push away the thought that the latter is what it is, and I focus on the fact that Jake is the sweetest boy I've ever met, and I focus on the question of whether he'll kiss me today or not. Am I even ready for that? I mean, it can't be that hard. I've read enough about kissing to get the gist.

What am I talking about? That's not the same thing.

Idiot. Don't overthink it. You'll ruin it. If he even wants to.

We walk back to our dorm, and as we pass the art museum, I tell him I've never been to a museum. He tells me about his favorite paintings, and how his mom loves The Starry Night, and how it's on her phone case, no matter how dorky that is, and how he wants to take her to see it in New York one day. I laugh and watch his smile grow as he talks about how his little sister likes to read.

"I think she'd really like you," he says as we enter our building and step back into the elevator. "She's kind of quiet, kind of shy, but she's one of the most creative people I've ever met. She wants to write her own books, one day."

I smile, trying to picture this little girl who pinkie-promises her older brother and likes writing. For a second, a pang of longing tightens my chest, but I push it away.

"Tell her I'll read them when she does."

He smiles as the elevator starts to rise, and I wonder if he's thinking about kissing me. But he doesn't by the time we reach our floor, and he doesn't when we stop in front of my door, but he does say,

"I had a great time today, Lyds. Would you, uh, would you wanna do this again sometime soon?"

"For sure," I say, and he grins at me, but keeps his distance. Maybe he's just waiting, which I do appreciate.

"Awesome," he replies. "I'll check when I've got practice this week and let you know. Maybe we can go to the museum."

"I'd love that," I reply earnestly.

We say our goodbyes, and the minute I turn around and open the door, still smiling like an idiot, I can hear Imani's voice loud and clear from within our room, and I know damn well that Jake can, too.

"Lydia!" she yells, "Tell me *everything!*"

Jake laughs, and I hurry into the room and shut the door behind me, beet red.

But, per her request, I do.

CHAPTER FOURTEEN

MY EXCITEMENT from my date with Jake spans the rest of the day, until my looming interview ruins it, which is scheduled for Monday afternoon after geology. About thirty minutes beforehand, I change into one of my dressier shirts, take a few sips of blood just in case, Google *how to do a job interview,* and try to slow my increasing heart rate with deep breaths.

I text Aiden before I leave, sending a simple and very calm-sounding *off to my interview!* to which he seems to read my mind and replies:

> aiden swanson: sweet! Try not to stress too much, Roarke is super cool and I already talked you up a lot lol so just be yourself :)
> Let me know how it goes!

I abruptly stop in the middle of the hallway and reread his text a few times.

Roarke? As in the Roarke I saw barely three hours ago?

Roarke is not a common name whatsoever, and I really

doubt there just *happens* to be two Roarkes working in the South Loop.

> me: roarke?

I text back, finally starting toward the elevators again, or else I'll be late.

> me: did he happen to mention if he knows me?

Aiden doesn't reply until I'm down to the main floor. Granted, he's in class, but I wish he'd pay attention less and reply to me faster; it doesn't take all that long to walk to the bookstore.

> aiden swanson: No, why do you think you know him?

> me: my english professor's name is roarke lol

> aiden swanson: No way! I didn't know that. I bet it's him, tell him he's a little shit for not telling me if it is

> me: oh for sure, cause thatll get me the job

> aiden swanson: lame

> I'm jk

> Good luck!

My heart is somehow pounding even more rapidly by the time I get to the bookstore, a little brick building with large glass windows and a sign jutting out from the side reading *EB's Books* that creaks in the wind. When I open the door of the bookstore, it's completely empty save for, yes, my professor, Roarke.

"Lydia!" he says, the light wooden floorboards creaking under his feet as he walks from a bookshelf packed with children's books. "I was hoping it was you, but when Aiden told me he was 'recommending his book-loving friend Lydia,' I didn't want to ask too many questions and be disappointed. Come in, come in! Let me show you around."

I smile, somehow both relieved that it *is* the Roarke I know and even more nervous because of that. I mean, just because I've seen him the past few Mondays and turned in some assignments for him doesn't mean he *knows* me. What if I reveal something he doesn't like in this interview and doesn't give me the job *and* hates me in class? I don't know what I *could* say that would get that kind of reaction other than, *by the way, I'm a vampire,* but who knows?

God, now I *really* can't screw this up. What was I thinking, *hoping* it was him?

I follow Roarke around the store as he rapid-fire tells me where each genre is, finally stopping in fantasy, which sits almost in the center of the small store. I scan the titles as he talks, telling me about how his wife technically owns the bookstore, but he'll do interviews and can stop in more often than she can because she's busy with their kids, two of which the store is named after, and "other life stuff."

"So," he says, "when can you start?"

I tear my eyes away from scanning the shelves.

"What?" is all I manage.

He grins, flashing those sharp teeth at me. "C'mon, Lydia, I've seen enough in your classwork to know you'd be a great fit here. I mean, your analyses go so in depth, and you're extremely timely in getting your work in. Not to mention the way Aiden raved about you, and I've come to trust his opinion over the last year." I hope he doesn't notice the heat rising to my cheeks at that. "Plus, we can always use the help. I'll just need a few things for your paperwork and your availability, but other than that, if you want the job, it's yours."

I'm flustered, to say the least. I've been here for what, ten minutes? I didn't have to interview, and I have the job?

What the hell did Aiden say about me?

But Roarke is looking at me expectantly, so I let my smile blossom through my shock and say, "Yeah, I'd love to work here. Thank you."

Roarke claps his hands together, making me flinch slightly from how loud and abrupt it is. He tells me what he'll need from me, paperwork-wise, and gives me his phone number so I can text him my availability. A customer comes in, the bell above the door jingling as we're finishing up, so Roarke speeds through the end of his speech after telling the person he'll be with them in just a minute.

"And, Lydia," he says, lowering his voice a little as the man wanders off into what I think is the nonfiction section, "just because I'm your professor *and* kind of your boss doesn't mean you can't come to me if you need anything, alright?"

I nod, wondering what exactly he means and why exactly he's looking at me as if he's trying to get me to understand something. I think back to that first day of class, how he felt so familiar. *Do* we know each other?

But instead, I just thank him again and leave, a little more pep in my step as I walk back to my dorm.

CHAPTER FIFTEEN

I END up being scheduled for my first shift on Friday: a closing shift with Aiden. Roarke tells me when I meet up with him to fill out paperwork the next day, because of how small the store is, they generally only have one or two employees working at once. He also tells me with a grin that he'll try and schedule me with Aiden as much as he can, which I can't help but smile about, too.

And so, when Friday rolls around, despite it being *work*, I'm excited, because it means:

1. Getting to be around books all day,
2. Getting to spend time with Aiden,
3. Getting to make money, and
4. Adding even a little more normalcy to my life.

Aiden and I walk to the bookstore together, talking along the way about school and whatnot, and it's just so *easy*. I can't help but feel even more secure that I made the right choice in coming here. For once, I'm—I think I'm *happy*.

"So, your job is gonna be to do whatever I tell you to do."

Once we get to the bookstore, I follow him up the small set of stairs leading to the front door. Once we reach the landing, he pulls out a set of brass keys. They all look the same to me, but the one he chooses successfully unlocks the door, which he holds open for me to enter first.

"And what if I don't wanna do what you tell me?" I ask.

The lights flicker on, flooding the entire store with warm lighting. It feels homey, and with Aiden here, it's even better.

"Then I think I have the right to fire you."

I smile as he steps toward me, having to raise my chin slightly higher to be able to look him in the eyes.

"You didn't hire me, so while you might have the right to *get me* fired, I don't think you can do it yourself. Am I wrong?"

"You're a smartass, that's what you are."

I laugh, and he slowly smiles. There's something different about him. He seems a little more relaxed somehow. It shows in the way he's joking with me, in the way that he lowers himself into the rolling chair behind the desk and props his feet on the desk. Even in the way he smiles at me seems more genuine.

"You'll be here for the most part, or—" He tilts his head toward the other rolling desk chair behind him, facing a smaller desk that faces the wall. The one Aiden is at faces out, complete with a desktop computer and a drawer for the cash register. "—back there. If you're sitting where I'm at, you'll pretty much be waiting here while customers are in the store because they'll come to you if they need anything. But if you're back there, you'll be the one shelving or helping anyone else find anything they're looking for. Or whatever other dirty work I have you do."

The corner of his mouth quirks up in a smile. "It's pretty simple. You'll get the hang of it." He pushes himself up from the chair. "C'mon. I'll give you the tour."

I decide not to bring up the fact that Roarke already gave me the tour, because honestly, I could really use it again. I want to know where everything is without having to read the signs.

"Over here," he says, "we have the new releases. These aren't organized by genre or anything. Just make sure you alphabetize correctly. Believe it or not, we had someone last year who couldn't manage to do that."

He stops abruptly in front of the first shelf, and I stop, nearly colliding with his back. I flush as I step back, keeping a respectable distance away from him. If he notices my sudden awkwardness, he doesn't say anything, much to my relief. He continues on with the tour, showing me where the fiction section is, the nonfiction, YA, children's, and so on, weaving between the short but high shelves.

I run my fingers along the spines of the books, feeling the smooth edges and the occasional raised letters of the titles. It's stupid, but there's something comforting about it—not just the reading part, where I can lose myself in the stories and no longer be *Lydia the vampire girl with no friends—well, a few friends now, actually*, but also just being surrounded by books, the atmosphere, the smell.

And Aiden, who seems to understand that more than anyone I've met, evident just by the way he explains and moves around like he's more comfortable here than anywhere else, surrounded by stories.

It makes me wonder. What secrets does *he* have?

"Any questions?" he asks, spinning around to face me.

I shake my head. "Don't think so."

"Good," he says. "Now, do you mind if I go—" My panic must show on my face, because he laughs. "I'm kidding, I'm kidding."

I shake my head, just barely fighting back a smile. "You—"

I stop myself, and Aiden raises a teasing brow. "Calling your manager names is another means for firing, Ross."

I grin at him, as innocently as I can, and I swear his heartbeat stutters.

"I didn't say anything."

Aiden grins, but then we're interrupted by the jingling bell above the door. "C'mon," he says, "Let's get to work."

I feel relaxed. Obviously, being surrounded by books helps, but Aiden is definitely a contributing factor. I find myself constantly with him throughout my shift, almost as much as I was on my date with Jake.

In just one shift, I think I get a pretty good handle on things. Still need to get used to the sales system, but everything else is pretty easy to understand. The hours fly by, and next thing I know, Aiden is showing me how to close up, and then we're outside.

"Nice work today, rookie," he says, locking the door. "You're a quick learner."

"Well, I had a great teacher."

He chuckles as we start walking back to our dorm. I like the sound of our footsteps falling in sync with each other.

"I heard about your date tomorrow," Aiden says. "The art museum, right? Jake seems pretty excited."

"Yeah," I say. "I'm excited, too. Mostly nervous, but—" I turn my face up to the sky; the days are getting shorter and it's getting darker earlier. No matter how much time I force myself to spend in the sun, I think I'll always prefer the still darkness of night.

Today's just been a good day.

"Don't worry about it," Aiden says. "'Cause trust me, think about how nervous you are, and then double that, and that's where Jake is at."

"What? No."

There's no way. He's so... *outgoing* and can just talk to

people. I have to think about everything I say for at least two minutes before I say it and it *still* usually comes out sounding stupid.

Aiden grins crookedly. "Oh, yeah," he says. "He seemed about ready to go on a fake date with Tripp or I to practice. I don't think I could've turned him down, either. I wouldn't wanna hurt his feelings."

Aiden smiles as I laugh, covering my hand with my mouth.

"He really likes you, Lydia," he continues. I swear I see his smile falter for a split second, but he turns his face away before I can tell for sure.

THE NEXT MORNING, I'M SITTING ON THE EDGE OF my bed, ready to go, two hours before Jake will be done with practice. Imani is out getting coffee with a friend, so I'm free to pace around the entire room, lifting my hands to my mouth to bite my nails before realizing they're still painted and lowering them before repeating it all again. I nurse a bottle of blood, too, even though, really, I should be okay after feeding while she was at Tripp's last night.

Imani comes back about an hour later, just as I've given up and started picking at the nail polish. She stops at the end of my bed, tilting her head and giving me a look that's half-exasperated and half-amused.

"C'mere," she says. When I place my hands in hers, she brings them close to her face, examining the damage.

"At least you're not biting your nails," she muses. She crosses the room and begins to rifle through the bin of nail products on the corner of her desk. "I used to bite my nails *alllll* the time in high school. Tripp, believe it or not, was the one who helped me and told me he used clear nail polish to help himself stop. 'Til his parents found it, and—"

She lets out a sigh, glancing up at me as I drum my fingers on my thighs, trying not to pick at my nails.

"He makes jokes about it, but they *are* really shitty. I can't wait until we can afford to get an apartment together. I mean, he hasn't been back home since he left for college, since he stayed with Jake all last summer and went home with him for holidays 'n everything. He's basically Jake's adopted brother at this point." Imani smiles a bit sadly, a pink bottle and a cotton ball in one hand and a smaller bottle of light blue polish in the other. "I admit, I was a little jealous that first year we were long distance and I had to share him with Jake, but he's so much happier here. He can be a little shit sometimes, *obviously*, but I don't know what I'd do without him, y'know?"

I smile softly, because quite frankly, no, I don't know, but it seems nice to love someone that much and to be loved that much in return. Both romantically *and* platonically—for Tripp to have Imani *and* Jake, two people who clearly love him unconditionally.

Will I ever get a chance at something like that?

Or, if I find someone I let myself fall in love with someday, will I scare them away if I tell them what I am?

Or is love just not possible for someone like me, if I don't suppress it, hide it like I've been doing? *Lydia the human* can be, at the very least, liked—that much has been proven to me. But can *Lydia the vampire,* who has bottles of blood stocked in her fridge? Who can't get too close to anyone without getting overwhelmed?

Imani unscrews the lid of the pink bottle, and I can't stop myself before I visibly cringe from the scent as it makes my eyes water. She laughs a little at my reaction, putting the cotton ball on the opening and flipping the bottle upside down as she walks toward me.

"I know, it stinks."

We sit on my bed and I hold out my hands, trying my best not to breathe too much, as she starts to remove the remaining, chipped polish from my nails.

"I can tell you're nervous. But you shouldn't be. Jake clearly likes you." She lifts her gaze, looking at me through my lashes. "Did you date anyone in high school?"

I flush. But there's no point in lying.

"Uh, no. No, I've never been on a date. Well, before Jake. And, I, uh, I've never kissed anyone before, either. Nobody, um... Nobody really liked me in high school, I think."

She just tsks and shakes her head as she moves on to carefully applying the new, light-blue polish. While she doesn't comment on it, I assume she gets fed up with how shaky my hands are because she takes the one she's working on and lowers it onto her thigh to steady it, which only succeeds in making my entire face heat up.

"Well, the people at your high school were *clearly* idiots and didn't know what they were missing out on," she says, not helping my already bright-red face. My tendency to blush so easily is definitely one human trait I'd be perfectly okay with *not* having.

Imani glances up at me through her lashes again, a smile playing on her full lips. "You up for a girls' night tonight? You don't have work, do you?"

"No work. And yeah. That sounds fun."

"Good. Listen, as much as I love those boys—" She doesn't even finish her sentence, and instead just gives me a look with raised eyebrows. I can't help but laugh.

"I get it," I say.

Imani finishes my nails, blowing on them gently to help speed up the drying. By the time we're all done, it's already about time Jake should be back.

And sure enough, a few minutes later, as I'm waving my hands to make sure they're dry, there's a knock on the door.

Imani winks at me as I get up to answer it.

"Hey." Jake grins when I open the door. "You all set?"

I nod, and after he says both hi and bye to Imani, and I make sure I have everything, we head to the art museum.

We end up going through every possible exhibit, and I feel myself relaxing a bit, settling into the calm of heartbeats and hushed conversations. My favorite exhibit definitely ends up being the miniature rooms on the lowest floor. They're like little dollhouse rooms, but with an insane amount of detail, and from different decades and centuries. Jake lets me take the lead, trailing behind me and pointing out his favorite details in each. Every second I spend with him, I feel myself letting some of my guard down little by little.

Before long, we're leaving, holding hands again as we walk down the sidewalk. I feel a flutter of nervousness in my chest as he rubs his thumb across mine, and his heartbeat is a little quicker than usual, too.

We decide to stop in Starbucks, where we settle into a two-person table in the corner. Because it's now later in the after-noon, it's not as packed as it could be, which is a relief on my senses. Instead, I can enjoy the richness of the coffee and the sweet scent of cookies and other pastries.

Jake sips his dark pink refresher as we talk. He, unfortu-nately, asks me more about growing up, to which I try and give the vaguest answers possible. Somehow, though, I'm able to steer the topic of conversation away from myself.

"It's you, your mom, and your sister, right?" I ask.

He's never brought up his dad—and I don't feel comfort-able asking yet. So, I'm a little surprised when he says, "Since I was thirteen, yeah. That's when my dad died."

"Oh," I say, quietly. "I'm sorry."

Jake shrugs one shoulder. "Yeah, I mean, it still sucks, a

lot." He laughs humorlessly. "I had to step up a lot in those years after he died, with my sister being so young and my mom being as torn apart as she was. I—" He looks away, and I realize this is really the first time I've seen Jake as something deeper than the happy-go-lucky golden retriever I've started knowing him to be.

"It's been a little more tough recently, 'cause she's having her bat mitzvah soon, and Dad died just after mine. It's like, I was so excited to be considered an adult, y'know, and then..."

He drifts off, clearly unsure of how to continue, so instead of saying *I'm sorry* again, I ask the question at the forefront of my mind: "You're Jewish?"

He nods, smiling a little, though there's obvious sadness in it. "Yeah," he confirms. "We're pretty casual about it." His smile turns a little sheepish. "We've also gained a little more distance from it all since Dad died. I don't think it was ever really intentional, but then I got older, too, and started focusing on other things, and..." He sighs. "I felt kinda guilty moving here for college, but my mom insisted they'd be okay without me." He huffs a humorless laugh, meeting my eyes again. "Told me that my dad would want me to live my life, and that's kind of the push I needed, I think. And, of course, moving here brought me to Tripp, who's more of a brother to me than a best friend at this point, so I really don't feel *as* guilty anymore, but at the same time, I do, y'know? I dunno, it's complicated."

He pauses, before shaking his head, that familiar grin coming back to his face, though it doesn't quite reach his eyes.

"Sorry to get so serious there."

"No, no, it's okay," I say, tapping my fingers rapidly, anxiously, on my thighs under the table as I decide to continue. "I, uh, I kind of understand. I've felt some guilt at leaving my dad, since it's only ever been us since—well, my whole life, but at the same time, I kinda want him to learn to live his life without me, y'know? He's... he's always put me first."

Jake nods slowly, never once looking away from me, even as I drop my own gaze under the intensity of his.

"I know what you mean," he says. "But, if you don't mind me saying, I think he doesn't need to learn to live his life *without* you. You're his daughter, after all, and he loves you." A smile tugs at the corner of his mouth. "I could tell that much from that first day I saw you guys saying goodbye. The distance and the space is important as you get older and everything, sure, but you'll still always be there for each other. That's kinda what I have to remind myself."

I stare at him, something tightening in my chest.

I wish I could explain to someone it's not so easy. That I've made Dad's life a hundred times harder just by *existing*. That I'd move across the country if it meant he could just actually live the life he deserves.

"Yeah," is all I say, toying with the peeling sticker on my cup. "Yeah. You're right."

We leave Starbucks soon after that, and I try my hardest to stay in the present with Jake, to stay outside my head. That becomes easier when he holds my hand again, when he asks me about what I'm reading, and when he tries to sneak up on a pigeon to grab it, despite my discouragement.

"I've been trying since last year," he whines when the pigeon flies away. "I want to sneak one into Tripp's room, at *least* before graduation. It's on my bucket list."

Our conversation in Starbucks still lingers in my head by the time we reach our dorm, but he has me laughing enough to where it's been pushed to the back of my mind. We're able to snag an empty elevator, and the second the doors close behind us, I think back to our first date, where we were in this exact same position. Me, on the left side of the elevator, leaning against the back wall, and him on the right side, leaning against the far wall.

And I wonder, yet again, if he'll kiss me.

What do I do if he does?

Oh, I don't know. Kiss him back? That was a stupid question.

He's looking at me now, a small smile playing on his lips as we pass floors three and four.

"What?" I ask, my voice small. His smile grows as he pushes himself off the wall. I swallow hard, hoping that my great hearing *is* just a vampire thing and that he can't hear my erratic heartbeat.

If only I knew these things for sure. It feels like my whole life is made up of guesses sometimes.

"Just—" He pauses. "Can I kiss you?"

My breath catches in my throat, and I realize his heart is beating just as fast as my own, as if he's just as nervous as I am. It's like our heartbeats are one and the same.

The elevator softly dings as we pass floor five.

"Yeah," I confirm, my voice breathy. His answering smile makes my heart flutter as he crosses the elevator to me. I let my eyes shut, not sure what to do with my hands, so I leave them at my side as I feel one of his hands cup my cheek. I lean forward, breathing in the scent of his cologne and blood and sweat and shampoo, and I feel his breath on my lips just a split second before his lips brush against mine, as if testing the boundaries before he really kisses me.

There aren't any explosions or fireworks or whatever else they talk about in romance books, but it's nice. His lips are soft and warm and gentle against mine, and they're gone all too soon. I open my eyes as he pulls away, the elevator doors sliding open on our floor—just in time to see his face split into a grin.

CHAPTER SIXTEEN

"Oh my God! How was it?!" Imani exclaims once I tell her about the kiss. She's perched on the edge of her bed, giving me her utmost attention. We're all set for our "girls' night" with Netflix open on the TV, the blinds drawn, and popcorn she used the boys' microwave to make—while I discreetly took a few sips of blood from one of my bottles, my body still thrumming from being that close to someone so human.

"It was nice," I say earnestly, and she squeals, clapping her hands and clutching them together by her chin.

"I'm *so* excited for you. Has he asked you to be his girlfriend yet?"

I shake my head. To be honest, I've been so wrapped up in the hand-holding and kissing that I haven't really thought about the making-it-official part.

Oh my God. Am I going to have a *boyfriend*?

Oh my *God*, do I tell Dad?

Will I have to introduce him to Dad? Will I have to meet *his* family? What if they don't like me? What if they think I'm boring?

"Idiot," Imani says. "I'll tell Tripp to talk some sense into him so he asks you already."

"Oh, you don't have—"

Imani grins wickedly at me, and I know there's no use in fighting her when she already clearly has her mind set.

Not even twenty-four hours later, Jake takes me out to lunch before my afternoon shift at work and asks me to be his girlfriend, and I say yes. I still haven't processed that I have a *boyfriend* and have been kissed *multiple* times now by the time I walk into work, to find Aiden already there, since he came straight from running errands. I'm really happy with how our friendship is building, and I hope that doesn't change now just because I'm officially dating one of his closest friends. Aiden brings out a different side of me; I *feel* different with him—a good different, and I'd be really disappointed if I were to lose that.

He's a little quieter than usual, but when I ask if he's okay, he just says that he's tired. But even so, the energy in the bookstore is a little off—all the way until closing that night.

Between work, classes, homework, hanging out with my friends, and spending disappointingly minimal time with Jake when he's not at practice or traveling for away games or one of the other hundreds of things he has to do for football, the next week flies by. I realize it's already mid-October, which means a few different things are right around the corner:

1. Midterms—math is completely kicking my ass.
2. Imani's nineteenth birthday—what the hell do I get her?
3. Halloween—Imani's making us do a group costume.

But my math problems will have to wait for later. We throw Imani a surprise party in the boys' apartment for her birthday, after Jake gets back from an away game, which leaves Tripp, Aiden, and I on decoration duty. Tripp takes the reins, and soon enough, the apartment is decked out in all things pink, all things glitter, and cardboard cutouts of popular vampires in media, from Gary Oldman as Dracula to the brothers from *The Vampire Diaries*.

I don't know how to feel about them.

But Imani's happy — she practically screams when she walks into the apartment. "You guys! Oh, my God. Oh, my *God*! It's Stefan and Damon!"

"Yeah, and they're going *straight* to *your* room after this," Tripps says, but with a smile as Imani launches herself into his arms. "They've been freaking me out, being in mine."

We do presents soon after she's settled down from being surprised and wearing her plastic tiara and birthday sash. I decided on a special edition set of the *Twilight* books, and when I bought them with my employee discount at work, Aiden teased me about stealing his idea. When she gets to my present, she tugs the bag over to her and says, "Jeez! This is heavy!" She wastes no time in pulling the tissue paper out, and as she reaches into the bag, she lets out a gasp. My cheeks hurt from smiling — and from fighting to keep my lips firmly clamped shut.

"*Lydia!* You *didn't*!"

She squeals as she shows the boys the box set, showing off every side of it. "Look! Look how *beautiful* they are. You're the *best*, Lydia! Thank you, thank you, thank you!" Once she sets them down, she flies across the room and gives me a huge hug. I laugh, wrapping my arms around her, feeling her rapid heartbeat.

After presents, she settles onto Tripp's lap and says,

"Oh! Oh, guys. I have our Halloween costume theme. Drumroll, please."

Jake drumrolls his hands on his lap. Imani grins and announces, after a pause for dramatic effect:

"Scooby Doo. The Mystery Gang. Isn't it perfect?"

"Only if I get to be Scooby," Jake says.

"Dammit, Hamp," Tripp all-but yells. "*I* wanted to be Scooby. But fine, I call Shaggy."

"Does that make me Fred, or do I get a choice of one of the girls?" Aiden asks, his leg bumping mine as he lifts his hips to shift his sitting position. My cheeks immediately flush, but I don't scoot away.

Imani grins, adjusting her tiara.

"Fight that one out with Lydia. *I* want Daphne, as long as that's okay with you, Lyds?"

"Yeah, yeah, I'm fine with Velma," I say, quietly, glancing over at Aiden. "Unless you *really* want her, then I guess I can negotiate."

Aiden sighs dramatically, but then smiles crookedly. "I *guess* I'll be Fred."

I learn that the Halloween party is being hosted by the girl-friend of one of Jake's teammates. Apparently, there's going to be "plenty of alcohol," in Tripp's words, which gives me a little anxiety, and prizes for different categories of costumes—which is why Imani—and now Jake—are insistent we look our best.

As soon as the party is over, I have the room to myself because Imani is sleeping over with Tripp—and her cardboard cutouts—so I curl up in my bed and start studying for my math midterm tomorrow. But apparently, it's not successful, because I wake up, fully dressed, at 3 A.M., on top of my notes.

That must have been an indication of how my midterm was going to go, because when my score is uploaded online Tuesday afternoon, as Imani and I are at one of the stores downtown to look for pieces for our costumes, my stomach sinks when I see I got a D.

I've already been doing shitty enough in the class, and now *this* tanked my grade. I'm fine with passing with the bare minimum, but if I fail the final, I'm going to fail the class. And I *know* that would disappoint Dad.

"This skirt would be per—You okay?"

I look up at Imani, who's holding up a red miniskirt on a hanger.

"Uh, yeah. Yeah." I tuck my phone back into the back pocket of my jeans. "I didn't do good on my math midterm. I'm just- I'm kinda worried about how I'm gonna pass, I guess."

Imani's mouth tugs down in a frown. "Ah, I'm sorry, girl. I'd offer, but I'm not great at math, either. Maybe there's someone in your class who can help you?"

I think of my math class. The only person I've spoken to is Xavier, who did offer to help me, but maybe he didn't really mean it. He was probably just being nice. But then again, maybe I'll gather up the courage to ask him. It's not like we're strangers — we're not friends who talk outside of class, but he's good company to have in class and walking home after, so I wouldn't feel *as* weird bringing it up again as I would with someone else in the class.

But it's still a *strong* maybe.

To get my mind off it, I take the skirt from Imani and go to a fitting room to try it on. I feel incredibly exposed, especially when it rides up on my thighs every time I take a step, but with Imani hyping me up, I cave and buy it.

The Halloween party is Thursday night, which I find a little odd, but it has something to do with the football team's schedule, and plus, *I* don't have classes on Friday, so I can sleep in; I just have to make sure I make my trip to the butcher sometime before Imani gets back from her class.

The thought about the trip to the butcher makes me a little anxious, because well, I'd never admit this to Dad, but

I'm out of blood. I don't know if spending more, er, *intimate* time with Jake has made my cravings worsen and ability to hold out for multiple days at a time decrease, but when I go to open my fridge Thursday, the morning of the party, I realize I took my last bottle from the fridge on Tuesday morning — or was it Monday? — and that there are none left in my freezer.

No biggie, I tell myself. In the summers in high school, when it was just me and Dad and I wasn't tempted by large groups at school, I could easily go four or five days between feedings. Dad hated it, thinking I was gonna lose it on him (even if he never admitted it), but it saved us money when I didn't go through blood as fast.

Plus, I remind myself, I'm going tomorrow morning. This is only what, the second or third day? I'll be fine.

I'll be *fine*.

CHAPTER SEVENTEEN

I'm not fine.

My stomach was already churning when the boys came over to collect Imani and I to head over to the party. Now, as I sit on the nearly empty train, I'm struggling to keep my mind on anything but the smell of blood filling the small car.

And, unfortunately, Jake isn't helping. His hand is on my thigh—revealed by this too-short orange skirt that rides up if I take too deep of a breath—which already makes my heart race. He's so close and warm, and his blood smells so good, I catch myself wishing he hadn't worn any cologne so I could just breathe him in—

No.

I lean against the window and press my cheek against the cold glass to try and distract myself, even focusing on the faint smell of pee that lingers in the air.

Jake is talking to Tripp, bringing up names of people I don't know, but who'll be at the party tonight. I'm glad he's not paying attention to me right now, so he doesn't ask if I'm okay.

My phone vibrates once in my lap, indicating I've got a

text. After pulling my hand away from Jake's, I turn it over, tapping the screen only to see that it's from Aiden.

> aiden swanson: you okay?

I respond, deciding to be as honest as I can:

> me: fine, just a little anxious

The three little dots appear within seconds, indicating he's typing, and a minute later, I get another text:

> aiden swanson: I know you won't wanna feel like you're dragging Jake away if you wanna leave, so you can always use me an excuse. I can fake puke very convincingly, believe it or not

And another:

> aiden swanson: It's one of my many hidden talents

I smile, and when I glance up at Aiden, he's already looking at me, the ghost of a smile playing on his lips. It feels like we're in our own little world, away from Jake and Tripp and Imani, who are all laughing about some story Jake's been telling about the boys' last Halloween together.

> me: i might have to take you up on that. just to see how convincing it really is

Jake nudges my arm, sliding his fingers through mine once again, and it's like I crash back down to Earth. I feel a little prick of guilt. I should try being more honest with him, too.

"This next stop is ours," he says, leaning to press a kiss to my temple, his lips distractingly warm against my skin.

Thankfully, the walk from our stop to the apartment isn't long because the air is chilly against my exposed legs, though it gives me something to focus on other than the human warmth surrounding me.

I can already hear and sense everything even as I step through the door, and my heart climbs into my throat. The music and the voices and the heartbeats and the stench of alcohol make the walls of the too-skinny hallway feel like they're closing in, constricting with the pulsing sounds.

Immediately, we get introduced to the host, who's dressed like Tinkerbell, her boyfriend and Jake's teammate, who's dressed like Captain Jack Sparrow, and other various people in a bunch of vastly different costumes whose names I've already forgotten. I look around the apartment, at the ten or so people gathered in a kitchen designed for two, pressed up against the counters and each other as they all try to talk over one another.

I try to decipher everything, ignoring the pain in my gut. There's the stench of perfumes and colognes mixed with sweat and blood and... pizza? I glance over to the tiny counter next to the fridge, only to see that yes, there's a pizza, though judging by the pace that the Superman standing next to it is devouring the two pieces he already has, it's going to be gone soon. Not that human food would help me right now anyway.

The Tinkerbell host, whose name I already forgot, too, ushers us into the living room. We get introduced to two more people: a girl with black hair dressed as a sexy Dorothy from the Wizard of Oz, her cleavage practically spilling out of her low-cut top, and—

"Nice fangs," Imani tells the boy dressed as a vampire, and he smiles at her, further exposing his fake fangs.

I look away, a little too quickly, and step closer to Jake. There's something about the fake blood smeared across his chin that hits a little too close to home, making the churning in my stomach worse.

Next thing I know, a little container is being pushed into my hand, which I'm soon told is a Jello shot. Mine is orange, but by the time I'm finished inspecting it, trying to figure out how to get it out of the cup, everyone around me has already downed theirs and is grabbing seconds from the tray that Superman is holding.

"You don't have to if you don't want to," Jake says as quietly as he can, leaning down to speak in my ear, his dog-ear headband sliding forward on his head. "But they aren't strong or anything, if that's what you're worried about. You can barely taste it."

I look into his face, at the gentle, reassuring look in his eyes, and decide to take the shot, but not before pushing his headband back on his head, which makes him grin. Once I finally unstick it from the sides with my finger and manage to get it to slide out of the cup, I realize he's right as I chew and swallow. It pretty much just tastes like normal Jello. Jake smiles before asking if I mind if he goes to take shots with some of the others and if I want to come with, and I say no to both, watching as he disappears into the kitchen, into the crowd that's growing bigger and louder and warmer by the second.

I turn toward Aiden, suddenly feeling lost. I don't know how to make small talk with any of these people whose names I don't know, nor do I really want to. The music that's blasting from a speaker is just noisy and nothing that I can even use to distract myself, and everybody's yelling over each other, and everyone smells like alcohol and sweat and pizza grease, and my stomach and my head are starting to hurt so, so bad.

"You sure you're alright?" Aiden asks.

"Fine," I say. "It's a little loud."

He nods, scrunching his nose in an oddly cute way, but I

push that thought out of my head immediately. "It's okay, you can say it. This music sucks," he whispers, and I laugh.

But my momentary distraction is shattered when Jake comes back and slides his hands along my waist to pull me back into his chest. I have to step away because of the overwhelming desire to sink my teeth into his exposed, veiny wrist.

As the night goes on, I accept a shot of liquid that I'm not even sure what it is, but I don't ask because I don't want to seem like an idiot. I practically have to choke it down because it tastes so bad. I can't feel the alcohol hitting me like it's clearly hitting everyone else, and everything is getting louder and more unbearable.

My vision starts going in and out and all I can focus on are the scents of sweat and blood and all I can see are wrists and the soft skin of necks and perfectly smooth skin peeking out from the edges of clothing teasing, teasing, teasing, begging me to have a taste, the veins in an arm or the soft curve of a thigh until my mouth is practically watering and my fingers are twitching in a way that's out of my control.

I'm just. So. *Hungry.*

Next thing I know, I'm standing in a little circle with Jake and a few others, and everyone is laughing, and a pair of arms slides around me. It's Imani, and as she hugs me, I breathe her in, and her hair slides to expose her neck. It shines with the sheen of sweat, and her pulse thrums just below her warm skin. And if I just tilted my face down just a little bit, I could just graze my lips against her neck and-

No. No, no, *no.*

I bite down on my lip, hard, and as my own blood pools in my mouth, I wrench myself out of her arms. I need a bathroom *now.*

Thankfully, it's empty. I barely manage to get the door locked before I sink to the floor, my back pressed up against the wall, a choked sob making its way out of me. Not that anyone would be able to hear, and not that it'd be safe for anyone to approach me right now anyway—not in the state that I'm in, as black spots dance at the edge of my vision, as I breathe in a deep breath, only to pick up all of the blood outside this door. I can still imagine how it'd taste, how it'd feel to sink my teeth into soft flesh, hot and flushed from drinking and dancing, and I know I need to make it stop *now*, and I know there's only one thing I can try to make it stop, even though I don't know if it'll work.

And I sure as *hell* don't know what I'll do if it doesn't.

I barely register how badly I'm shaking as I lift my arm to my mouth, pressing my lips to my own skin, cold and clammy and nothing like what I'm craving so badly, but it'll do. I'll do anything as not to hurt anyone on the other side of the door, even if that means doing something I've only done once, over a decade ago, back before we knew what I am. As long as it satisfies me in this moment, that's all I need.

As long as it's not someone else.

I open my mouth, letting it rest against my arm for a second longer before letting my fangs pierce through my flesh, pain shooting through my arm and forcing my eyes shut, but the warm, thick, sweet blood that floods my mouth only a second later makes the pain worth it. I suck on my arm, my eyes rolling back as I feel the tension leave my body, my shoulders relaxing as I slouch, hunching over my arm, focusing on nothing but the blood, leaving the human side of my body only to enter it again, satisfying the monster in me, slowing my heart rate.

With a gasp, I pull my mouth away, gasping for air as I lower my arm to my lap, stretching out my legs in front of me and leaning my head back against the wall. I don't dare look down at my arm, but I can already feel the skin healing, closing up the holes and making it appear as if I didn't just do what I did.

But even if the monster feels *slightly* better, I still need to get out. For my sake, but mostly for theirs.

Once I control my breathing, the piercing pain in my head dulled to a still-unbearable ache. I push myself off the floor and look in the bathroom mirror. I turn on the faucet, wetting the tips of my still-shaking fingers so I can clean the already-dried blood off my lips and chin, and use my index finger as a makeshift toothbrush to clean the blood off my teeth. The entire time, I stare back into the hollow eyes of my reflection, studying the deep purple bags under them, but a part of me is thankful for those bags.

I splash my face with water, and once I'm convinced that I look a little less terrible, I unlock the door with a shaky hand and let myself out of the bathroom.

"There you are!"

I barely step out of the bathroom before Imani is there, grabbing my shoulders and making me look at her. Her hands lift to cup my cheeks, turning my face from side to side, but I remove her hands as gently as possible.

"Are you okay? Did you puke?" she asks. "I'll get you some water. Go sit in the—"

I shake my head vigorously. I don't want to stay here and be coddled. I want to go back to my room where I'm safely locked away from others. As I'm searching for an excuse, I see Aiden pushing through the throng of people that have gathered once again in the kitchen, our eyes meeting as he does.

I wonder if he knows something's wrong. But when he comes up from behind Imani, he leans down over her shoulder to yell to us over the music and voices that seem to be getting louder and louder, holding eye contact with me the entire time.

"Hey, I think I'm gonna head out early."

My chest tightens. He knows. He's saving me from making the call.

Before I can even think of what to say, Imani swivels around to look at him, pointing over her shoulder at me.

"Take Lydia with you. She's not feeling good. As long as she wants to leave, of course."

Aiden lifts his eyes from Imani's, as if asking for confirmation, and I nod at him—just before Jake comes bounding from behind, his smile dropping as he looks between the three of us. His hair is sticking up every which way, his cheeks are bright red, and his eyes are glossy, so much so that part of me wants to stick around solely to make sure he gets back home okay. But I know I can't—for his safety.

"I'm not feeling the best," Aiden explains. "Lydia's gonna head back with me, too."

"Are you okay?" Jake immediately asks, pushing past Aiden and Imani to get to me. I can smell the alcohol on his breath. "I can—I'll go with ya, I wanna-"

"I'm fine," I say, hiding my shaking hands by gripping the hem of my sweater. "You can stay. Aiden and I will be fine."

Aiden and I exchange another look that seems to get by Jake and Imani, both of whom clumsily kiss us both on the cheek and instruct us to text as soon as we get back so they know we're okay and that they'll be Ubering back relatively soon. My stomach churns, and for a minute, as I start to follow Aiden through the kitchen, I think I might puke blood all over the tile floor and people's shoes.

But we make it out okay, and I feel a hell of a lot better as soon as we step foot out of the stifling apartment and back into the crisp night air. I welcome the cold breeze on my bare legs, and I even roll up my sleeves and pull my hair into a low ponytail to feel more of it. I can feel Aiden's eyes on me as we walk along the cracked sidewalk, and finally, as we approach our train stop, I look up at him.

"What happened in there?" he asks, and I immediately look away to pull my Ventra card out of my wallet—which I'd kept securely strapped in the waistband of my skirt—but mostly, I just can't look into his eyes and lie to him.

"Same as the football game," I say as casually as I can muster, still avoiding looking at him as I scan my card and push my way through the turnstile. "I got a little claustrophobic, which usually leads to nausea."

"That's it?"

I swivel to look at him as he makes his way through the turnstile after me, my eyes searching his face for any hint he knows what I am. Almost subconsciously, I tug my sleeves back down my arms, as if there's a trace of what I did.

"That's it."

He doesn't respond right away, even as we climb the two sets of stairs that lead up to the train platform. He doesn't respond in the few minutes we wait for the train, along with a couple who appears to be eating each other's face off, and an old man, all of whom I can sense, but it's not bothering me as bad as it might've before, not when I can still feel my heart beating in my chest, despite what I did. I know Dad would hate it if he found out. But he's not going to find out, and there's no point in feeling guilty or gross about it, because guess what?

I didn't hurt anyone. And that's what's important.

Aiden finally responds once we settle into seats on the train, side by side, so close that our knees touch. Some of the ache in my chest eases.

"Lydia, um, if there's anything you'd ever like to talk about—"

"I'm fine, Aiden," I interrupt, not wanting to hear it. I just want to be in my bed. Alone.

I hear him respond, his voice barely audible, only after I lean my head back and rest it on the back of my seat.

"Okay," he murmurs, and I swear I hear a note of disappointment in his voice just as the train takes off.

CHAPTER EIGHTEEN

I DO my best to act normal after Halloween, and I think everyone buys that I just didn't handle my alcohol well.

Except Aiden—which is why I do my best to distance myself from him. Just slightly, but enough to limit our time alone to avoid questions, which is hard because of work, but it also disappoints me because of how much I like talking to him. But I can't do that again. I *can't* be that stupid. Because what if it happens again, and there's no time to escape?

What if it was Imani?

As the weeks pass, Jake's football season starts to come to a close, so while I try to be cautious, especially since Halloween, it's nice to see him more. And if I'm being honest, sometimes it's just nice to sit with him or have his arm around me while we do homework—as long as I've fed. I also don't do any better in my math class, though I keep a close eye on Xavier, thinking about what Imani said about asking for help and about his offer at the very beginning of the semester.

I don't want to have to take it. But my pride aside, I know I need to.

Another thing I don't think about until it's brought up in a phone call with Dad is Thanksgiving.

"Are you coming home for Thanksgiving? Should I come get you?" he asks one evening, while I'm lying in bed, the room to myself.

"Uh." I fiddle with a string hanging off the corner of my pillowcase. "I—"

I haven't thought about it. I've been preoccupied with an idiotic mistake I made and a class I'm close to failing. Oh, by the way, I have a boyfriend now, whose humanness sometimes overwhelms me too much. No biggie.

"Or I could come to you," he says. "We could go out. I'm fine with not cooking." He chuckles, and I realize he sounds uncharacteristically cheery. "I could meet those friends of yours, too, if any of them will be in town. What 'dya say?"

"Uh, yeah. Sure. That sounds good."

"Remind me of their names again, so I'm prepared. I remember your roommate–Ma–Marcy? Macy? No—"

"Imani, Dad." I pause, rolling onto my side. "There're Aiden, Tripp, and Jake who live across the hall. But, uh." I brace myself, squeezing my eyes shut as I force the dreaded words out: "Jake is, uh, Jake's, uh, kinda my— my boyfriend, now."

If I couldn't hear his breathing, there'd be dead silence on his end.

"Jake. I remember now. The one you work with at the bookstore? That's—"

"No, no. Ah, the football player."

More silence, in which I can only hear the quickening of my own heart with each second that passes.

"That's great." I can't miss the apprehension in his voice. "He's good to you?"

I let out a little breath of relief. "Yeah, Dad. He's really sweet."

"Does he—"

"No." I already know what he's asking. "He doesn't know. Nobody does."

"Okay." Long pause. "Well, we'll talk more when I see you for Thanksgiving. I'm looking forward to meeting him."

Hopefully he's gone home for Thanksgiving by then.

"Yeah, yeah. That'd be great."

I find out, shortly after that phone call, that Dad and Jake will not be meeting this time around, because Jake and Tripp are leaving the day before Thanksgiving to go to Jake's house for the short break. Imani is leaving a day earlier, and Aiden says he's planning about the same thing as me, so he'll be around.

I make a mental note to keep far away while his parents are in town. I don't need them shooting daggers through me while Dad's here, who I *know* will jump to conclusions.

Not that I didn't, too, but still. I had to get it from somewhere.

The morning of Thanksgiving, I get ready way too early, dressed up in a nice, maroon-colored sweater that's a little big on me and black jeans. I even curled my hair a little—the best to my ability. That's something Dad definitely was never able to teach me, though thanks to a YouTube video, I don't do terrible. After putting on some light makeup, too, I feel pretty and normal enough to send Jake a picture of myself with a caption, *Happy Thanksgiving :)*, and his response makes it worthwhile.

> jake hampton: BABY! You look gorgeous wow

> jake hampton: You're so pretty

> jake hampton: I miss you already! Tell your dad I say hi

He then sends me a picture of himself, in the kitchen, holding up a thumbs-up with a caption that says he's helping make something called a kugel.

Just then, I get a text from Dad, which says:

dad: Here.

I feel surprisingly relieved when I meet him at the front doors and he pulls me in for a tight hug; I hadn't realized how much I actually missed him.

"So, how's everything been?" he asks. He's dressed in a nice, light-blue button-down and black slacks, his hair neat. There's something different about him, in the way he smells, in the way he holds himself. He's even completely shaved, instead of the usual stubble he wears.. Between this and his cheery attitude the other day when we talked...

Did he meet someone?

Not that I would know how to bring that up. I'll let him approach that subject, if it's true, and if he's ready.

The thought tightens something in my chest. I'm happy for him, don't get me wrong, but...

If I weren't around, he could've done this a lot sooner.

Have I really been holding him back from happiness?

"Uh, good," I say, to answer his question. "I've been good. Busy, with finals coming up and everything, but yeah. I, uh, I really like it here. Do you wanna see my room?"

Dad smiles. It even seems like his smiles come easier, nothing like the tense Dad that left me here months ago. "Lead the way."

On the elevator, I explain that most of my friends are gone, so he won't get to meet them. As the doors slide open on my floor, he asks,

"And this *boyfriend* of yours? When do I get to meet him?"

I flush. "Well, he's—"

I stop, because as I look down the hall, I see Aiden leaving his apartment. He's dressed nicely, in jeans that are paired with a tucked-in, olive-green button-down, the sleeves of which are pushed up to his elbows. If I'm being honest, the casual yet dressy appearance looks really good on him. He glances over, smiling at me, and I can't help but return it. I also feel really guilty for kinda trying to avoid him when he hasn't done anything wrong—he was just concerned about me.

"Hey," he calls as I approach. Dad lingers a few steps behind me.

"Hey. Where are you headed?"

"To meet my parents. They're waiting in the parking lot, and we're going out to eat. They made reservations at some ridiculously fancy place, so I'm probably underdressed, but.." He looks down at himself, grinning sheepishly, and I swear his cheeks are slightly pink when he looks back up at me.

"You, uh, you look nice, though," he adds, his heartbeat increasing a little.

My heart stutters in my chest; there's something about the shy, almost hesitant way he says it.

And then I remember Dad is still here.

"Thanks. Um, you do, too," I say, quietly, before clearing my throat. "Uh, this is my dad. Dad, this is Aiden. He's the one who I work with at the bookstore."

There's a faint look of surprise on Dad's face as he holds his hand out to Aiden, who shakes it and offers him a smile.

"It's nice to meet you, Mr. Ross."

Dad's grin only grows. "No need to be so formal. Call me Keith. But it's nice to meet you too, Aiden."

"Text me later if you're not doing anything," Aiden adds to me just before leaving. "I've been bored out of my mind."

I smile at him and tell him I will before he disappears

around the corner to go to the elevators. Dad doesn't say anything until we're in my room, the door closed behind us.

"He isn't your boyfriend?"

"*No*, Dad. Jake is. He's at home right now, so you won't get to meet him."

I stand in the corner by my bed, watching as Dad assesses the room. There's a beat of silence until he says,

"You sure?"

"Yeah, I'm *sure*. What do you even mean by that?" My face feels like it's on fire.

Dad just smiles faintly. "Nothing, nothing. So, tell me more about this mysterious Jake, since I'm not going to get to meet him."

He sits on the edge of my bed as I do, telling him some basic facts about Jake and his family. Dad stays quiet throughout, nodding, and as I talk, I'm kind of hoping *me* talking about *my* boyfriend will segue into him talking about this new person he's probably dating.

But it doesn't. It just segues into exactly what I expected:

"He sounds like a nice kid. I look forward to meeting him. But, Lydia, just remember, I had a baby at your age—"

"Oh, my God, Dad." Even though I expected it, it doesn't make it any less uncomfortable. "No. I mean, we're not—I'm not—We're taking it slow, okay? Really, *really* slow. And we don't even know if—" Dad knows I don't get a period. He also knows I don't even want kids. But what I *do* want is to get away from this topic as soon as possible. "Just... don't worry about it, okay?"

Thankfully, we have to leave to make our reservation, but a more uncomfortable topic comes up in the car.

"Have you thought about telling him?"

As we sit at a red light downtown, I look out the window at the other cars and the few people walking out and about— less than usual, that's for sure, but it's still relatively busy. It's also a surprisingly nice day, with the sun shining overhead, making it a little less cold than a normal late-November day. Still, Dad has the heat cranked in the small car, making it a little stifling. I reach out, pushing one of the vents away from me.

"I mean, I've thought about it, but I'm not gonna."

"Why not?"

The question catches me completely off guard. I whirl around to look at him, raising my eyebrows, as the light turns green.

"What do you *mean*, why not? What good could possibly come out of that?"

Dad sighs as he changes lanes.

"I've been doing a lot of thinking since you left, and, well, how do I say this... Hearing you talk about your friends and your classes and everything you've been doing lately, and how happy you seem, it just makes me think that maybe I... well, maybe I coddled you a little too much."

I try not to look too shocked as he continues, staring straight ahead at the road, so I look out the windshield, too, watching cars speed in front of each other to change lanes.

"It also made me think that maybe... maybe I never approached this right, and I made you feel ashamed of your-self, which was never my intention. Your... being... being what you are is nothing to be ashamed of, kid, and, well, I—I'm sorry if I made you feel that way."

I almost want him to stop as I blink back tears, but at the same time, I think we both need this.

If he knew about my close call at Halloween, though, he might not be saying this, and my heart twists at the thought of that.

"I think that... if they really are good kids, and you trust them, you could tell them, if you're comfortable. Especially, I mean, now that you're dating this Jake boy... It's good to be able to talk to your loved ones about things, you know? To be able to be honest with them." He clears his throat. "All I ask is that you do make sure they really care about you and you really do trust them, but I don't want you to—I don't want you to feel like this is something bad. It's just something you need to be cautious about. And I think I haven't done the best at differentiating that." He pauses. "Does all that make sense?"

I nod, but when I realize he's driving and isn't looking over at me, I force out a little "yeah" so he can't tell I'm trying not to cry.

For the rest of the short ride, Dad makes an abrupt and slightly awkward subject change, asking me about my job at the bookstore, which I gladly entertain, telling him about customers I've encountered, opening and closing the store with Aiden, and Roarke.

When we get to the restaurant, I swallow past the lump in my throat and try my best to enjoy Thanksgiving. Dinner itself is good, a buffet-style, so I'm able to pile on all the mashed potatoes onto my plate that I want. I definitely stuff myself a little too full, but I'm in a significantly better mood by the time Dad and I leave the restaurant, seeing as I opened up to him a bit more about our beach trip almost two months ago, football games (excluding when I went into sensory overload and puked in the bathroom) and a few other little events. *He* even opens up to *me*, telling me about going to football games in high school with my mom, who, as I'm just now learning, was on the dance team and would dance at halftimes.

I feel a little closer to him than I've ever felt in the past eighteen years.

The dreaded moment comes, though, as we're walking back out to the car.

"I can't believe I forgot to tell you," he says. "I wanted it to be a surprise, but I don't think I can keep it any longer. There's someone I can't wait for you to meet."

I'm sure she's great. But I can't help but feel like this new side of Dad, this *happy* side, is just because of her, and not just because he came to some new conclusions about me since we've had some time apart.

My heart sinks a little as he starts to pull out his phone. I wonder if I know her, and that's why he's showing me a picture instead of just telling me.

Until he turns the screen towards me, and I feel like a complete, total idiot as I look down at a picture of a dog.

A puppy, actually. A small, black lab.

He smiles at me, eyes brighter than I've seen them for the first time in—well, ever, maybe.

"You leaving also made me realize how lonely it is in the house without you around, and how I don't even really have anyone else to talk to." His smile is sheepish. "I figured it was due time to get another dog, and I found this little girl at the shelter and couldn't resist. I think you'll love her. Her name's Bella—she's such a sweetie, and super energetic. Not that I could ever replace you, but—"

I hug him before he can see the tears welling in my eyes.

Dad's arms wrap around me, and I breathe in the familiar scent of him, making sure I'm not going to cry before pulling away.

"I can't wait to meet her. She's adorable."

The energy in the car is significantly lighter as Dad drives me back to my dorm, and I almost don't want to leave.

Maybe he's right. Maybe I should tell them.

Not now.

Eventually.

Maybe.

He gets out of the car when he pulls in front of my building to give me one last hug. I watch him drive off, smiling as I catch him waving at me, before I go back inside. As I'm waiting for the elevator, I decide to text Aiden.

me: are you back from dinner yet?

I get a text back within a minute.

aiden swanson: Look up

I whip my head up, looking toward the front doors just as the elevator dings with its arrival. I smile at Aiden, who's walking through the door. As the elevator door opens, I step forward, holding it, and he does a little half jog to catch up to me.

"Look at that," he says as the elevator doors slide closed. "Perfect timing."

"I know. How was dinner with your parents?"

He sighs, and I can practically feel the irritation radiating off of him.

"The food itself? Superb. My parents? Same as always. If not a little worse, somehow. They want to know every single detail about everything I've done and everyone I've seen. And not in a just-making-conversation way. As if I didn't survive my entire freshman year."

I grimace. Even Dad's not that bad. "Sorry."

He shrugs as the doors slide open on our floor.

"It's whatever. I'm used to it. How was yours? Your dad seems cool, based on the thirty seconds I met him earlier."

"It was really nice, actually."

"You sound surprised."

We stop in front of our doors, the hallway separating us.

"I guess I am. He, uh, he was really protective growing up. But I think he's realized that, like, I can make my own way in the world, I guess. And that I'm not a total loser and actually have friends."

Aiden laughs a little. "That's great. You seem—you seem happy. It's, uh, it's nice to see."

I nod, feeling my damned cheeks warming. "I am. It feels nice."

"Would you be interested in ruining that by watching *Dead Poets Society* with me?"

I laugh. At least he's honest.

"I've never seen it, but sure."

Aiden gives me an incredulous look. "*Lydia.*"

"I already said sure!"

"I'm vetoing your sure by telling you you *have* to."

I laugh again, and he grins at me.

"I don't think it works like that, but *fine*. Let me change, and I'll be right over."

I change into a hoodie and the sweats I sleep in, take off my makeup, and throw my hair up into a ponytail. When Aiden lets me into his apartment, the scent of him and popcorn fills my senses in a way that's comforting.

"You know," he says, leading me to the couch, where a giant bowl of popcorn sits on the coffee table, along with two cans of Coke—I can't help but smile to myself when I see that, seeing he remembered when I told him Coke is my favorite pop, despite caffeine not doing anything for me. Another vampire thing?

"You really ought to make a list of everything you haven't read, watched, or done, and in the next, well, two years, we'll do it all. We'll call it something stupid, like *Aiden and Lydia's Bucket List Extravaganza*." Aiden sits on the far end of the couch, turning sideways to put his legs up.

I don't know if it's because it's been a good day or if I just randomly feel a lot lighter, but I laugh out loud at that, taking a handful of popcorn from the bowl and mirroring his sitting position.

"That is stupid, but I like it." I pop a piece of popcorn into my mouth. "Why only the next two years, though?"

"Because I graduate in two years," he says, "hopefully. If I ever figure out what I actually want to major in. Or do with my life. Y'know, any of that important stuff." He looks down, picking at something on the thigh of his pants. "It just feels like I don't belong anywhere sometimes, I guess, so it's hard to figure that shit out."

"Trust me, I know exactly how you feel."

He looks back up at me, his gaze soft as silence stretches between us—a comfortable, understanding sort of silence. But he breaks it by throwing a piece of popcorn at my head.

"C'mon," he says, grabbing the TV remote as I exaggeratingly rub my head, mock-glaring at him. "Let's cross this movie off the list."

CHAPTER NINETEEN

AIDEN DIDN'T WARN me about how much I was going to cry while watching the movie. I don't even know how late I was there, since we got talking after the movie and he told me he had to hold me hostage until I helped him finish all the popcorn we made, even though I stayed long after the bowl was emptied.

We hang out a few more times over break. We see the huge Christmas tree lighting in Millennium Park the day after Thanksgiving, but we stand across the street, away from the crowd, clutching cups of hot drinks from Starbucks. It starts to snow, too, and even though I hate snow, normally, it's kind of magical in that moment. Snowflakes get caught in Aiden's curls and we try to catch them with our tongues.

I'm in a great mood when Imani, Tripp, and Jake finally get back from being home for break.

"I'm taking you ice skating," is one of the first things Jake says to me when he's back.

We're sitting on my bed. He pulls my hand into his lap, drawing shapes on the back. He just grins at whatever look is on my face—probably some sort of horror. Am I even coordinated enough for ice skating?

"I've never been, but the rinks just opened, and I've always wanted to go. Aiden and Tripp were too *cool* to go with me last year."

I can't help but smile. "Are you saying I'm not cool?"

Jake grins back, lifting my hand to press a kiss to the back of it. "I'm *saying* you're just about as cool as me. Which, no, isn't very cool."

The casual intimacy of the gesture makes my stomach flutter even as I laugh softly. It's been almost two months since we've been together, and I feel slightly guilty in the sense we've made little progress physically—if not gone backward instead, especially since I've been particularly scared about something happening after my Halloween situation.

I'm terrified about hurting him, even though I made sure to feed right before I knew he was coming back. And with my stress about classes and finals in only a few weeks, and making sure I feed, there's a lot to think about, but then I think about my talk with Dad and my good—*great*—weekend with Aiden.

"Fine," I say, deciding to tease him back. "I suppose I'll go ice skating with you even if you don't think I'm cool."

His face lights up adorably at that, and my chest tightens. I like him a lot, I do, and he's sweet and too good for me, but like Dad said, I'm not bad. This thing, this part of me, doesn't make me *bad*.

Right? I've never hurt anyone. Only myself, and that doesn't really count.

So sure, I'll try something new and go ice skating. Especially if it makes Jake happy.

I even lean forward and kiss him—which, I rarely initiate any sort of contact or affection, but I can work on that, too. He eagerly kisses me back, hands cupping either side of my face, stroking my cheeks with his thumbs.

I want to do something more, push my boundaries a little, but I'm not sure what to do until his hands slide down to rest at the slight curve of my waist.

He's close, so close and warm, and when I move to straddle his lap and his breath hitches. Something stirs deep within me, both my human and vampire sides reacting. It's a risk, but feeling his arms snake around me, pulling me closer, feeling his body against mine, it's all such an utterly human experience and desire, but pushing through it is his heartbeat that thuds in my ears, under my fingertips, blood pumping through his veins, warm and close and soft, and what would his skin taste like? What would it feel like to break the skin with my teeth and—

I pull away, breathing hard and keeping a hand on his chest to keep some distance, and when I open my eyes to look at him, it's almost worse: his hair sticking up from where I ran my hands through it, his cheeks flushed.

Oh my God, what was I *thinking*? The feeling that just passed over me—it was just like at the party. But—but I was starved then. I took all my precautions. I shouldn't have any problem now.

"You okay?" he asks.

"Yeah," I start to say, "sorry, I—"

I *what*? Thankfully, I don't have to figure it out, because there's noise coming from the door as if someone is fumbling with their key card.

I realize that since Imani knows we're in here alone, it's probably her way of warning us that she's coming in.

I scramble off Jake just before the door opens, and I catch him pulling a pillow over his lap. As Imani and Tripp walk in, I take deep, steadying breaths; Tripp smirks at Jake as Imani jumps back on her bed and starts in about a Christmas market of some sort she wants us all to go to before we leave for winter break in a few weeks.

"Speaking of which, are we celebrating tonight, Hamp?" Tripp asks, flopping down on Imani's bed and lying across her legs. She makes a face and pulls them out from under him.

"Celebrating?" I repeat, looking over at Jake.

"Tonight's the first night of Hanukkah," he says. "Last year it was during finals week, so Tripp and Aiden celebrated with me. It wasn't a huge thing or anything. We just made some food and lit the menorah I have."

"And gifts," Tripp adds.

Jake smiles sheepishly. "Yeah, they gave me gifts. Even though I told them not to."

I start to panic a little. I should've thought about this—I knew Hanukkah was this time of year. Do I get him something? Multiple things? Is it too late? Do I get my other friends' Christmas presents before break? Is that something friends do?

"But yeah, I was probably gonna make something and just light the menorah tonight. If you'd wanna come?"

I smile at him. "Yeah, sure, of course. I'd like that."

He turns. "Imani?"

She grins. "Of course! Anything I can help make?"

We end up in the boys' kitchen, but I stand off to the side with Aiden while Jake, Tripp, and Imani start the food. Turns out Jake's mom sent him with some ingredients to help start him off, but they have to run out and buy some other things, so I stay back with Aiden, who tells me a little more about their celebrations last year (which included getting drunk off wine and eating little chocolate coins), and confesses that Tripp loves to cook and is great at it, though he doesn't flaunt it, like most things he's good at.

I see the proof soon after; he's a natural in the kitchen, starting off with a dish called matzo ball soup, he said Jake's mom taught him last year, and with some help from Jake, it turns out amazing. After we eat, he lights the menorah and then teaches us a game with a little wooden dreidel and foil-wrapped chocolate coins he calls gelt.

We sit in a circle on the floor in the living room, laughing and eating the gelt, and at one point, I look around at all of them, their faces illuminated by the glow of the candle and the one kitchen light that's on in the next room.

I realize, then, as I sit cross-legged between Aiden and Jake, my knees touching both of theirs, feeling more at peace than ever, that when I'm able to put my differences aside, that is what a family probably feels like.

THE NEXT DAY, SINCE I FEEL LIKE I'M ON A ROLL IN life despite my little makeout-session-freakout, I ask Xavier after class if he'd be willing to help teach me a few things before the final. He agrees with no hesitation. He's busy most of the upcoming weekend, and is only free when I'm at work, so we agree to meet in one of the study rooms in our building the next weekend, right before finals, after I get off work that Sunday night.

"Where do you work, by the way?" he asks me as we walk back after class, snowflakes sticking to the fabric of his black beanie and melting almost immediately after they land. His cheeks and the tip of his nose are flushed from the cold.

"Um, EB's, it's a bookstore down the street. I'm there a lot 'cause obviously the money's nice, but I really like it, too, since I love to read."

"Oh, that's awesome," Xavier says, flashing me a shy smile. "Maybe I'll check it out while you're working sometime. I'm not a huge reader, but I was as a kid, so I'm really trying to get back into it. If you have any sci-fi recommendations, send 'em my way."

"Oh, for sure." I smile back.

I'm in high spirits by the time I join my friends for night two of Hanukkah. I end up getting Jake a few gifts, which I give to him over the next few days—nothing big—but he hugs me with all his might and tells me how much he loves them each and every time. That weekend, we went ice skating in Millennium Park, and it's honestly beautiful. The rink is right under the Bean, and since we go when it's dark, the night is lit by the city lights. And the rink isn't even too packed. It's really a beautiful night.

Jake goes in with confidence but ends up being hilariously bad—not that I tell him that. He clutches on to the side railings for dear life, inching along even as I start to get a hang of it, adjusting surprisingly quickly to balancing and sliding around on thin blades.

"Come on," I say, reaching out my mitten-covered hand to him.

He looks over at me, wide-eyed, and I stifle a laugh. He finally ventures a few inches from the wall, grabbing my hand —only he moves a little too jerkily, a little too fast, and only succeeds in losing his balance and propelling his body too far forward, knocking both of us down, my body colliding with the cold, hard ground.

"Oh, my God, baby, I'm so sorry," he says, scrambling to his feet and almost losing his balance again, holding out a hand to help me up. I wave him off, giggling despite the dull ache in my knee.

"It's okay. As long as you stick with football, I think we'll be good."

He laughs, and once I push myself up from the ground and grab on to the side for balance, he wraps an arm around my waist from behind, leaning over to kiss my cheek. Between our layers of coats and jackets, I barely even think twice about our closeness.

"I love it when you give me shit."

We're both laughing and sore by the time we leave, but I'm glad we did it. Really, really glad, actually.

That same night, as we walk back to our dorm, holding hands and basking in the beauty of the city at night, Jake brings up a question that catches me off guard.

"Lyds," he says, slowly, only continuing when I look over at him. "I was wondering if, uh, maybe you'd wanna come stay with me over break? I know you celebrate Christmas, of course, so I totally get it if you wanna go be with your dad, but my mom and sister would love to meet you, and Tripp'll be there, and yeah." He smiles shyly. "Maybe if you'd even wanna fly out for a little while? Again, no pressure or anything—"

"Yeah, yeah, sure," I say, without thinking, too shocked by the idea. "I'll talk to my dad about it."

Jake's face lights up, and as soon as the words are out of my mouth, I start to question if it's really a good idea or not. Being here with my own private fridge and a schedule I can control is one thing, but going to someone's house for a few weeks?

Maybe I can pack a cooler. Yeah. I'll do that. Or I could just tell him. And then I don't have to hide it.

Nope. Nope, nope, nope. I'm not ready for that. Not when things are so good as they are.

They're only good because you're lying to everyone.

I'm not *explicitly* lying. I'm just not telling the full truth. That's... not as bad.

I'll just be careful.

And now that Dad seems to trust me, he'll be fine with it, right?

It'll be fine. It'll be good, and fun, and it'll feel like I'm a normal girl visiting her boyfriend's family.

Yeah. Yeah, it'll be good. I'll just be extra careful.

But as we near the end of the semester, I don't get to

spend as much time as I'd like with Jake or any of the others between everyone working on final papers and studying for exams and work, but the week after ice skating, the Saturday before finals, the five of us go to the Christmas market, buying snacks and hot apple cider and hot chocolate and ornaments for the makeshift Christmas tree the boys had put up in their living room, which is actually a four-foot-tall artificial palm tree with lights strung on it, courtesy of Tripp, who seems really proud of it. By the end of each day, I'm exhausted and crash without having to take a lap around the floor or read first.

In fact, I'm in such a good mood that I call up Dad the night of the market and ask him before I can chicken out of it, but my heart still thuds rapidly from anxiety as I let the words tumble out all in one breath, "Would-you-mind-if-I-possibly-go-stay-with-Jake-and-his-family-over-winter-break-at-least-for-a-little-bit?"

I feel a sharp stab of guilt almost immediately after the words leave my mouth, and it gets even worse during the few beats of silence before he answers, during which I have to check to make sure if he's actually still on the line or not.

"You're an adult," he says. "I trust you if you trust yourself."

After a few more minutes, after we finish talking and I reassure him about twelve more times that I'll do what needs to be done to make it work, I rush over to the boys' apartment and tell Jake that I can go. He pulls me into a big bear hug, my face getting pressed against the soft fabric of his dark blue sweater. I have to pull away as it starts to get a little too much, starts to make my stomach twist and ache.

The stress of finals—specifically my math exam—presses down on me, and I bring my math notes to work that Sunday, trying my best to rifle through them and make sense of anything I possibly can so that I'm not *completely* hopeless when meeting Xavier tonight. Aiden and I close at seven, but Xavier can't meet til nine, which kind of sucks, but hopefully meeting later means all the study rooms will be free. While I really should've asked him for help around midterms, I appreciate him attempting to teach me a few months' worth of math in one night—more than he knows, probably. Maybe I'll buy him a gift card or something to thank him. For where, I don't know, but I owe him big time.

I'm sitting at the desk, bent over my notebook, moving my pencil along a problem I copied down in class, trying to figure out the steps, but my brain just can't comprehend it. I hear the bell ring, distantly, indicating a customer has walked in, and as their scent fills my nose, my whole body goes alert, the hair raising on my arms, my stomach aching.

I look up from my notebook, resting my pencil on the page as I smile at the customer, letting my eyes follow the old woman as she veers toward the children's section, her sweet-smelling blood filling the store.

I swallow, discreetly trying to take shallower breaths through my mouth. Why have I not been bothered with Aiden in here? We've been here together since noon, and while we've barely had any customers today, his presence still should have set off alarm bells.

When did I feed last?

My heart sinks as I stare at my notebook, listening to Aiden talk cheerily to the woman as I try to figure out the timeline. I've been going on Fridays to pick up more blood, but I didn't this week because... because Imani didn't go to class. And I didn't go yesterday, obviously, but that's fine, I have more in my fridge, I think, and I was with them yesterday and working on my paper Friday, and I've been so tired at night and...

I'll feed right when I get home. I guess I've been ignoring it, suppressing it, too distracted by, simultaneously somehow, my rising stress levels and how well things have been going. It's happened with human food, too, so it's not all that surprising. There have been plenty of times I'm too engrossed in a book and realize I haven't eaten dinner.

Maybe Dad's reminders in high school *were* more helpful than I thought.

But it's fine. I'll feed before meeting Xavier, which'll be good because it'll help me focus, too.

The woman approaches me with a stack of four children's books. I hope my voice doesn't sound as strained to her as it does to me as I help her check out, trying to rush her along, but she keeps telling me about her grandkids and other things I don't care about. I just need her and her scent to get out of here.

I let out a breath as soon as she leaves, slumping in my chair and leaning my head back to look up at the ceiling. I smell Aiden, of course, but it doesn't affect me. It doesn't make my stomach turn and make me clench my jaw and make me tense every muscle in my body—*ever*. I can always relax around him.

But *why*?

"You okay?"

I bring my head forward, looking at Aiden, who's still standing by the children's section, a book in his hand. I remember from when I was younger, about fairies. He glances down at it before pushing it onto the shelf where it belongs.

"Uh, fine," I say. "Just... my stomach's bothering me a little. That's all."

His eyebrows furrow.

"Sorry. That sucks. If you wanna head home, I can handle—"

"No, no, no, I'll be fine," I assure him, but I try to assure myself, while I'm at it.

The corner of his mouth quirks up, but it doesn't reach

his eyes. "Just try to puke *away* from the computer if it comes down to it, okay?"

I smile back, and it comes a little easier than expected. "Or what, you'll fire me? You can't, just so you know."

Aiden fully grins, reaching to flatten his curls. "When I *do* get that power, eventually, because of how much Roarke obviously adores me, I'm gonna put that first on my list, just so *you* know."

"Mhm." I spin in my chair, letting the toes of my Converse drag on the floor. "I'm sure, Aiden. I'm sure."

CHAPTER TWENTY

I GO into a slight panic when I get back to my room and realize my fridge is empty.

And slight might be an understatement.

Imani is in her bed, scrolling on her phone, so I'm forced to go into the bathroom to calm myself down. I lock the door, sliding down and putting my face against my knees, taking a few deep breaths to slow my pounding heart.

I wouldn't be so panicked if I could go first thing when they open tomorrow, but I have English I need to be at, and I can't skip because it's finals week, and what if Roarke asks questions? Would he believe an excuse as weak as *I'm sick*? I guess I'll run between that and geology with some sort of excuse, but do I really have time?

I have to have time. I'll make time.

I ignore the sharp pain in my stomach, the sluggish way I move, when Jake knocks on my door at eight the next morning, asking me about work. He tells me him and Tripp are meeting some of the guys on the football team in one of the other dorms to hang out for a bit. I force a smile when he goes in for a kiss, holding my breath the entire time.

An hour later, as I'm gathering my supplies to study, Imani asks, "Hey. Are you okay?"

I straighten up, maybe a little too quickly, because a flash of pain pierces through my skull. "Yeah. I'm fine. Uh, I'm kinda cramping, is all."

"Ah," she says, but I can't say she looks entirely convinced. "I got some ibuprofen if you—"

"No, no, I'm okay. I gotta go meet Xavier."

I repeat my mantra of *I'm fine* the whole way to the study room, which is down the hall from the elevators, another hallway down on the left, past the lounge I found my first night here, and at the very end of the third hallway. There're a few rooms, and I spot Xavier immediately through the little window in one of the doors—we appear to be the only people using any of these rooms tonight, which I can't complain about. Everyone else must be in their own suites for the night or pulling late-night study sessions in the library. Finals season has made the hallways dead after a certain time.

That means I only have Xavier to worry about. But I don't have to, because I'll be fine.

"Thank you for helping me," I say, once I greet him and close the door behind me. "And so late. It means a lot."

"It's really no problem," Xavier replies, somewhat shyly, as he pushes his glasses up the bridge of his nose.

Between the close proximity of the room and my current situation, the scent of Xavier's blood seems even stronger than usual, and it's very, very distracting.

Xavier pushes a folder and one of his textbooks across the table so they're out of our way. We're seated on the same side of the tiny, two-person table so he can show me his notes, and I can follow each problem he does step-by-step, and so he can see what I do clearly and stop me when I inevitably screw up.

"We'll start with unit five," he says, opening the first textbook and flipping through the pages. "That's where you started having problems, right?"

I confirm, and he starts talking about what we'll cover within unit five, but every time he moves his hands—which he does a lot when he talks—his painfully noticeable, blue veins are all I can pay attention to, even as he flips open his red notebook to a blank page about three-quarters of the way in, mechanical pencil in hand as he starts to copy down the first problem, explaining each component as he writes it on the paper.

I nod slowly, trying to follow along, but at this point, it's overwhelming. It's like walking into a middle-school girls' locker room just after PE where all the girls douse themselves in perfume. So when you walk in, it's just an overwhelming mix of different perfumes that all smell good but you can't seem to escape it because it's everywhere and it makes me want to smell it but I know I shouldn't because my stomach pain starts worsening to the point where I think that maybe I should've taken some of that ibuprofen, because maybe, *maybe*, it would've eased the pain a little, but does ibuprofen work on vampire-specific issues? I've never even taken ibuprofen before—I usually just drink blood, and my physical problems go away.

And I doubt it would help. Because there's only one thing that'll help right now and it's flowing in both me and Xavier, but I *can't*, I need to focus on those stupid little numbers and symbols that don't make any sense or else I'm going to fail this goddamn class and I can't do that.

But I can't stay here. I need to excuse myself, to do what I did on Halloween, so I can actually focus on what he's saying instead of all of his words blending together.

I eye his hands as he moves the pencil across the paper in very clear, defined handwriting. The slope of his neck, the blemish-free skin, the heartbeat thudding beneath his skin, loud and clear, ringing in my ears, teasing me. He sets down the pencil on top of the paper and moves his hand back to the textbook, and I have to just interrupt him, to give him some excuse to get away, to tell him I have a raging headache and I need to grab ibuprofen, and I'll be right back. He won't know. Nobody will need to know. And then I'll be fine.

"Hey, Xavier?"

Time seems to stop as the scent of blood grows stronger until it becomes the only thing I can smell. Xavier lifts his finger, a drop of blood welling on it.

"Ouch," he says, smiling sheepishly. But I can barely hear him, because I zero in on that sweet, red, red blood, and before I can even think, I feel myself moving.

Vampire Lydia takes control.

I can hear a tiny little voice at the back of my head screaming *stop* as I knock Xavier to the floor, the chair falling with us. He struggles against me, but he's weak, easy to pin down as I kick the chair away, hearing it *crack* against the wall. I straddle his waist and push his head to the side, exposing his neck so I can sink my fangs into him. I break through the skin with ease, like scissors through tissue paper, and *oh*, it's even better than I thought it would be, so much better than the pork blood, so much sweeter and fresher, and there's so much *more*. It keeps coming, filling my mouth endlessly, and Xavier stops fighting me, and he goes limp. I shut my eyes as I suck and suck and suck, feeling a surge of strength and *aliveness* I've never felt before, and oh I feel so much better, so much stronger, and—

Oh. Oh my *God. Xavier went limp.*

I throw myself off him, wiping the back of my hand across my mouth as I stare at his body, at the two holes in his neck.

He's not moving.

He's not moving, and I can't hear his heartbeat anymore,

and oh, no no no no no why isn't his heart beating? He can't be dead. I can't have *killed* someone, no no *no* no no—

"Xavier," I say, like an idiot, grabbing his arm and shaking him.

No response.

I slide my hand up his arm, to his neck, past the two puncture wounds from my fangs, which are still dripping blood, and it smells so *good,* and I'm aching for more, but I have to check for a pulse.

My hands shake as I press my fingers against his pale skin. Was he this cold a minute ago? He couldn't have been this cold a minute ago, because he had a *pulse* a minute ago, and oh my *God,* I killed him, oh my God oh my God oh my God, I killed him.

I stare at him, holding my hands slightly above his body because I'm not sure what else to do. My whole body shakes, but I'm not sure if it's because I just murdered my classmate or because I've never had this much energy in my life and my body doesn't know what to do with it.

I could run a marathon right now.

But I have to get rid of Xavier's body first.

Oh, my God, his body.

How am I supposed to get rid of his body?

Jake? I can't tell Jake. Sweet, hardworking Jake can't be an accomplice to murder. And he can't know what I am. He just can't. Not yet—not like *this.*

Tripp? No. No way.

Imani? There's a strong possibility she would believe me if I told her what I am, but I don't know if she would be the best help when it comes to disposing of a body. And she can't know like this, either. It has to be right.

Aiden?

"Aiden," I hear myself say, my phone pressed against my ear, but even though I'm saying it, it sounds like my voice is a million miles away. I know I need to just *say* it because if I stall too much, someone will find me kneeling next to Xavier's body with his blood on my teeth and on my hands, and I can't explain that to just anyone.

How did I let this happen?

"I need your help," I say, and it sounds like I'm about to cry because I *am* about to cry. I might actually already be crying because his body is blurry now, and my entire body is shaking so much it hurts, but I can't stop it. "I was studying with Xavier, and something happened, and he went limp, and I think—I think he's—"

"I'm on my way. Don't go anywhere."

The line goes dead before I can even register Aiden's calmness or lack of questioning—just that he's on his way, and that's all I need right now.

Oh my *God,* how am I gonna explain this to him?

I do my best to run my tongue along my teeth and lips to get rid of as much blood as possible as I check Xavier's pulse every few seconds, as if it'll come back. How could this happen? How could I let this happen? Please, please, please tell me this is a nightmare, that I didn't really do this, that I—

"Lydia." I hear my name, feel hands under my arms, pulling me to my feet, away from Xavier, and to a corner of the tiny room. I realize Aiden brought something—a large bag that looks familiar, as he sets it on the ground next to Xavier—

"That's Jake's," I manage to say.

"I'll replace it. I needed something big enough for the body."

Did I say he died on the phone? Watching Aiden roll him into the extra-large football bag with ease, watching him have to bend some of his limbs and wrap his elbows and knees with some sort of tape or something he brought, and it hits me again, like a punch straight to the stomach.

I killed him.

I killed someone.

I killed someone who I asked for help, who would still be alive if I weren't an idiot and he wasn't so nice. I should've just done it before I left and not taken the risk, and I should've acted sooner, and now he's fucking *dead.*

I think I'm going to be sick.

Once Xavier is secure in the bag, Aiden hauls it over his shoulder. He turns to me, his curls a bit unruly, but the look in his eyes is surprisingly controlled.

"Lydia, I need you to help me. We're going to the lake, but I need you to just open the doors for me and keep calm until we get there. We can't draw suspicion. Can you do that for me?"

I nod, not wanting to tear my eyes away from his because something deep in me tells me that all the bad feelings will come back full force if I look away.

He nods back at me, firmly. "Then let's go. But wipe your mouth on your sleeve before we leave."

Once I look presentable enough according to Aiden, we leave the study room, and everything hits me in full force again. We're alone in the elevator, but I convince myself on the ride down that the security guard at the front desk is going to stop us on the way out and ask us what's in the bag and then not only will I—rightfully—get in trouble but Aiden will too because I dragged him into this and why did I drag him into this, he's been such a good friend to me and whydid-Idraghimin—

But they don't. They pay no attention to us.

And then we're out of the building and the fresh, freezing night air hits me along with soft flakes of snow. I'm shaking again, and I feel like I'm about to burst out of my skin.

Why is he so calm? How did he know how to handle a dead body?

Has *Aiden* killed someone before?

It takes too long to get to the lake. Every step, I try and convince myself I'm going to wake up any second, or that a police officer is going to come running up to us and rip the bag from our hands and haul us off.

Aiden keeps talking, but I can't listen. I can't focus because everything is brighter and more colorful and louder, and I'm so very aware of every inch of my skin. I can feel the blood rushing through my veins, and I feel like I'm on top of the world, until I remember the cost this feeling came at and where he is. I tighten up inside and everything goes completely numb, and I can't breathe deep enough, and I think maybe I'm actually dying, maybe human blood is poisonous, and the whole thing is a myth, and I'm getting what I deserve.

Because it's night and it's cold, the lakefront is abandoned. And because of that, I watch as Aiden checks every possible direction before he tosses the bag out into the lake where it sinks amongst the flat slabs of ice floating on top of the dark water.

Where Xavier sinks.

Gone forever.

CHAPTER TWENTY-ONE

I SIT on the edge of the lakefront trail and stare out across the dark water, not knowing what to say or do or think.

I feel like I should be panicking more or something, or at least reacting in some way, but maybe I already got all of that out of my system. Or maybe what I did is just so terrible I'm never going to really be able to process it and I'm just going to have to live in this state of numbness for the rest of my life, knowing I killed someone, knowing I just took an innocent person away from his family and friends and all the people who loved him because I'm a monster who doesn't know my boundaries or how to control myself.

And that's why I can't figure out why Aiden is still sitting next to me. Or how or why he's so calm about all of this, as if he wasn't washing blood off his hands less than five minutes ago. As if he didn't just dump a body into a lake for someone he met less than six months ago, and as if he knows the whole story even though he hasn't asked a single question.

I barely process the cold pricking against my skin or that Aiden is saying my name, trying to get my attention. But when I do finally look at him, there's worry etched deep in his face. I wonder what he's seeing on mine. If I look as numb as I feel, both mentally and physically, or if he can see the energy thriving beneath that, as the human blood in my system lights me aflame, making his eyes brighter and greener, even in the darkness.

"Let's get you inside," he says, and I feel myself shaking my head, almost involuntarily. The thought of having to face anyone else after this makes me want to vomit. My stomach is already churning, and it only gets worse when I start to think about the blood that coated my hands when I felt for a pulse and his eyes, open and scared and unseeing.

My stomach surges, and I lean over, letting myself vomit into the water, my throat burning as it comes out of me, liquidy and dark. Aiden pulls my hair away from my face, holding it even after I'm done, as I'm dry-heaving and sobbing, finally, tears and snot and drool and all, the ache in my chest tight and unbearable.

His hands slide from my hair to my arms, pulling me back against his chest gently, and I feel his body, his warmth, and his heartbeat, and I need to get away before I hurt him, but I don't want to, and—

Why isn't he scared of me? Why didn't he call the police?

Why does he seem to know exactly what happened already? Why was he so prepared?

A wave of calm passes over me, and I lean further back into him, letting myself relax in his arms as I wipe the remnants of my breakdown away with my sleeves.

As if he knows what I'm thinking, he says, his voice soft and close to my ear:

"I'm... different, too, Lydia."

I whirl around to look at him, unsure if I heard him right, and at a loss for what that means if I *did* hear him right, because I don't know if "different" covers it. I'm half of a monster.

Aiden swallows, his Adam's apple bobbing. He's clearly nervous about whatever it is he's about to tell me as if I didn't just practically tear someone's throat out with my teeth. He *should* be nervous—to be around *me*.

"It's... It's a long story, but I feel like you should know. Can we go somewhere?"

I study his eyes, bright against his flushed cheeks, and the way his shoulders hunch against the cold, and I nod. He looks relieved as he stands, holding out a hand to help me up, which I hesitantly take. That wave of calm washes over me again as his stone-cold fingers close over mine.

It's only when we're sitting across from each other at a corner table in the dimly-lit Taco Bell down the street from our dorm and I'm sipping anxiously on my large Baja Blast and he's picking at his bowl of potatoes does he begin to explain, his voice quiet so the workers can't hear us over the music.

"I was homeschooled until high school, which you know," he says, shoving the potatoes around with his fork. "My parents were always super protective of me, kind of kept my interactions with other kids to a minimum. And I'd always tell them everything—not that there was anything to lie about or not tell them, since I was around them pretty much twenty-four-seven. But when I was fourteen, I was allowed to go to public school for the first time. The night before my first day, my parents sat me down and told me, basically, that I should just be quiet and keep to myself and interact with the other kids as little as possible, or else they'd find out I was different."

Dad told me that, too—at age eight.

"They told me I couldn't lie—not in the sense it was important to be truthful, but that I was incapable of doing so. They said that other kids would cheat and lie, but that was against my nature, and warned I might be drawn to playing tricks on them, but I couldn't, or else I'd get in trouble. And that other kids didn't have pointed ears and—"

"What?" I ask. Aiden glances around before pulling his mess of curls aside so that I can see the tip of one of his ears. And sure enough, it's got a slight point to it, but nothing that looks unnatural.

And what does that have to do with anything?

"Other... others exist, Lydia," he says, keeping his voice so low that to any human ears it would probably be barely audible, "and I'm one of them. I'm—I'm Fae."

My heart stutters in my chest. Fae? I've read enough fantasy novels to understand that refers to faeries, and to know there are many variations of them in fiction. But—

What?

"My parents knew," he continues when I'm at a loss for words. "They—they've had run-ins, apparently, with va— with, um, your kind before. I never have. I never even knew your kind—"

"Don't call it that," I say, my voice hoarse. They're not *my kind*. I'm still half human, and that's what I'm trying my best to hold on to right now. Because if I don't have that, then what am I? I'm just the monster. I'm just the—the *thing* that killed Xavier. That's it. So, hearing Aiden say that—though I know his intentions are good, seeing as we're in public— threatens to send me deeper into the spiral I'm balancing on the edge of.

"I'm sorry," he says, and I can tell it's genuine. And not just because he apparently can't lie. "But I was just saying I never knew they existed. I never knew *anything* existed, and I probably wouldn't if my parents didn't *have* to, well, teach me how to act before I went to public school. And so, after you, my parents explained it to me that apparently, they could sense it on you, despite your human qualities being so overbearing. It's like... some sort of familiarity, they said, being around another being like us. Feeling like you know them. And I did feel that, that day we met. I just didn't understand it at first. They also..." Shame clouds Aiden's expression. "They told me to stay away from you. That you'd cause nothing but trouble for me, if you ever... lost control."

I take my mouth off my straw, which I had been subconsciously chewing on and poked holes in, and lean back in my seat, taking slow breaths to steady the churning of my stomach. A chill washes over me. They were right, after all, and *I* was right, because that's why they were looking at me like that when I met them. Because they *did* know.

I have so many questions. Is Aiden immortal? Does he have powers? Do his parents have powers?

I make a conscious decision not to beat myself up more and voice my thoughts that his parents were right and that he *should* stay away from me, because selfishly, I don't want him to. If he understands even the *slightest* bit what it's like to be different, I need that kind of support. Because sure, I can talk to Dad about normal vampire stuff—not Xavier, never Xavier —but he doesn't *understand*. He never can, never will, and that's not his fault.

"Do you have—" I lower my voice, "—powers?"

Despite everything, the corner of his mouth quirks up, and I'm almost glad for it.

"Not that I know of. In fact, my parents like to talk about it as little as possible. We kind of pretend it doesn't exist in my household."

I let out a little sigh, watching a drop of condensation run down the side of my cup. I don't get it. Why not talk about it if *they're* Fae, too? Being Fae doesn't seem like it directly affects Aiden's life too badly, besides the lying thing. It seems kind of cool, actually, if it's anything like the books I've read, with magic and everything. I'd switch with him any day.

Except no, I wouldn't. I take back that thought almost

immediately. I wouldn't put him through this awful existence. I wouldn't willingly do that to anyone.

When I lift my eyes to meet Aiden's, a little spike of anxiety settles in me, and yet another question pops into my head.

"Are you sure? Do—do you have, like—" I lower my voice again, this time mostly out of embarrassment."—*calming* powers?"

Aiden cocks his head slightly. "Huh?"

I grab my straw, swirling it around in my half-empty cup, just so I don't have to make eye contact with him, my face flushing.

"It's just, like, whenever I'm around you, or make eye contact with you, or like, touch you like at the lake, it just kinda feels like... I'm able to relax. More than would be normal, I think." I pause, glancing up, and there's something so soft in his gaze that makes me look away again. When he doesn't say anything, I blabber on, "Maybe that sounds stupid, maybe I'm just imagining it because we're—we're friends and it's easy to be around you and tell you stuff and I—"

"Lydia." His hand closes over one of mine that's resting on the table, and I feel it again, unmistakably. When I finally tear my eyes away from his hand and risk looking to meet his, that look I saw before is gone, replaced by something a little more...

Pained?

And I feel that, too. Something in my chest.

"I feel it now," I breathe.

He jerks his hand away, looking at it as he flexes his fingers.

"I—I don't know. They never told me about anything like that."

He's obviously telling the truth, so I drop it, feeling a little embarrassed, but I'll take this over—

I close my eyes, letting out a shaky breath as my heart

twists so, so painfully. "What do I do? Oh my God, Aiden, I..."

"Nothing," he says, so firmly that I open my eyes. "It happened, and it's over, and we took care of it."

A tear slides down my cheek as I try to steady my breathing.

"He's—"

His hands close over mine. A little bit of the pain eases as I choke back a sob. "I'm here, okay? I'm not going to tell anyone. We're in this together, you and me."

He smiles faintly, though it doesn't reach his eyes. "And remember, I can't lie."

He lets go of my hands, but only to stand up and throw his garbage away. When he comes back, he stops next to the table and holds his hand out to me.

"C'mon. Let's go home."

CHAPTER TWENTY-TWO

THE NEXT MORNING, when I wake up from the dazed, half-asleep state I settled into for the night, it takes a minute for everything to come back.

I immediately run to the bathroom to puke up the remainder of everything I consumed in the last however-many-hours.

Including Xavier's blood.

Aiden, in a very un-Aiden-like way, practically ordered me to go straight to bed when we got back last night and immediately headed back to the study room. I couldn't let him go alone, so I caught up to him, and between the two of us, we made sure the room had no evidence of what happened, though we couldn't do much about the chair that had a bent leg from where I threw it against the wall, along with the wall's matching dent. Just being in that room again made me queasy, the backs of my eyes burning with tears.

"Did you know?" I had asked, not really wanting to know, but needing to at the same time. "Did you always think I'd do something like this?"

He looked over at me while setting the chair back up and

pushing it in, his expression unreadable. I still couldn't—and still, this morning, can't—quite wrap my head around the fact he's a faerie. In fact, that's what I'm focusing on to keep myself from completely spiraling, because if vampires obviously exist, and Fae exist, what else is out there?

Familiarity. Like you already know them. Haven't I felt that before?

And is that why I've never been drawn to his blood like all of my other human friends?

"No. My parents had... well, they told me vampires can either drain people completely, if they don't stop themselves, or they can change them." He had chuckled, humorlessly. "I don't know why I'm telling you this. I'm sure you know."

I shook my head. "No. I really don't. My—Well, I was raised by a human."

He chewed on the inside of his cheek. "Right. Okay, well, they told me they'd never seen anyth—anybody like you before, and they weren't really sure how your, uh, cravings would work, but that regardless, they thought you were dangerous. Even as I got to know you, I knew I... I don't know. It was always in the back of my mind to be prepared, I guess. And I'm really sorry about that."

"And... Halloween? Did you know it wasn't the alcohol?"

He shrugged. "I suspected. And obviously, I don't know if it all affects you besides what my parents have told me, but I always kinda assumed it's why you hate large crowds. So, that's why I covered for you, as truthfully as I could."

He paused, finally pulling his gaze from the dent in the wall and meeting my eyes.

"How *did* you handle it? On Halloween?"

I thought back to sitting on the cold tile floor of the bathroom, my back against the door, shaking, as I suck my fangs into my own arm.

"I just took a minute to calm down," I said, tearing my

eyes away from his, fiddling with the hem of my sweater. "Focus on myself instead of everyone else."

Even if he didn't buy it, he didn't ask any more questions.

I groan as I slump against the bathroom wall, my stomach churning.

"Lydia! You okay, girl?"

"Fine!" I call back, wiping at the tears sliding down my cheeks as I take deep, steadying breaths that soon catch with a sob as I think about Xavier—not that I've stopped.

At what point does his roommate or friends contact the police to report him missing? At what point do I get myself taken to jail as a murderer and Aiden as an accomplice?

It was only a matter of time before I ruined my own life. Before I ruined someone else's.

But *why* was I so stupid?

Why did I have to drag him into it? Why didn't I recognize the signs and hang back and feed off myself first? Why didn't I excuse myself sooner? *Why do I think I can handle this?*

Once I brush my teeth and push the thoughts far back enough to feel like I can compose myself and face another person, I leave the bathroom to see Imani sitting up in her bed, her eyes still half-lidded with sleep.

"Sorry," I murmur, not quite able to meet her gaze. While the effects of pure human blood have worn off slightly, I still feel like everything is brighter and louder and just... *more*. When I do look at Imani, I can practically see every pore on her face.

"Don't be sorry!" she says. "Can I do anything? I can run down to the food court or CVS or—"

"No, no, I'm fine."

I take a shaky breath, and all I can picture is Xavier. My hands pin his wrists down to the floor. The feel of him underneath me, so warm and alive one second, and the next—

I need to get out.

I'm not hungry anymore—Xavier solved that.

But I just—

I need out.

"I think I just—I just need some fresh air," I manage, already grabbing blindly at the clothes in my closet for an outfit so that I can escape outside and feel the cold air on my skin. Before I leave, Imani tells me to be safe just before I let the door slam shut behind me. I hear the concern in her voice, but I can't. I can't answer any questions, and I shouldn't have brought my coat because I'm too hot and why is the elevator taking so long and I can't get a deep enough breath.

I keep my head down as I get on the elevator, which is thankfully empty, tears blurring my vision. I can't go to class. I can't. I don't have an exam; I only have a paper, which I already did, so I'll just email it to Roarke and tell him I'm sick and can't go. I'll tell Jake I'm sick and can't go. I can't even breathe by the time I push open the doors of my dorm, gasping for air and unable to see because of the tears. The air is cold but not cold enough, and I want it just to seep through my skin and stick to my bones until I can't feel anything anymore.

What did I *do*?

Why couldn't I just be *normal*?

If my mother didn't cheat, I wouldn't be like this. I would've grown up and got to go to grade school instead of being in the hospital every other damn day because I was living half-dead and I would've made friends and actually learned how to interact with people instead of overthinking every word that anyone said to me and I would've gotten to experience normal things and I wouldn't have to hide things and I could've just been happy and not fucking hated myself.

Or maybe, *maybe*, if it had to be this way, if I was always destined to suffer like this, in this body, then maybe my biological father could've stuck around and helped me understand what I am instead of being left guessing for eight years. Until *I* had to figure it out myself.

I hate it. I hate myself, and I hate that I let it get that bad and that I wasn't responsible, and I ruined a life because of it. *Lives.*

I'm a monster.

I pull my coat off as I walk, draping it over my arm and pushing the sleeves of my hoodie up to my elbows to feel the cold bite against my skin.

The cold helps, numbing my fingers and face and my toes through my beat-up Converse that aren't all blocking the snow or slush, soaking my socks. But it helps because then I don't have to feel anything, and I don't have to think about—

Stop.

I end up walking to the butcher, where I'll get enough for every day this week and for—

Shit.

Shit, shit, *shit.*

I'm supposed to be leaving at the end of this week. For Jake's house. With Tripp and Jake and his mom, and sister, and I can't. I need to find a way out. But then they'll ask questions, and Dad will ask questions, but I *can't.*

Shit.

I'm teetering on the edge by the time I leave the butcher, trying to control my breathing, trying to figure out how I'm going to back out of this trip, but first, I have my geology exam where I'll have to see Jake, and I have my math exam tonight. How am I supposed to go when I know Xavier's seat is going to be empty and that it's my fault he won't get a future?

Was he supposed to have a final this morning? At what point does his roommate or his professors or his mom report him missing? How much time do I have? How much time does Aiden have? I can't go, but if I don't, I'll fail, but if I go—

Imani is gone by the time I get back, so I get into bed and

stare over at her side of the room, my limbs aching as the warmth returns to them. At one point—around ten—there's a knock on the door, and when I drag myself out of bed to answer, I pull it open to see Jake, standing with a CVS bag and a bouquet of flowers. He smiles at me, and my chest tightens so badly I can hardly breathe.

"Hey, baby," he says. "Thought I'd check on you and bring you a few things. You okay to go to geology?"

"Yeah," I murmur. "Thank you."

"Let me know if you need anything else." He smiles again, but his concern floods it. And I only feel worse.

After the door is shut, I peer into the bag and see there're two Gatorades and two cans of soup, my chest tightening.

I set the bag and flowers on my desk, get back into the bed, and flip over, staring at my blank, white wall, my comforter pulled up to my chin, until Jake knocks on my door again, forty minutes later.

I feel like a zombie, listening to Jake talk on our walk there. I can barely bring myself to look at him, and somehow, an hour later, I manage to turn in a completed exam and walk back, listening to him talk about the questions he wasn't sure about and asking what answers I chose.

I think I answer him. I'm not sure.

I get back into bed the second I get back, kicking off my shoes and getting under my comforter. I still feel like a zombie when I finally drag myself out of bed around six to go take my math exam. My stomach growls, protesting at the fact I haven't eaten any human food today, but I ignore it and start shoving my notebook and pencil case into my backpack to leave.

I don't even know why I'm bothering to go. I'm going to flunk anyway.

Somehow, I end up in my math classroom, in my usual

seat, trying my best not to look at what used to be Xavier's. My professor calls attendance, and I wait to hear his name.

And she says it.

Followed by silence.

And then she moves on. She just moves on, as if it's perfectly fine he's not there and he's dead and in Lake Michigan, all because of me.

And then she's passing out the exams, and there're so many pages. I look at the first question, and okay, maybe this won't be so bad, but at what point does he end up in the news? At what point do people start to ask questions?

My pencil slips from my hand, slides over the edge of the small desk, and clatters on the floor. I lean over to pick it up, hands shaking so violently I can barely write. How long have I been staring at this question, problem number five? The little black numbers and the symbols that accompany them drift in and out of focus, taunting me, and I skip it, but I know Xavier would know it, he'd probably be halfway through the exam already, and I'm sure everyone else is, too, but I can't think because I look at the numbers written in my handwriting and see Xavier's handwriting and the blood welling on his finger, a perfect bead of red. I see the drops sliding down his neck, his parted lips, his unmoving chest.

"Time's up, Lydia."

I look up, forcing my eyes away from the page. My professor is standing in front of my desk, looking at me. The room is empty. I look back down, registering I somehow got to the second-to-last page.

I rise from my seat, handing her my test, and start packing my things.

I end up back in my room. Back in bed. Staring at the wall. My phone vibrates behind me on the desk, indicating I'm getting texts, but I ignore them. I close my eyes, and the next time I open them, the room is dark. Imani softly snores from across the room, and moonlight streams in through the window. I close them, but all I see is red red red numbers, Xavier's face, Xavier's hands, Xavier's neck, and my stomach aches for human food. I need it to stop. I need everything to *stop*.

The days start to blend together. I sleep during the day sometimes, and sometimes I sleep at night, but sometimes I'm awake at night, staring at the wall, trying to block out the noise, trying not to feel. I don't get out of bed except to use the bathroom and go to my exams when I absolutely have to.

I don't go to work, and I lie to Roarke when he texts me, checking in to see if I'm okay and telling me my essay got a perfect score. Imani and Jake check in on me, and I lie to both of them, too, telling them I'm sick and can't remember when I ate last. Aiden checks on me and brings me books, and when I try and humor him and try to read, I end up staring at one word. My eyes unfocus, and I let my mind go back *there*. And then it's Thursday.

Jake comes over, and he's asking me if I'm still okay to go on the trip to his mom's, and I can't say no because they bought the ticket for me already. His mom and sister are excited to meet me, and I can't say no when he's looking at me like that, even when all I really want is to lie here and rot for the rest of my life like I deserve. And I need to say no for his and Tripp's sake, and Jake's mom and sister, and everyone in the airport and on the plane, but I can't say no because... I just can't.

Because maybe this is my chance to prove I'm still human.

That I can still be good.

And so, I hear myself say okay.

CHAPTER TWENTY-THREE

I WANT to take back my "okay" as I'm spending Friday packing.

I want to get back in bed.

I want to get off the train and turn right back around before we even pass one stop to get to the airport.

I want to get off before I'm even on the plane.

I want to leave as soon as I'm *on* the plane.

I tried to shove it all down and act like everything was normal and that I was just sick—and because of that, I agreed to go to Chinatown to a restaurant Friday night to celebrate the end of finals and hang out one last time before Tripp, Jake, and I left the next morning. After consuming nothing but crackers and Gatorade and water all week—and blood, which is even harder to get down now—the food in front of me made me nauseous. It was a place called a hot pot, chosen by the boys, so the workers brought us a pot of broth and a bunch of different meats and tofu, and vegetables to cook in the broth ourselves. Tripp and Jake seemed to be getting a kick out of it. Music played quietly, and I could hear the sounds of bubbling broth, the clinking of metal chopsticks, the fizzing of pop. And, still ringing in my ears, the sound of chair legs scraping, a body hitting the floor, and my name.

The lack of a heartbeat.

I stayed quiet during dinner, barely following the conversations as I pushed a piece of broccoli around my otherwise empty plate with my chopsticks. Aiden acted normal, only contributing to the conversation every so often, like he normally does, but occasionally bumping his leg against mine under the table as if just letting me know he was there.

They were talking about Christmas, I think, and for Jake, what his family usually does during the break, since they don't celebrate Christmas. I heard Imani talking about how her and her brothers are master gingerbread house decorators or something like that, but I completely lost any hold I had on the conversation as soon as I lifted my eyes from my plate.

My gaze immediately met a man's, middle-aged, walking down the aisle next to our booth—like he was already staring at me.

Instantly, I got the feeling I knew him.

He was tall with dark-brown or black hair and neatly trimmed facial hair to match, a stark contrast from his pale skin, which looked even paler because of the full black ensemble he had on: dress pants, dress shoes, and a black trench coat. But his eyes—his eyes were almost as dark as his hair, the color of his irises blending in with the pupils, and the way he looked at me sent a shiver down my spine, because he looked at me like Tripp always does.

Like he was trying to look into my soul, to figure out my deepest secrets. Or worse—like he already *knew* my deepest secrets.

And it was made even worse when the corner of his mouth tugged upward in a barely-there smile, and gave me a nod, as if he felt that familiarity, too.

I haven't stopped thinking about him since. I mean, he had to have been *something*, right? Fae, like Aiden?

A vampire?

And now—on the plane I forced myself to get on because there's no way I could've gone home and faced Dad after what I did—I think the only reason I'm not sent into a complete mental breakdown is because Jake insisted on buying himself, Tripp, and I matching bears from the Build-A-Bear vending machine in the airport as "an early Christmas gift", and because I got the window seat.

I clutch my bear to my chest, staring out the window the entire time, the pressure building in my ears and head. Jake, who sits squished in the middle, asks me every so often if I'm feeling okay, if I need a drink, if I need something, anything.

At a certain point, I just tell him I'm going to try and rest —an excuse to close my eyes, rest my head against the window, and not speak. I hear him and Tripp talk in low voices, other conversations, other heartbeats, the roar of the plane, the flush of the toilet, everything, everything, *everything*. I think about Aiden, about the man. I think about these people and their lives and how they can probably exist without despising it.

I'm miserable almost the entire flight, except for when I nibble on pretzels. When we finally land, people start clapping, the plane bouncing and rolling to a stop, and it's too loud. I have to squeeze my eyes shut, trying to somehow prevent the piercing headache that's starting to make my head throb.

Tripp snorts. "White people," he mutters.

"*You're* white," Jake reminds him.

"Not *that* white," Tripp grumbles back.

Jake holds my hand as we exit the plane. As much as I'm tempted to tear my hand away, to limit contact between us, I need to act *some*what normal. I've been too *gone* all week.

I don't think he buys it, though. I'm not acting normal

enough. Not after ice skating and the market and all of the good we had *before.*

"Mom says they're here," Jake says, as we head to baggage to get our suitcases, looking down at his phone. "So, we'll grab our stuff and find them. You okay, Lyds?"

I look up from my own phone, where I'd been typing out a text to Aiden.

"Mhm. 'M fine."

He turns away, and I glance at Tripp, whose gaze lingers on me before turning away, too.

We grab our suitcases when they come around the belt, and I linger behind as Jake and Tripp weave their way through the airport, Jake occasionally glancing back to make sure we're both still with him. He gives me a smile each time, and I force a small one back.

Before long, we near an exit, and I hear Jake say, "There they are!"

I look ahead, and sure enough, there's a woman and a girl standing by a pillar near the doors, waving in our direction. And as we near, the resemblance becomes clear; his little sister, Anabelle, has the same brown hair—shoulder-length—the same facial structure, even the same thin, angular eyebrows, but there's a childlike softness to her face, too. Unlike Jake, her eyes are a dark brown—which reminds me of that man from Chinatown—and so are Jake's mom's, but unlike that man, their gazes are light, happy.

Anabelle runs forward. She's a small, thin girl, and when she practically jumps into Jake's arms, he lifts her and swings her around with ease, both of them laughing.

My chest tightens. I watch as Tripp lets go of his suitcase, stepping forward into Jake's mom's outstretched arms.

"Oh, I missed you, too, Tripp," I hear her murmur. "I hope you've been behaving yourself."

"Of course not," he replies, smiling.

She turns to me next, a warm smile on her face.

"And *you* must be Lydia," she says, and just like Jake, her smile lights up her entire face. My chest tightens even further as I try my best to return her smile, hoping it doesn't look as forced as it feels. "I've heard so much about you. It's nice to finally meet you, honey."

I let her hug me, her embrace soft and warm. My heart pounds in my ears, because even though I downed the last of the blood in my fridge before we left this morning—two full bottles, which I almost threw up after—I still feel like I can't get too close. Like if I make a wrong move, something will happen.

And I'll ruin another life.

I look over at Anabelle, who Jake has since set down, and she offers me a shy smile and a wave. I force a smile back, and she almost immediately turns to Tripp, who ruffles her hair as they fall into step together.

I stay to the back, watching them lead the way, Anabelle with a little skip in her step as she animatedly talks to Tripp about something, and Jake, who gives his mom a side hug and a kiss on the cheek.

This is fine. I can do this.

I swallow past the lump in my throat.

Just push it down, Lydia.

CHAPTER TWENTY-FOUR

THE HAMPTONS' house is somehow exactly what I expected.

The siding is brown, but the roof and window frames are dark green. The front yard is small, split by a sidewalk that leads to a small porch with a rocking chair. There's already a car in front of us in the driveway, parked in front of a small garage. As we pull closer to it, I see the license plate reads **JAKEYH2.**

Despite the hollow feeling in my chest, the corner of my mouth tugs upward.

"Nice license plate," I say, quietly. Jake leans forward, shooting me a huge smile past Anabelle, who we put in between us in the backseat of the small car. I add, just for good measure, "Was **JAKEYH1** taken?"

Tripp snorts a laugh from the front seat.

"Actually, yes, it was," Jake replies.

"He was very distraught," Joanne says in a stage whisper, and Anabelle giggles as Jake protests, "I thought it was original enough!"

We all get out of the car, and I take up the back as we head to the front door.

Joanne's keys jingle as she sorts through them for the house key. I take the opportunity to look around: the neighborhood is pretty, everyone's yards still coated with fresh blankets of white from the most recent snowfall. And it's quiet. It kind of reminds me of back home—but if I think too much about home, I start thinking about Dad, and I can't think about Dad right now. Not when I'm not sure how I'm ever going to be able to look him in the eye again.

"You okay?" I startle at the sound of Jake's voice, low and close to my ear. "You were quiet on the car ride. And the plane." A smile tugs at the corner of his lips. "Which isn't bad," he adds. "Quieter than usual is all."

"'M fine," I say. "Just... nervous. Sorry."

That's partially the truth. I *am* nervous. Because my head's not in the right place to make a good impression, as much as I want to, because both Joanne and Anabelle seem so sweet and Jake cares about them so, so much, but I can't escape from that study room. And because I know I'm not going to be able to get my hands on blood over these next few weeks, so I know what I'm going to have to do, and even though I know it's not right, and that it's not the best option, I deserve it. I deserve the pain and the feeling it brings me.

But at the same time, I've come to terms with the idea that maybe this trip could help me as much as it terrifies me. I need to regain my grip on my human side.

Because I'm losing her.

"Don't be," Jake whispers, and I let him press a kiss to the top of my head as Joanne gets the door unlocked. "Just be yourself and they'll—they'll think you're great, just like I do, okay?"

I nod, following the others into the house. It smells

comforting; some sort of warm, cinnamon-y scent floods my nose. Jake quickly jumps ahead to give me the tour, taking me down a little hallway to show me the kitchen and the living room. Everything is *warm*, from the dark brown of the couches that match the dark wood of the kitchen cabinets, and compared to Dad's house, it's so... lived in.

There's proof of *life*. There's pictures on the walls, and as Jake leads me back down the hallway so he can show me what's upstairs, I pause so I can look at all of them: there's a much younger Jake in a football uniform, smiling and red-cheeked, his hair plastered to his forehead, cradling his helmet in his arms. There's a much more recent Jake, posing in his graduation gown, his high school diploma in one hand and making a thumbs-up with the other. Next to him stands Anabelle in a light blue dress and two braids, making two thumbs up, just like her brother, wide grins on both of their faces. There's individual pictures of Anabelle, too, from what looks like preschool graduation to her in a soccer uniform, and there's family pictures—like a candid one that looks like it was taken on a night of Hanukkah with a young Jake reaching forward toward the menorah, and another at a beach, of the kids when they were younger, and behind them a smiling Joanne, and next to her—

"That's Dad," Jake says, seeing what I'm looking at.

"You look like him," I say, and it's true. It seems both Jake and Anabelle got most of their features from their dad, but Anabelle got Joanne's dark-brown eyes, whereas I can see—in some of the better-lit photos—that his dad's eyes were lighter, like Jake's. They even have the same smile.

Jake's smile grows.

"A lot of people have said that. And I like hearing it. I just... I hope I can be even half the man he was, too."

My heart cracks.

"You are," I say, quietly. "I'm sure you are." He finally looks at me, something a little sad in his eyes, and smiles.

"Thanks, baby," he replies, and I let him wrap his arm around my waist and pull me close so he can press a kiss to the side of my head. I close my eyes, trying to give in. Trying to remember it's Jake and that the living, breathing human next to me is exactly that: living and breathing.

But I still have to step back before too long, nodding toward the staircase.

"So, what's upstairs?"

"Right," he says. "C'mon. I'll show you where you'll be sleeping."

There're four bedrooms and one small bathroom upstairs; Jake tells me that Tripp usually gets the guest bedroom, but because I'm here, I'll be sleeping in there, and Tripp will bunk with Jake in his room. The thought of getting the privacy of my own room again after about four months of sharing sounds like heaven—especially now.

After the tour, we go back out to the car to get our suitcases, and Joanne calls in pizzas for us for dinner. I take one look at the red sauce and my stomach churns, but I manage a few bites so nobody asks questions—which I almost immediately throw up after we all head upstairs for the night.

I tell Jake I'm tired and gonna head to bed early, and the concern in his eyes is clear.

"Okay. You sure you're okay?"

I tell him I am, and that I'm just tired from the trip. He doesn't press me any further. I *am* tired, so it's not a total lie. I'm exhausted. And while I don't feel that familiar hunger yet still, I don't want to wait until I feel it. I don't want to—I *can't* —risk that. Even after feeding extra this morning, so much it made my stomach ache in protest of my lack of balancing blood and human food.

"Okay," he says, pressing a quick kiss to my forehead. "If you get hungry, you can grab something from the kitchen. I didn't see you eat much at dinner."

The backs of my eyes burn with tears at the fact he noticed.

"No, I, um, I think the stomach bug I had is still bothering me. My, uh, my appetite's not all back yet. But thank you."

He nods, seeming to buy that.

"That makes sense," he says. "If you want anything better for your stomach, like soup or something, we should have some in the pantry. Don't be shy." He smiles lightly, but it doesn't quite reach his eyes. "Take whatever you need. I want you to start feeling better."

I do, too. But I don't know if that's possible.

Not when every time he touches me, I'm sent back there. Imagining *his* skin, growing cold under my touch. I imagine laying my palm against *his* chest and not feeling the steady thud of his heartbeat.

"Thank you," I say earnestly.

He lets me go after that. After I shut and lock the door, I go to the bed, huddling under the thick comforter without bothering to change my clothes, clutching my bear to my chest. I pull out my phone, checking the texts I got but didn't look at earlier.

I have two replies to texts I sent earlier, one to Dad and one to Aiden, both after we got off the plane. Dad sent a *"Great. Thanks for the update,"* and Aiden sent an encouraging *"You got through it!!"* to which I couldn't help but smile at. I send Dad a quick update that we made it safely to the Hamptons' and everything is fine, and then I open my thread with Aiden.

me: hi. how's being home?

I set my phone down next to me on the bed, staring blankly at the light blue painted wall, listening to the sounds I can hear. Something howling in the distance, a dog barking, and, much closer, heartbeats and whispers and the sound of running water and the flutter of a page turning. My phone buzzes with texts after what feels like an hour, but could have easily only been a minute.

> aiden swanson: Honestly? I miss not being home. My parents are being overbearing per usual

> aiden swanson: I think I'm gonna start looking to get an apartment over the summer so I can stay in Chicago and not have them breathing over my shoulder every second. Plus I can just keep working at the bookstore

> aiden swanson: But how are you?? How's Jake's?

My thumbs hover over the keyboard for a few seconds before I finally type out a response.

> me: if you get an apartment in chicago, not only will you be away from your parents but you'll also be closer to me :)

I hit send before I can overthink the smiley face, adding a second text:

> me: it's okay. i'm kind of exhausted and i haven't been all here but i'm trying my best. better than this last week. and jake's mom and sister are really sweet

The three dots almost immediately pop up, showing he's

typing. I watch the time change from 9:36 to 9:37 before his replies come through.

> aiden swanson: I know :) trust me you'll be sick of me by the time summer ends

> aiden swanson: That's good that you're better. That's really good. But remember not to push yourself either. Just take it one day at a time. Everything's gonna be okay

I stare at those texts. At the smiley face. At "everything's gonna be okay."

I wish he were here.

I wish I could tell Jake.

I close my eyes, physically feeling the guilt ache deep in my ribcage before I text back.

> me: i could never be sick of you

And then, before I can stop myself:

> me: i wish you were here

The second I hit send, I wish I could unsend it. It's too vulnerable. But then again, nothing can really be worse than getting rid of a body together, right?

That's not funny.

I pull the comforter up over my head, and an anxiety-filled minute later, he replies:

> aiden swanson: Me too

> aiden swanson: Jake wouldn't hate you if you told him you know

I wouldn't blame him if he did.

But either way, I can't tell him now, at his house. His family comes first, I know that. And if he knew I could potentially be a threat...

I blink away the tears that threaten to spill and abruptly change the subject, telling Aiden I'm tired and need to go to sleep.

I shouldn't have come here. I throw the comforter off my head, sitting up and looking down at my arms, turning them around. There's a pit in my stomach, and I need *something*— probably human food, but I just can't risk it. Ever again, but especially not here. I can't do that to Jake.

I lift my right arm to my mouth, supporting it with my left, and I bite. Pain shoots through my arm, and as I suck, and even though I have to pull away and gag when I start thinking about Xavier, how he went limp underneath me, it's better that it's me than someone else.

And that's why, as the days pass, every day, after faking smiles and being present in conversations, after escaping off to my room for the night, I feed on myself. Even though I don't *need* to feed every day or even every other day, I can't get as much from myself as I would my blood from the butcher, and plus, it just makes me feel better, knowing that the only person I'm hurting now is myself.

And I text Aiden every day and every night, but I don't tell him. And I keep Dad updated, sending him pictures of the snowman we built with Anabelle and of the Christmas lights we drive around and see the evening of Christmas Eve, for Tripp and I's sake, just so he doesn't suspect that I'm falling apart.

Texting Aiden makes me feel better. Maybe it's because he knows, and so he doesn't ask me if I'm okay like everyone else does. He just treats me normal and asks how things are going and teases me, and sometimes even manages to get a laugh out of me. One that's not forced, so people think I'm okay.

I get caught when Jake is driving us around. Anabelle and Tripp are in the backseat, pointing out someone's huge house that's decked out in Christmas lights over almost every inch, and I'm in the passenger seat, leaning my head against the window and glancing at my phone whenever it vibrates. I accidentally huff a laugh, and Jake looks at me.

"What is it?" he asks.

"Oh, uh, nothing," I say. "Aiden just texted me something funny about a book he's reading."

"Ah. He's probably going nuts being stuck with his parents, huh?"

"Yeah." I let a smile tug at my mouth as I think of all the complaints Aiden's been texting me over the last week, keeping me distracted, telling me about all the questions his parents have tried bombarding him with—some about me, specifically, and how he's "coping" with the vampire girl next door.

If only they knew they were right about me. That I'm the monster they suspected me to be.

"He, uh, he seems pretty fed up with them already. He said he might be getting his own apartment for the summer just so he doesn't have to deal with them."

Jake chuckles, his face illuminated by the white and red and green and light blue Christmas lights outside. He reaches over to my lap to take my hand, and I let him, as much as I want to pull it away when he presses a kiss to my knuckles. Because his lips are warm and he's breathing and he's alive. He's *alive*, and that's not a bad thing. It shouldn't make me want to jerk away from him.

Because it's better than the alternative.

But him being alive makes me remember that what happened to Xavier is possible.

It's a never-ending cycle I can't escape.

That night, when we get back, I play my part. I say good-night to everyone, and I even let Jake kiss me on the lips for the first time all week, instead of swerving and avoiding him. I even give Anabelle a hug when she shyly offers one.

Everyone's alive. Everyone's breathing.

Except Xavier.

As soon as the guest bedroom door is shut behind me, I sink my teeth into my arm, stifling a sob against my skin.

CHAPTER TWENTY-FIVE

THREE HOURS after I lay down to go to sleep, I'm still staring at the ceiling.

I've already gone through my daily rounds of Googling Xavier, of searching his name on social media just to see if there's any notice of him missing, of anyone looking for him. There isn't. I don't understand.

And I can't close my eyes, because every time I do, I see his face, his hands, his blood. I feel him, I smell him, I taste him.

I finally get up, trying to make as minimal noise as possible as I pull the door open and make my way down the dark hallway and staircase to the kitchen.

I flip on the light, cringing back as my eyes adjust. A snack couldn't hurt, seeing as I've barely eaten human food in... well, I don't know how long, even though I do feel guilty for raiding Joanne's food. Then again, Jake *did* offer.

I unlock my phone after choosing a bagel from one of the cupboards. It's open to my messaging app, displaying the now-embarrassing-to-look-at string of texts I sent to Aiden earlier, once I realized sleep wasn't an option. I quickly close out of my messages, but instead of going back into the spiral of checking every social media app I have, I just stare at the home screen, at the little icons of colors that start to blur as I picture Xavier's face.

Xavier. I'm already forgetting the exact color of his eyes.

The sound of his voice.

"If you're waiting for Santa," says a voice from behind me, "then I have some bad news."

I turn around, facing Tripp and his crooked smile that I forcibly return, despite the hollow feeling in my chest. I must have been so deep in my thoughts, within myself, I didn't even sense him approach.

He's shirtless, dressed only in gray sweatpants. Even his feet are bare despite the cold tile floor of the kitchen. His dark hair is messy, unkempt, as if he were tossing and turning in bed just before coming down here.

"Is it the fact that he isn't real," I ask, deciding to play along, "or the fact that if he is, he'd skip us since we're in a Jewish household?"

Tripp fakes a look of disappointed shock. "What do you mean he isn't real?"

My returning smile comes a little easier, but it still doesn't feel convincing as I turn and pick up half of my bagel. Tripp brushes past me, putting one hand on my arm to keep me where I am as he reaches over to steal the other half of my bagel. I stiffen under his touch, but I hope he doesn't notice.

"Hey," I protest.

But he ignores me, chewing thoughtfully.

"I was the one who ruined Santa for my little brother," he admits, and I perk up slightly at the offhand mention of anything family related. It's not like Tripp to mention his family past a depressing, self-deprecating joke, so to see the fond look in his eyes as he recalls the memory grabs my attention.

"How old was he?" I ask.

"Five, I think," Tripp replies, wiping a crumb away from the corner of his mouth with his thumb. "Which would've made me eight. He cried the entire morning, even while he was opening presents. My parents were pissed."

"You did it *on* Christmas?" I ask, incredulously, and the corner of Tripp's mouth quirks up. "That's pure evil right there."

"Oh, I know," he says. "But trust me. Over the years, he made up for it."

I don't question what that means as Tripp finishes off his half of the bagel. I just watch him, taking in the little scars and marks and proof he's lived: that line across his chest and stomach, the burn mark just above his right collarbones, the scar that's visible under the dark hair on his left arm, his snake tattoo.

"Are you okay?" he asks, and the question throws me wildly off guard.

It's a question I've gotten from everyone else, but one I've never gotten from Tripp, because why *would* he ask? We aren't particularly close. He's my boyfriend's best friend. I'm his best friend's girlfriend and his girlfriend's roommate. That's about the extent of our relationship. We may be in the same friend group, but are we really *friends*?

Maybe he knows, somehow, that I'm hiding something. That I did something. Maybe he hates me and just hasn't said anything to keep the peace.

"Jake worries about you, y'know," he says when I don't answer fast enough. "Says you've been off in your own world for like, the last two weeks. And he says he knows you're lying to him, that you're not telling him what's actually wrong. Why won't you tell him?"

Because I murdered someone, Tripp.

But I'm saved from having to figure out an actual answer, thanks to my phone vibrating on the counter behind me. It's Aiden, finally replying to the texts I sent him earlier during my mental breakdown, long before Tripp came down here.

But when I turn back to look at Tripp and notice the hard look in his eyes, the furrow of his eyebrows, I know he saw Aiden's name lighting up my phone, too.

I ask, "What?"

"You and Aiden have been awfully close lately. Do you talk to *him*?"

My heart sinks. Does he think—

I shrug, trying to appear nonchalant, but I know Tripp can see right through me.

Tripp wouldn't take it well. There's no way he would.

Not when he would do absolutely anything for Jake. Or Imani.

And if he knew I was a threat to both—

"We mostly talk about books," I say, which isn't entirely false. "I lent him a few over break, so he probably just finished one. Or he complains about his parents, like I said earlier."

"Hm." Tripp doesn't sound the slightest bit convinced. But what am I supposed to say? Thanks for thinking so little of me. You assume I'm cheating on Jake with one of his *closest friends*?

I want to leave. Tears burn at the backs of my eyes, and I want to leave before I start crying in front of him, because then he'll really think I'm cheating. If only I could tell him, just to rub it in his face.

I just want to leave. I want to go home.

No, not home. Because Dad can see right through me, too.

I just want to disappear off the face of the earth so I can't hurt anyone ever again.

"I know you're hiding something," he adds, and my stomach drops.

His eyes narrow, and he opens his mouth to continue, but

before any words can come out, another voice comes from the dark staircase:

"I hate to break it to you guys," Jake says, "but Santa's not coming."

"Dammit," Tripp says, continuing to stare almost threateningly at me while addressing his words to Jake. "Looks like we're out of luck, Lydia."

"Damn," I agree, tearing my eyes away from his as Jake comes around the corner, his eyes half-lidded with sleep, his hair sticking up in every direction, and grinning, completely, utterly oblivious to the fact that his girlfriend and best friend were *this* close to getting in a fight. But little does Tripp know, we'd be on the same side.

"If I made a pizza, would anyone eat some with me?" Jake asks, already opening the freezer.

"I think I'm gonna go back to bed," I say at the same time Tripp says, "Sure."

He gives me the side eye while Jake's back is turned.

"Suit yourself, Lyds," he teases, but leans over to kiss my temple and ask, "You alright?"

"Fine," I confirm, ignoring Tripp's burning gaze. "I was just having trouble sleeping. The silence is deafening."

The corner of Jake's mouth quirks upward as he steps away from me to start pulling the plastic wrapping off of the pizza, only to succeed in getting frozen pieces of shredded cheese all over the floor. He curses under his breath, but both Tripp and I immediately kneel down to help clean up. I can, again, feel Tripp's eyes on me, but I, again, avoid looking at him entirely.

"I know. No sirens or car horns or random screaming to lull you to sleep here," Jake says as Tripp and I stand up.

As Jake puts the pizza in the oven, I finally look at Tripp. He furrows his thick, dark eyebrows, and I just purse my lips and turn back to Jake.

"Enjoy your pizza," I tell him. "Make sure to save some for Santa, though."

Jake grins. "Will do."

He leans forward, obviously with the intention of giving me a kiss, so I swallow my anxiety and peck his lips in return.

He's fine. He's alive. You haven't hurt him.

"'Night," I say, once we pull away, getting a "'Night, baby," in return.

"'Night, Tripp," is what I say to Tripp, and I earn a pointed "Goodnight, Lydia" in return.

As soon as I round the corner and start heading back up the stairs, I pull my phone out of my waistband to check the text from Aiden. Well, *texts*, plural.

> aiden swanson: Hey, I'm sorry I didn't see these right away. Let me know if you're okay

> aiden swanson: And it's okay. You're gonna be okay. You're not gonna hurt anyone there

> aiden swanson: Call me if/when you can. Or just text. I just wanna make sure you're alright

I glance back down the staircase as I hear Jake laugh loudly at something. I figure I probably have time to call Aiden, as long as I'm quiet. I make my way back into my room, closing the door behind me as I tap Aiden's contact. It only rings once before he picks up, before I can even cross the dark room to my bed.

"Hey," he greets me, his tone hurried, and I realize just how much I worried him.

"Hi," I whisper, and I swear I hear him release a breath of relief upon hearing my calm voice. My chest tightens a little at the thought of him stressing over whether or not I was okay.

"I'm sorry if I scared you. I got cornered by Tripp in the kitchen, and then Jake came down, and I couldn't answer right away."

"It's okay," he sighs. "You're okay, though?"

"I'm fine."

There's a stretch of silence before Aiden continues, so long that I pull my phone away from my ear to make sure the call didn't disconnect.

"What do you mean you were *cornered* by Tripp?" he asks, slowly. "Does he suspect something?"

Yeah, that I'm cheating on Jake with you. No biggie.

"No, no, I should've phrased that better. He just, uh..." I trail off before blowing out a defeated breath. There's really no point in lying to Aiden. Not at this point.

"Yeah," I admit. "He does. Not in regard to—" I pause, not able to say his name out loud quite yet, but I know Aiden knows what I'm saying. "But, like, he thinks I'm hiding something. I'll, um, explain more later."

It sounds like Aiden sucks in a sharp breath through his teeth.

"Okay, well, it's just Tripp. I'm sure he'll lose interest in trying to tear you apart. When he can't figure someone out, he usually drops it. Eventually."

But this?

"Okay," is all I can bring myself to say.

I roll over from my side onto my back, so I'm once again staring up at the ceiling. I can hear something from downstairs that sounds suspiciously like a fork falling onto the tile floor, and I can hear a toilet flush from the direction of Joanne's room. As much as I want to disappear so I can't hurt anyone, I don't want to be alone. The loneliness is so much worse; it's when everything starts coming back. And the overarching silence is still too loud, and I feel too alone without Imani's heartbeat and quiet breathing across the room. And my chest contracts, almost painfully, when I think about having to hang up with Aiden, even with Jake and Tripp downstairs. Maybe, before, I would go down to Jake, tell him I can't sleep, and ask him to stay with me.

But I can't do that now. I can't risk that.

"Aiden?"

"Yeah?"

Guilt weighs on my chest. "Will you stay on the phone with me 'til I fall asleep? I just... I can't..."

There's another long pause. I twist my fingers in the sheets anxiously, my other hand still holding the phone to my ear as I await his response, each second that ticks by making me regret even asking. I prepare for the humiliation that will come with him saying no, that it's crossing a boundary.

But I'm just asking him as a friend. Friends do this all the time, don't they? Friends who know your deepest, darkest secret and then some, when your boyfriend doesn't, because you can't tell him.

But then Aiden says, with glaring reluctance, "Yeah. Yeah, I can do that."

"I don't mean to make things weird," I say, hurriedly, Tripp's accusations at the front of my mind. "I just—"

"Hey," he says, gently. "I get it. Trust me."

I roll back over onto my side, plugging in my phone before setting it on the bed next to me. I let my eyes flutter shut, trying to picture anything else so that my mind doesn't go straight to—

I think of Aiden. His eyes, his smile, him sitting across from me in Taco Bell, pushing back his curls to show me his pointed ears.

That man, his dark eyes boring into me.

Aiden. How relaxed I feel with him.

Dad. Who trusts me, and whose trust I broke, even though he doesn't know yet.

Xavier. Blood trickling out of the bite wound on his neck.

Jake.

Tripp.

Imani.

Xavier.

My chest starts to tighten. No. No, no, no.

Breathe. Everyone in this house is alive and breathing.

"Aiden?"

"Yeah?"

"Goodnight."

He chuckles softly, and the last thing I hear before I let myself drift off to sleep is his voice, quiet and tender:

"Goodnight, Lydia."

CHAPTER TWENTY-SIX

I ACTUALLY GET a decent night of sleep, making the next morning a little easier to bear, which mostly is spent by us lounging around the house. Anabelle puts on one of her kid shows, which Tripp becomes almost comically invested in, staring at the screen intently while curled up in the corner of the couch. I can tell our discussion last night is still on his mind, based on the way he didn't even bother to look at me when he clipped out, "Morning, Lydia."

While he chuckles along with the laugh track, Jake pulls me into the kitchen where a small gift bag and two wrapped, rectangular presents sit on the table.

"Jake," I say, my cheeks flushing. "You didn't have to get me anything."

He smiles. "It wasn't me," he says, guiding me over to the table. "Santa decided to stop by last night after all."

When I give him a look, he just smiles bigger. "It's no biggie, I promise. I wanted to. It *is* Christmas, after all, and even if we don't celebrate, you guys do. I got Tripp something, too."

I start on the green gift bag, pulling the excessive amount

of red tissue paper out until I finally reach the gifts inside. There's a beautiful leather-bound journal with a strap, accompanied by a pack of my favorite pens. I turn the journal around in my hands, opening it and running my hand over the lined pages before smiling at Jake, my chest tight.

I don't deserve this. Any of it.

"This is perfect," I say, keeping my voice low. "Thank you."

He just smiles and tells me to open the other two. I pick up the first, listening to Anabelle and Tripp in the next room, who, by the sound of it, have started to argue about something relating to the show. Jake huffs a laugh, shaking his head as he listens in, too. I attempt to open the first wrapped gift, the shape and size of which is suspiciously the same as a book. The wrapping paper is black with pictures of Snoopy all over it, but as I turn the present around to try and find an open edge to tear it off, I realize Jake has taped nearly every edge.

"I don't think you used enough tape," I say, and he just laughs, taking the present from my hands.

"My mom always says less is more," he says, tucking his finger under the tiniest loose edge of wrapping paper. "I've never believed her."

He pulls upward on the edge, but the sound of him sucking in a breath and the smell of blood, close and fresh and sweet, fills my ears and nose at the same time, and I feel my entire body stiffen as if it's reacting on its own, even as my mind screams *no no no no no no*—

"Paper cut," he says, bringing his finger up to his lips, sucking at the tiny slice on the pad of his finger. I stare at it as he pulls it back, at the purely red blood welling on his fingertip.

The chair crashes against the wall. My hands tighten around his wrists, holding his arms down. He writhes under me.

The walls are closing in further and further and further. Lydia, stop, stop, stop, Lydia, please, stop, Lydia–

"Lydia. Baby. You okay?"

I focus back in and realize it's Jake saying my name, that I'm in the kitchen, that he's set the present down on the table, and his hands are now on my arms, holding me steady, concern filling his brown eyes.

I'm not there. I'm not back there. Jake is in front of me, alive.

He's okay. He's okay, he's okay, he's okay.

"Fine," I say once I find my voice, but it comes out rough, my chest so tight that it hurts to breathe. "I—Sorry, I just— um, the—I got really dizzy for a second."

"Sit, sit," he says, guiding me into a chair at the table. "Have you eaten today? You look really pale." As he sets a cup of water in front of me, my eyes find the slice on his finger, minuscule and bloodless now, but I still feel nauseous and I still have to tell myself I'm not there and that Jake is not Xavier and that he's here and he's alive and he's breathing and every- thing is okay.

But Xavier should be opening gifts at home right now.

Where do his parents think he is?

Does he even have anyone who cares?

I think back to the first day I saw him—my first day here. The way his mom scowled beside him like she'd rather be anywhere else. Is that why he hasn't been reported missing? Does the only person he *might* have not care enough to wonder where he is?

"I—I don't know. I had some of a bagel last night. Sorry. I'm okay. I just—I just got dizzy."

He says I have nothing to be sorry about, not looking at all convinced that I'm really "okay," but once I down the cup of water—which just churns in my stomach and burns my throat, threatening to come right back up—he seems to relax a little, sitting in the chair next to me.

I assure him once more, for good measure, that I'm okay before starting to open my two presents, mostly to just distract both of us from what just happened, when really, I just want to go to bed and pull the covers over my head and never see anyone ever again. The first one is, in fact, a book—one I mentioned I've been wanting offhandedly once, but since we don't have it in stock at EB's, I haven't gotten around to getting it for myself yet. I thank him, earnestly, before opening the last present, which is a box that contains long, fingerless gloves, and I can't help but smile a little when I see them, because I know exactly what they're for—all the times I've been reading or doing homework around Jake, and he's grabbed my hand and mentioned how cold my hands are.

My chest aches even more at the memories. When I could be slightly more carefree with him. When I wasn't sent back to that study room, every time I touched him.

"Thank you," I say, turning over the soft, black gloves in my hands. "These are perfect. Thank you for all of it."

One of his hands comes to rest on my knee, and I resist the urge to jerk away, hoping the strain doesn't show on my face.

"I'm glad," he says. "I'm really glad. I'm also really happy you decided to spend break with me, even though you haven't been feeling great. It means a lot, really." He pauses, eyes searching my face. "Merry Christmas, Lyds. Now I'm gonna make you breakfast, though," he says, pushing himself up from his chair. "I'll get you more water, too. Do you want pancakes? I think we have pancake mix—"

"I'm okay with anything," I assure him, though the ache in my chest doesn't subside, the panic still lingering just under the surface, even as I open my new journal and start doodling on the first page as Jake rifles through the cabinets, trying to find the pancake mix.

I set my pen down and pull my phone out of my pocket as I take another sip of my water, hoping the nausea subsides soon. I see I already have three texts to answer: one from Dad, and another two from Aiden.

Dad's is accompanied by a picture of the puppy wearing a Santa hat and says:

> dad: Merry Christmas to my favorite daughter! Call me sometime today if you can. Love you.

I text back that I'll call him later before opening the two from Aiden.

> aiden swanson: Merry Christmas Lydia. Just so you know, I forgot to charge my phone last night because of us being on the phone all night, so it died. I hope you feel bad. Terrible, actually. I hope you got coal too

I smile to myself, genuinely, at his complete dorkiness as I read the second:

> aiden swanson: I'm jk. I love lying over text. It gives me such a thrill. Feeling better today?

I text him back:

> me: first of all jokes on you because santa didn't come at all

> me: seriously though, i really appreciate you staying on the phone with me last night. it helped a lot. and yes i mean i was feeling a little better but also not really anymore because jake got a paper cut and it messed with me

> me: any plans for today? what'd santa
> get you?

After hitting send, I text Imani Merry Christmas, and she texts back almost immediately, wishing me a Merry Christmas in all caps and telling me she loves me and she hopes I'm having a good break, accompanied by exactly three exclamation points and four heart emojis, two red and two green.

I hear sizzling coming from the stove, so I look up at Jake who flips two of the pancakes, his back to me. Even through his t-shirt, I can see the way his back muscles move as he moves, and I let myself stare at him for a minute, trying to picture a life where I could just be with him like a normal girl.

I look down at my phone, hesitating for a second before opening the text thread with Dad.

"Jake."

He turns, and I can't help but notice the flicker of worry on his face, gone in an instant.

"Yeah, what's up?"

"Wanna see the picture my dad sent me of his puppy?"

Jake's face splits into a grin, just like I'd hoped it would. He walks around to the back of my chair to lean over my shoulder. I hear him chuckle, and he presses a kiss to my temple before straightening back up.

"Adorable. I can't wait to move out of the dorms and get a dog of my own."

"I know. Your golden retriever? Or do you think you'll wait?"

He grins, and there's something a little more relaxed in his face.

I need to try harder to act like I did before. I need to separate again and deal with vampire Lydia on my own time. At least for him, of all people, until I can actually tell him.

If I do tell him, now.

"Oh, man, you know how much I want my golden. I don't think I *can* wait much longer."

He looks down at his phone as he flips the pancakes in the skillet, and adds, "Did you see what Imani just sent to us?"

"Huh? No," I say, not even realizing I'd gotten another notification. Sure enough, there's a link in our group chat sent by Imani, accompanied by a text that makes my stomach drop.

> imani: see?? i've been TELLING u guys
> vampires are real!!!

I open the link faster than I've ever done anything before, to see it's an article, highlighting a few attacks that happened in Chicago over a few days just last week that police are suspecting are linked, where the victims—three of them, two women and a man—were found dead in alleyways with what were seemingly bite marks in their neck. My eyes scan the article over and over, but nothing is said about the attacker; apparently, they were long gone by the time the victims were found. The writer ends the article by asking—in a way that's clearly joking—if vampires have been real all along.

I can't breathe.

"Great."

I look up to see Tripp leaning one shoulder against the kitchen doorway, looking at his phone, too, an amused smirk lighting his features. I look back down at my phone before either Tripp or Jake can see whatever's written on my face because while I'm not sure what it is, they're going to see I'm clearly not as amused by this information as they are.

I stare at my phone screen, trying to process, to control my breathing, to make sense of what I just read.

Tripp sends in the group chat:

> tripp daniel: Babe you know I love
> you but...

Imani responds not even thirty seconds later:

imani: they said it not me!!!!

My phone vibrates again, but this time, it's not the group chat; it's Aiden, texting me privately. I tune out Tripp and Jake, and everything feels hotter, and my chest tightens, and I can't get a deep enough breath.

It wasn't me, obviously. I'm not that stupid. I killed Xavier; as much as I hate to admit it, even in my head, it's what I did, but it's the *only* thing I did. He's the only one whose life I ruined.

So, who did *this*?

And why *now*? Why couldn't this have happened even a month ago, when I was in a better mental state? When I didn't feel like breaking at the drop of a hat?

I open my message thread with Aiden as I try not to hyperventilate, the letters swimming in my vision.

aiden swanson: I saw what Imani sent. Everything's gonna be okay, it wasn't you. Just remember that. This is not related to you

aiden swanson: But to answer your question, get this. Santa brought me a Barnes and Noble gift card. A hefty amount too. Am I being a traitor by using it?

aiden swanson: I just noticed you sent two questions. To answer your FIRST question, my only plan is to start on one of the new books I got and eat way too much chocolate. I'd definitely recommend

I know he's trying to make me feel better by distracting me, but it's not working. Not right now, not when I feel like I'm suffocating. And I don't even know why—Aiden's right, I didn't do anything to these people, but it can't be a coincidence, can it?

Who else is out there? Do they know what I did? Did they find his body somehow? Did I start something terrible?

Is this somehow my fault?

> me: what if it is?

Is all I text back to Aiden for now.

I feel hollow, even though Jake and Tripp have moved on and Jake is teasing Tripp about getting so into Anabelle's show, to which Tripp responds with some choice language just in time for Joanne to come down the stairs and scold him, just in time for the smoke alarm to start blaring in my ears because Jake forgot about the pancakes, and everything is too loud and the small kitchen is suffocating and I can't *breathe* I can't—

The only response I get from Aiden is

> aiden swanson: Call me.

I excuse myself to the bathroom as Joanne and Jake work on Jake's disastrous burnt pancake situation, the scent filling my nose, and even though I can feel Tripp's eyes on me as I leave the room, I don't care. I lock myself in the upstairs bathroom and sink to the cold tile floor, leaning back against the door as I dial Aiden with shaky fingers. He picks up before the first ring is even over.

"Lydia," he says, and it's when I hear his voice I burst into tears.

CHAPTER TWENTY-SEVEN

We spend the rest of Christmas Day watching movies and drinking hot chocolate while under thick blankets on the couch. After a short talk with Aiden where he tried his best to calm me down over the phone by reassuring me we'll figure it out together and distracting me (successfully this time) by telling me about the book he's reading, after shortly feeding on myself in the bathroom, and after Joanne banned Jake from the kitchen so she could actually make us pancakes (which I had no appetite for and only managed a bite or two), I'm now sitting curled up next to Jake—just close enough so we're barely touching but not far enough for him to ask questions—despite the terror that's coursing through me.

Dad is right. I shouldn't have come here. I shouldn't have even gone off to school in the first place—maybe I should just break up with Jake and drop out and move back home to live with Dad again and block all their numbers.

Maybe I shouldn't even do that. Maybe I should just save up to get my own place and live alone and become a hermit so I can never hurt anyone ever again. Because, inevitably, the truth would come out and Dad would be disappointed in me all over again when he was just starting to see me as a responsible adult. Which I thought I could be, which I convinced both of us I could be, but I'm not.

I'm a monster.

My chest tightens as Jake rests his hand on my leg under the blanket that we're sharing.

All of them are clueless about who I am and what I've done—except for Tripp, who potentially agrees I'm a horrible person, but for the wrong reasons.

But I can't tell him. I can't tell any of them.

Maybe before. But now?

I can't. I can't I can't I can't.

I let my eyes close, listening to Jake's heartbeat over the others', feeling the warmth of his hand on my leg. It's good; this is what I want. I want him alive. Breathing.

Why can't I just enjoy that?

Why does everything have to be so fucking hard?

Why couldn't I have been born as anyone—anything—else?

"You tired?"

I hear his voice, a quiet whisper only for me. I open my eyes, looking over at the gentleness in his eyes, waiting for my answer. I just nod; it's not a lie.

I'm tired. I'm exhausted. Of everything.

I just wish things could be easy. I wish I could be normal. I wish I didn't have to overthink every move, and I just wish I could feel what it feels like to not hate my body.

Jake smiles a little, and it makes me want to cry.

"C'mere then." It's more of a question than anything.

And I need to try. So, I scoot slightly closer, resting my head on his shoulder, trying to swallow the bile that threatens to rise. He's warm and soft, and I can hear his heartbeat, and I'm not hungry, and he's safe. He's safe and this is okay. He's not Xavier, and I'm not back in that room. I'm not going to hurt him. I'm not going to hurt him. *I'm not going to hurt him.*

He kisses the top of my head, and I let my eyes flutter closed, fighting back the image of Xavier's eyes, wide and unseeing.

CHAPTER TWENTY-EIGHT

I'm almost relieved when it's time to leave. I feel a twinge of regret when I have to hug Anabelle goodbye and see how clearly disappointed she is we're leaving, but at the same time, it's for the best. Joanne tells me she hopes she'll see me again soon, and that I'm welcome anytime.

I can feel Tripp's eyes on me the entire time.

The second we arrive back in our dorm after a morning full of sitting in the airport and flying and Ubering, I let my suitcase fall to the floor and collapse in my bed. I need to get more blood, and *soon*, so that I can finally stop feeding off of myself—which I definitely don't think is helping how drained and exhausted I feel—but right now, I just want to be alone while I can, before Imani gets back tomorrow.

But at the same time, I don't want to be alone, because my head just keeps replaying the sounds and the visions and the feelings over and over and over to the point where I can't even close my eyes, where I stare blankly out the window and try to focus on something, anything else. I need Aiden here, because he's the only one who gets it. He's the only one who can possibly even start to understand the crushing weight that makes it harder to breathe every single day, and I just need *something* to distract me from all of this, but this is different than anything I've ever faced before, because what can distract you from the fact that you're a Goddamn *murderer?*

So, I partake in the only distraction I can think of. I roll over, facing my blank, white wall. I turn my face into my arm, and I sink my teeth into my flesh, letting the pain take over.

I DECIDE THAT THINGS WILL BE BETTER THE next day.

They have to be — or else I'm going to drive myself insane.

For one, I'm back to a routine. I go early in the morning to buy more blood, and while I'm gone, Aiden gets back. And in the afternoon, we have work together. I don't think I could be more relieved to see him. I feel some of the tension leave my body the minute we make eye contact for the first time in a few weeks as I open my door for him. When he smiles at me, I think I smile genuinely for the first time in weeks, relief blossoming and easing the ache in my chest.

He doesn't bring up anything we discussed over break, and neither do I.

At work, it's quiet for the first few hours, and Aiden tells me that this is normal: the post-holiday season slump. So, I settle back in my seat and try my hardest to force myself to work on an assignment I have due before classes even start next week—some essay about our knowledge of Victorian times for the literature class I'm taking. It's a completely wasted effort, too, because I lose my train of thought every word or two I manage to type. What classes would Xavier be taking this semester? He did say he wasn't much of a reader, even though he told me he'd stop by the bookstore at some point to say hi.

Which he never got a chance to do, thanks to me. Along with the miles-long list of every other damn thing he'll never get to do, thanks to me.

But he still hasn't been reported missing, and there's no obituary online. Why does it feel like he just never existed in the first place, and that I'm going crazy, remembering someone that nobody else seems to? Like I'm locked into my own personal nightmare, and nobody else can even validate the monster that I am because they don't know, and they'll never know what happened to him?

Every time the few words I've typed start to blur in front of me and my sweater sleeves feel too heavy on my arms and I start to feel like I'm really about to lose it again, I look for Aiden. Sometimes he's shelving, sometimes he's just pacing around the store, sometimes he's helping the few customers that we do get—my heart jumping whenever I see someone male with dark hair. But I look at Aiden, and as if he can sense it, he'll look at me, and the corner of his lips will pull up in that little smile that makes me think that maybe, just *maybe*, I'll get through this.

A few hours in, after the sun has already set and the book-store is lit by nothing but the buzzing, headache-inducing fluorescents, the dreaded bell above the door jingles. I inwardly sigh, but plaster on my fake customer-service smile none-theless, only for it to drop immediately once I see—well, *sense* —the customer that walked through the door.

Because it's him. The man from the restaurant, from right before break. I *know* it's him because the way he looks at me, like he knows who and what I am and what I did, is exactly the same as the last time I saw him.

Only this time, because it's just me, him, and Aiden, I realize something I didn't realize before.

He's missing a heartbeat.

Thankfully, as I try to remember how to form words, Aiden comes to my rescue with a "Hey, welcome to EB's. Are you looking for anything specific today?"

"No," the man says, the corner of his mouth tugging upwards in a pleasant, closed-lip smile as he raises his eyes from mine to meet Aiden's, who's standing behind me, his hand gripping my shoulder—reassuringly or protectively, I can't quite tell. "I'm just browsing, thank you."

"Of course," Aiden replies, though there's an edge to his usual customer service voice. I imagine he can also sense the man is maybe-probably-definitely a vampire, but we can't talk about it with the man *here*, because if he's anything like me, he has supersonic hearing and can probably hear every shallow breath and stutter of my heartbeat way too loudly.

And what other explanation would there be? His skin is pale, if not paler than mine, and his cheeks aren't flushed like they should be after coming in from the cold, though it could just be the awful lighting, or maybe just the contrast of his hair and eyes and clothes. He's dressed extremely similar to the last time I saw him, in all black: dress pants, dress shoes, and a long, black coat that just *looks* expensive, snowflakes still melting on the fabric on his shoulders and in his dark hair.

But there's no mistaking the missing heartbeat. There's mine, obviously, and Aiden's, which has a certain rhythm that's familiar to me at this point, so familiar I push it to the back of my mind as if it's nothing but a ticking clock. And Aiden's blood, too, is something I never notice anymore. But what I do know is no matter how much I try to discreetly sniff or inhale to try and pick up a distinct scent on this man, I can't.

But if that's the case and this man is truly a real, full, *actual* vampire—

Was it him?

Was *he* behind the attack in the news?

And why would he be here now, unless—

No, y'know what? I can't go there, or else I'll send myself into the panic that I'm teetering on the brink of. Maybe he just wants to buy a book. This is a bookstore, after all. And the other time, at the restaurant, he just wanted to eat.

But he's a vampire—normal vampires don't eat, right?

So, he definitely knows about Xavier. He *has* to. Or why else would he be looking at me like that?

Oh my God oh my God oh my *God*.

Aiden and I watch, both of us deadly still as he disappears off into the fiction section as casually as ever, but I can't relax. I can't breathe, actually. Every breath I try to take feels hollow, and my throat feels tight to the point where I'm going to start gasping for air soon.

Aiden's hand squeezes my shoulder gently, and my heartbeat starts to slow. A shiver runs down my spine as his breath tickles my ear.

"I'll keep an eye on him," he whispers, so quietly even I can barely hear him. He straightens back up, removing his hand from my shoulder, and moseys toward the fiction section, trying to look casual, but I can't miss the slight set of his jaw or the way he stands straighter than usual.

I finally tear my eyes away as I hear him striking up a conversation with the man, staring at the computer screen that's still open to the essay I was working on, trying to take deep breaths as discreetly as possible. I let my hands hover just above the keyboard, pretending like I'm thinking about what I'm doing, when really, I'm just trying not to think about the fact Aiden is alone with my potential vampire-stalker behind the horror shelf, which I hope isn't symbolic of something that's about to happen.

I risk a glance over only to see a glimpse of their heads over the shelf. Aiden's taller than the man by a few inches, their heads bent over something, and their tones are unhurried—friendly, even, even though I can't bring myself to focus on the conversation itself as my own heartbeat pounds in my ears.

Maybe he doesn't have bad intentions. Maybe he's just trying to approach me because he knows what I am. Maybe he can sense me—or Aiden, even—in the way Aiden's parents sensed me, even though I have a heartbeat and blood running through my veins; I can walk in sunlight and stupidly thought those things would make it so I could live my life without anyone finding out what I am.

I hear Aiden chuckle, and the tension in my shoulders releases ever so slightly. I'm totally overthinking this. I even brought myself to type another word for my essay, the clacking of the keyboard keys sounding way too loud.

I straighten up when I see them starting to come over, a book clutched in the man's hands. Aiden's eyes meet mine for a split second, and I can tell by the look in them—which, thankfully, doesn't seem to be alarmed—he's trying to tell me something. But then the bell jingles again, and in comes an old woman with a cane who almost immediately asks for Aiden's help finding something, and of course, I'm left alone to deal with the man, who's looking at me in that *way* again. And of *course*, my heart rate shoots up... again.

"Find everything okay today?" I ask him, my voice hollow and far away as he sets his book down on the counter so I can scan it. As he says yes, I glance down at the book, my stomach twisting as I read the title.

"You ever read this one?" he asks. I shake my head as I ring up the book, trying to find my voice.

"No," I mumble, my mouth dry. "Just seen the movie."

"Mm," he says, his voice pleasant as if he's asking about the weather. "I have as well."

He continues, even as I deliberately avoid eye contact with

him, taking his card and watching his receipt print out after I swipe it.

"Decent movie, if you choose to ignore the inaccuracies."

I'd really, *really* like to think he's just talking about the inaccuracies from the book to the movie, but some stupid little voice in me tells me to clarify with him.

"You've read the book before?" I ask, tearing his receipt from the machine to hand to him, finally raising my eyes to his, which are so dark I can't tell his pupils from the irises.

He smiles slowly—only this time, he smiles with teeth, and I know for a fact he can hear when my heart stops, because there they are: two long, white, perfectly-pointed fangs.

"No," he confirms. "I think you know what I mean."

He tells me to have a good day in that same oh-so-casual tone before taking his receipt, tucking it in the front pocket of his pants, and leaving with his copy of *Dracula* tucked under his arm.

CHAPTER TWENTY-NINE

I STARE out the Starbucks window blankly, fixating on a stop sign across the street that hangs crooked on its post. "I need to know who he is."

Beside me, Aiden spins his near-empty cup around absent-mindedly, the ice shifting.

"I'd be careful," he says. "He didn't seem like he meant any harm, but you never know. You're right, though; he clearly wanted you to know he knows about you."

"But why?" I ask, not expecting an answer, but merely just to say it all out loud. "And how? Unless he's been, like, following me, how would he know where I work? Or who I am? I mean, he saw me at the restaurant, and maybe he picked up on me there, but... How would he know where to find me again? And why would he want me to know that he knows?"

I look back out the window. The streets are almost abandoned now that it's dark out. We came here straight after closing, and we weren't—well, *I* wasn't—quite ready to go back to the dorm after that, especially now that Imani's back, who'll inevitably ask me about how break was. I don't feel like talking about much of anything right now, besides this, which I just can't wrap my head around.

"If he has good intentions, maybe to let you know you aren't alone," Aiden suggests. "If he somehow has been following you and knows who you are, then maybe he knows you've never met anyone like yourself before. Maybe he wants to help. But I'd still be careful."

"If he knows what I am," I say, "then he knows what you are. Right?"

I look back over at Aiden, who nods slowly, meeting my eyes.

"Sure. Probably. Why does that matter, though?"

"It doesn't," I admit. "I just..." I groan and press the heels of my palms against my eyes. "Why *now*? Do you think he—"

Aiden answers before I even finish my sentence, and I'm grateful for it, so I don't have to force the words out.

"How *could* he know? There hasn't been anything about... *him* in the news, no missing person report or anything. Which I think is odd, sure, but it's good for us. And I mean, besides those articles about the attacks, which have nothing to do with you—"

I pop up, turning to look at Aiden, who grimaces, as if he realizes, too, he let a plural slip.

"*Articles*? What do you mean, *articles*? There was only the one that Imani sent us, wasn't there?"

Aiden doesn't answer, and I know now it's because he can't lie to me.

"*Aiden.*"

"Lydia," he says, dropping my gaze and swirling his ice around again, only clearly guiltily this time. "I didn't, uh, want you to worry—"

My heart drops to the floor. "Show me."

The tight, aching feeling in my chest only worsens when Aiden pulls up article after article, my eyes scanning text about people found dead in alleyways, streets, parks, all with the same bite marks on them, all dated within the same week—the week after I killed Xavier.

I don't see how it *could* be connected, but I don't like the coincidence.

I tear my eyes from Aiden's phone to meet his, which are still full of guilt.

That man.

He has to be connected, right? Why else would all of this be happening *now*, when everything was so quiet, so *good*, before—

"Can we go back to the bookstore?" I ask Aiden.

His eyebrows pull together, but before he can ask why, I say, "He paid with a card. We can get his name at least, right? And from there, I mean, there's Google and social media and stuff."

Aiden chews on his lip. "Yeah. Yeah, we can do that. But, can I ask what you're planning on doing once you figure out who he is?"

I stare at him as I try to think of an answer. If I'm being honest with myself, probably nothing. I'll probably just obsess over it even more, continue to drive myself crazy over why he seems to be following me, and wonder how much he knows.

But I'll least I'll have a name.

And it'll distract me from Xavier.

The corner of Aiden's lips pulls upwards in clear amusement.

"You don't know."

"I don't know," I confirm, and I can't help but smile. "But maybe it'll give us something, right?"

Aiden shrugs, eyes searching my face.

"It's worth a shot. Just..."

"Please don't." I shake my head, not sure what he's about to say, but I have a feeling I don't really want to hear it.

Whether it's telling me he's worried about me, or that he doesn't want me to do anything drastic, or whatever else that'll make him sound too much like Dad, I just don't want to hear it. And I think he realizes that, because he smiles sheepishly.

"Fair enough." He stands from the stool, holding up his ring of keys. "Let's go."

On the way back to the bookstore, I get a text from Jake, and I send him a quick reply telling him we got some new shipments we're sorting, so I'm working a little late. As I tuck my phone back into my pocket, chewing on the nails of my other hand, Aiden looks back at me as he unlocks the front door.

"What?" he asks. I can't help but wonder at what point we've gotten close enough where he can tell when something's wrong by the slightest of movements.

Then again, getting rid of a body together will probably do that.

But at the same time, I'm still convinced Aiden has some sort of faerie-emotion-powers that he just doesn't know about. So maybe it's that. Who knows anymore?

"Just, uh, just Jake. I lied to him and told him we're working late."

"Must be nice." Aiden opens the door and shoots a grin at me over his shoulder. A laugh erupts from me once I realize the meaning of his joke, and it occurs to me we've never really joked about our—about *this* before. I've made jokes to Dad (none of which he ever found funny), but it's become harder to make any sort of light of what I am recently. But hearing Aiden...

I don't know. It makes it a little easier, I guess.

"I guess it is. I mean, if you can look past the crushing guilt."

Aiden chuckles as I follow him into the dark bookstore—

he doesn't flip the lights on like usual, which I suppose is smart—and over to our desks.

"Touché," he says, leaning over the desk, placing one hand on it for balance as he turns on the little tablet we use for purchases, the screen illuminating his face with a white glow. I lean next to him, our arms brushing, and as much as I know I *should* move away, I lean a little closer, calm settling the tension in my body.

"Alright," he mutters under his breath. "It was, what, about five?"

"I think so. It was dark, so after four-thirty." I pause, watching as Aiden scrolls through all the transactions for the day. "I, uh, guess the thing about vampires not being able to go out in sunlight is true?"

Aiden looks over at me, smiling slightly, and I hope he can't notice the slight flush on my cheeks at how close we are.

Don't give Tripp more evidence, I remind myself, clearing my throat and looking back at the tablet. Aiden turns, too, and since we didn't have many customers, he lands on one that sounds like our guy and snorts a laugh when he reads the name.

"Not to sound like an idiot, but what's funny?"

Aiden looks over again. "You're not an idiot, Lydia. You just need to brush up on your classics."

Before he can continue, I grin—teeth and all. "*Wow.* Remember what you said to me when we first met about being pretentious? I've never *actually* thought that until you let those words leave your mouth."

Aiden drops his head, laughing, and I can't help but laugh, too, leaning against him a little further, and I feel something, something *strong* yet gentle, something that seems to spread throughout my very being and stick to my bones.

And it's gone when he moves away.

"Maybe you should lie a little more often," he says, but

I'm trying to process what just happened. He definitely has some sort of emotion power. He *has* to. Because whatever I just felt wasn't my own emotions. I felt it, so strongly, and then it disappeared like *that.*

Can he alter other people's emotions *and* share his own? Do his parents have any idea?

"No, it's just, his name is Bram. Bram Davelin. And he's a vampire, obviously, and who was the author of *Dracula,* arguably *the* most influential piece of vampire media ever? Bram Stoker. It's just—what?" He finally looks at me and notices me staring.

I shake my head. "You—I just felt what you were feeling in that moment. Just now. I—You definitely have some sort of... some sort of *something.*"

Aiden immediately looks away toward the screen, straightening up.

"Uh, I don't—I don't know. Maybe. But wouldn't my parents tell me about something like that? They would have to, right?"

I drop it, letting the conversation move back to where it was, because he obviously feels weird talking about it, but I mentally add *Aiden's possible faerie powers* to my list of things to distract me from my own issues.

And number one on my list now has a name: *Bram Davelin.*

Aiden moves the keyboard so he can use the computer to Google his name, but something catches my eye under the keyboard.

"Hold on," I say, pointing. "What's that?"

Aiden follows my finger, sliding what looks to be a little black card the rest of the way out from under the keyboard. He flips it over, and I lean over slightly so I can read it.

It's a business card for a bar called The Last Drop, which is spelled out in golden letters. Underneath, in a slightly smaller font, it says Bram Davelin's name followed by the word "owner," a phone number, and an address—for a building only a few streets away from our dorm.

"Did you see him leave this?" Aiden whispers, as if we aren't the only two people in here, but I feel compelled to whisper back.

"No, not at all. But, he obviously left it for me, right?"

Aiden's returning look says enough.

It looks like I'm going to be taking a trip to The Last Drop.

CHAPTER THIRTY

I HAVE to wait a few days until that Friday, but Aiden and I make a plan to go to the bar. I have to convince him to let me go alone, but he makes me promise I'll text him if I feel even the *slightest* bit uncomfortable or if something feels sketchy. I also have to lie to escape from Imani and Jake, who I tell I'm going to get notes from someone in my psychology class.

I make sure to tell Jake when he's not with Tripp, because I don't need Tripp being even more suspicious of me, though I suspect word will get around to him, whether it's from Jake or Imani.

I'll cross that bridge when I get there.

For now, I bundle up in my coat and hat and down about a half a bottle of blood in preparation for—well, I don't know, exactly, but I also don't know what I'm about to walk into.

When Aiden and I looked up the bar online, it seemed pretty normal with raving reviews from seemingly normal people. Apparently, it's been around for a really, really long time—and I wonder if Bram has been, too.

It's windy, snowing, and dark on my walk. The cold numbs my cheeks and nose, but within fifteen minutes, I arrive at my destination, heart pounding hard. Aiden made the point to remind me I might not be able to get in if they don't believe I'm twenty-one or older, and seeing as I'm a terrible liar and look pretty much my age, I don't see this being very likely.

But it's worth a shot. Who knows if I'm ever going to meet anyone similar to me ever again?

There's also the fact I don't know what I'm going to say to him. I go through all the possibilities in my head as I walk down the final block: the dimly-lit street that's only illuminated by one flickering street lamp, finding the small, dark building tucked between two others that have *for rent* signs in their windows. The only indication I'm in the right place and not about to walk into a situation that'll have me on a true crime documentary is the red neon sign that says the name of the bar—The Last Drop—the pounding bass of the music coming from inside, and the general sense of humanness I can feel, which is kind of reassuring.

Then again, I might still be walking into my very own true crime documentary.

Hell, if he somehow knows about Xavier, then it's already started.

But I'll worry about that later. What do I say to him?

Hey, so, uh, you're a vampire, too. Yeah, no shit. He knows that.

Hey, I'm a vampire, but like, not fully. What's that about? Are there more like me? Do they hate it, too?

How do you deal with it?

Why have you been following me?

Are you an undercover cop who knows about Xavier? Can vampires even be cops? Maybe if they work the night shift, right?

Is that a stupid question? That's a stupid question.

They're all stupid questions.

I wish Aiden were here. But I *have* to do this alone. This is my problem, not his.

I already crossed a line by dragging him into the Xavier mess.

I fight against the wind to pull open the door, immediately being hit with warmth and scents and sounds and just—*everything*. As my eyes adjust in the dim lighting, it feels like I've stepped out of a time machine. From the chandeliers to the black-and-white photographs of jazz artists, nothing about the place exactly screams *21st century*. Or even *late 20th century*.

It's a lot bigger than it looks on the outside, with the actual bar counter sitting at the far wall, leaving room for small wooden tables to fill the space between it and the leather couches that line the back wall to my left. It's packed with some people sitting at the tables, others dance or just stand off to the right in an empty area, and there are some who sit at the little stools at the counter. There's heartbeats and laughter and sweat and blood and alcohol galore. I look around, unsure of where to go or what to do or who I should or shouldn't talk to. As I reach to my back pocket for my phone to text Aiden, something along the lines of "SOS," and take a step toward the bar counter, I hear a deep voice to my right.

"Hold on just one second there, Miss."

I turn, having to tilt my face upwards to be able to look the man in the face, who can only be described as tall, beefy, and terrifying. He's dressed in all black, but all I can really focus on is his outstretched hand.

"Your ID?"

Oh, God, this was a terrible idea. I look down at my purse, unzipping it and blabbering, "Oh, my ID, yeah, of course. Sorry, it should be *right* here. I—"

"Listen, sweetheart, if you don't have ID, I can't let you in."

I continue to rifle through my purse, keeping my burning face turned away from the bouncer's, as I try to think of what

I can do, my pounding heart louder in my ears now than the music.

I can't just give up and leave, not that I'm already here. Meeting another vampire is right at my fingertips, and I have so many questions. I *can't* leave, and I can't cry, but judging by the burning in my eyes and my real ID that loudly proclaims I am, in fact, only eighteen, it looks like I'm about to do both.

"Ah, there you are."

This new voice comes from behind me, and when I whirl around, I look into the face of the very person I'm looking for.

Bram Davelin.

I swallow past the lump in my throat as I give him a quick once-over. He's dressed the exact same as when I saw him last, in his black suit-and-tie getup that looks way too fancy for this setting, and not a hair out of place. But he doesn't look at me. He looks at the man, a slow, easy smile pulling the corner of his lips. I strain to pick up something from him, but I can't manage to find a heartbeat, a distinct scent of blood, nothing. The only scent he seems to bring to the room is... smoke?

"Thank you, as always, Rick, for being so diligent, but she's with me. No need to worry about ID," he says, his voice smooth. He speaks as if every syllable comes naturally to him, as if he's rehearsed every sentence a million times over. "Now, if you'll excuse us."

Rick doesn't bother to hide the displeasure on his face as Bram puts a hand on my arm to turn me around. I stiffen, hoping the sound of my pounding heart isn't too obvious to him.

Maybe I did walk into something I shouldn't have.

Bram drops his arm and tilts his head as an indication to follow him through the throngs of people. I do, assessing all the customers we pass, seeing if I can pick up on anyone else like him, but I can't focus over all the other sounds and scents in here. We walk past the right side of the bar to a black door with a sign on it that says *employees only*. Bram reaches into the pocket of his pants, pulls out a ring of keys, chooses one, and unlocks the door, stepping aside and holding it open with a splayed hand for me to enter first.

Oh, God.

I should turn and run. That'd be the logical thing to do.

Maybe Rick was trying to save me. Maybe he knows. *Maybe—*

But still, I enter, stopping just inside the room and looking around as he flips on a light from behind me, though the room is still dimly lit from the single overhead light—or it could be that the walls are painted a dark gray, making everything seem darker.

As I hear the click of the door shutting behind me—my heart rate spiking —the pounding music and laughter and chatter from just outside becomes considerably quieter, as if the room has some sort of soundproofing—the office, I should say, because that's what it is. It's tiny, probably about the size of Jake's bedroom. A desk sits in the middle of it, a black chair on the far end, and a plain gray folding chair on the side closest to me. Behind the desk, on the far wall, is another black door, just like the one we walked through, only it doesn't have a sign on it. To either side of the desk are floor-to-ceiling book-shelves, leaving just enough room between them and the desk for one person to walk through, and both bookshelves are packed. I notice plenty of classics, and honestly, as I rapidly skim the shelves, I can't find a book that looks like it was published any later than the mid-1900s.

On the floor, next to the bookshelf to my right, sits a stack of what appears to be records, the one sitting on top a Frank Sinatra record. As I look around for any sort of photos or personal objects that might indicate whether he's a serial killer or not, he passes me and lowers himself into the desk chair, opening the top drawer and pulling out—

A pack of cigarettes?

I'm fully aware I'm gawking as he plucks one out of the pack, pulls a lighter from the top drawer, lights the cigarette, and takes a drag, blowing smoke from between his pursed lips. He looks up at me then through his dark lashes, quirking an eyebrow as he holds the cigarette lazily between two fingers.

"Take a seat, Lydia. Do you smoke?"

Lydia. He says it so... assuredly.

Even though I never told him my name.

I shake my head as I lower myself into the cold, hard folding chair, and he nods approvingly, placing the cigarette back between his lips. He leans back in his seat, the chair rocking back with his weight.

"Good, good. Horrible habit, really, but it's the one I was never able to drop from my human life. The inner workings are slightly different now, of course, and then again, it can't kill you if you're already dead, right?" He smirks, clearly proud of himself, but I can't even begin to form words.

What the hell is this?

"Forgive me," he says then, leaning forward, resting one elbow on the desk as he extends his hand to me. "I remembered I haven't had the chance to properly introduce myself. I'm Bram Davelin."

I take his hand, hoping my face doesn't betray my surprise at how cold his skin is—colder than mine, which *I* thought was cold, compared to the warmth of Jake and Imani and Aiden. His handshake is firm, and once I pull my hand away, he leans back again, taking another slow drag as he looks at me. I try to hold his scrutinizing gaze, but it's hard. I clench my hands together in my lap, hoping they'll stop shaking. It's too eerie, my own being the only heartbeat in the room. My blood being the only blood in the room. In a very, very small room. In which I'm alone.

With a vampire.

A real, *actual* vampire. I feel like a fraud compared to him, and I can't tell if that's a good thing or a bad thing.

"Let's start with you," Bram says, as I try to make my face devoid of my unease. "I'm sure you have questions. I have questions, as well, but we'll have plenty of time for that later."

Later?

He has questions?

But he's right—I have all the questions in the world. One being, *are you going to kill me?*

Once I finally find my voice, I bring myself to ask, "Why did you—how did—why me?"

Bram chuckles, cocking his head, and I get a glimpse of his sharp canines.

"When I saw you for the first time at the restaurant, I couldn't believe it. Because you looked human, you felt human, but at the same time, I could sense it on you. People like us, as I'm sure you know, can sense each other. And it was faint, but it was there. I was sure of it. I couldn't understand how it had happened, to be quite frank, so I decided to keep tabs on you until I could approach you. And the more I thought about it, about your existence, it began to make sense to me..."

He trails off, but I stay quiet, because he clearly has more to say. I can see it in the twitch of his mouth as if trying to hold back a smile, in his dark eyes.

"Because why else," he says, "would you look so much like *her*, unless you were my daughter, Lydia?"

CHAPTER THIRTY-ONE

My stomach drops to the floor.

My…

I don't know why I'd always assumed my biological, vampire father would be long gone, out of the picture, always someone whose presence would be lingering at the back of my mind for the rest of my life, but someone who I would never be able to get answers from.

And if he was just lying for shits and giggles, he wouldn't have made that comment, that I look so much like her—my mother—unless he knew her.

Oh, my God.

I'm glad I'm sitting, because the room seems to sway as Bram chuckles.

"I know, it was shocking for me, too. After all, there has never been such a thing, at least outside of fiction." He smiles crookedly. "A child, conceived by a vampire father and human mother, born with characteristics from both sides? It's unheard of, but here you are, Lydia." He pauses to take a drag from his cigarette, but I'm too much at a loss for words to take the moment to ask him any questions.

"I wasn't aware your mother was married when we met," he says, his dark eyes unreadable. "And when her obituary stated she left behind a newborn... I always assumed, though the timing was close, you were her husband's child. After all, I wasn't aware I could produce children in this body. But how else could you exist, like this, if you weren't mine?"

I feel a flare of anger deep inside the pit of my stomach, directed toward my mother. I've already had some sort of resentment toward her my entire life for abandoning Dad and bringing me into the world, but to not even tell Bram, either, she was pregnant with a child that *could* potentially be his? If everyone wasn't left in the dark, maybe...

I don't know what could have been different. But maybe something.

I could have been different.

I love Dad, I do, and I'm thankful for all he's done for me, but what if I could have been raised with an understanding of what I am? Someone who could understand me, guide me, *help* me?

Maybe then what happened to Xavier wouldn't have happened, and I wouldn't feel like such a goddamn *monster*.

"You're angry," he notes, his voice calm and casual, as if he were pointing out a butterfly. "Tell me why, Lydia."

This is too much. He may be my biological father, but he's a stranger. I can barely open up to people I *do* know.

But, maybe it's worth a shot.

"I just..." I suck in a deep breath, trying not to screw up my face in disgust as I inhale the cigarette smoke that lingers between us. "I wish I'd known, I guess? 'Cause, like, Dad—my —Keith—"

Bram smiles lightly. "I understand. Go on."

I laugh nervously, though nothing about this situation is funny. "He, well, he did his best, but he's never really under-stood what I am, and so I guess *I've* never really had the chance to understand it, either, and I just..." I sigh. "I feel like, I guess I feel like I was robbed of a lot of years of not... not feeling the way I do about myself. And that might've been different if... if I knew you."

He quirks an eyebrow. "And how *do* you feel about yourself?"

I feel heat rushing to my cheeks.

"Ashamed," I admit, quietly. "Like... I don't belong anywhere. I *did*, for a while, with my—with my human friends, but..."

But then I got lost in acting human, and I killed Xavier.

Bram doesn't push me to explain further. He just nods, leaning forward and putting out his cigarette in the little black ashtray at the corner of the desk.

"But with them, you're playing a role, correct?"

I nod.

A smile plays on his lips. "I can understand. I play a role here every day. To the majority of my customers, I'm your average, human, business owner, and ownership of this bar has been passed down through my family for centuries. But to others, well..." He smiles fully, fangs and all. I look at them, wondering how he consumes blood, how often.

Wondering if he's ever bitten anyone.

"I'm myself. I'm their leader, someone they trust, someone they can look to to guide them through this new existence. We have quite the history, Lydia, and if you want to learn, I'm more than willing to teach you."

He looks at me expectantly.

We, he said. He's their leader. There's a community here, right under my nose, and their leader—my biological father— is willing to bring me in, to teach me about the side of me I've been running from my whole life.

But he doesn't seem to hate it.

So, maybe I can learn not to, too.

I swallow hard, clenching my hands together in my lap, and nod.

"He's your *DAD*?"

"I *know*." I refused to tell Aiden anything about my meeting with Bram since I got back to my dorm last night, since I wanted to wait 'til we were alone at work, away from the rest of our friends and anyone who could potentially overhear. Now, we're opening the bookstore, and it's a quiet, snowy Saturday morning, so for now, we have the place to ourselves.

"That's insane. How did he find you?"

"Right place at the right time?" I put a stack of new, extra YA books under the shelf. "He said he could sense it on me, the—you know, and when he realized how much I look like my mom, he just pieced it together, I guess. I'm still not sure how he found out I work here, but isn't it weird?"

"That's *nuts*." Aiden stretches from where he stands, a few shelves over, by our small collection of biographies. He seems even more appalled by the fact that Bram is my father than I did, which I find funny. He rakes a hand through his curls. "So, what's the deal, then? He's just a bar owner who happens to be a vampire, or—"

"I mean, kinda." I pick up the half-full box that sits at my feet to take over to the romance section, but Aiden takes it from me before I can even take a step. I follow him across the store, saying, "He told me about how there're all these vampires who have been living in the city for, like, a century, just living amongst humans, and how it's the same across, like, the entire country in all these big cities. Like, people are just living alongside vampires and have no clue. And there's like, a leader for each region or something, and so Bram is the leader for all the Chicagoland vampires. Like, they have these meetings and get together, and like, it's this whole *community*, Aiden. And nobody knows about it. They just, like, live their lives after dark. Isn't that insane?"

Aiden grins at me, his eyes crinkling at the corners.

"I think that's the most I've ever heard you talk in one go," he teases me, but when my cheeks start to heat, he adds, "It's—keep going. I didn't mean that in a bad way. At all. So, like, what do they talk about at their meetings? Do they have like, bake sales and cookouts or—"

I laugh. Usually, I hate even *thinking* about my—my vampire side, but... I don't know. Last night, Bram told me how incredible my existence is about ten times, and then there's Aiden, who'll listen and encourage me and...

I haven't decided if I'm going to tell Dad. I'm leaning toward no, but...

"He didn't really specify, but he said the next one they have, he wants me to come, if I'm ready to meet others. Obviously, it's still crazy to me to meet a full vampire, and he said he has a lot more to tell me before then, since it's in, like, a few weeks, but I don't know. My worst fear, my entire life, has been people finding out about me. And then when—when *that* happened, I..." My voice drops off, getting a little quieter. Aiden has since abandoned his shelving, his attention fully on me, his gaze so tender that I have to drop my own, looking down at my boots.

"I felt like it was over, y'know? Like, I'd done the worst thing I'll ever do in my life. And I mean, I *did*. But, like, you don't hate me for it, or for what I am, and Bram doesn't hate me for what I am, and..." I raise my eyes to meet Aiden's. "What if that had to happen so I could meet him and finally begin to learn to live with myself? I don't think I'll ever be able to forgive myself for it, but..." I suck in a shaky breath. "We talked about playing roles. And he told me he has to play a role to his customers at the bar, but when he talked about how freeing it is to be himself with the others, and I thought about... well, I thought about how I feel when I'm with you, since you know, and what if I could have that all the time, with others like me? Well, kind of like me, but y'know? Who understands what it's like to—to exist differently? Because they don't- they don't see it as a bad thing. So maybe..."

I bring my thumb to my mouth, chewing on the nail. "Sorry for rambling."

Aiden shakes his head. "There's nothing you need to apologize for. I—I can understand it. I think I'd do the same if I had the opportunity."

"Don't you?" I ask, leaning down to take a book from the box, glancing at the author before finding its place on the shelf. Aiden follows my lead, grabbing a few to shelf, too. "I mean, your parents—"

"I've learned not to talk about it," he interrupts, not meeting my gaze. "When they told me for the first time, I had so many questions. I'm sure you get that. But they shut me down, said it wasn't important, and that my life would be easier if I could learn to live a human life. It would never affect me, they said, besides the lying thing obviously, but I should just let it go. Which is easier said than done when you tell your son that he's something he thought was pure fiction his entire life." The last part comes out in a mutter, half under his breath, and he shoves a book on the shelf with a little extra force.

He sighs, turning to me. "But I did. I learned to live with it, and then I met you, and now, now I see how it feels for you to get some sort of explanation for what you are. Like, for things to make *sense,* and..."

"I could ask Bram," I offer, reaching out to touch his arm. I feel a spark of something—something just as strong as the other day, but on the complete opposite end of the spectrum; something deeply—deeply *lost*, almost. But it's gone almost as quickly as it arrived, as I drop my hand, to the point where I question if I really felt it or not. "If your parents knew about me, I don't see why he wouldn't know about you. Or maybe you could meet him for yourself? Officially, this time."

Aiden looks at me, his mouth quirking in a smile that doesn't reach his eyes.

"You don't have to do that for me, Lydia."

I smile at him—fangs and all. Something softens in his expression.

"And you didn't have to help me with—with Xavier, Aiden." Saying his name out loud is hard, and I think Aiden knows that, because he smiles softly at me—encouragingly. "But that's what friends do, right?"

His smile grows into a full-out, almost adorably boyish grin that makes something twist deep inside me.

"I think friends do a lot less, actually," he says. "Not that I had many before coming here, but—"

"Not surprising," I tease, and Aiden lifts an eyebrow as if challenging me to continue. I grin as I say, "I can picture you, pretentious little Aiden with all his *classics*—"

"Dear God," Aiden laughs, shoving me lightly on the shoulder as he passes.

CHAPTER THIRTY-TWO

I START SNEAKING off to the bar as often as I can.

Each day, I grow more and more eager to learn. Bram tells me stories. Sometimes, he'll bring me snacks or drinks from the bar, even after I remind him I'm only eighteen. He usually just smiles and winks at me, letting me know he won't tell anyone. He brings me something new every time I agree to it, and I hate how much I like the drinks—I can't even taste the alcohol in them, but they *work*, unlike my first attempt at drinking back on Halloween. But they're usually strong and sweet and almost addictive, because by the time I leave some nights, it feels like everything is brighter and louder and I feel more *alive*. Almost like I did that night... after Xavier.

One night, Bram tells me about how he was Turned, as he calls it, as they all call it.

"You know of the Great Chicago Fire, I assume?" he asks, at our third meeting. When I nod, he smiles lightly. "I was in my late thirties, no wife, no children, and stuck in your average businessman lifestyle. Things were very different back then. I was trapped in a burning building, and I thought that was it. That my life was over, and I had never really *done* anything with it. Until I was saved. I don't remember it actually happening; I think I was unconscious already. But I remember waking up when I wasn't expecting to, feeling like an entirely different person. All my burns were gone, and I felt stronger. I thought I was dead." He smiles a little. "*Actually* dead, in Heaven, or wherever we go when we pass. But then I was introduced to the vampire who saved me. He was the leader at the time and explained I was on the brink of death when he found me, so he pulled me out and risked his own life to save me. I'm sure you've heard that fire is deadly to vampires, and that is true. It's one of the few things, like sunlight, that can kill us. But he was good, and still, he saved me that day."

"What happened to him?"

Bram waves a dismissive hand. "He passed, tragically, and I took over the Clan. We have vampires from almost every decade since I was Turned, vampires of different ethnicities, backgrounds, you name it, Lydia. But none like you." He smiles slowly. "I cannot wait for them to meet you."

He gives me a tour of the bar one night, showing me every closet, every nook and cranny, and even a huge room upstairs with a stage and an empty, hardwood floor that he explains used to be a theater, but they use it for their meetings now. I can't help but note he doesn't show me what's behind the door that sits on the other wall of the office, but I just assume it's personal. Maybe his bedroom; he never suggests he lives elsewhere.

As I spend more time with him, I start to tell him things. Information seems to tumble out of me in his presence, and at our fifth meeting, in the first few days of February, I ask him about other beings.

He sees right through me, smiling at me as he sits on his side of the desk, feet propped up on the corner, his usual cigarette hanging out of the corner of his mouth—though this time, it's not lit.

I've never thought to ask him how exactly he can smoke without working... without working *anything*. But then again, apparently vampires are fertile, too. A lot of things have seemed impossible to explain lately, so I let it be.

"The Fae, you mean?" He pulls his feet off his desk, leaning forward. "That friend of yours in the bookstore. You're asking about him, aren't you?"

I blush and nod, and Bram just smiles. He does that a lot, even if I don't understand what exactly it is that he's smiling about. Something is just always amusing to him.

He leans back in his seat, crossing his arms over his chest.

"Ah, well, this is something that was going to come up in due time. You see, the Fae and vampires have a history that goes way back, over centuries. At least in the States, we do. But the Fae—and please don't be offended, because I'm sure your friend is good to you—were selfish, malicious, and cunning creatures, and wanted the land to themselves. It's just in their nature, you see. They drove our kind out, despite the Treaty we had signed dividing up the land. It got bloody, and the Fae did everything in their power to eliminate us; burning our houses down, driving us out into the sunlight. Those who survived fled, and as I'm sure you can guess by this point, settled amongst the humans and were forced to live under-cover. The Fae continue to preoccupy those lands, which is why your friend's presence is so rare, and why you're likely to never meet another faerie in your day-to-day life."

"Oh." That's not what I was expecting to hear. Faeries drove vampires out? I think of Aiden, who's really my best friend at this point. Do I tell him? I have to, right?

Bram rubs a hand over his beard.

"Your friend... I'm sorry, what's his name?"

"Aiden," I say softly.

"Aiden," Bram repeats, thoughtfully. "Was he raised Fae?

Or was he raised similarly to how you were—primarily human?"

"Human," I answer. "His, uh, his parents don't even really like talking about it, I guess. Whenever he's asked questions, they... They're not open about it like you are. They've always shut him down, so he really doesn't know anything."

Bram clicks his tongue, nodding. I wish I could tell what was going through his head, but honestly, he's hard to read.

"Pity," he murmurs. "Well, I'd like to meet him sometime."

As time passes, I find it easier and easier to tell him things that I've either kept inside or only ever have told Aiden. He always lets me start, every time we meet, and every question I throw at him, he answers; every story I feel like telling him, he listens. I tell him about growing up with Dad, about wishing things went differently with my mother, about feeling conflicted about whether I should come clean about what I am to my human friends, but why I can't—Xavier.

I tell him about Xavier one night when I'm feeling partic-ularly vulnerable, when it's riding on my conscious a little harder, when I can't look at anyone with dark hair or slumped shoulders or a shy smile. Lately, most days, I know it's not good to linger on it, but the days it hits me and I skip class because I can't get out of bed without the guilt crushing my chest and making it hard to breathe, I know I'm only worrying Imani and Jake more than they already are about me.

So I cave, and I tell Bram, because even though Aiden doesn't hate me for it, Bram is the only person I have right now who might understand how it actually feels.

It's hard to relive it, and I have to stop a few times to collect myself, but he listens patiently, nodding, taking drags from his cigarette. I tell him how it felt, how it's left something hollow and empty within me, how I wonder every day why I haven't heard anything about him being missing or his body being found, how I've hated myself for it.

"It's... a difficult thing," he says, eyes on his cigarette as he taps it on the edge of the ashtray, clearly choosing his words carefully. "Over the years, I've had my fair share of, well... To be frank with you, Lydia, I have both Turned and drained many. In the first few days a vampire is Turned—we call them newborns—well, it's almost as if they blackout and attack blindly, getting blood wherever they can find it, and often that results in draining bodies fully, as opposed to Turning, where some blood is required to still be in the system so our venom can latch on to it. But those first few days, it's when we're at our most dangerous, and coming out of that, well, it's difficult. It weighs on the conscious, knowing what you've done. But at a certain point, you have to let go. It's tough, but what happened does not make you a bad person. It's just a part of who you are."

That's what Dad told me, too. Before. I have a feeling he wouldn't still tell me that if *he* knew what I did.

I chew on my thumbnail, the fleeting thought going through my head that I should ask Imani to paint them again before I chew all my nails down to the quick.

But then I think of those articles.

"How often do... are... people Turned? And do you find the vampires who did it? Are there ones who aren't a part of your Clan?"

Bram chuckles, putting out his cigarette. "You're a very inquisitive young woman, Lydia. It's nice to see."

In the silence that follows, I debate whether or not to point out that he didn't answer any of my questions, but I just stay quiet and wait. I've noticed sometimes he'll take these long pauses, only to continue just as I'm about to say something to fill the silence. It's like every single word is calculated, as if he doesn't want to even risk saying something wrong. I don't think I've ever even heard him stumble over his words.

Sure enough, after folding and unfolding his hands on top of the desk, he continues. "If, in the account that somehow the newborn is not a part of the Clan already, I will send my most trusted out to follow attacks and bring the newborn to me. More often than not, they're very complaisant because they're confused as to what happened to them, and we, of course, offer them explanations, shelter, and blood. Some, of course, go back to their homes if they live alone, but others cannot, so I always assist those in need. There's no telling what humans in their lives would do if they found out, but they are always safe with me, and I always make sure to tell them that."

I nod slowly, taking it all in. Just as I'm about to open my mouth and ask about the attacks back in December, a noise comes from behind the door behind Bram—as if something fell, but only complete and utter silence follows, other than the sound of my quickened pulse. I flinch at the noise, and Bram stiffens, but only for a split second, so fast I'm not sure if he actually reacted or not. The next second, he's standing up from the desk and giving me one of his lazy smiles.

"It's getting late, Lydia. I have some things I have to attend to. But you'll join me again tomorrow?"

I slowly push myself up, trying not to look too confused as his abrupt ending. Usually, he'll let me talk until *I'm* the one saying it's late and that I should go, and then he'll walk me out.

I eye the door; what made that noise?

"Uh, yeah, I should be able to."

"Good, good. Be safe out there and have a good night."

But even as I stand out in the street a moment after Bram leaves, from somewhere inside, I swear I hear the very heavy slam of a door.

"SO, YOU'RE TELLING ME FAERIES ARE ASSHOLES."

It's a Wednesday afternoon, so Aiden and I walk to class together; we both have class at one o'clock in the same building, and I take the time to fill him in on the things Bram has told me in our meetings over the last few days. I haven't had time alone with Aiden since work on Sunday, and these aren't things I want to text.

I cringe as a train roars overhead.

"I mean, yeah, basically. He said you're probably fine, though."

Aiden huffs a laugh, tugging his beanie further down, so that only a few curls escape from the bottom. "I'm honored that I've gotten the vampire dad seal of approval."

"*Shh*," I hiss. "And no, not yet. He wants to meet you."

Aiden's eyebrows fly upward. "He wants to meet *me*? Why?"

I shrug. "To see if you're an asshole for himself? I don't know, but I'm meeting him again tonight."

Aiden's mouth twists to the side.

"What?" I ask.

"It's just... Jake and Tripp have started asking me what's up with you. Everyone knows something's going on, Lyds, and I..."

Aiden trails off, and I sigh heavily, watching the other people walking down the street, disappearing into the places we pass, like Dunkin' Donuts and Harold's Chicken. Ever since Xavier, and especially since meeting Bram, my mind's been stuck in one place. But Aiden's right; I need to manage my time better. Tripp's already suspicious of me as it is, and Jake...

Jake's been nothing but good to me. And I know I haven't

been all there, even in the few times we *have* hung out since school's been back in session. It hasn't been all my fault, either —he has his workouts and whatever else he has to do for his off-season on top of homework, and since I have homework, too, and I *have* been working a lot, though that's mostly to spend time with Aiden, but I do need the money because I've been back to making my weekly butcher runs, and...

These are all excuses. That's all they are.

But it's also been hard because, well, now that I know what Aiden is, since we've come to the conclusion I'm not drawn to his faerie blood for some reason, I feel...

I feel safe with him. And with Bram, too, of course.

They just understand in a way that nobody else will ever be able to, even if I did tell them and they took it well.

And as much as I hate to admit it, being alone with Jake, or even Imani, just makes me think of Xavier.

"You're right," is all I say, quietly, that familiar ache returning to my chest.

"They wouldn't hate you," Aiden says. "Trust me, I get why you don't want to tell them, but they wouldn't hate you for it."

I don't say anything as we reach our building.

With Bram, and with Aiden, I'm finally, for the first time in my life, finding it a little easier to exist as vampire Lydia. But with that, it's becoming a little harder to play my role of human Lydia.

Only this time, I'm still hurting people because of it.

No matter what I do.

SOMETHING IS DIFFERENT WHEN I WALK INTO THE bar hours later. Bram is waiting for me just inside the entrance, making small talk with Rick. The bar thrums with its usual energy just past us.

"Lydia," Bram says, shooting me one of his usual smiles. Surprisingly, he's dressed in a dark gray dress shirt tonight, as opposed to his usual black. He's really branching out, I see.

I'm a little relieved to see him after talking with Aiden earlier and settling myself into the realization I'm never going to be able to split myself evenly between either side of myself. I've been in a bad mood all evening, curling up under my comforter and mindlessly scrolling through social media, texting Jake occasionally when he sent me a few texts about how boring the class he was in was.

Bram leads me to the office, just like every other night, but as we approach it, instead of reaching out and opening the door, he turns around to face me.

"Lydia," he says, his face unreadable. "When I first reached out to you, I was... hesitant. I wasn't sure how receptive you would be of learning about your identity, but I've been very pleased. Because of how well this is going, I... Well, there's someone I would like you to meet. And I think that now, you're ready."

My palms immediately grow sweaty. Who? It has to be one of his most trusted—however, the hell he put it, or else why would this be such a big deal? Has he been telling these other pe—vampires about me? And they're obviously a full vampire, whoever I'm about to meet, because there's no presence I can detect from the other side of that door. Which makes this all the more terrifying.

I nod at Bram as firmly as I can, but the second he turns his back to reach for the doorknob, I wipe my palms on the front of my coat. Should I be dressed better to meet this person? Hell, I'm wearing leggings and a hoodie under my coat. I really hope that—

The door swings open, and Bram steps to the side. The

person stands up from where they were sitting in the chair I usually sit in, turning, and I think there's a good chance I might pass out.

Because I know her. I don't *know* her, but I know the long, chestnut-brown hair, the soft, round face, the porcelain-white skin. I know those wide, light-blue eyes because not only do I see them in the mirror every single day, but I've seen them in pictures, I've seen them squinted with a smile alongside Dad's in their wedding photo.

My stomach sinks, and from somewhere past the ringing in my ears, I hear Bram say,

"Lydia, I'd like you to meet your mother."

CHAPTER THIRTY-THREE

SHE SAYS my name with a hesitant smile as Bram goes to stand next to her, placing a hand on her back, and when I see the fangs, it all sinks in.

She's been alive this entire damn time.

Well, not *alive*, but—

Rage boils deep inside of me, stronger than I've ever felt before, but I don't know who I'm more furious at. *Her*, for truly abandoning Dad and I, or *him*, for lying straight to my face after I told him, after I *trusted* him with how I felt—

"Lydia." It's Bram who says my name this time. "Allow us the opportunity to explain. Please. I know this is a lot—"

Oh, is that right? He *knows*?

I look at him, at a complete loss for words, before looking back to her. Vampires—full vampires, at least—stop aging when they're Turned—that's a common fact in fiction that Bram confirmed is true. And since it's like looking in a mirror, she had to have been Turned...

"How?" I ask, not trusting my voice for any more words than a few at a time, but really, not knowing what the hell to say, either. "When?"

Her wide blue eyes leave mine, looking at Bram, waiting for him to speak. And he does, but I continue to stare at her, biting down on my lip.

"Well, you see, I wasn't lying to you when I said I assumed the baby—you—were her husband's. After all, your mother and I only—It only happened once, between us."

I wonder if my disbelief and disgust is showing on my face. Who knew, after all his rehearsed, smooth-talking bullshit, that the one topic able to make him stumble over his words would be sex? I almost want to laugh about it.

"I always assumed, too, that vampires were not fertile. There had been no proof we could be, given the minimal interactions between our kind and humans, so a vampire impregnating a human... It was unheard of. It wasn't until your mother's body started, well, failing, that we suspected anything."

I look back at my—Genevieve. This woman standing in front of me, this *girl,* she's not my mom. Her eyebrows are pulled together in such human-like distress I have to turn my gaze back to Bram.

She had *eighteen years* to fix this. To come back, to apologize.

It's too damn late.

"Failing?" I can't help but ask, directing my question at Bram.

"Yes." He glances at Genevieve, who looks at her feet, wringing her hands in front of her in a nervous gesture that feels uncomfortably like I'm watching myself. "We've chalked it up to the idea that you—your vampire half, that is—were killing her from the inside, draining her of her energy and, likely, blood. It's a miracle she made it as close to full-term as she did."

Dad never told me that. He told me I was born early, but he never mentioned how bad the pregnancy was. He's mentioned it was hard for doctors, in our years of hospital visits, searching for any answers as to why I was such a weak child, but we never talked about it, not like this.

"My—Keith, he said. She died during childbirth. He saw her, dying. So how—?"

"And that much is true. She did. I will spare you the details, but though it was difficult, I was able to Turn her and take her back to Chicago with me by the time she woke up, with nobody finding out she was missing, including Keith. After your mother woke up, we had lengthy discussions about what action to take. We decided, with Keith in the picture and believing she was deceased and not knowing who I was—as well as the fact it was more likely you were completely human than not—it would be easier to let him keep you. We did discuss trying to find you eventually, just to check in on you. But then, of course, you came to us." He smiles lightly, and it makes my anger flare. I can't even wrap my mind around this —it feels like I'm in some sort of sick nightmare.

She was alive. Just sitting here, waiting. They both were, knowing about me, knowing there was a *tiny* chance I could *maybe* be part-vampire, and they didn't do *shit*, leaving Dad and I to struggle.

And for what? Because they were scared to get caught? We needed fucking *help*.

I blink, trying to fight back the tears that start to burn my eyes out of frustration. I stare up at Bram, taking in his calm, controlled expression as I search for something to say that won't make me end up in tears.

"And if I didn't? If I didn't just *happen* to come to Chicago for school? Somehow, I doubt you really would've come looking for me." My voice cracks and my heart sinks. I take a breath before continuing, letting the words spill out, having to tear my eyes away from Bram's as my vision blurs with my tears. "I was in Chicago for almost four months before we saw each other at that restaurant, and it was after the worst had already happened. If—if there was any time I needed you, it was then. It was *before* I hurt anyone! But no, no, *you* waited to show up when the damage was already done, when it was fucking easy for you, so you wouldn't have to do the work of actually looking for me, right?" I suck in a sharp breath, but it doesn't seem to go anywhere; my chest is too tight to accept the air. I look at Genevieve, ignoring the way my heart twists sharply when I register the glossiness of her eyes.

"And you—*you* didn't even bother to show up. I don't even care, but y'know who deserved the truth from you? Dad. My *real* dad, the one who actually loved me and raised me, even though *you* two fucked up!" My words break off into a sob, and I can't breathe, and I need to leave because I can't be around them anymore, but I just cover my hands with my face as I cry because Xavier is dead, and it could've been *avoided*.

And *Dad*. What am I going to tell him?

Am I going to tell him anything?

"Lydia."

I feel a hand on my upper arm—Bram's. I don't pull away when he tugs me into a hug, as strange as it feels, as angry and frustrated and sad as I am, with both him and Genevieve.

I try to take deep breaths to steady myself, to stop the tears from pouring from my eyes, and push down the rising humiliation that I completely lost it in front of them. As soon as I pull myself together, I step back from his grasp, wiping at my eyes. I can't bring myself to look at him, even as he starts to speak.

"I'm truly sorry it had to happen like this, Lydia. All of it. I want you to know that you can still trust me. Everything else we discussed, about our community here, it's all true. And talking with you, getting to know you, has been such a favorable experience for me, as I hope it has been for you." He takes one of his slow pauses as I sniffle, staring at his shoes as nothing but my heartbeat thunders in my ears. "Admittedly, I didn't know if you could handle meeting both your mother and I at the same time, but I did not think about how it might affect you, and I apologize. But, if you will, please take a seat. I have something else I want to tell you about, if you feel prepared for it. If you need time and space to process this, I understand, but I ask that you hear me out first."

As much as I hate to admit it, I can understand where he's coming from. If all of it was dropped on me at once, I would've... I don't know. I'm just exhausted. That's what I do know.

But still, I sit.

Bram pulls a chair from the room behind him into the office for Genevieve and sets it on his side of the desk for her before lowering himself into his usual chair.

"Thank you, Lydia. I believe I told you we—the Clan— hold meetings. We have one coming up on Friday, February fourteenth. These meetings are very special because they allow us to all get together and work toward our goals. I think, now, you're ready to attend, because as I said before, I'm very proud of how receptive you've been to learning about all of this. If you'd like to bring your Fae friend, too, he is more than welcome to come. It's a formal event, so dress nicely. It would mean the world to me—and your mother—if you were to attend."

He wants me to come to a Clan meeting.

He's proud of how I've handled everything so far.

The word sinks through my skin and latches itself to my bones. *Proud*.

He wants me to come.

But I'm mad at him. I'm mad at Genevieve.

My gaze slides over to her, and her expression surprises me a bit.

Because she doesn't look pleased, or *proud,* like he does. Her eyebrows are knit together again, and there's something unreadable in her wide, blue eyes.

If I didn't know better, I'd say she almost looks scared.

My hesitation prompts Bram to stand up from the desk. "I would love to show you something on your way out, Lydia, if you'll allow me?"

When I nod, Bram guides me out of the office without so much as a word to Genevieve, a hand pressed firmly between my shoulder blades. I'm just exhausted and confused and I hope whatever this is, it doesn't take long—I'm sure my face is blotchy from crying.

Standing just outside the office, he points toward one of the bartenders: a gorgeous, dark-haired woman who moves behind the bar with undeniable ease, as if it's second nature. Her arms are covered with brightly colored tattoos.

"That's Casey," Bram says, low and close to my ear. "She has been with the Clan since '05, but she was Turned in... oh, the '90s, I believe. One of our best."

My eyebrows raise. *She's* a vampire? She throws her head back as she laughs, mixing up a drink for a customer. Seated at the bar, a man laughs with her.

She looks so... so... *normal.*

I don't want to take my eyes off her, but Bram turns me toward the other end of the bar, where people are dancing.

"That man? That's Angelo." The man in question is dancing very, er, *closely* with two women. "He has been with us since 2015. He enjoys, as I'm sure you can see, getting close to some of our human patrons, but he knows his limits."

Bram points out more vampires: two women doing karaoke, an older man sitting at the bar, a bouncer who comes to swap with Rick. The whole time, I'm at a loss for words. I never would've guessed. I mean, they all look so... so *normal,* so integrated into this little community here.

He walks me to the door, but my mind is racing. These people... they understand, don't they? They know what it's like to hide, but they don't let that stop them from living.

Well, kind of.

We stop just before the entrance.

"This is your home, too, if you want it to be, Lydia. With the rest of us." He pauses. "Including your mother and I."

I think back to Genevieve, still behind that office door, and my chest aches. God, I'm still pissed. I'm really pissed. But that was the past, right? This...

This could be a part of my future.

Bram smiles lightly. "And, please, let me know about the meeting. Your decision doesn't have to be made now," he says, but I shake my head. I've seen enough.

I want a chance to fit somewhere.

"I'll be there."

"WHAT DO YOU MEAN BY *ALIVE*?"

"She's a vampire, Aiden. She's been a vampire this entire time."

"Holy shit."

"I *know*."

Imani is at her Wednesday night class, Jake is working out with some of the football guys, and Tripp is in his room, so Aiden's over in my room, spinning around in my desk chair as I give him a recap of the night, from Bram dropping the bomb of Genevieve being alive to inviting me—and Aiden—to this vampire meeting, leaving out my breakdown.

"That's—" Aiden shakes his head. "Are you gonna tell your dad? Like, your *dad* dad. Not Bram, obviously."

"Thanks for the clarification," I tease, and Aiden smiles

sheepishly at me. "But, no. Maybe. I don't know. I just don't see it doing any good. Like, I think he'd be crushed. And understandably. *I* was, and I didn't even know her or love her like he did."

Aiden nods thoughtfully, slowing his spinning to a stop and pulling up the hood of his green hoodie.

"No, yeah, I get that." He tugs on the strings absentmindedly, scrunching up the hood around his face, and I can't help but smile a little as I watch him. "Will you tell him about Bram, at least? Ever? I mean, you definitely don't need to, but if you're gonna have a relationship with this guy, you might wanna think about it. It's up to you, obviously."

I sigh.

"I know. I have thought about it, and I think I might, but I don't know if I'm ready yet. He'd ask a ton of questions, and I'd probably have to tell him about Xavier, and I'm not ready for that, either, since he'll probably want me to drop out of school when he learns about it. And I can't say I blame him."

Aiden cocks his head at me.

"If he does and you need to escape, just come live with me in my apartment. I could use a roommate." He grins.

I ignore the weird feeling his smile gives me.

I think I'm getting pretty good at ignoring things.

CHAPTER THIRTY-FOUR

I DECIDE I NEED A BREAK. I can't think about Bram or Genevieve or vampires or Xavier or the fact my mother is "alive" or wonder how Dad would react if next time he called, I said, *oh, hey Dad, by the way, in the last month I've met my biological vampire father. Oh, and Mom's alive! Isn't that fantastic? They only left us hanging for, oh, almost nineteen years.*

I decide I can't think about anything anymore, actually, or I'll have to check myself into a mental institute, so when Jake asks me if I want to come over and do homework with him the next night, when I don't have class or work, I actually say yes. It hits me I actually really miss him and his normalcy and how normal he makes *me* feel—more often than not.

But I make sure to down a bottle of blood before I go over to his room.

We do actually get a bit of work done, but soon enough, he says, "I hate this. Truly. I hate this."

He's staring at the textbook in his lap, his glasses perched on the end of his nose. When I look up from the book on my lap to the open pages of his textbook, I see numbers. A lot of numbers and a lot of letters and symbols that look like pure torture to me.

And I see Xavier, hunched over a similar book. Xavier's glasses, sliding down the bridge of his nose.

I suck in a breath, pushing the image out of my mind. Nope. Nope, nope, nope.

I reach out, pushing Jake's glasses up the bridge of his nose, hoping that will help change the image in my mind, and it does, because Jake looks up at me and smiles, his voice soft when he speaks.

"Thanks, baby. Hey, c'mere."

He wraps his arms around me, kissing the top of my head as I lay it on his chest and listen to the steady beating of his heart.

"What're you working on?" I ask.

"Calculus," he sighs. "And it sucks. I don't know why I did this to myself. I mean, I know why. But still."

I wrap my arm around his waist. "Have you thought more about changing your major?"

He sighs, his chest heaving against my cheek, and I let myself curl a little further against him, enjoying his warmth as long as I remind myself he's going to stay this way, warm and alive.

"I just, I don't know. I still don't really know what I'd change it *to*. I mean, I like science a lot. I'd love to like, work hands-on in a lab or whatever full-time, but... I'm still not sure. I think I'm just pushing off committing to making a decision." He chuckles a little. "I know if I'd just *do* it, I wouldn't have to stress about it anymore, and it probably wouldn't be as big of a deal as I'm making it out to be. But it's that first leap that's the hardest, y'know?"

"For sure," I murmur, my mind going directly to—well, all my secrets.

What if Dad's right? What if Aiden's right? What if I just

tell everyone what's been going on, and like Jake said, it wouldn't be as big of a deal as I've made it out to be?

But he's right, too. It's the first leap that's the hardest.

And, Xavier...

"But," Jake continues in a much more cheery tone before I can think of anything more to say, "I don't feel like thinking about that right now. What d'ya say we plan our date for Valentine's Day? It lands on a Friday, so that means we can do whatever for however long and don't have school the next day. And we have your birthday to think about, too. I was thinking—"

I squeeze my eyes shut. *Shit*. The meeting. Why didn't I realize it's on Valentine's Day? Why would Bram have it on Valentine's Day? Does being a vampire mean you can't have any romance in your life?

To be fair, that's what I thought. But—*ugh*. I want to go scream into my pillow.

Before he gets too far ahead of himself, I force the words out. "Um, can we do it on the fifteenth instead?"

Jake's eyebrows pull together slightly. "What?"

I feel my cheeks start to warm, not wanting to repeat myself.

"The fifteenth?" I ask, my voice small and timid. "It's just, I have this project for my psych class, and—"

Which isn't technically a lie. I do. It's just not due for like, two weeks. But I can't use work as an excuse, or else he might try and visit me there.

He would, definitely. He'd pull some sort of romantic gesture—bring me flowers, or—

God. I'm awful.

Jake sighs. He *sighs* at *me*, and my heart starts to pound. Great, I've pissed him off. Or disappointed him. Which one is worse? I'm not sure. Then again, have I not been disappointing him every day since Xavier? Him and myself and every single other person in my life, and *why can I not just disappear off the face of the Earth already?*

"They're busy every other day," I continue, my voice just as small and pathetic sounding. "And I said sure to meeting, because I didn't think about what day it was until just now, and—"

Jake closes his eyes, and I take that as my cue to stop talking.

"It's fine," he says, opening his eyes, but his barely concealed exasperation tells me the exact opposite. "We'll do the fifteenth."

He turns away to his textbook, flipping to the next page. I watch him for a minute as he spins his pen between his fingers, his eyes scanning the pages, but he's doing it so quickly I doubt he's actually reading the problem.

"Jake," I finally say, "I'm sorry."

He sets the pen down on top of the pages of his textbook and runs his fingers through his hair, causing it to stick up in every direction once he finally lowers his hands. He turns his gaze on me, finally, and I'm surprised to see something in his hazel eyes that's not disappointment or anger or really even the frustration from just a few seconds ago. Something more like... hurt?

"It's not... It's not about changing the date. That's fine, I don't mind that. You've just been so distant lately, Lydia. Every time I think we're okay again, or we have a good day, something else happens. It's like something changed right before winter break. Just—is there—did I do something? Do you not want to be in this relationship anymore? I—"

"No, no, of course I do," I interrupt him, reaching out for his hands. He lets me put my hands over his, which are resting on top of his textbook, but when I meet his gaze, it's hard to look him in the eye. "I just—"

Before Xavier, I might've taken the leap right here and now.

But now, I can't find the words quick enough. I don't know where I'd start.

Jake's eyes search my face, and when I don't finish my sentence, he pulls his hands out from under mine, along with the textbook, so that he can continue flipping through it. He picks his pen back up, too, tapping it distractedly against the page, the *tap tap tap tap* filling up the silent room.

"It's—Things have been... hard," I say, quietly, resting my hands in my lap.

That's an understatement.

"I can tell," he replies, just as quietly. His eyes quickly scan the page he's on before flipping to the next, *tap tap tap tap.* "And I want to help you. I really do, because I care about you a lot, Lydia. But I don't know how to help you if I don't know what's wrong."

I resist the urge to pull the pen out of his hand as he looks back to the book—*tap tap tap tap.*

"It's not... It's not easy."

That stupid textbook feels like a roadblock in this conversation, but maybe it's better that he refuses to look at me. Maybe if I don't look at *him*, I can actually squeeze the words out.

My chest tightens painfully at the idea of saying it. Of putting it out there, right here and now.

What would he say? What would he do?

I can't. I can't, I *can't.*

"Relationships don't work without communication," he says, slowly, his eyes still fixated on the page he's open to. "And... It's just hard. Some days we're okay, like today, and we can hang out and cuddle and laugh, but then it could be the next day, and it seems like you don't want me to touch you. I just want to understand. And if there's something bigger going on that you feel like you can't talk to me about, then... if you need to talk to someone else, that's okay. That's really, really okay. I just... I need to make sure *you're* okay. With or without me."

I swallow past the lump in my throat, tears threatening to spill as I search for words—*any* words. It feels like there's hours of silence between us as he finally looks at me, and whatever he sees on my face makes him push the book off his lap and pull me back to him.

The minute my face meets his chest, the tears start to flow. He holds me tightly, stroking my hair and back, kissing the top of my head.

"Whatever it is, baby, you can tell me. I'm here, okay? I'm right here."

Xavier, eyes blank and unseeing.

His blood, staining my fingertips as I search for a pulse.

Sinking my teeth into my own arm, knees up to my chest, listening to Jake and Anabelle and Joanne and Tripp sleep soundly in the other rooms.

Sitting across from Bram in his office, hearing him tell me that he's my biological father.

Xavier, sinking to the bottom of Lake Michigan.

"I'm sorry," are the only words I manage to get out. "I'm sorry."

"I'm right here," he continues to murmur as I calm down. "You're okay, sweetheart. I'm right here."

Once I feel like I'm composed enough to form words, even though the ache in my chest is like there's a ton of bricks making it impossible to breathe properly, I force myself to pull myself back and look at him. He looks... he looks *sad,* concerned, and he won't let go of my hands, his thumbs brushing against the backs of mine.

"There's just... there's a lot going on recently," I manage. "Like, um, family stuff, too. And I know, I know I haven't been fair to you, and I'm sorry, but... once I process it all myself, I promise I'll tell you. I'll tell you everything. I promise." I lift my eyes to his. "I—Thank you. For sticking with me."

He nods, tugging on my hands to pull me in enough to kiss my forehead. "Hey, thank *you*. I'm sorry for getting frustrated earlier. I know... I mean, I can tell, whatever this is, it's a lot deeper than I thought. But I... I care about you, a lot, Lyds." He reaches up to tuck my hair behind my ear. I tilt my head into his touch.

I don't deserve this boy.

What will he think of me? Of what I've done?

"Just know, whenever you're ready, I'll be here. And even when you're not and you just wanna get milkshakes, I'll still be here." He smiles lightly, and I smile back, wiping my eyes. I have cried *way* too much these last few days.

"Milkshakes sound great right now, actually."

Jake visibly perks up, and I can't help but laugh, some of the ache easing in my chest. "Man, I was *hoping* you'd say that. What d'ya say we order milkshakes and fries and then we can watch whatever cheesy romcom you want?"

I smile, finally allowing myself to just be in the moment with him.

To be a normal girl with a normal boyfriend. Just for a moment.

"You just wanna get out of doing your homework."

He grins at me, closing his textbook for emphasis. "*Absolutely*. But I also wanna cheer up my beautiful, amazing girlfriend."

I lean in, giving him a quick kiss.

"Then milkshakes and cheesy romcoms it is."

CHAPTER THIRTY-FIVE

Once Jake and I settle in with our food and movie, it *almost* feels like before Xavier, and I'm able to lose myself for a bit, pushing everything to the back of my mind. Tripp knocks on the door at one point and comes in to ask to borrow Jake's laundry detergent, and I can't help but notice he seems surprised I'm here.

"Oh. Hey, Lydia," he says once his eyes land on me, curled up by Jake's side. The two of us haven't talked or seen each other really since winter break. And maybe that's been kinda intentional on my part, because every time I see him, I think about his accusations.

So, maybe I'm a little glad he walked in and saw us on our way back to where we were before. But I know we never really will—*I* will never get back to where I was before that.

As Valentine's Day and the meeting approach, over the next week, I feel more and more anxious each day. I mean, what if the Clan doesn't like me? Or will they think my existence is as miraculous as Bram does?

And, *shit,* I have to see Genevieve again.

Thursday afternoon, Imani texts me on her way home from her first class and asks if I want anything from Panda Express. And when she comes back, we each sit on our beds and dive into our food. I realize this is probably the longest we've spent together all week apart from sleeping, and I think she realizes that, too, because she smiles sheepishly.

"Sorry for being gone all the time recently," she says, quietly, and the way she's looking at me makes me wonder if she heard something from Tripp about his suspicions. I mean, if I thought *my* best friend was being cheated on, I'd tell...

Well, my best friend is Aiden. And I'd probably tell him.

Nevermind.

I drop Imani's gaze, stabbing my flimsy plastic fork into a piece of broccoli.

"It's okay," I say.

"I just feel bad. I mean... if something's goin' on with you that you don't wanna tell Jake or even Aiden, you can talk to me. Girl code, and all that." She smiles, but I still see the concern in her face, and my stomach twists with guilt. "Or, if you don't, I totally get it, and we'll have a movie night in or have a girls' night out, just us. Just say the word."

My next smile comes a little easier, because honestly, that sounds nice. I just don't know if my head would be in it right now.

We talk a bit about Valentine's plans and my upcoming birthday, but Imani finishes her food quickly, already having to head to her next class. She rushes back across the room to grab her backpack, swinging it over one shoulder with so much force I watch in fear of her knocking herself out.

"I'll take the trash out later, so don't worry about it. You work soon, right?"

I nod. "Aiden and I close tonight."

As soon as she's gone, I finish my food, wanting to take a shower before work, considering I know Aiden will want to leave soon. I turn the water to scalding hot, trying not to think too much about anything besides the water practically burning my skin and making the bathroom look like a sauna. I dress simple, not caring too much about how I look today, but the minute I open my closet door, I realize I *still* haven't gotten a dress for tomorrow night.

Shit.

I can go after work. I'm sure Target will have something, right? Not that I want to go all the way to Target at eight at night, but...

Maybe I can convince Aiden to come with me.

I get dressed and ready for work in my usual sweater and jeans, finishing up just in time for Aiden to knock on my door. I pull open the door, and he smiles at me.

"Ready for yet another *enthralling* day?"

I smile back. Aiden steps back as I step out of my room, closing the door behind me and making sure it's locked before we start down the hall.

"Some of us enjoy the bookstore, Aiden."

We reach the elevators, and it comes almost immediately after Aiden presses the button. I step forward to get into it, but Aiden shoves me aside before I can, so he can get in first. I laugh, and for a minute, I forget about the event tomorrow that I still don't even really know what to expect from, and my breakdown in front of Jake and the fact that now everyone obviously knows I'm just really not doing great.

"Any chance you're up for a Target trip after work?"

Aiden looks across the elevator at me, pushing his curls back from his forehead.

"Let me guess. You don't have anything for tomorrow?"

I smile sheepishly.

"*Yes*, Lydia, I'll go to Target with you."

"Great," I say, just as the elevator doors slide open on the first floor. Aiden lets me out first, but we walk side by side out of the building and down the sidewalk, snow falling softly. I look at Aiden, at the snowflakes that have landed amongst his curls, and at the soft red flush of his cheeks and the tip of his nose. "You have to come up with an excuse, too, y'know."

"I know, I know. I'll figure it out." When we get to the bookstore, Aiden sits me down at the cash register while he shelves and does inventory. There aren't any customers, so I get up and walk over to where he stands in the young adult section, putting away a few new books. I grab some of the books from the box by his feet and start looking for where they belong. I can feel his eyes lingering on me even as I kneel and start to put the books away, so I look up, raising my eyebrows at him.

"What?"

Aiden shakes his head. "Just thinking about tomorrow," he confesses. "I doubt they'll actually ask me where I'm going if I just disappear, but just in case, I'll probably just come up with something like, I didn't want to be around all the couples since I'm single and lonely so I just walked around the city and splurged on Valentine's candy to eat all alone." The corner of his mouth tugs upwards in a crooked smile that makes my heart twist.

"That's so depressing of you," I say, shelving books of my own, "but I guess it works."

"What?"

"When's the last time you dated someone?"

"Oh, man, I mean, high school, for sure," Aiden says. "But even then, it was like, one girl for... nine months or so, junior year. Nothing serious."

I raise my eyebrows at him, pausing with the book halfway in its spot on the shelf.

"*Nine* months at what, like, sixteen? So, what's serious to you, then, Aiden?"

He grins, a hint of mischievousness in his smile.

"Meeting her parents. It's even better if it's at some fancy event, and they're v—"

I shove him as I pass, and he just laughs and laughs and laughs.

I can't help but grin as I walk away, my cheeks warm.

CHAPTER THIRTY-SIX

AIDEN and I decide to go to EB's to get ready for the meeting —we agree both of us leaving the dorms in formal clothes on Valentine's Day, *together*, would raise some red flags, especially when I'm supposed to be meeting classmates to work on a project.

I make sure to say bye to Jake before I leave, who's alone in the dorm for the night, which makes me feel even worse about the whole thing.

I'll tell him. I will.

Just—not now.

Aiden got a head start to the bookstore, because we also agreed that in the very, very small chance someone who knows us or Jake were to see us together right outside the dorm...

We just decided to play it very, *very* safe tonight.

It's a chilly night, and the dread is already starting to sink in at the mere thought of having to ditch my thick, comfy jeans and sweater for a dress that barely hits mid-thigh.

I wonder what Aiden will be wearing.

I push the thought out of my head as I reach the bookstore, the lights shining through the big windows and illuminating the sidewalk. I look in as I climb the stairs, and I definitely see Aiden's familiar blond curls, accompanied by—

"Lydia! Long time no see!" Roarke exclaims as I push open the door.

I smile sheepishly. He's right, after all—I haven't seen him in a while, since I was gone for all of winter break. He hasn't been in at the same time as me since then, and, well, I skipped his last class because it was the day after...

"Yeah, I know," I agree, before excusing myself to the bathroom, making a face at Aiden as I pass. He grins at me, and just as I close the bathroom door, I hear Roarke asking what we're up to tonight.

I kick off my shoes and tug my clothes off as quickly as I can, goosebumps rising on my exposed skin as I hear Aiden fumble for a truthful-but-not-too-truthful answer. I step into my dress, pulling it up and immediately tug it as far down my thighs as it'll go, which isn't very far.

I glance up as I step into my heels, not able to avoid my reflection in the mirror that hangs over the sink, and stop in my tracks.

Huh.

I take the risk to turn sideways, letting my eyes trail over my body. The fabric clings to my skin like I was expecting, but it doesn't make me feel as uncomfortable as I thought it would. Because I look—

—*good*?

This dress actually makes me look like I have some curves, and even though I know someone with a body like Imani would look much better in it, I *feel* good, too. I feel... feminine.

For now. When I step out of this bathroom and have to have other people look at me, it might be a different story.

Oh, God, *Aiden's* going to see me in this. What will he think? Will he say anything? Will we just ignore it?

Why do I think he'll care?

Do I *want* him to care?

I tear my eyes away, squatting down to rifle through my bag for the makeup I brought, doing some quick eyeshadow and mascara. Once I shove everything back in my bag—and decide I look actually *pretty*—I put my coat back on, which pretty much hangs down to where my dress stops and makes it look like I'm not wearing any pants, sling my bag over my shoulder, and open the bathroom door.

"Aiden says your dad owns a bar," Roarke says, almost immediately. "Which bar?"

Aiden gives me a wide-eyed, slight shake of the head that screams *I gave as little information as possible.*

I don't see the harm in telling Roarke, though. I mean, he's probably been to The Last Drop before, or at least knows about it. And to almost everyone, Bram is just a guy who owns a bar.

"The Last Drop," I say.

My heart drops as Roarke's expression immediately changes, his smile vanishing. I exchange a glance with Aiden, who's clearly just as confused as I am, until Roarke says:

"Your dad is Bram Davelin."

"Yeah," I say, wiping my sweaty palms on my coat. "Yeah, I mean, I was raised by my mom's husband, so I didn't really, like, *meet* him 'til this year, but yeah. He's... You, uh, you know him?"

Roarke sighs, and I try to catch Aiden's eye, but he's not looking at me now. He's staring intently at Roarke, and I get the sense he's about to say something. And I think I know what, but I don't want him to say it because what if Roarke *doesn't* know? Maybe he just hates Bram because he kicked him out of the bar one time or something.

"You know what we are, don't you?"

And he said it.

I stare at him, willing him to get better at telepathy.

But then Roarke nods, and my stomach drops.

"How?" I ask.

He swallows, glancing down at his watch. "How much time do you two got?"

CHAPTER THIRTY-SEVEN

"WE DON'T," Aiden says. "If we want to be on time, we need to leave now. But—"

"Then it'll have to wait." Roarke blows out a breath, and as much as I know we need to leave to be on time, I want to sit him down and ask him a million questions.

How does he know?

How long has he known?

Is... *he* something? I rack my brain for—

That's *it*. That first day we met, in class. He felt familiar, just like Aiden and his parents. Of *course*. How could I have forgotten that? Is that why he singled me out, telling me specifically I could come to him if I needed anything? Because he knew instantly like I wasn't human, either.

But then what *is* he?

He's definitely not a vampire. Fae would be my only other guess, but... wouldn't Aiden have picked up on that?

"I know you have questions, and I promise I'll answer all of them. When do the two of you work together next?"

I glance at Aiden for confirmation. "Sunday?"

Roarke nods. "Okay. I'll come in then, and I will tell you two everything. Just, for now, be careful, okay?"

Be careful?

A chill rolls down my spine. But Roarke doesn't say anything more, and it's only when we're outside, on our way to the bar, that either Aiden or I speak.

"What was that? What *is* he?" I swivel to look at Aiden, an uneven portion of the sidewalk catching my toe and making me trip. Aiden grabs my elbows and steadies me, and I swear I hear a rise in his heart rate as he removes his hands from me, but not before he slides my bag off my shoulder and slings it onto his instead.

"I don't know. I have no clue. But that was the only thing I could think of when he reacted like that about Bram. But he's not—he's not a vampire, obviously. At least not a full one. Is he like you, do you think?"

I shake my head, so lost about this whole situation that I barely register the freezing wind against my bare legs. "No. No, I don't think so. And he's not—he's not like you?"

Aiden chews on his lip.

"I'm like, ninety-nine percent sure he isn't. But he's gotta be something. I... I haven't thought too much about it since, but when I met him last year, I did get that feeling like I knew him. I just didn't know what it meant yet."

"Me, too," I say, eager to hear that I haven't been alone in it, but I can't believe *I* didn't put two and two together sooner.

I guess I have had a few other things to worry about.

"But why'd he say 'be careful?' Does he know something about Bram?"

"I guess we're about to find out," Aiden says, nodding ahead of us. "Isn't that the bar?"

It is—thankfully, because my toes and legs are numb and my

fingers ache from the cold, but now, I have a sense of rising panic inside of me, tightening my chest. Bram may be a liar—or at least avoidant of telling the full truth—but he wouldn't intentionally put me in harm's way. After all, his whole thing is *helping* people.

So what the hell is Roarke talking about?

There's a sign on the black door—a neat handwritten note from Bram saying something along the lines of that he's sorry, but due to unforeseen circumstances, the bar will be closed on Friday, February fourteenth.

"He said the door would be unlocked," I whisper—not quite sure why I'm whispering—as I reach out and turn the handle, and sure enough, it is unlocked. I glance back at Aiden, who looks significantly more unnerved than he did just a minute ago, but still, he follows me into the bar.

It's almost just as dark as outside. The main portion of the bar is only lit up by one of the chandeliers, its candles flickering in a way that feels a little too ominous. Bram is nowhere in sight, unlike every other time I've come here. But the heat washes over me, which is nice, and being in here for barely a minute already has me itching to take off my coat.

"Are you sure we're in the right place?" Aiden whispers from just behind my shoulder, now clutching onto my coat. I have to swallow my laughter at how he's holding on to my sleeve and letting me take the lead like he's a child. It's cute, really, and gives me something to focus on other than Roarke's words echoing in my head.

Be careful.

"Yeah," I whisper back, now mostly because our voices already sound too loud in the silent bar. "He said it's in the other room, upstairs. I saw it when he gave me a tour once."

He allows me to steer him toward the office, where Bram said we could put our coats and any other belongings. That door is unlocked, too, and I step in first, flipping on the light, which buzzes overhead.

Aiden sets my bag down onto my usual chair and begins to unzip his coat. As he shrugs it off, I see he's wearing a plain black dress shirt, the top two buttons undone. I've never seen Aiden in all black like this, considering that's normally Tripp's thing, but it works for him. It really works for him. I hesitantly begin unzipping my coat, my anxiety about wearing this dress returning to the pit of my stomach, as Aiden hangs his on the back of the chair and starts to roll the sleeves of his shirt up to his elbows.

His eyes slowly widen at the sight of me. I immediately avert my gaze, hanging my coat on the back of Bram's chair, my face burning. I risk a glance back up at him, only to see he's fiddling with his coat, adjusting it on the chair, and he's as red as I suspect I am.

"You look good," he chokes out, meeting my eyes again.

"So do you," I say, quietly.

I look away, clearing my throat as I yank down my dress from where it's ridden up on my thighs, and run my fingers through my hair one last time.

Before I start spiraling into all my worries about the night all over again, I lead Aiden out of the office, our arms brushing as I pass him in the tight space, and follow the wall to the door I've only been through once before

Our footsteps and our heartbeats are too loud, but as I approach the door, I swear I hear another—slower and steadier. I halt in my tracks, fingers lingering on the cool doorknob, trying to figure out why it sounds like it's coming from above us, instead of out on the street.

"What is it?" Aiden whispers from close behind me.

But just as quickly as I heard it, it starts to fade, like whoever it belongs to is walking away.

"Nothing," I say, pulling open the door. "I just thought I heard something."

Is there someone else like us here, with a heartbeat?

Someone else like *me*?

No, no. Bram said he had never met anyone like me before.

I push it out of my mind and begin the ascent up the dark staircase, which is only wide enough for one person at a time. And of course, thanks to the minimal light and the heels I'm not used to walking in, I misjudge one of my steps and stumble, nearly falling forward. The only thing that stops me from completely biffing it is Aiden, one of his hands gripping my arm, the other clutching my waist.

A warm, nervous energy spreads through my entire body, and I can hear his heart, pounding, as if he just ran a marathon.

"Thanks," I whisper, not daring to look over my shoulder at him as I clutch the handrail.

"Want me to go first?" he whispers back, his hands—almost hesitantly—leaving my body, the warmth along with them.

"No," I say, carefully climbing the next few stairs until I reach the landing, which veers off into another set of stairs to my left. "Who's gonna save me when I fall again?"

Aiden chuckles

"Aren't vampires supposed to be more graceful than that?"

I grin at him, fangs and all, despite my growing anxiety at the fact that at the landing just above us sits another black door. The glow of light leaks through the cracks, meaning only a few more steps separate us from our destination. I've seen this room before; it's not scary.

At least it wasn't when it was empty.

No. No, this is nothing to be *scared* of. Just because this is the first time I'll be in a room of people who know what I am doesn't mean I'm about to be judged for it. Bram wouldn't have invited me otherwise.

This is a community. This is what I want.

Aiden's smile falters just enough for me to register his

nervousness again, and for me to understand he's really only holding himself together for my sake. I take his hand, but unlike earlier, he doesn't pull away as we begin the ascent up the next few steps, Aiden right behind me, still holding my hand, his fingers wrapped tight around mine, as if he's holding on to me so tightly so that I can't leave him to whatever's awaiting us behind this door.

I stop at the landing, taking in a deep, slow breath. Aiden doesn't say anything, but instead, squeezes my hand reassuringly, and after I've finished telling myself neither of us is going to die, that these are people like me and can handle a heartbeat or two, I open the door.

CHAPTER THIRTY-EIGHT

WE'RE MET by the dim lighting of crystal chandeliers and a roomful of people. An overwhelmingly full, abnormally quiet roomful of people. But not people, exactly—vampires.

I pull Aiden into the room behind me, keeping him behind me as if I can shield him from them, as if he's not six feet four to my five feet six. But hardly anybody even looks in our direction as we walk in, and if they do, their eyes merely linger on Aiden before darting away, as if they'll get in trouble for staring. It gives me time to look around the room, to study the layout.

There are circular tables—too many to count, with about five or six people per table. Everyone is dressed like us, though some of the men are in full tuxes and some of the women are in what appear to be ball gown-style dresses. I recognize a few familiar faces from the last night I was here: Angelo, who seems to be flirting with the women at his table, and Casey, the bartender, her tattoo sleeves bright. When we make eye contact, she offers me a smile, her fangs on full display.

Across the room from us sits the stage I remember from last time, only with its heavy, red-velvet curtains drawn this time. I wonder if that will be in use tonight, if Bram will be up there.

But what makes my stomach churn is—well—everything else. I've gotten so used to ignoring the sound of heartbeats everywhere I go—fast, slow, even, some stuttering—but under the chatter and laughter that fills the large room, there's silence. I've gotten used to it with Bram, but in a room full of so many people that should have so many different heartbeats, it's so, so much worse.

And the smell. Oh, *God*, the smells.

It's unmistakably coming from the wine glasses that sit in front of each vampire, each filled with a dark, thick, red substance, and I know well enough by this point, I know how to distinguish the scents; I know this type didn't come from a butcher.

So, then, who did they get it from? And how?

I know they can hear my heart practically beating out of my chest as a cold sweat begins to break out over my skin.

I can't do this.

I can. I can. It's just like the first day of school, that's all. It's different, and different takes some getting used to, but different isn't bad, right? I mean, even Dad said that.

I can't do this.

I feel Aiden's hands gripping my upper arms, grounding me, my body relaxing ever so slightly, as if he understands exactly what's going through my head. And I'm sure that he does. And now, I'm here, and they're sipping human blood and laughing and talking with each other as if they don't even care who it came from or what had to happen to the human in order to obtain it.

And I did it, too. I'm no better. I attacked Xavier and I liked the way his blood tasted and the way it made me feel before I came to my senses and realized what I was doing.

Or maybe it's not human blood. Maybe it's just...

No. What am I thinking? What *was* I thinking, coming here?

If they drink human blood so casually, how can I ever fit in here?

But there's Bram, walking toward us from the front of the room with long strides, hands in the pants pockets of his tux, and his usual relaxed smile on his face. When he reaches us, I try to mirror his easy smile, but I can't, and my heart is pounding in my ears, and all I can see are Xavier's eyes, blank and unseeing, and the blood that coated his neck and my mouth in those wine glasses, and I feel like I'm going to puke.

The only reason I'm still upright is Aiden, who has both hands clamped firmly around my upper arms.

"Aiden, right? It's nice to meet you, officially," Bram says, smiling over my head at Aiden.

Aiden replies in a completely collected and relaxed tone, reaching out one of his hands to shake Bram's. As he does, he pulls me back from in front of him to his side, wrapping his free arm around my waist in one swift, casual motion, as if he's simply moving me out of the way so that he can introduce himself properly to Bram instead of keeping me from completely falling apart, my knees already starting to wobble.

"I'm so glad you were able to make it," Bram says, still smiling and displaying those pearly-white fangs, now turning his attention to me. I'm able to force what I hope is a convincing smile at him, though at this point, after all our meetings—after our *last* meeting, especially—I'm sure he knows well enough I'm losing it.

"Me too," I say, my voice shaky.

Aiden's hand moves from my waist to my upper arm, which he rubs up and down casually, yet reassuringly, that usual calm that comes from him lingering at the edges of my panic, keeping it contained.

"I've got seats for you two up at the front with your mother and I," Bram explains. "Best seats in the house."

He turns, waving a hand for us to follow, and we do, Aiden keeping his arm around me the entire time. I feel people's eyes on us as we pass, walking down the main aisle through the tables, as if they were too polite to stare when we could see them staring.

I take a slow, steadying breath as we walk, and Aiden squeezes my arm. Sure enough, at the center table in the front row sit only four chairs, one of which is occupied by Genevieve. And I can't help but stare as she gets up from her seat to greet us, a pleasant, red-lipped smile curving her lips, but not reaching her eyes.

She's one of the few dressed in a long gown, only hers is a bright, and honestly beautiful, red that matches the color of her lips. She pulls it off annoyingly well, the neckline dipping in a low V that almost reaches her belly button, and the long, flowing skirt with high slits down either long, pale leg that separates the skirt into two sections. Her long, brown hair is curled, the front parts pinned back to put her round, blemish-free, beautiful face on display, and her piercing blue eyes—*my* eyes—stand out even more than usual, thanks to the dark grays and blacks of her eyeshadow and mascara, which matches her thin, black heels with straps that wrap around her ankles.

Dad. What would he think right now?

"Lydia, you look lovely." Her voice is soft, pleasant, and grinds my gears, even more so when she shifts her gaze to Aiden.

"And you must be Aiden."

When I look at Aiden, it occurs to me that this is the first time that he's seeing my—Genevieve. Realizing that when I said I look like her, I mean it, and realizing for while, she may be around forty, she still physically looks our age. He's not hiding it very well, either, even as he very obviously tries to recover from his shock with a smile and a greeting.

"We have refreshments," Bram says lightly, once we all sit around the table, all around one side, so that we can turn towards the stage with ease. "But, well—" He eyes Aiden, who smiles casually.

"I ate before I came."

Bram flashes a grateful smile at him.

"Lydia?"

I wave my hand, not even wanting to hear my options. Wanting to shove down the betrayal of my body, which is practically begging for a taste, remembering the way that I felt after Xavier, the *aliveness* that sat like a black sheep amongst the horror and guilt.

"Do you have water?"

"We do." Bram waves over a waiter, who's holding an unlabeled bottle of dark red liquid. I pull at a string on the black tablecloth as he asks the waiter to run downstairs and get water for Aiden and I. The waiter obeys without a word, but eyes Aiden and I before leaving. I wonder what they all know about us.

A beat of silence passes as if nobody knows what to say with Aiden sitting here. Or maybe it's me, because of the way our most recent meeting went, and we're all just reminiscing about how I broke down into ugly sobs. Because I know I am.

"Nice place you've got here," Aiden finally says.

Bram seems grateful for it, because he jumps into an enthusiastic explanation of when the place was built, how he used to work here back in the day, yadda yadda yadda—all stuff I've already told Aiden. I eye Genevieve as Bram explains and Aiden listens attentively, only to see she's gazing somewhere past us.

Just then, I hear it again, faint and quiet under the chatter: a new heartbeat.

I turn in my seat as slowly and casually as possible, just in time to catch a glimpse of someone dressed in all black slide out the door Aiden and I had walked in. Is there another human here? Or someone who can at least pass as human, like Aiden or I?

I look at Genevieve, searching her face for some sort of hint as to who it could have been, but she looks at Bram, her lips curving into that placating smile of hers.

"Dearest," she says once there's a pause in the conversation, "what would you say about me taking Lydia for a stroll around the building while we wait?"

Bram smiles one of his easy smiles back at her, though like hers, it doesn't reach his eyes. "Don't be silly, darling, we're just about to start. Plus, she's already seen the entire building. We wouldn't want to bore her." He flashes a smile at me before turning back to Aiden without missing a beat.

I jump as the waiter sets down glasses of water in front of me and Aiden, condensation sliding down and onto the tablecloth. I glance at Genevieve, trying to understand what just happened, but she's got a smile plastered on now, looking up and saying something to the waiter.

As if Aiden knows I'm unsettled, as he listens to Bram talk about renovations, he reaches out under the table and rests his hand on my thigh, calming some of my unease. I swallow hard, hoping my face doesn't betray the way my bare skin prickles at the contact. I look away, pretending I'm merely studying the room as I set my hand over his, seeking the comfort I so desperately need right now.

And that's when I hear them.

Heartbeats that aren't mine or Aiden's.

Multiple this time—and they're quick and frantic, and then they're gone. I hear the muffled collision of the waiter's pen against the plush carpet, but he's already walking away.

Genevieve picks it up and discreetly tucks it into her lap, nodding along to whatever Bram's saying to Aiden.

Something doesn't feel right. Actually, nothing feels right. I hoped I would come here and blend in, fit in, just like the vampires seem to do at the bar every night. Just like they seem to fit together here, laughing and drinking. But instead, I've never felt more exposed.

I squeeze Aiden's hand tightly, and he squeezes mine right back. Only a few minutes later, after the waiter has come back with a glass of blood and a napkin for Genevieve, Bram excuses himself and rises from his seat, beckoning Genevieve to walk with him to the front of the room.

"Alright, everyone," Bram calls. His voice immediately brings the room to silence. I can't help but be impressed—past the anxiety that has my stomach in knots—he's able to control a room so easily. It occurs to me I haven't seen *this* Bram yet— the well-respected clan leader. *I've* only gotten the privilege of seeing absent father Bram—or not, I guess.

I reluctantly pull my hand away from Aiden's, folding them tightly in my lap once I feel everyone's eyes in my direction, even though I know they're looking at Bram and not at me. And at Genevieve, who plasters a perfect, complacent smile on her face, her pearly white fangs gleaming as she stands with Bram's arm around her waist. Looking at them now, it doesn't feel like they're my parents. Bram, maybe more so because I've already allowed myself to think of him as my father, but with his role and importance as a leader, he still feels so distant. But looking at Genevieve, specifically... She feels like a classmate. Someone I have to deal with because she's there. Someone who I can't get a read on.

I can't help but wonder—who would I be if I were raised by them instead of Dad?

Even just thinking the question threatens to send me into the downward spiral I'm already teetering on the edge of. I push it deep into the back of my mind where it sits with the thick scent of blood, the unnerving deadness of the people surrounding me, and the unexplainable heartbeats that don't seem to have a source, except for that one, that person who disappeared.

"I am pleased to welcome you all to the first Initiation of the year."

Initiation?

At that, there're a few whoops and claps to which Bram pauses and smiles. A perfect picture of relaxation and easygoingness.

"Yes, yes, very exciting, I know. We've got a very promising group of new additions to our clan who are so very eager to prove themselves to you. As always, I expect you to welcome them in and treat them with the utmost respect. I'm also looking to increase the number of Initiations we do this year. I have some exciting new information to share with you in due time, but for now, without further ado, relax, and enjoy the show!"

There's applause as Bram and Genevieve make their way back to their seats, but I keep my hands firmly folded in my lap. I look over at Aiden, who's clapping slowly and hesitantly, and when I catch his eye, he just shrugs at me.

The lights in the room dim further into near-blackness, and as they do, the curtains pull back to reveal the lit-up stage. And in the middle of the stage, under the hot, bright lights, sits a woman in a wooden chair. She appears to be in her thirties with light-brown hair. But as I study her further, I realize just how wrong the scene is.

Her eyes are closed and her head is cocked to one side as if she's sleeping. But she's held upright by the thick rope tied around her middle, securing her to the back of the chair. Her legs are tied to the chair legs, and while her arms are behind the back of the chair and out of sight, I suspect her wrists are tied, too. There's a piece of fabric tied around her head, in her mouth, to gag her. Her makeup is streaked down her face in black, like she was crying, and my stomach turns and my palms start to sweat as I breathe in the scent of her sweet blood, as I hear her heartbeat, slow and steady, pounding in my ears.

Human.

Totally, utterly human in a room full of vampires.

Aiden's hand is already back on my thigh before I can reach out for him. I gratefully clutch his in both of mine, my eyes glued on the stage as I watch her start to stir. Her head lifts, her eyes fluttering open, and I watch in horror as she whips her head around, her eyes adjusting to the light, and once she realizes she's on a stage, bound to a chair to be tonight's entertainment, she starts to thrash and scream, as well as she can with the gag in her mouth.

I squeeze my eyes shut, gripping Aiden's hand so tightly I'm sure that my nails are digging into his skin. As if that will shut out the screaming and the sound of wood scraping against the stage as she tries to shift her chair, to escape, to do *anything*.

Her screams get more panicked, somehow, and I open my eyes, only to see someone else has joined her on the stage, and I swallow down the bile rising in my throat as he crosses over to her. This man can't possibly be more than a few years older than Aiden and I, but he's not bound to anything; he's free to move as he pleases, which happens to be right toward the woman, who's staring at him in complete terror. His dark hair offsets his pale skin, and when he grins maniacally at her, I see the gleam of his fangs in the bright stage light.

No, no, no.

But I can't tear my eyes away. I can't bring myself to even shut them as he kneels at her side. I can practically feel his hunger radiating off of him, because I know the feeling. Because I've *felt* that uncontrollable desire to sink my fangs into the pulsing veins of a human, to taste the sweet, thick blood, to feel the power and satisfaction that follows a feeding. But now, all I want to do is throw up or look away or get up and run or *something*, but I watch. I watch as he reaches around with one hand and rests it on the side of her neck that's furthest from him, holding her in place as she screams and sobs and thrashes. I watch as he puts the other hand on her thigh as he licks a slow stripe up her neck before finding that perfect spot where he pauses, his lips brushing her skin. I watch as his grip on her tightens, his lips part, and his long, white fangs are bared. I watch as he tilts his head just enough to get that perfect angle to sink them agonizingly slow into her flesh. I watch as his lips clamp onto her skin as he sucks and she screams one last, horrible scream, as if the sound was ripped from the very depths of her.

Did Xavier scream?

Did my hunger make me so deaf to his humanity that I couldn't even hear him scream?

She goes limp, her fight finally over, but I know she's not dead. Not *dead* dead, anyway, because he didn't suck long enough to drain her. I know she'll wake in however long it takes for the process to be complete, but that when she wakes, her life will be over. And the worst moment of her life will be forgotten by all of these people who saw it as nothing but Friday-night entertainment.

The man tears himself away from her, standing and facing the crowd. I'm distantly aware of applause roaring in my ears, of Aiden saying my name, but I continue to stare as the man's lips part in a wide, proud smile, his white teeth stained red.

My body is stiff. I can't move, and I can't bring myself to look away even as it happens again. And again. And again and again. As a new victim—some older, some younger—is brought out on stage, tied up, and a newborn vampire is released on them, to prove their worth to the clan. To prove they don't care about ending an innocent human's life, not if it means that they'll be respected and have new members for... for *what*? What's the point of this?

But what's worse? Turning them and forcing them to live this new, immortal life in a world they most likely never knew existed, never able to go back to their family and friends because of what they are, or downright murdering them, like I did?

I feel the heat in the room pressing down on me, and I'm aware of Aiden's gaze, of him trying to get my attention, trying to get me to leave or react to him or something, but I can't. I can't, because all I can see is the girl on stage who looks like she's a high schooler turning a boy who looks my age, if not younger, and I see myself and Xavier. I see Xavier spinning his pen between his fingertips as his eyes scan the problem I had set in front of him, and I see my eyes leaving the problem and finding his veins, feeling the steady, addictive pulse of his heartbeat in my ears and my throat and everywhere in my body. I see the pen sliding out from between his fingers as I dive, my hands pinning his much larger arms to the ground. Feel his struggle as I straddle him and bring my lips to his neck, the scent of his blood and sweat and his *aliveness* just daring me to have a taste. I hear my name, I hear my name come from his lips over and over and over and–

"Lydia."

Green. Aiden's eyes. My name on Aiden's lips. Not Xavier's. It's Aiden's hands clutching my arms, holding me in place in front of him. And we're outside. In the cold. I'm not in the hot stage room anymore with the inescapable scent of blood filling my nostrils. I'm not in the study room with Xavier.

I'm outside with Aiden. Aiden, who's warm and alive and has a heartbeat.

And it's snowing.

I turn my face up toward the sky, closing my eyes to feel the chill and the snowflakes falling onto my face, only to melt once they hit my skin. But I have to open my eyes, because the moment I close them, I see it. I see it all, and I hear it, and I smell it.

I'm outside with Aiden. I'm outside and I'm with Aiden.

The rest is over.

I'm not sure if it's me telling myself the words or if Aiden is saying them to me and I'm just repeating them in my head, but once I slowly come to my senses, I jerk away from his grasp and sit against the nearest wall I can find, which thankfully, is only a few steps away.

I shrug off my coat—not entirely sure if I had put it on myself or if Aiden put it on me when he got me out of there, whenever that was—and toss it next to me, needing to feel the air on my skin, not caring if I get hypothermia or frostbite or whatever else I could possibly get from wearing nothing more than a short dress and heels in the middle of February in Chicago.

"Lydia," Aiden says, kneeling in front of me. He puts a hand on my knee, which I've pulled up close to my chest, but I reach out and push it away. His skin is too hot. I need the cold. I need the cold and numbness, and I need to be able to breathe properly, but every breath feels too shallow, and I need something to smell so the scent of spilled human blood isn't stained in my nostrils. And I need Aiden to stop looking at me like that, with concern and worry and pity because he may understand what it's like to have a secret and to have your life burdened by your identity you know nothing about but he'll never know what it's like to not be able to get too close to people in fear of hurting them or having to resort to sinking your own teeth into your own skin just so you don't hurt someone else, just to feel the pain so that someone else doesn't have to.

I wish I could go back to not knowing. I don't want this anymore. I'll never fit in with them, and I'll never fit in with humans, and I'll never fit in anywhere.

"Lyds," he says, softer.

"Don't call me that," I snap, suddenly aware of the tears sliding down my cheeks, blurring my view of Aiden, who continues to kneel in front of me, but I could care less.

Because it makes me think of Jake. It makes me think of Jake and the fact I've been a shitty girlfriend for months now because I can't push everything down and not care and be good for him. He does so much for me, cares so much, and I've repaid him by avoiding deep conversations with him at any cost and pushing him away. I need Jake not to care. I need Aiden and Imani, and my dad, to not care so I can just disappear off the face of the earth and never hurt anyone ever again. Because that's all I ever do, is hurt and disappoint and hurt and—

Aiden reaches out for me, and I jerk away from his touch again, not able to meet his eyes.

"Don't," I croak, my voice scratchy. "I don't wanna hurt you, too."

He starts to say my name again, but when I shake my head viciously, he stops. The cold has crept into every pore, numbing every inch of my arms and legs, and face that's exposed to it. But the numbness is better than feeling. I'll take the numbness any day.

"I hurt my dad first, because I killed my mom," I continue, letting the words spill out of my mouth as I wrap my arms around my legs and fixate on a spot on the ground to Aiden's right. "And I hurt him every day after by not being normal and by being a reminder of my mom and what she did, and even if he says it's okay and I'm okay, I'm still just his freak daughter, who he can't have a normal life because of. And I hurt Xavier and Xavier's family and friends and every person who has ever loved him. I hurt Jake by shutting him out more and more every day and not telling him the truth about me. I hurt Bram and Genevieve by not being the perfect vampire daughter they've been waiting for, and not just saying it's okay that they left me. And I don't wanna hurt you, too. I can't. Not you."

I allow myself to meet Aiden's eyes, so green against his red face, so red from the cold I've kept him out in, and a wave of guilt passes over me.

He's done so much for me; what have I ever done for him?

And I cry. Like, really cry, rasping sobs that shake my whole body. I let Aiden pull me to him this time, enveloping me in his arms. I let the cold seep into my skin and I shake from it as he pushes my hair back from my face and tells me I'm a good person, one of the best he's ever met, but I don't think I can believe him. I feel that calm that he brings me, lingering on the edges of my being, but it can't break through. I hurt too much. But I let him—once I'm drawing in slow, shaky breaths, and once the tears have mostly stopped—pull my coat back on, wrap his scarf around my neck and over my mouth and nose.

I let him take my hand in his and lead me down the quiet, snowy streets to our dorm, praying for the numbness to return so the ache in my chest can go away.

I'd rather be numb for the rest of my life than have to feel this way. Maybe I do just need to rip off the band-aid and tell Jake, tell Dad, tell everyone so they can stop caring about me and see me for the horrible person I really am.

I tuck my other hand into my coat pocket only to be met with something that feels like paper. I pull it out to see it's a napkin, stopping and taking back my other hand from Aiden so I can unfold it.

"Lydia?"

"One second." I sniffle, struggling because I can't feel my fingers, but when I do, I see that it was written on with pen, in neat, loopy handwriting I've never seen before. But I know immediately who wrote it, who snuck a pen and asked the waiter for a napkin, and who I can remember now hugged me goodbye before Aiden pulled me out of there.

My chest tightens, and I can't breathe again.

Run while you can
- Mom.

CHAPTER THIRTY-NINE

I WAKE up in my bed. I know where I am even before I open my eyes, thanks to the unrelenting mattress under me when I roll over onto my stomach and the clean scent of my freshly washed pillowcase. And for the briefest of moments, I'm in the blissful space between sleep and consciousness.

But then I remember.

Roarke's warning, the freezing cold, the inescapable smell of blood, the horrified screaming. The inability to breathe, weight crushing down on me, the tears, the pain, the numbness, the *note*.

And Aiden, leading me down the hall to my room—which was empty, thankfully. Aiden, who snuck to his room and got me his little heater and extra blankets, no matter how much I insisted I was fine. Aiden, who unbuckled my heels with his own numb, shaky fingers, who got my pajamas out of my closet and waited while I got changed in the bathroom. Aiden, who—despite the horrific night, despite the emptiness inside of me and the confusion and the wanting to disappear —was able to get a laugh out of me when he wrapped me up in one of the blankets like a burrito.

When I roll back over, reaching out to my desk and pulling my phone—which is plugged in, even though I don't remember plugging it in—toward me. Sure enough, there're five texts: one from Imani, three from Aiden, and one from Jake.

I open the one from Imani first, which was from last night:

> imani: staying over at tripp's tonight. be
> safe getting home! :)

The one from Jake is from this morning, and I feel a fresh stab of guilt when I open it:

> jake hampton: Let me know when you're
> up. I have something for you. We still on for
> tonight?

I text him back, pulling my bottom lip in between my teeth as I roll onto my back so that both of my hands are free to type a response.

> me: i just woke up, but you can come over
> if you want. yes, we're still on for tonight, as
> long as you still want to

I need a distraction. I need to not let myself go back to that place I went to after Xavier, staying in bed and not eating and not speaking to anyone.

I need to be better.

I need to *tell him.*

And I'm not like them. Xavier was an accident; a horrible accident. But it wasn't on purpose or for fun or entertainment.

I'm not like them.

But I think of Genevieve's note, hidden between the pages of the book I'm reading right now.

Run while you can.

Be careful.

Run.

I need to hear what Roarke says tomorrow at work, because apparently he—and Genevieve—know something about Bram that I'm being left in the dark about.

Something beyond his murder shows, I assume.

My phone vibrates with a response not even a minute later:

> jake hampton: Of course I want to. Be right over :)

My chest tightens, and I decide to down a bottle of blood before he gets here. And to distract myself, so hopefully I'm not in tears when he knocks on my door, I open Aiden's texts, which are from the middle of the night, a few hours after we got back, and long after I had fallen asleep.

> aiden swanson: I know you're asleep, so text me when you wake up. I want to make sure you're okay. I also know that you're gonna want to apologize for last night, but you don't need to. It's not your fault. The most important thing to me right now is knowing that you're okay. Or that you'll be okay

My chest tightens further at that. Maybe it was a bad idea to read Aiden's texts before Jake gets here. My eyes drift down to the next blue bubble of text, sent thirty-two minutes after the first.

aiden swanson: I keep thinking about what you said. I'm not gonna tell you that you'll never hurt me, and I'm not gonna tell you that I'll never hurt you. It's not realistic. But I will tell you that even if you hurt me or I hurt you, we'll just pick up the pieces and put them back together. I'm not leaving you to go through any of this alone

And the last, shortest text, which came through two minutes after the previous one:

aiden swanson: You aren't getting rid of me that easy Lydia

I blink back my tears, taking a few deep, slow breaths to calm myself, and just in time for the knock on my door. I decide I'll text Aiden back later; I'm kind of at a loss for words right now.

In a good way.

I glance at myself in the mirror, running my fingers through my bedhead and wiping at my eyes one last time before opening the door. There stands Jake, dressed in a football hoodie and jeans, but what really draws my eye is the wide, somewhat nervous smile on his face and the bouquet of pink and red roses he holds out to me.

My heart breaks.

An image flashes in my mind of thick, dark red liquid in wine glasses.

"Thank you," I whisper.

"Of course," he says. He pulls me into him, resting his cheek against the top of my head. I wrap my arms around him, still clutching the flowers. His heartbeat thuds against my ear.

What if, last night, he'd been up there? Or Imani, or Tripp?

No. Don't.

Maybe I need this. Maybe I need to take a step back again, which I haven't really done since... since Xavier. I've let my vampire side rule me ever since it happened, and so maybe I just need to play human again, and better, this time.

But maybe I don't have what it takes to give myself fully to either side.

No. Tell him. You need to just tell him.

He deserves it.

And when am I going to talk to Bram next? What do I say when he inevitably asks me my thoughts about the whole thing? Does he know how badly I shut down? I don't remember much of what happened between the last turning and ending up outside with Aiden. I blacked out, sent back to those moments with Xavier.

Not now. Not now, Lydia.

Be here, be present. With Jake, who's okay and alive.

He pulls back, holding my face in his hands. I hold his gaze, no matter how badly I want to look away, because I feel like he'll be able to tell that something's wrong. But then again, maybe he won't notice, because something's been wrong for months now.

Maybe this is just who I am now. Forever stained by what I did.

He kisses my forehead again, my nose, and finally, my lips. His hands come to rest on my hips.

"How was your night last night? Did your project go okay?"

I let out a small sigh, looking down at the flowers. They're gorgeous, and they smell so good. But the images come back as my eyes trace the curves of the red petals.

And I see the red that stained that man's teeth as he smiled at the crowd with pride.

The red stained on Xavier's throat. On my hands.

"It was okay," I say. "I've just been looking forward to

today, though." I look up at him just in time to catch his smile. "How was your night?"

Tell him. Don't make it a Xavier situation where it becomes too late.

"Not bad. Aiden disappeared for the night, so I watched some shitty reality TV in peace while Tripp and Imani were at dinner and went to the gym for a bit when they came back. I missed you, though." He smiles again, leaning forward to kiss me before adding, "What d'ya say we plan our date for tonight?"

I twist in his grasp and set the bouquet down on top of my bookshelf before turning back to face him.

"Hold that thought," I say, holding up my index finger. "Can I shower first, and then we plan?"

Jake shakes his head, grinning wider. "No. You absolutely may not shower."

I smile back at him as he lets go of me and goes to lie down on my bed. I turn to open my closet, letting my smile drop only when he can't see my face anymore, my mind screaming at me to just *tell him tell him tell him.* I carefully pick out some clothes, being conscious of the fact that we're going on a date, so I choose one of my favorite sweaters. I snag my phone off the desk, make the conscious decision to lean over and kiss Jake's cheek before I head to the bathroom; his answering smile warms something inside of me.

Once I'm in the bathroom, I unlock my phone, which is still open to the text thread between Aiden and I. After thinking of a response for a solid minute, I finally text back:

me: thank you

Then, in a separate message:

> me: i'm still going to apologize for last
> night. for dragging you into that with me
> and for everything after. thank you for
> helping me though. for always helping me,
> even when I probably don't deserve it.
> you're too good to me, that's for sure

And one last one, which says:

> me: how are you? are you okay? after
> seeing all of that?

He must have been on his phone when I texted, because
the bubble with three dots pops up almost immediately after I
send the last text, indicating he's typing. While I wait, I turn
on the shower. I look down at my phone when I see Aiden has
replied in two separate texts.

> aiden swanson: I'm not too good for you.
> Nothing and nobody is. You deserve all the
> goodness Lydia

My cheeks start to burn as I read the second:

> aiden swanson: I'm okay. A little shaken up
> sure. But don't worry about me. Try to relax
> and have fun with Jake today. You deserve
> it. And don't try to tell me that you don't

I smile to myself as I text back:

> me: thank you. you have any plans for
> today?

> aiden swanson: I have a date

He replies, and I ignore the weird twisting feeling inside
of me.

me: a real one?

After a second, I add,

me: don't let her take you to any events that her parents host. especially if they're vampires

He types for an aggravatingly long time, and I bite back a smile, the weird feeling disappearing once he responds:

aiden swanson: Yes, a real one. And don't you worry about me. It's just with this stack of books on my nightstand. I'll make sure to stay far away from any vampire novels though

me: loser. have fun :)

I finally step into the shower, the water scalding against my skin, turning it red, but I don't care. It feels good, different from what I wanted from the numbing cold last night that finally only left my system with Aiden's heater and being wrapped in the blankets he brought me.

But I wash quickly, trying to scrub away any remnants of last night that may remain on my skin. Because being here in the shower means being alone with my thoughts, and I don't want that right now. I want to let Jake distract me, and I want to work on things, and I want to have a good day for once.

And then to possibly tell him and ruin our relationship.

Once I get out of the shower, towel-dry my hair, put some light makeup on, and change into my jeans and sweater, I walk back into my room to see Jake still lying on my bed, scrolling on his phone. Draped over his legs is a dark-blue blanket—one that came from Aiden last night.

"Hey," he says, smiling over at me. "You look pretty."

"Thank you," I reply quietly, smiling back.

He lifts his head, nodding toward the blanket.

"This blanket's really nice. Super soft. Looks familiar, too."

My stomach turns.

"Oh, I got it from Target," I say, as casually as possible, but I turn away, just in case my face is betraying my lie. "That's probably why it looks familiar."

I look back over my shoulder as I close the closet door, watching as Jake stretches, his sweatshirt rising up and exposing a strip of his stomach as he stretches his arms above his head. I let myself admire him for a second. I cross the room to join him on the bed, curling into his side and snuggling against him. He wraps an arm around me, pulling me even closer to him. As I close my eyes, resting my head on his chest, I try not to think. About anything, but especially not yesterday.

There're a few minutes of silence. Comfortable silence, where I'm able to focus on the steady rise and fall of his chest.

"I know it's annoying and I keep being indecisive about it, but I think I'm really gonna change my major," Jake mumbles quietly, as if he's half-asleep. "I've been thinking a lot about it since we talked about it last."

"It's not annoying. To what?" I ask.

He stays quiet, absentmindedly stroking my still-damp hair.

"I'm thinking biology. There're a lot of options from there, but I've always just really liked it, too."

I prop myself up on my elbow. "That'd be neat. I think you should go for it."

"Yeah. That's what Belle said, too," he sighs, looking at the ceiling.

I smile at the thought of Jake getting encouragement from his little sister.

Finally, shifting his gaze back to me, he continues, "I think it's just the leap that's freaking me out. Like it's not even that big of a deal, and if I *do* it, it'll be done, and I don't have to stress anymore. But it's just the *doing it* part I can't seem to get myself to do, y'know?"

I stare at him, trying to figure out how to say he just put into words exactly how I'm feeling about my situation of telling him without actually telling him yet.

Unless...

"Yeah," I opt for. "Yeah, I get it. You're right, though. You just have to rip off the band-aid, and then things will be better."

"Before the school year ends, for sure," he murmurs, a beat of silence passing before he adds, "What about you? Are you doing okay with... whatever's going on?"

No. It's just getting worse.

I sigh instead. "It's... complicated. Really complicated. But I'm okay. I just wanna spend the day with you." I pause, fixing my eyes on a scratch on the wall as I force out, "Not right now, but can I... can I tell you some of it later?"

I wonder if he can hear how loud and fast my heart is pounding as he answers, "Of course, baby. You can tell me anything." I feel him shift a bit under me, so I turn my own head so that we can look at each, trying not to think about my own impending doom.

But this is for him, I remind myself as he kisses my forehead.

He deserves to know.

CHAPTER FORTY

Jake ends up taking me to the restaurant in Chinatown. While we're there, I try not to think about the last time and how it was the start of Bram being in my life, and how I still don't really know why he was here in the first place.

I let Jake take pictures of me when he insists I look cute, and I even give him the okay to post the ones I approve of. We sit across from each other at a little corner table and share Crab Rangoons and eat the huge portions of food we ordered, and he tells me him and the others have something planned for my birthday on Monday, and I do my best to just lose myself in every word that comes out of his mouth.

We walk around after dinner, the sky dark and the wind chilling both of us to the bone. He slips on a patch of ice on the sidewalk and almost falls as we walk back to the train station, and we laugh, and I try not to think too much about *can I tell you some of it later?* until later actually comes.

But as our day out comes to an end, later approaches way quicker than I'd like.

When we get back to downtown, we stop for milkshakes

at the little burger place next to our dorm and then head up to Jake's room.

"Hey," he says, as he closes the door behind us and I perch on the edge of his bed, sipping my strawberry milkshake, "what did you wanna talk about? About whatever's going on?"

My stomach drops.

Now? I can't do it now. We've had such a good day, and I've felt better about what happened last night. It's basically Valentine's Day, and he's already made birthday plans for me, but he *deserves to know*. I'll tell him, I swear I will. I'll tell him after I find out whatever Roarke has to say about all of this and when I hopefully find out what Genevieve's *run* means.

I'll tell him.

I *will*.

But then what do I tell him now? *Just kidding, didn't really mean it when I said I wanted to talk about it. Rain check? Even though I've been taking rain checks for the last two months? What's another week?*

But I'm not going to feel like it in a week, either. Or in two weeks. Or a month.

No matter when I tell him, I'm always going to feel this crushing anxiety, making it impossible to get a deep enough breath.

Jake smiles, but it's more like a grimace, and I can feel my heartbeat growing faster by the second.

"Is it bad? I mean, I know it has to be bad, so I understand if you don't wanna talk about it, but... I just wanna understand, Lyds. And help, if I can."

I'm a vampire. Well, half.

I attacked someone. I killed someone and I dumped his body in Lake Michigan.

My dad—my biological vampire dad—invited me to his murder show last night. So, hey, if you ever see a guy who only wears suits and looks kinda ominous but talks really smooth but is also a big liar, stay away!

Oh, and my mom's alive.

And I don't know who to trust anymore.

And I'm not ready to lose you.

I look at Jake and see that curtain opening, and I see him strapped to one of those rickety wooden chairs, only it's me on the stage with him. And past the hot, blinding stage lights, in the crowd, I see Tripp and Imani and Joanne and Anabelle and Aiden and Dad. And then it's me in the crowd, only I'm strapped to a chair in an empty room, and Jake is on stage, strapped to a chair, and I have to sit there, helpless, and watch as he struggles and screams as someone sinks their fangs into his neck.

It's for Jake's safety. It's for his well-being.

I'm not Bram. But I'm no better than him and his skirting around the truth if I don't make myself say the words right now.

My vision starts to blur with tears. Jake immediately starts over to me, but I hold out my hand to him, swallowing past the lump in my throat before I say it, forcing the words out as fast as they'll come, because if I just get them out, I can't go back:

"I'm a vampire. And I... I did something really, really bad to someone."

I blink past my tears, trying to slow my breathing so I don't send myself into a panic attack during Jake's silence, as the corner of his mouth twitches up, then down, and up again, clearly trying to gauge if I'm kidding.

"Half," I add, clutching my melting milkshake in both of my shaking hands.

Jake's mouth moves, struggling to form words, before he finally says,

"I'm... I'm sorry, what?"

My stomach churns, and I start to think that maybe I shouldn't have drank so much blood earlier or ate so much Chinese food or maybe I should've never come here in the first place and stayed home with Dad or better yet, moved somewhere far away and threw my phone in the ocean so I would have never hurt anyone.

I bite down on my shaking lip, drawing blood, before I start.

I tell him everything from my perch on the bed while he remains a few steps away, staring at me the entire time, as I start from the *very* beginning, filling in the gaps of my childhood, confessing to being scared of hurting him but caring about him so much and wanting to feel normal, Xavier, and Bram and Genevieve, but I leave Aiden out of everything.

It's not my place to tell anyone what he is.

Jake is silent when I'm done. I bite the inside of my cheek, hard, and clutch my cup so tightly the domed lid pops off as I wait for a response—*any* response, bracing myself for:

I'm calling the cops.
You're disgusting. Get out.
Freak.
I hate you.
"Um..." he says instead. "Okay. Alright."

He nods slowly, eyes focused somewhere past me, as my heart pounds so hard and so fast I think I might be going into some sort of cardiac arrest.

"What?" I manage.

"Okay," he repeats. "That's... I mean, I've just been wracking my brain for months, and I figured... Not to sound like an ass, but I thought maybe you had depression or something and didn't wanna tell me, which I totally understood, and I wanted to respect your space because I know how hard that can be, first *and* second-hand, so I'm just... I'm sorry. I'm just trying to process. This really blindsided me." He cracks a smile.

A smile.

I stare at him, watching as his smile falters slightly.

What?

"Can I sit with you?" he asks. I nod, still at a loss for words as he sits about six inches away from me on the bed. I turn to face him, and he holds out his arms to me.

And the floodgates open.

"I still... I still want this. I still wanna be with you," he murmurs into my hair as he holds me. "I just need time to process everything. And try to understand. I hope that's okay."

I pull away, wiping at my eyes and nose.

"Yeah, yeah. Of course." I meet his eyes. "It'll be okay if you... if you don't, either. I get it. I mean, what I've done is..." I trail off, swallowing past the lump in my throat.

Jake shakes his head, grabbing both my hands in his, tightly. "Lyds, it's not like you've been hiding an entirely different personality. You're still *you,* and I still—care about you and have had so much fun being with you. The way I'm looking at it... Things are still the same. It's just, now there's a little extra about you I know, and now you don't have to hold that in around me. So things can be better for both of us, I think. And I mean..." He sucks in a breath. "You're not a bad person, I know that, Lydia. I know—I can *tell* what happened to Xavier wasn't, like, intentional. Like, I'm not gonna tell you anything you don't know about it, and I won't lie to you and tell you that that's not a little... much, for me, but I understand now what was going on with you that whole time. And I can understand why you wouldn't want to tell me. That's not easy. None of this is. I just need to wrap my head around it, and it might take me a while. I don't think I'll ever *fully* understand it, but I'm not planning on going anywhere.

Because I really care about you, and it means a lot that you trusted me enough to tell me all of this." He closes his eyes and shakes his head, opening them again just to smile at me, and I feel myself starting to tear up again. From shock, from *relief*, and from the millions of other emotions I'm feeling and not feeling right now.

"I do have a question, though."

I figured he would, considering I covered a hell of a lot in a very short period. Still, I can feel my anxiety ramping up as I wait for him to say it.

"Do you really think this is the second-best city? For—for vampires?"

I laugh through the tears rolling down my cheeks. I had forgotten about that comment Imani made. It feels like forever ago, now. Long before I knew how much things were going to change—for better and for worse.

"You know what?" I say. "It's not that bad."

CHAPTER FORTY-ONE

I END up staying the night with Jake, which is a first. We spend most of it talking, the most we've done in months—well, *I* spend most of it talking and explaining, and he listens attentively, nodding along and asking all kinds of questions, his face only illuminated by the flickering glow of his TV, the volume down so low even I can barely hear it.

"Do you have all the like, advantages, then, too? Like the increased speed and strength?"

I chew on my lip as he draws shapes on my arm with his fingertips.

"I'm gonna be honest, I don't really know. I guess besides the obvious things, I've spent so long trying to avoid it that I never really consciously thought about stuff like that. But I never did track or any sports, so I've never really had anything or anyone to compare it to, if that's what you're asking."

Jake smiles lazily, his blinks slowing, letting his head rest on his pillow. I can tell he'll be out in a few minutes, and I can also tell it's going to be one of my near-sleepless nights, considering it's nearing three in the morning and I'm still wide awake, reeling from all the emotions of today.

"We should get you on the football team," he murmurs, his eyes closing. "You'll be showing up the guys in no time."

"Mhm." I laugh softly, watching him for a minute or two, until I'm sure that he's definitely asleep.

He knows.

He *knows.*

Everything.

And instead of being handcuffed and taken away, instead of any of the other hundreds of scenarios I came up with, I'm here, in his bed, and we're okay.

THAT AFTERNOON, ON THE WALK TO WORK, I TELL Aiden about spilling my guts to Jake.

"You told him?" he asks. "Everything?"

"Not everything. Not about you," I quickly clarify. "Like, he knows you know, but he has no idea you're not human. I wouldn't do that to you."

"I know you wouldn't. Thank you." The breeze rustles his curls. "I mean, you told him about—Xavier?"

I nod, and Aiden's eyebrows lift. Our arms brush as we walk, and I can see the bookstore down the block, my stomach twisting at the thought of whatever the hell Roarke might have to tell us.

But at least I'm with Aiden.

"That's—That's big, is all. That's great, Lydia. Do you feel any better?"

"A little. I mean, yes. I do. Obviously, part of me is still worried he thinks I'm disgusting and is just too nice to tell me, but I'm also worried about whatever we're about to hear from Roarke. Especially after, y'know."

"There's no way Jake thinks that. I get being worried

about Roarke, though." Aiden starts to smile. "Would you rather bet on what he is? I have a guess, and I want to rub it in when I'm right."

I can't help but laugh. "*No.* I hate when you're right."

Aiden and I head inside the bookstore, just as a few customers leave, along with the girl who was working the morning shift, leaving the store empty, except for Roarke, who sits behind the front desk, feet propped up on it.

"Happy Sunday, you two," he says, cheery as always. For once, I want him to skip the cheeriness and just tell us what the hell is going on.

"Happy Sunday," Aiden says. "So, what do you know about Bram Davelin?"

Roarke chuckles and stands up.

"Cutting right to the chase. I get it. First, tell me. What happened at that meeting you went to Friday night?"

Before I can even think of what to say, Aiden retorts, "Tell us what you are, first. And how you know what we are?"

Roarke just grins at Aiden, who returns his gaze with an unwavering stare. I'm impressed because I can tell he's not going to budge, and this isn't a side of Aiden I've seen often. I've really only ever seen him get stern when, well, he was instructing me not to lose my mind the night of Xavier.

"Alright, alright. Well, I picked it up on both of you, immediately. Aiden, you were easier to pin down—when you came in for your interview last year, I knew you were Fae. I've had experience with them, and if you know what you're looking for, it's as obvious as if it were written on your forehead. But it's tempered down on you, definitely. A glamour, I'd suspect, since Fae love throwing those around."

Aiden opens his mouth to respond, his eyebrows tugging together with confusion, but Roarke turns to me.

Glamour? I know that word—I've read enough fantasy books. From what I know, it's like a magical illusion. But,

Aiden, glamoured? Who would have put it on him? And why?

"You, Lydia, were difficult. That first day in class, I knew I picked up something on you, but it took a few classes before I thought I figured it out. I've never met—or even *heard*—of anyone like you before. You're both human *and* vampire. Is that correct?"

I just nod. Roarke nods, too, glancing between me and Aiden as he continues, "You see... I'm a werewolf."

A werewolf. I don't know why I'm as shocked as I am, seeing as I know both vampires and faeries exist and apparently live right under our noses, so it only makes sense that werewolves would, too.

At this point, who knows what else is out there?

"That's what I thought," Aiden says. I fight back a smile—I'm glad I didn't take that bet. He winks at me, and I feel my cheeks start to heat up. "How does that work, then? Do you have control over it? And how do you know Bram?"

Before Roarke can answer, the bell jingles as a mom hauls a toddler through the door. Roarke immediately greets the woman and asks if she's looking for anything specific. I step closer to Aiden as Roarke leads the woman to the children's section.

"How'd you know?"

Aiden grins, tilting his head for me to follow him around the desks, lowering himself into the front chair. "I did some research yesterday. I was too curious. They're one of the other most human-passing beings I could find, besides us. I've never paid any attention to the moon cycle, though, so that was tricky. I really didn't have any evidence. It was just a good guess."

"A good guess that still would've won you the bet. Good thing I didn't agree to it." I smile, nudging his foot with mine, and he smiles back, pushing his a little harder back.

The woman walks up with a stack of board books in her hands. As Aiden checks her out, scanning each book, Roarke hangs back, squatting down to talk to the kid, a little, brown-eyed girl with wispy hair who smiles gummily when he makes a face at her.

A *werewolf.* I can't wrap my head around it. Who knows how long he's been living this way, working with his wife on the bookstore, working as a professor, and hiding this huge secret. He's even mentioned he has kids of his own. Do they know? Do they understand what their father is?

A few more customers come in and out before Roarke is able to tell us anything more.

"Like vampires, you have to be bitten to be Turned," he says, sitting on the edge of Aiden's desk. I scoot my chair closer to Aiden's, until our armrests bump into each other. "I was bit back in... it would've been '96. I was sixteen, and my friend lived out in the country. His house was surrounded by trees, and no one ever wanted to go out there after dark, but we were dumb kids and they dared me to, without a flashlight. It was the full moon, so I figured I had enough light to go in there for just a few minutes, long enough to appease them. And, well." He shrugs.

"I couldn't hide it from my parents for long, obviously, because there's no controlling the transformation at the full moon. They ended up kicking me out. I didn't know where to go, so I just started walking. Every full moon, I'd pick up on a very specific scent, and I'd follow it. It eventually led me to the Fae Lands."

"Fae Lands?" Aiden sits up a little straighter.

"The Fae Lands," Roarke repeats, nodding at him, "are—were—areas where people like us could co-exist. Fae took up the majority, divided into the four seasonal Courts, and even a territory for those who were Courtless, but for a time, werewolves lived there, and vampires, too. Now, true to its name, only Fae live there."

I think about what Bram told me, how vampires were driven out.

How Fae were the problem.

Knowing what I know now, about his little habit of excluding vital information, is that even true?

"But, anyway, I settled in amongst the Courtless Fae and other werewolves—people like me who didn't have a place at home anymore, or, for the Courtless Fae, those who didn't have better opportunities due to the nature of their birth. You see—and I don't know how much of this you already know, Aiden, so feel free to stop me at any point—"

"I don't," Aiden interjects, obviously completely in awe. "My parents haven't told me anything."

Roarke doesn't look surprised, like I was expecting. He just nods and carries on.

"Well, like I was saying, I settled in with people who were like me. I joined a pack—just like regular wolves, werewolves, we form packs. I'm a part of one, even now, though it's different than the one I was in back then. Any day outside of the full moon, we watch out for each other, care for each other. We're friends—but on the full moon, no matter where we are, we search each other out by scent. Watch out for each other for the night. I won't get into the exact logistics now, but...

"I learned a lot from the people I was living with. You see, while werewolves have a lifespan comparable to humans, Fae are immortal, just like vampires. Many of the Fae I was living among had been alive when vampires still lived there, hundreds of years prior, so they were able to tell me the history."

"Why did they leave?" I ask.

"*Immortal*?" Aiden echoes.

I need to know if Bram told me the truth about at least this one thing.

Because if not...

Roarke's mouth twitches in amusement.

"Yes, Aiden, immortal. And, Lydia." Roarke turns his gaze on me. "When vampires and Fae first agreed to share the Lands, in a signed treaty, vampires agreed to only feed off animals. Fae also offered them any humans that happened to make it through the glamour that shrouds the Lands. But the vampires quickly got dissatisfied—there just wasn't enough blood for all of them, so before long, they started attacking Fae.

"The Fae were infuriated by this, so they took it upon themselves to not just evict the vampires from their portion of the land, but attack them back, instead. They burned down their homes—anyone who survived the fires was driven out into the sun and died that way. And the few who survived fled and scattered throughout the country. It depends on who you talk to; some blame the Fae, some the vampires. But anyway, it was quiet for years, with only Fae and werewolves living in the Fae Lands. Until... well, let's see, I was twenty, so it was 2000. Only about four years after I'd moved to the Fae Lands myself.

"One summer night, I woke up to screams. I didn't understand what was happening until I went outside and saw dead bodies scattered across the grass. Some were Fae I had gotten to know over the years, with bloody holes in their necks."

I shift in my seat, seeing those poor humans strapped to those chairs, hearing their final screams.

"Others, stakes were driven through their chests. I'll spare you both the details. But it didn't take long for me to put two and two together that someone had gathered a group of vampires together to attack, and all sides were taking casualties. I lost members of my pack because it wasn't the full moon, and we were essentially defenseless. Those who survived left the Fae Lands. There was no point in being there if we weren't being guaranteed protection, and most of us felt we'd be safer living among humans, in hiding." Roarke sighs. "The Fae faced major losses, too. Not only were many killed, but the Summer Court king and queen fled—they couldn't risk their chances with a newborn, I suppose, but their Court was left in shambles, scrambling for a new leader. In Fae culture, as a royal, abandoning your Court is seen as the worst possible thing you could do—and they did it.

"But anyway, ultimately, whichever vampire had led the attack was unprepared, because most of the vampires were killed, and the survivors backed off."

My stomach sinks to the floor. I can see it in Roarke's eyes before he even says it.

"I later learned the leader's name was Bram Davelin."

CHAPTER FORTY-TWO

I feel Aiden's and Roarke's eyes on me, but I can't look at either of them. He didn't tell me all the details of vampires being driven out of the Fae Lands, but at least what he told me was close to the truth.

But of course, yet again, he *conveniently* left out that he organized an attack on the Fae...

The year before I was born.

And Initiation... it has to be connected, right? Is he planning to do something again?

I explain what Aiden and I witnessed Friday night. Roarke listens intently the entire time, his face taut and serious.

"And—" I glance at Aiden, who nudges my foot with his gently, nodding at me in encouragement, even the slight touch enough to ease some of the tension in my chest. "—my... I found a note in my pocket. From my—my mom. She's been with him since, well, since I was born. It said to 'run while I can'. Do you think..."

"That she's absolutely right? I do, Lydia. Bram is dangerous, and he's dangerous in the way that he gets you to trust him, and soon, whether you know it or not, you're trapped in his web. It sounds to me that with the massive amount of Turning he's doing, he's trying to replenish his numbers. Possibly to attack again, but I can't say for sure. What I *can* say is that you should stay far away from him, Lydia."

I sink lower in my chair, fixing my eyes on the analog clock on the wall, watching the seconds pass, *tick tick tick tick.*

They're right. I know they are—Aiden, Roarke, Genevieve.

Yet part of me—the part that desperately wanted to fit in like the vampires at the bar and melted at the *word* proud—still wants to hear it from Bram himself.

I WAKE UP THE NEXT MORNING TO MY PHONE buzzing with texts every few seconds. When I roll over and grab it off my desk, I see the group chat is blowing up. Plus, I have some individual texts, all wishing me a happy birthday, while the group chat is just mostly Jake talking about how I better prepare myself for my party tonight in a bunch of separate texts.

Dad is the first person I reply to—he says to check my email, and when I do, I see that he sent me a digital Barnes and Noble gift card. I thank him, and then text Jake, Tripp, and Aiden back and thank them, too. Imani rolls over then, grumbling about the group chat before smiling sleepily at me and welcoming me to being nineteen.

Dad and I never made a huge deal out of my birthday, and I always liked that. He'd usually just get me a gift and a little cake we'd share, and we'd spend the evening watching my favorite movies.

So, really, tonight is my first ever actual birthday party—

which I definitely don't mention. I just wish I could get out of my head and enjoy it a little more.

At work yesterday, we didn't talk much more about the whole thing, but on the way home, Aiden stopped me in the middle of the sidewalk, snow falling softly and settling in his curls, his cheeks flushed from the cold.

"Are you thinking about going back there?"

I couldn't lie to him, so I just nodded.

"I just... I want to understand," I'd said. "I mean, aren't you going to confront your parents? Don't you want to ask them about all the stuff Roarke said?"

Aiden chewed on his lip.

"I mean, of course I do. But... you heard it yourself, from someone who's seen firsthand what he orchestrated. He's dangerous, Lyds."

"I just want to see if I can get an idea of what all of this is for, and then I'll never go back there again. Okay?"

He just nodded, and neither of us brought it up again for the rest of the night.

But for today, for my birthday, I decided not to tell anyone I don't really need a party, especially because Jake and Imani have seemed so excited about it. So, when it comes time to go over to the boys' apartment, I let Imani assist me in doing my nails and makeup, and hair. Once we're done, I'm in black jeans, a dark blue tank top I borrowed from her with matching nails and makeup, and my hair curled in loose waves. I feel pretty, and when I admit to Imani as much and thank her for helping me, she pulls me into a tight hug and says she's happy to help and that I'm always beautiful.

That familiar guilt settles into my stomach like a rock, weighing me down, as I inhale the scent of her blood and perfume, my stomach churning, despite the blood I'd downed earlier in preparation for tonight.

Aiden knows, Jake knows. And they're both still here.

But Imani? Tripp?

Once I'm dressed and ready, I feel a little better about the party and try to let myself take it as a welcome distraction from everything else. I vow to myself to not think of Bram, of Genevieve, of Roarke, of Xavier, and Initiation and what I'm going to hear whenever I see Bram again.

Once Imani is ready, we head across the hall to the boys' apartment. Tripp answers the door, greeting us with a "ladies," before pulling Imani in by the waist and giving me a polite nod and a "happy birthday, Lydia."

Jake runs up next, practically shoving Tripp out of the way. "There's the birthday girl," he says, waiting until Tripp and Imani head into the living room to add, "Everything okay?"

I nod, giving him a small smile before letting him pull me into a kiss.

Aiden is in the living room sitting on the couch, and he gives me a small, almost shy smile—our relationship in front of others is so different than what we are normally.

Though nothing about our relationship is normal, really. I can't help but wonder what things would be like had I not called him on the phone that night and asked for help.

There's a variety of snacks and pop, and we soon settle in to play Mario Kart on Tripp's Switch, which he hooks up to the TV. Since I'm the birthday girl, they let me pick the courses, passing around controllers every few rounds so everyone can have a turn playing, and before long, I'm not thinking about Bram or Xavier or Genevieve, and it feels just like it did before—*before*.

Almost.

A few hours later, we wrap up. Imani tells me she's going to stay the night with Tripp, and before I leave to go to my room, I say bye to Aiden and let Jake kiss me goodnight, who asks if I want to stay the night with him, but I—honestly—tell him I'm tired. I'm exhausted, really, so hopefully, I'll be able to just pass out after my insomniac night last night and my day filled with almost *too* much information.

And after I've changed in my room, my earbuds in and playing some soft instrumental music, I think that's it, and I had probably one of the most exciting birthdays of my life—until there's a knock on my door. I pull my hair back into a low ponytail as I peek through the peephole, my suspicions confirmed:

It's Aiden.

I open the door, smiling up at him and noticing he has a brown paper gift bag in his hand.

We didn't interact much tonight, besides a few shared smiles across the room from my seat on the couch, and where he eventually ended up moving to the chair, so that both couples could sit next to each other. I was a little disappointed because I couldn't sit next to him, but he made up for it by making faces at me whenever I hit him with shells or bananas.

"Hi." I step aside so that he can come in, eyeing the bag as he passes me. I insisted to everyone that they didn't need to get me anything, but of course, they did. They all pooled on getting me a few different things—including another Barnes and Noble gift card, which I'm looking forward to spending even if it is a betrayal of EB's—and I got a little flustered as I thanked them all, my face hot with everyone's attention on me.

And now here's Aiden, the little shit, with something *more*.

"I know you said no gifts," he starts to say, as he sits on the edge of my bed, "but I already had this idea and then Jake came to me with his ideas and obviously I wanted to be a part of that, too, so, yeah. And, uh, here."

I take the gift bag from him. It's medium-sized, and surprisingly heavy. I eye him suspiciously as I set it down on my desk and pull the tissue paper off the top, him watching me, slightly pink-cheeked the entire time.

In the bag are four books. Hardcovers.

I start pulling them out, about to reprimand him for spending so much money on me, but he speaks before I can, explaining as I look at the cover of the first book, realizing it's one I've read a few times already. And as I pull out the other three, I realize they are, too.

"You've mentioned each of these a few times," he says, almost shyly, from where he sits behind me. I study the books, listening. "And, well, I know we don't read the same genres but, I mean, they seemed special to you and so... I've spent the last month or so reading them and, uh, if you open them—" I open the first one up, and my heart melts. "—all those notes and highlighted parts and underlines are things that stuck out to me. And those are in each of them. I just—I guess I just wanted to let you know that I, uh, I hear you and—"

I'm hugging him before he can finish his sentence—because I'd rather hide in a hug than start crying—my arms around his neck and my face buried in the crook of his neck and shoulder. His arms slide around my waist.

"Thank you," I murmur, my chest tightening, hoping he understands that really, I'm thanking him for everything he's done for me. Not to mention the fact he went out of his way to read *four* of my favorite fantasy and romance books and annotate them for me to read when he doesn't even like fantasy or romance all that much.

Fantasy, I understand, because he's explained that, because he's been living it his whole life, he likes to escape through other genres. But I guess it's always just worked differently for me, because in the fantasy books I read, it always works out for them. They always find a place they belong with people they belong with.

And, honestly? Aiden's that for me. Even if it's not in the

way I thought I'd find a place to belong when I came here in the first place, because I thought I'd have to hide myself to belong.

I couldn't ask for a better best friend.

"Of course," he murmurs back, his hand rubbing up and down my back, and I *feel* it. I feel something so strong and safe and warm—something that's his—that I could stay here in his arms all day and just bask in it.

But I can't. Because the door starts to open.

I practically jump back, pulling my arms from him and putting them behind my back as Imani walks into the room, a light but wary smile curving her full lips.

"Oh, hey Aiden," she says, her tone as cheery as usual. "I didn't know you were in here."

"Uh, yeah." He stands, tugging his hoodie down and shoving his hands in the front pocket. "I just had a few books for Lydia. I can go if—"

"Oh, no, no, no, you're good. I'm just grabbing a few things."

I can't read her face as she crosses the room and disappears into the bathroom. After grabbing a few things from there and her side of the room, she scurries back out, calling to us to have a good night. I look at Aiden, who's still standing, and he looks at me, his cheeks flushed. My own face feels hot, but I'm not exactly sure why.

"I should—"

"Yeah, yeah."

I thank him again, and he gives me a somewhat shy smile as he wishes me happy birthday again and leaves.

The second the door closes behind him, I let out a deep breath.

CHAPTER FORTY-THREE

THE WEEK PASSES WAY TOO QUICKLY, MOST of which I spend re-reading the books and reading Aiden's annotations with a huge grin on my face, and I'm actually feeling kind of okay. Because when I'm reading, I'm not thinking about what my plan is this weekend.

I spend Friday night with Jake, lying on his bed, staring up the ceiling as he comes back from the bathroom. Since I told him, since he understands a little more now why I've been acting the way I have, the topic of the... physical side of our relationship (and lack thereof) came up, and I saw the realization hit him like a ton of bricks.

"Oh. *Oh.* You've been worried about hurting me?"

I nodded, feeling my face grow hot. "Yeah. I mean, I've never felt like I was *close* to hurting you, but I didn't wanna take the risk, and I didn't know how to explain it, because it's not like... It's not like I don't *want* to, like, try, and—"

He cut me off with a kiss. Which turned into... some other things.

After he comes back from the bathroom and kisses me,

and asks what I'm thinking, I tell him I'm planning to go to the bar tomorrow.

"It feels like I'm not seeing the big picture of what's really going on with him and his Clan. So, I want to hear what he says about it. And then I probably won't ever see him again."

Saying the words out loud, strangely, makes my chest tighten.

Because as angry as I've been at him, as betrayed as I've felt, I was *glad* to find him. That short period of time, when he started putting puzzle pieces together for me, telling and even *showing* me how vampires lived, hiding their true identities, just like I was. I didn't feel so alone—there was something comforting, after Xavier, about sitting in his office and having my questions answered.

Or so I thought, I guess.

"Is anyone going with you? Is it safe?"

"I'll be fine," I say, curling against his side when he joins me on the bed. "It'll be a Saturday night, so the bar will be open. There'll be tons of people around."

"Okay," he murmurs. "But you'll call me if you feel unsafe?"

"Of course." *That's* a lie. After what I saw last Friday, I don't want Jake anywhere *near* Bram. Or Imani, or Tripp.

Oh, shit. *Or* Aiden, after what I know now.

I have to do this alone. I'd already decided that, but now, I really have to.

"Thank you." Jake kisses my head, and I can hear the drowsiness in his voice. I listen to his heartbeat, thumping steadily, more reassuring now than anything, now that I'm staying on top of my feedings better than ever, now that I don't have to lie about going to butcher—at least to him—and now because of what I've seen. "I..."

"Hm?"

"Nothing. I'm exhausted." He laughs a little. "'Night, baby."

I'M JITTERY ALL THE WAY TO THE BAR, PICKING OFF my nail polish as I walk and trying to run over what I'm going to say in my head, the night cold, wind biting and stinging my cheeks.

I know the truth, I'll say, bursting through the door. *I know that you led an attack on the Fae Lands and were responsible for so many deaths. So tell me, now, everything else you've been hiding, or I'll call the vampire cops on you!*

Vampire cops? No, scratch that line. That's stupid.

He'll tell me everything, and it'll be horrible. And then he'll say, *Please, Lydia, forgive me.* And I'll say, *no, I'm done with you and your lies,* before standing up from my seat and storming out, leaving him shocked, one of his stupid cigarettes tucked between his fingers. And then I'll go home, tell Imani and Tripp, and then we'll all hang out and I'll be happy and probably never tell Dad about any of this.

I should at least tell him I told Jake, though. He'll be happy to hear that, I think.

Maybe.

Admittedly, I've been really bad at keeping in contact. I really just text or call when he initiates, but y'know what? After tonight, that'll change.

After tonight, everything will change.

Everything will be better.

I hug myself tighter against the cold wind that seeps right through the fabric of my coat and hoodie. Thankfully, I can see the bar up ahead, neon light on, and I can already feel the bass of the music thumping in my chest.

I stop just outside the door.

I could always come back another day.

No. *No*, Lydia, rip off the band-aid. And then go home and rip off the other two band-aids, and then everything will be okay and fine and—

Open the door.

I have to force my hand out to yank open the door, which fights against the wind. As soon as I step inside, I'm met with a comforting blast of heat, along with the sounds and scents that I've become so familiar with. And to my right, Rick, the bouncer, just like always.

He looks at me, eyebrows furrowed in confusion.

"Hey, kid," he says. "Bossman expecting you?"

"Uh, yeah. I mean, he said I could stop by." I can't fathom how Aiden has gotten through life without the ability to lie.

Rick nods, glancing over his shoulder toward the closed office door. I feel the presence of people entering the bar behind me; he looks back at me, cocking his head towards the office.

"Go on ahead. You can just go in. He might not hear a knock with everything else going on in here."

I thank Rick, starting to weave my way through the crowd, warm bodies brushing up against mine, the pure humanness in this place always borderline overwhelming. My chest tightens, thinking about the vampires among us, the potential I thought was there.

But I just can't fit in with people who are okay with something like Initiation.

I stop in front of the office door, raising my fist to knock before I remember what Rick said. I strain my ears, trying to differentiate between all the voices I'm hearing, all underneath the music, but it's only when I lean a little further toward the door I'm able to pick up on what sounds like Genevieve's voice, followed by what I assume is Bram's, though it sounds different.

More... tense. Angrier, almost.

And is that a heartbeat?

I need to just go in.

Rip off the band-aid, Lydia.

I take a deep breath, yanking the door open. My gaze lands on Bram first, but only long enough to see him fly from his seat, palms braced on his desk, an unlit cigarette between two fingers. Genevieve sits on the side of the desk closest to me, twisting in her seat, but I barely skim her face before my eyes land on the person sitting next to her.

The breath is knocked out of me.

I hear Bram say my name, asking me what I'm doing here, just barely over the ringing in my ears.

Skin, paler than I remember, and I would know, because I've been tortured by the images of him in my head every day for the last two months. His hair, still dark and curly, and his dark eyes, no longer framed by his dark-rimmed glasses.

And when he smiles, I see them:

Short, yet obviously pointed canines.

Just like mine.

"Good to see you, Lydia," Xavier says.

CHAPTER FORTY-FOUR

I'm speechless.

"Lydia," Bram says again, but I can't tear my eyes from Xavier. I'm not even sure if it's *him*, because, well, I felt him, dead.

I watched Aiden toss his body into the lake.

Even if it is really, truly the Xavier I thought I killed, and he's really, truly here in front of me—

Why is he *here*?

"Lydia," Bram repeats, forcing me to look at him. And for the first time, I see something on his face, in his slightly widened eyes that tells me that for once, this wasn't a part of his plan. That I shouldn't have come tonight, in his mind, and I'm seeing something he didn't want me to see.

"What is this?" I force out, the room seeming to spin under me. I feel hands on me—soft, gentle, guiding me into a seat, and I realize it's Genevieve, her hands lingering on my shoulders before she steps away, standing where I just was.

I whip my head toward Xavier, now sitting beside me, and my stomach churns. The last time we sat next to each other was in that *room*, blood welling up on his finger, and I can still smell that blood now, still sense his heartbeat, calm and steady unlike my erratic one, but there's that familiarity lingering on him, the one that makes the hair on the back of your neck rise to let you know there's someone like you in the room.

I did this to him.

Oh, my *God*.

I made him like me.

"Lydia, I wasn't expecting you tonight." Bram's voice has shifted back into that light, casual tone he always uses, but there's nervousness lingering on the edges, I can tell. He lowers himself back into his seat, reaching for his lighter.

"How did this happen? How long have you known?"

I look at Xavier. "You were—I mean, we—"

"Zipped me into a bag and dumped me into the lake? I know." He grins, and even looking at him in this close vicinity, seeing all the features that tell me he's obviously Xavier, I can't connect the two. Because this is Xavier, but it's not the shy, quiet Xavier I met in math class. There's confidence around this Xavier, as he leans back in his seat, crossing his arms over his chest.

And he's *alive*.

Sort of.

"So—so—" I stammer out, still unable to form a complete sentence. "How did you—"

"I woke up in said bag, well—" He looks over to Bram for confirmation. "We worked out that it must've been only a few hours later. Something about your venom working quicker than a regular vampire's, since it only overtakes half the body and leaves them partially human still. But anyway, my panic and newfound super-strength made it easy for me to fight my way out of the bag. I could barely remember what happened besides you knocking me to the ground. But somewhere between that and my first attack, I was able to piece things together."

First?

"I went haywire," he continues, through my horrified disbelief. "I needed blood so badly. So, I get it. Don't think I'm holding anything against you for what happened to me. But it was only after my first couple of attacks and hiding the bodies and all that I really came to my senses. But by then, one of Bram's Clan had found me and brought me back to him. I told him everything. He asked what you looked like, and when he brought out Genevieve, I told him you two could be twins, and that's when he told me you were their daughter and explained that whole situation. So, he asked me to help him keep an eye on you until he felt it was appropriate to approach you. He knew how you were raised, so he didn't want to bombard you with everything at once. Especially because he didn't know how you'd react to knowing you Turned someone.

But anyway, I had a good enough grasp on myself to go back to school, so I made up the finals I missed and finished out the week. In one of my classes near the end of the week, I heard your friend—Imani, is it?—talking about how your group was going to Chinatown that night, so I told Bram, and we went there. He wanted to see you for himself, and the second he laid eyes on you, he said he could just tell you were his. Right?"

I can't breathe.

Bram nods, taking a drag on the cigarette.

That night... Xavier was there, too? This whole... this whole *nightmare* could've been cut short by two months if I would've just *seen him*.

My stomach churns, and I think I might throw up.

Xavier grins, turning back to me.

"He then asked me what the best way to approach you would be, and I told him the bookstore. But at that point, I'd guessed you'd be gone for winter break, so he had to wait. But since then, we've been testing the limits of half-vampires—dhampirs, that's the official name—and it's really amazing, Lydia. I should thank you, really."

I stare at him, unable to comprehend.

Thank me?

They knew the entire time.

He knew, and even after I opened up to him about the sick feeling that's never gone away and the nightmares and the panic attacks, he never thought to say, *Oh, by the way, you didn't kill him, you Turned him. And he's right around the corner. Xavier, come on out!*

This is it. The nail in the coffin.

My chest is so tight I can't pull in a satisfactory breath. I might as well put it all out there at this point, right? No point in keeping secrets anymore, now that his biggest secret has been revealed.

"I came here tonight," I say, my voice coming out with a shockingly hard edge, "to tell you I know you led an attack on the Fae Lands you never told me about. Is that what Initiation is for? Are you trying to build some sort of army? Why else would you attack innocent people and—"

"*Enough.*"

I flinch at his tone, even though he just barely raises his voice. He leans back in his seat, the cigarette smoking between his fingers, his eyes dark and unreadable.

"I have been debating whether or not to tell you ever since we met, and I was leaning toward no after seeing how you reacted at Initiation, but I suppose the truth is out. I do not know who you heard this from, but yes, as you put it, I led a failed attack on the Fae Lands just before your mother and I met.

"I had heard about the history of our species, and I didn't think it was fair we were the only ones forced into the human world. I felt it was wrong, so once I took over the Clan and felt I had the numbers to make a statement, we attacked. But, I can admit when I'm wrong."

I want to laugh.

"I was unprepared. I thought I had enough vampires, but our numbers were nothing compared to the Fae, many of whom have specialized powers, as well. I came back discouraged, but with the goal of one day trying again. At the end of the day, I simply want a safe space for vampires instead of us being forced to hide our identities amongst humans. You understand that, don't you, Lydia? My intentions have always been pure—it's just the means of getting there cannot always be clean. You'll learn that as you grow older."

I want to punch him.

"So?" I say. "Are you building an army or not? You still haven't said what Initiation is for."

Bram quirks an eyebrow, amused, and I *really* want to punch him.

"The reason behind Initiation," he says, slowly, "is to get our numbers back to where they used to be. But also, for newborns to prove to the rest of the more experienced members of the Clan they are capable of and willing to assist the cause by performing their first Turning in front of everyone."

I want to throw up.

"And we handpick our new members carefully," he continues. "We follow those who live in the city and watch them, choosing those who may need a better life, those who are struggling or may not have any loved ones anymore. Or, of course, in the rare instance a rogue vampire is Turning people, we take in their victims. It's not as sinister as you're making it out to be. We aren't *attacking* people, as you put it. Both sides are benefitting."

I open my mouth, but decide against arguing with him, closing it again. I know that any argument I *want* to make will just come out scrambled and weak-sounding, anyway.

"But," Bram says, pausing dramatically to take a pull of his cigarette, "now, everything has changed, and it's all because of you, Lydia." He smiles. "You see, dhampirs have the strengths of vampires, and none of the weaknesses that allowed us to be picked off so easily by the Fae. They used our aversion to sunlight and fire to their advantage, yet dhampirs have the ability to move during the day; something they would never expect, especially given you still possess the increased speed and strength. I believe we have truly found the answer here, and I never would have known had it not been for you Turning Xavier. So I, too, thank you, Lydia. Soon, vampires and dhampirs alike will have a safe haven once again."

The silence that follows is suffocating.

He wants to make a half-vampire—dhampir—*whatever* army to attack the Fae again...

And he seems confident it'll work.

And it's my fault.

"So, what?" I ask, my voice sounding hollow and far away. "You're gonna just have Xavier Turn a bunch of people? What if it fails again? Why don't you just... make the Vampire Lands or something? There's gotta be *somewhere* you can go, if your intentions really are that *pure.* Why attack innocent Fae?"

The corner of Bram's mouth quirks.

"One question at a time, please, Lydia. Though I do love how inquisitive you are. Let's see—first, no, it is not possible to create a new safe haven, at least for us. You see, the Fae Lands, to any average human passerby, look like miles and miles of unused farm land. Not so far from here, actually. That is because Fae have the ability to glamour; that is, use their magic to disguise, and therefore, protect. We do not have the ability the glamour, and so any land that we tried to claim as our own would not be truly protected from humans. We would have to get Fae to do that for us, and, of course, that will never happen. And as for the attacking, to put it quite simply, as the phrase goes: I believe they deserve a taste of their own medicine. They killed hundreds of us. Why should we be kind after that?"

Bram pauses, thankfully giving me a minute to process all of that. My stomach drops, and I know they can all hear my heart pounding.

"To answer your other question, essentially, yes. Xavier will begin, and once our dhampirs start to multiply, then I can send more and more out. However..."

"We want your help." The words explode out of Xavier, as if he's been waiting for his one line in this morbid play.

Bram gives him a look, and Xavier instantly goes quiet.

"While it's plenty possible for Xavier to begin the process on his own, as they say, the more, the merrier," he continues. "If we had another set of hands, just to start... And you have shown, clearly, you have the restraint to stop yourself. Yes, it's eerie at first, but knowing you wouldn't be *killing* them—"

"No," I interject. I can't even believe what I'm hearing—that they'd even *suggest* it to me. That *Bram* would, knowing damn well how I've reacted to every instance of... of all of this. "No, I—no. I can't. I'm not doing that. I don't want any part of this."

Bram's expression darkens, his eyebrows lowering.

I want out. I want to get out of here.

"I know that you've adjusted to human life, Lydia, but I also know that it's difficult. Always worrying about whether or not your loved ones will accept you, and even when they say they do, they will never truly understand. You will always be out of place. I even understand if you felt uncomfortable at

Initiation, one of the sole people with a heartbeat in the room.

"But imagine, living amongst people *exactly like you.* Not vampire, not human, but both. Understanding exactly what you've gone through, how you feel—something even I cannot understand, nor your mother, Keith, nor that Fae friend of yours. But Xavier here; he is *exactly* like you. Born from your very own venom. Just, for a moment, Lydia, imagine being surrounded by people like that."

And I do.

And I push it away the moment it becomes tempting—which is about three seconds after I start thinking about it. But then I start thinking about what would have to happen to achieve it. So, I just swallow past the growing lump in my throat and shake my head, not trusting my voice.

Bram stares at me a moment longer, and I let him win, dropping my gaze to my hands, shaking in my lap.

I want to get out of here.

I need to get out of here.

"Very well," Bram says, his voice back to that light, pleasant tone he always uses. He stands, and I take that as my cue to stand, too, but not without glancing at Xavier and Genevieve, who I almost forgot were behind me this entire time.

"As disappointed as I am, I understand. You're still young, after all, but my invitation remains open, if you find yourself changing your mind, or even if you wish to come back and talk. It has been a pleasure to get to know you, Lydia, and I wish you the best of luck. I take it you can see yourself out?"

This is it?

I nod, at a loss for words. Xavier offers me a small smile. Genevieve looks at me, her face screaming that she wants to say something, but as usual, she stays quiet. Instead, as I reach for the doorknob, she grabs my other hand, squeezing it and giving me a little nod.

The words from her note flash in my mind:

Run.

What if I put too much blame on her?

What has she gone through, with him, all these years? Guilt settles over me.

So, I squeeze her hand back, and I leave.

CHAPTER FORTY-FIVE

As soon as I'm outside, I hear my name, and I whirl around, coming face-to-face with—

"*Aiden*? *Jake*? What are you doing here?"

Jake grins at me, glancing at Aiden before he says,

"We were worried about you. I mean, I was, so I brought it up to Aiden because you'd mentioned he knew you were coming here tonight, and we agreed to just..."

"Hang around and make sure you were okay," Aiden finishes.

I look at the two of them, bundled up in their hands and coats and scarves, and between them going out of their way to *follow me* and make sure I was okay, and all the emotions of tonight, tears prick at my eyes.

But no. I'm not going to cry. Nope, nope, nope.

"Thank you," I say.

"So, how was it? Are you okay?"

"Did he give you actual answers?"

I glance between them, and then at the bar, my heart still hammering. "Let's... start walking first."

It's only when we're a few blocks away I let the bomb

drop, picturing his face in my mind, still not believing it myself. "Well, first of all, Xavier's alive."

Aiden actually stops in his tracks. "What do you mean Xavier's *alive*?"

I tell them mostly everything, censoring myself a bit because of Jake not knowing about Aiden, but I get the main points out: Xavier's been alive this entire time, and because of it, Bram is planning to build a half-vampire army.

"Is there anyone you can tell?" Jake glances between us as we walk. "I mean, this has to be out of your hands at this point, Lyds. This sounds dangerous."

I glance at Aiden. To be honest, I'd love to hear from his parents—if they lived in the Fae Lands at any point, they might have connections there still, people who could be warned and do something about this. But, obviously, I can't say that now.

"I have one person in mind," I say, looking at Aiden again, hoping he's gotten better at mind reading and can tell I'm talking about Roarke, who I think is our other best bet. "But I know, it is dangerous. Don't worry, I don't wanna be involved in *any* way."

We stop for milkshakes and fries before going back up to our rooms, and as much as I want to beeline for bed, I eat with the boys, Imani and Tripp joining us for a bit. Afterward, I ask Aiden if I can talk to him for a bit.

"You wanna talk to my parents, don't you?" he asks, before the door to my room is even shut.

"I do," I confirm, telling him my thought process. As he listens, he gazes out the window.

"I don't know," he says, and I can tell in his voice he's frustrated, and I know it's not with me. He rakes his hands through his hair. "They really haven't told me *anything*, Lydia. I learned more from Roarke the other day than they've ever told me. But…" He sighs. "I guess it's worth a shot, isn't it? If it means helping the Fae who still live there."

"I think so." I pause. "I don't know if it'd help at all, but I can be there with you when you talk to them about it. I know I always feel better when you're around."

My cheeks start to warm as soon as I say it, even more so when he starts to smile, his entire face softening. His smile really can light up a room.

"Yeah, same here." His smile falters a bit. "I'll have to think about it, though. Mostly because I just don't trust my parents to behave and not make snarky comments about you."

My heart twists at the thought of—of all people—Aiden's parents hating me, just because of what I am.

But instead, I smile a little.

"Trust me, after everything I've dealt with from my *own* parents, I can handle a few comments from yours. Just let me know when you're ready."

He leaves after a little while longer, and once I'm alone, I lay down on my bed and close my eyes.

Xavier's alive.

I'm not a murderer.

Bram is trying to start a half-vampire army.

Genevieve might not be as guilty in this whole situation as I thought.

Aiden knows. He's still my best friend.

Jake knows. He's still my boyfriend.

I'll tell Imani and Tripp. Soon.

Dad loves me.

I'm gonna be okay.

CHAPTER FORTY-SIX

THE WEEKS START to fly by. I'm just back to worrying mostly about telling Imani and Tripp and getting back on track with my schoolwork. I can relax a little. Jake and I start hanging out more, and I see a lift in him, too, after he talks to his advisor and gets encouragement about changing his major.

Aiden and I spend time together at work, but he's started coming around to my room sometimes when the others are in classes to bother me while I'm doing homework or borrow books. We've agreed to wait a bit to talk to his parents—he signed the lease for the apartment he was looking at, the move-in date is May first, and he wants to wait until after he's settled in to confront them. I get it, I do—it's a big deal for him.

And in the blink of an eye, it's my six-month anniversary with Jake.

Six months.

In the long run, it's not *that* long, but it feels long to me.

Jake takes me out to dinner to a place we've never been before, and it's more upscale than anywhere I've ever been, so I do my best to dress up a bit, Imani curling my hair for me. I think about telling her as I'm staring at our reflections in our bathroom mirror, but I decide against it, knowing I wouldn't want someone telling me anything shocking while holding a burning hot rod to their head.

At the restaurant, there's both an upstairs and downstairs, but Jake and I are seated on the lower level, at a booth in a corner, our table dimly lit by an overhanging light I could reach up and touch. I look around, taking in the bar, the oven where a worker is sliding pizzas into, the scents of pasta and pizza, and the sounds of glasses and silverware clinking and laughter.

Six months. I watch Jake as he studies the menu, feeling like something is clenching my heart.

Admittedly, I've been so caught up with everything since... well, *forever,* but especially since we met, that I haven't given the future any real thought.

School is over in just over a month, and not that we *need* to see each other all the time, but we really haven't... not, since I spent winter break with him. That's three months apart, and then we come back, and then—and then what?

They will never truly understand.

Jake accepts me now, but...

At what point does this stop working? At what point can he not handle the blood drinking and my inability to really, truly be physical with him and the knowledge we're just always going to be so, so different?

At what point can *I* not handle that?

You will always be out of place.

"I think I'm gonna get one of these pastas," Jake says. "I just have to look up what these Italian words mean so I don't sound like an idiot."

I laugh a little. "I think I'm gonna do the gnocchi."

Jake raises his eyes at me from his menu without lifting his head.

"What'd you say?"

"I'm getting the gnocchi?"

"Is *that* how you pronounce it?"

Jake doesn't believe me until he finds a YouTube video of the pronunciation of *gnocchi*, but by then, the waitress has come and gone, and we've ordered our food. Talking with him has gotten my mind off some of my worries a little more, until after we've gotten our food, and he brings up this summer.

"You've gotta try this, babe," he says, pushing his plate toward me.

"Sure. You wanna try some of my *gnocchi*?"

He gives me a look, but says, "Of course I do." After he's done chewing, he adds, "I'd love to come visit this summer. See you, see Aiden, meet your dad." He twirls another noodle with his fork. "And of course, you're always welcome to come visit my house again. Tripp, I think, is staying for the summer. But there'd be no problem… getting anything you'd need, I'd just make up some sort of excuse. My mom and sister would love to have you back, though. And so would I, obviously."

He laughs, almost nervously.

"'Cause I, uh… well, I love you, Lyds."

I look at him, and he looks at me, and we're both looking at each other as his words bounce around in my brain, but I can't seem to grab on to them and get my mouth to work to say something back.

Love?

He *loves* me?

Do I love him? I like him, and I trust him, and we have fun together. But is that *love*?

The seconds tick by, and my heart rate increases, and I can't make my mouth form words. And the waitress is here, asking if we need anything, and thankfully, Jake turns to her, and I hear him tell her no, we're doing fine, over the pounding of my heartbeat in my ears.

After she's gone, I hear myself say,

"I'm sorry."

Oh, my God, Lydia.

I'm SORRY?

"I—I didn't—I'm—"

"Hey, hey, it's okay." I can see it in his face; it's not, and he's just trying to hide his disappointment with a smile that's twitching at the corners. "If you're not there, you're not there. I'd rather you not say it than say it and not mean it, y'know?" He lowers his fork, holding out his hand across the table. When I take it, he adds, "I just wanted you to know. That I do."

He loves me.

I squeeze his hand, offering him a smile, trying to ignore the painful force that's clenching my heart hard.

"Thank you," I say, my mouth listening to my brain, thankfully.

Even if it's not what I know he wants to hear.

CHAPTER FORTY-SEVEN

I LAY STARING at the ceiling until the sun starts to light up the room again.

More than once, I open Xavier's contact in my phone, staring at it, staring at the little box that says "message". I could—I could text him, something along the lines of,

don't go through with it

don't help him

get out

run

i'm sorry for what i did to you. i'm sorry i'm the villain who did something awful to you and turned you and left you for dead, literally, and he's the hero who found you when you needed help and took you in but that's not how it is and he's planning on hurting a lot of people and you can't help him because if you help him then it's my fault this is happening

But I don't.

And more than once, I think about what it would be like if Bram wasn't, well, Bram. And he was good, and Genevieve actually looked happy in his presence, and they really did want to help me explore vampire life without dragging innocent people into it against their will.

I could've had a family.

I still could. What if...

No. No, if I went back, he'd just try and convince me to help him create his army. We could never go back to the way things were at the beginning, before I knew about Genevieve, about Initiation, about his attack on the Fae Lands, and about Xavier and about his new plan.

I can't go back. Ever.

And I don't need to. I try and convince myself, turning onto my side and tapping my phone screen just in time to see it turn from 7:03 to 7:04 A.M. I fix my eyes on Imani, her back facing me, but I can hear her steady heartbeat and quiet breaths.

I don't need them, I try and convince myself, because I have my friends, and I have Dad.

So why does it hurt? Why am I not angry, and relieved, and just glad to be done with him like I thought I would? Why do I still have the urge to go to the bar, to watch him light a cigarette, and ask him a million questions?

Why can't I just let *go*?

By the time Imani starts to stir, around 9, I've decided I'm going to tell her. I'm going to tear off my last two band-aids, telling her and Tripp, and then things will be fine and I'll be totally free, and maybe then I won't hear Bram's voice echoing in my head that I'll always be out of place.

"Can I tell you something?" I say, sitting up in my bed, as soon as she says good morning to me.

She squints at me from across the room, rubbing one of her eyes. "Yeah, 'course. How long have you been up, anyway?"

I tell her I just didn't sleep well, because I mean, I didn't.

And then, partially delirious from my utter lack of sleep, I tell her.

Everything.

She stays quiet, letting me pour everything out. And when I'm done, I brace myself, only for her to say,

"Thank you for telling me, Lyds. I was really hoping you'd feel comfortable enough one day."

I—

What?

I open my mouth to ask what she means, but she gets there before I can.

"I saw some trash from the butcher one day and put the pieces together, probably around... Halloween, maybe? I'm not exactly sure, but—" she smiles brightly, "—you know, I've always believed there's more than just humans out there, so to anyone else, I probably woulda sounded crazy and like I was jumping to conclusions, but it made sense to me. But would I have felt really silly if you came to me with any other explanation? Absolutely." She laughs a little. "But it's no big deal, Lyds. It doesn't make me think any differently of you. Actually, I, uh, set that article around Christmas time, hoping maybe you'd open up to me. Since you seemed to be having a hard time, and I wondered if it was related..." She smiles sheepishly. "But I have about a *thousand* questions, if you're up for it."

I open my mouth to respond, but when no words are able to come out, I just offer her a smile—a *real* smile, fangs and all —and nod.

She's known.

For *months*.

And she hasn't treated me any differently.

I always thought that if anyone might not react badly to it, it'd be her.

I just never thought she suspected almost the *entire time*.

When she holds her hands out to me, offering me to come over and sit on her bed with her, I quietly pad across the room, mirroring her position by sitting cross-legged across from her.

"I—" I do my best to get my brain to start working again. "I—You would've been the first person I told, I think, but... It's always been something I've been... ashamed of. I, um—" My voice drops, barely audible to even my super-hearing ears. "I was scared you'd hate me for it."

Her gaze softens. "Oh, Lydia," she says, and I try to blink back the tears starting to blur my vision as she reaches out and takes my hands into her baby-soft ones. "You know I love you no matter what, right?"

There's that word again. *Love.*

I'm *loved*.

The tears start to fall, and she doesn't hesitate to pull me into her arms, so my face rests in the crook of her neck, breathing in her blood and the warm vanilla scent I've begun to associate with her, listening to the steady *thump thump thump* of her heartbeat. She rubs a hand up and down my back, and the words *you will always be out of place* are a little quieter in my head.

"And I'm here no matter what," she says.

Once I recover, I pull away, wiping my eyes and blubbering an apology. She just smiles warmly, reaching out and wiping a tear from my cheek with her thumb.

"You've *gotta* stop apologizing for things you don't need to apologize for," she murmurs.

"Believe it or not," I say, "you're not the first person to have told me that."

Imani laughs. "One more thing," she says, resting her hands in her lap and intertwining her fingers. "This might sound stupid, but... Do what's best for *you*, okay? Don't do anything just 'cause other people think it's best for you. Put yourself first, okay? You deserve it."

I nod, wondering if any of my confusion shows on my face. She's definitely right—that's something I need to work on. And does she know that, or is she referencing something specific I'm not getting the hint of?

I brush it aside, holding out my own hands to her, spreading out my fingers and displaying my bitten-to-the-quick nails.

"*One* more thing," I say. "I'll answer any questions you have. But will you paint my nails?"

Her returning grin lights up her entire face and says more than words ever could.

One more band-aid left.

I WAIT A WHILE, THINKING ABOUT NOT TELLING HIM, but almost immediately pushing that thought out of my mind. That wouldn't be fair, and plus, the whole point of telling my *entire* friend group is so I don't have to tiptoe around it anymore.

Though it's *very* tempting.

After a few gruesome midterms that I do better on than expected, spring break comes, and I stay and work through, as does Aiden. It's nice to not have classes and to goof around with Aiden at work all day, and then have movie nights with him and Imani in their apartment at night since Jake and Tripp went to Jake's for the week-long break.

It's nice to relax, and to be *me*, alternating between romcoms and horror movies and Doordashing way too much food with two people who know what I am and still want to be around me despite it.

But when Tripp and Jake get back, I know it's time.

Aiden holds me accountable that night I decide to do it,

since Jake is out with some of his football friends, letting me into their apartment and only disappearing into his room once he's watched me knock on Tripp's door like I asked.

Maybe if Tripp and I have actually *talked* for more than two seconds since… well, Christmas, my heart wouldn't be about to burst out of my chest, and my hands wouldn't be shaking. But we're not *close*, and he probably already hates me, and if he doesn't already hate me, then what if he hates me after this and—

"Oh. Hey, Lydia." He looks surprised to see it's me when he opens the door, his hair pulled back in a tiny ponytail at the nape of his neck. He leans against the doorframe, crossing his arms. "What, uh, what can I do for you?"

"Can we talk?" The words burst from me. Like always, I just need to get myself to the point of no return before I can back out of this. I need to just say the words, and then I can explain and answer any questions he has. And Imani told me he'd probably have more than her—because he, in her words, "will definitely not believe me at first."

My anxiety spreads through my entire body as Tripp quirks an eyebrow.

"Yeah… you okay? You need water or something? You look like you're gonna pass out, and no offense, but I'd rather not deal with that."

I laugh, but it comes out as more of an awkwardly nervous cackle.

He might be right, actually.

"No, I—I just—I know you think I cheated on Jake, but I'd never do that to him. But… I have been hiding something." I watch the confusion grow on Tripp's face, probably wondering what I could possibly need to confess to him. I squeeze my hands into a fist, feeling the pain of my nails against my palms, and rip off the band-aid.

"I'm part vampire." His blank, blinking stare makes me

panic, so I dive into the details. "My mom cheated on my dad with a vampire, and now, here I am. I thought I was okay hiding it from everyone but then I did something really terrible, so I started to distance myself from Jake and then you thought I was cheating on him, but I couldn't tell you the truth because Jake didn't even know, and I didn't think you would even believe me, and I—"

I only stop when Tripp grabs my shoulder, squeezing his eyes shut for a second.

"Okay, okay, slow down. I'm gonna need a drink for this."

He gently moves me to the side, passing me to go to the kitchen, where I watch as he opens the fridge and pulls out a bottle of wine. I'm not sure how they even *got* that, considering Tripp's the oldest of us all at twenty, and I never would have pegged him as a wine drinker. But apparently I'm wrong, because he pours himself a very, very full glass of the clear liquid before glancing over his shoulder.

"Want some? It's peach moscato. You can't even tell it's alcohol."

I just nod, my heart still thundering in my chest.

Tripp grabs a second glass and pours me a much smaller glass than his, which I'm thankful for. He turns, handing mine to me as he takes a sip from his own, leaning back against the kitchen counter.

"Now, if you don't mind, I'm gonna need you to explain a little more."

He stays quiet throughout my explanation, his expression completely unreadable. I outline things from the beginning like I did for Imani, from growing up in hospitals—not understanding what could possibly be wrong with me before doing my own research based on the books I was reading, the books I was seeing myself in—to now, finally meeting my biological family to cutting them off within a few months. And of course, I only mention Aiden when I need to: that he helped me with Xavier that night, and he's been the only one who's known for most of the time, my grief bringing me closer to him and distancing me from Jake.

Once I'm done, I lift my glass to my lips, hoping it's not too obvious to Tripp it's shaking in my hand. He was right, though—the wine is good, and I try to focus on that to distract myself from the fact he's not saying anything, and *why won't he just say something already?*

Finally, he lets his eyes close. And he says, "Jesus Christ."

I can't read his tone, either; I don't know if it's *Jesus Christ, this girl is a lunatic,* or *Jesus Christ, I was so wrong,* or some other variation I can't think of right now because my mind is whirling, and *I just wish he'd say something else.*

And he does. He opens his eyes, and he says,

"Well, first of all, I'm assuming you're not kidding because that's too crazy of a fucking story to make up. I do have a thousand questions, but before that..." He shakes his head. "Shit, man, I'm sorry. I—damn. I get why you wouldn't tell anyone that. Any of it. But... I had no idea you were going through it *that* badly. I'm really sorry, Lydia. I didn't mean to throw accusations at you and make shit harder. I hope you know that. I really was just looking out for Jake."

I feel my emotions betraying me, that familiar lump growing in my throat, and the backs of my eyes starting to burn with the threat of tears. So instead, I tear my eyes from his, looking down at the floor myself, at my own socked feet.

"No, yeah, of course, I get it."

He sighs heavily, making me look back up at him, only to see that his eyes are closed again, rubbing the bridge of his nose.

"It's just... I don't know how much of my sob story you know, but I think I can understand the whole hiding-and-shitty-biological-parents thing more than you know." He looks at me, and there's a hint of pain in them I've never seen from Tripp. "I mean, you know I don't talk to my parents, and that's because they're homophobic assholes. And I'm bi, and I wasn't ever gonna tell them, but my brother found out and, well, did. They laid off a little on the comments once I started dating Imani, but then things still didn't get better, so I pulled my grades up, got accepted to college, and met Jake. He was the first person I really came out to after my parents, and I was terrified. And I know there're so many people who don't care, but, like, it's horrible each time. Like, I always brace myself for people to react like my parents did. So, I think I get it, kinda.

"But, anyway, once Jake found out about everything, he didn't hesitate to invite me to his house, every single school break. The Hamptons became my family, fast. Joanne accepted me without a second thought, like I was just another son of hers, and treated me more like a son than my own mother ever did.

"So, when I saw how close you 'n Aiden were getting... and it seemed secretive, I just—I don't even know, man. I jumped to conclusions because *I* felt betrayed, *for* Jake. He's been nothing but good to me, especially, but to everyone around him, too. I couldn't see him get hurt, so I lashed out. But, anyway, don't worry." He cracks a smile. "I'm in therapy for all that."

I stare at him, unsure of what to say. This was the last thing I expected from this conversation, even more than being caught off guard by Imani knowing—to be leveled with, to be understood?

Aiden knew, understood how it felt to move through life with a huge secret, knowing you aren't and will never be the same as your peers, no matter how hard you try.

Jake stood by my side, suspecting something was amiss, but waiting until I was ready to open up to him, caring about me throughout it all. And then, he accepted me for who I am. He *loves* me for who—what—I am.

Imani knew, too, and accepted it, all the while waiting until I was comfortable and ready to tell her.

And Tripp... Tripp understands the hiding, the family complications, the fear of others' reactions. And he wasn't disgusted with me, didn't laugh or accuse me of lying.

I blink back my tears.

Maybe Bram was wrong. Because no, none of these people are *exactly* like me, but why do they need to be? Why can't we just understand and accept each other in the ways that work for us? I do have a place—with them.

"Aw, c'mon, man, don't cry. I don't care that you're a vampire or part vampire or whatever. I just can't deal with crying. I take back what I said. I'd rather you pass out than cry."

I laugh, instead, rubbing my eyes, and Tripp chuckles, too, before tilting his head back and finishing off his wine.

"Now, before I bombard you with questions, I need to do something."

I watch as he walks away, back into his room, and I see Aiden's door crack open. He peeks through, smiling and giving me a thumbs up.

I figured he'd be eavesdropping. Hell, I would've, too.

It feels like the ton of bricks that has been sitting on my chest all year is gone—mostly. There's still the ache when I think about Bram and Genevieve and Xavier, but that's something for Roarke, and maybe for Aiden's parents.

But especially not for now.

Tripp comes out of his room, waving a fifty-dollar bill. He glances behind him, tilting his head at Aiden.

"C'mon, Swanson. I have a bet to fulfil."

"You still have the bet going?" Aiden emerges fully from his room; I give him a look, confused, but he ignores me as we —as I, blindly—follow Tripp out of the apartment.

"Well, I've never been proved wrong until now, have I?"

Crossing the hall and knocking on my door, Tripp winks at me, holding up the money. "Thanks a lot for this, Ross. I'm out fifty bucks now."

Imani opens the door, her curly hair down. Tripp doesn't say anything; instead, just holds up the bill, and Imani grins, snatching it from his hand.

"Oh, my God, I forgot about this! I love you so much," she laughs, wrapping her arm around Tripp's neck as he leans in to kiss her cheek. She grins at me over his shoulder. "When we first met, we started talking because he made fun of whatever vampire book I was reading at the time, and I told him that if it ever came out that vampires were real, I wanted fifty bucks. And he agreed."

I smile at her. "You're welcome, then."

I glance at Aiden, who mouths,

You did it.

I smile at him, fangs and all, and his eyes soften, something in them making my own heart twist.

"You guys are all hanging out without me?"

The voice makes me tear my eyes away from Aiden, turning to see Jake walking down the hall.

"That's what happens when you betray us for your other friends, Hamp," Tripp calls, Imani still in his arms. I smile at how cute they are, and Imani catches my eye and grins back.

It feels like the beginning of the school year, but better, this time. Because now, I'm not *Imani's roommate Lydia,* and I might not even be just *Lydia.* I'm *Lydia-who-just-so-happens-to-be-part-vampire.*

And that's okay.

CHAPTER FORTY-EIGHT

When Jake suggests another beach trip for the weekend before we all move out for the end of the semester and after Aiden's moved his stuff to his new apartment—a cute little one-bedroom we all go with him to see—I'm not as hesitant to agree as I was months ago.

The sun is still too bright, the sound of laughter and heartbeats and roaring waves and cawing birds overheard still fill my ears, and the sand is still too sandy.

And I'm not as anxious as I was the first time around. Because they know, and they accept me for it, and I'm still here with them.

And I'm able to, when Tripp casts me a sidelong glance as I start to pull my t-shirt over my head, joke and tell him not to worry, that I'm not going to turn into ash. The corner of his mouth tugs upward into his crooked smile, and he says, "Oh, thank God. I was worried about the cleanup."

He runs off toward the water before Imani can scold him.

Jake asks me if I'm coming, peeling off his own shirt as Imani runs off after Tripp, and when I tell him that I am, he runs after her.

I glance at Aiden, who's already looking at me.

I look back at him, at his unruly curls, at the freckles that cover his cheekbones right under his eyes that are really only visible in the sun, and at the way he smiles at me, slowly, his eyes crinkling at the corners, all the tension in my body releasing.

"Now that you've told everyone about what you are," he says, "we can work on number two on the list."

I raise my eyebrows at him, trying to fight back my smile. "What *list*?"

He grins. "Your list of secrets. Now, we have to get you to learn how to swim."

My eyes widen. I forgot I told him that.

"Hell, no." Aiden starts to laugh, finally moving to take off his own shirt. I look away, towards the lake, where Imani, Jake, and Tripp are all a way in, dunking under the water and splashing each other and laughing. "I've gone this long without knowing how to. I think I'm fine. But you wanna go out there?"

He looks at me, grinning as he says, "Not really."

I laugh, and something softens in his expression as he holds out his hand to me, palm up. I rest my hand on top, curling my fingers around his, and we take our first step into the bone-chilling water.

Together.

CHAPTER FORTY-NINE

"I can't believe this."

The next Thursday, after a week full of exam stress, Imani sits on her bed, far enough back so that her feet aren't even touching the ground. We both look around the room, which is, quite honestly, depressing.

Gone are the pictures and the lights and the TV and Imani's pink rug I got so used to seeing; the room is once again empty and white and boring, for the most part, besides my laptop and notebook and a few other things I need for my last final tonight. Boxes are piled in the corners, and while it looks like it did when I first moved in, the atmosphere is completely different.

I was optimistic then, I guess. Anxious, mostly, but optimistic and glad to be able to take control for once. Little did I know how quickly that would all go to shit, or how I could have avoided a lot of the pain I went through by just telling everyone about what I am.

I really do have some of the best friends. And I'm not quite ready for us all to go different directions for the whole summer. Aiden is closest, which is great of course, and Jake and Tripp aren't *too* far away, but Imani is going to be all the way across the country, and I'm going to miss her more than I had anticipated—especially now that I've let my guard down with her in the last week, more than it's been down the entire year.

"I know," I say. "Me neither."

She frowns, and I'm worried she's going to cry, because if she does, I'm not sure I'll be able to properly comfort her. But at that moment, I'm saved, because there's a knock on the door.

When I open it, I smile wide at Jake and Aiden. Jake comes in first, giving me a quick kiss on the forehead before passing me to hug Imani, who's definitely on the verge of tears. Aiden and I look at each other before he tilts his chin toward Imani, who's wiping away tears as she pulls back from Jake. I hear them talking in low voices:

"Has he texted you back yet?"

"No," Jake replies. "No, I haven't heard from him since he left for his last final this morning."

Imani sighs. "Damn. I wanted to say bye one last time before I have to leave for my flight, but at this rate..."

"I'm gonna miss you, Lyds, but I'm not gonna cry about it," Aiden says quietly, and I smile at him, something squeezing my heart at his own soft smile, and the stutter in his heartbeat.

I'm gonna miss him. I'm *really* gonna miss him.

Wordlessly, I step forward and wrap my arms around his waist. He doesn't hesitate to hug me back, and as we embrace, I feel it. I feel whatever it is he's feeling, lingering at the edges of my skin, something strong and safe and relaxing, and if Imani and Jake weren't standing on the other side of the room, I might just let myself stay in his arms a little longer.

My cheeks burn as I pull away, and I pray it's not noticeable.

"You better come visit," he adds.

"Oh, I will." I pause, then add, trying to hold back my smile, "You really think you'd be lucky enough to go an entire three months without me bothering you?"

Aiden grins. He's still not convinced he has emotion powers, but I am. I can only hope that when we ask his parents for help about the whole Bram situation, Aiden's glamour comes up, too.

We agreed to push off our talks further, with finals and move out and all. Since Aiden will still be living in the city, it'll be easy to meet up with Roarke, but I know why he's pushing off his talk with his parents.

I get it, I do. But I keep reminding him that I'll be there for him, with him, every step of the way.

He glances at Jake and Imani—Imani's smiling, though there's still worry pulling her brows together.

"You never *bother* me, Lydia," he says, only looking back at me when he says my name, and sure enough, I'm betrayed by tears pricking at the backs of my eyes when he adds, "And you know that has to be true."

"Don't get all sentimental on me just because we're gonna be an hour apart instead of five steps," I say, swallowing past the growing lump in my throat. I definitely wouldn't have gotten through this year had it not been for him.

And to think, everyone knew we'd get along before we even met, but little did I know he'd become my best friend.

After we got rid of a body together.

A body of someone who wasn't even *dead*.

I'm never gonna get over that.

But even so, I'm done with them. I don't have to worry about that anymore, now that everyone knows and I don't have to keep my need for blood a secret. We'll tell Aiden's parents, and Roarke, and I'll never talk to Bram again, and it'll be okay.

It's what needs to be done.

"Technically, it's more than five steps since my room is on the far side of the apartment, but..."

"Shut *up*," I laugh, and Aiden grins at me, his nose scrunching slightly.

"I'm gonna have to leave," Imani sighs, walking across the room to us. She stops next to Aiden, leaning against him and giving him a side hug, and he hugs her back. "Let me know if anyone hears from Tripp, will you? I'm sure he just let his phone die, but still..."

"Of course," Jake says. "I'm sure he did, but I get it. I'll text you right away." He steps forward to give her another hug when she lets go of Aiden, who side steps away. "Have a safe flight. You need help carrying stuff down?"

She shakes her head. "No, no, my parents are coming up. They should be here soon." She pauses, a frown tugging at the corners of her mouth. "I'm gonna miss you guys so—"

"I've already had enough sentimentality for today," Aiden pipes up, holding up his hands. "Sorry."

They all laugh, but when Aiden smiles specifically at me, something twists inside of me. I look at Jake, who smiles at me and tugs me over to his side, his arm settling over my shoulders. Ever since he told me he loves me on our anniversary, he hasn't said it too many times since—I think he doesn't want to overwhelm me. I also think he's waiting for me to say it, but...

I can't bring myself to.

I care about him deeply, and now that we're going to be doing long distance for the summer, I just...

No. I'll worry about that later.

It feels a little wrong, having our little goodbye hug circle without Tripp—who I feel significantly more comfortable with now that he knows, and he's even seemed a little more comfortable with *me*, now that he let down some of his guard, too.

It feels nice to not have to feel like I'm tiptoeing around him anymore. Or anyone.

Dad is coming first thing tomorrow morning to help me move out, and I've been talking with my friends—Aiden specifically—about whether I should come clean to him about the specifics of what's been going down since, well, Xavier. Since I haven't seen him, it was a lot easier to hide my depressive episode because of Xavier from him, and then there's Bram, and, well...

I'm worried about how he'll feel if I tell him about Genevieve.

Because I know if I felt how I did, he'll feel ten times worse, and I don't know that I want to put that on him.

But at the same time, now that I know how good it feels to be free, I don't want any more secrets. Not between me and my friends, not between me and Dad.

Besides the secret I'm keeping for Aiden. Because that's not mine to tell.

Once Imani brings her parents upstairs, the boys and I help them move her stuff downstairs, and once we're done, she hugs us each again, fully in tears this time. And after she's gone, and it hits me that I'm not going to see her again for a few months—unless she visits this summer—something aches in my chest.

Jake is leaving tomorrow, too, and I'm actually looking forward to seeing Joanne and Anabelle again, now that I'm... okay. And Aiden... well, Aiden's technically moved out, but for the last few days of finals, he was still using the dorm. So it'll just be a matter of saying bye to him. Which will still be hard. Even with him being only an hour away.

Aiden, Jake, and I head back upstairs together, and instead of going back to my depressing room, I head into their apartment with them to kill some time before I have to leave for my exam.

Jake suggests we watch a movie, to have "one last movie night before we all go home."

I agree, even though I *probably* should study for my last exam. Jake sends Tripp a text in case his phone *isn't* dead, telling him our plans and that if he hurries back from his exam, he won't miss much of whatever we pick.

We settle onto the couch with me in the middle. Aiden's in charge of the remote, propping his feet on the coffee table, turning on Netflix, and scrolling quickly enough through the categories that he must have something in mind.

Jake's body starts to shake with silent, barely suppressed laughter as Aiden makes his choice.

"Wow," I say as he hits play on the first *Twilight* movie. "*Wow*, Aiden."

"Imani's gonna be pissed we waited 'til she left," Jake says, squeezing my hand.

I grin and shake my head, my eyes on the screen, but enjoying the feeling of sitting here, between two people who I deeply care about, and who care about me, too, despite what I am. *Because* of what I am, because it's a part of *me*.

And because they still love me for what I am, maybe I can learn to, as well.

EPILOGUE

IT'S A BEAUTIFUL NIGHT, and a beautiful end to the semester.

It's going to be weird, going back to my room and seeing an empty side of the room for a night, but at least I'll get to see the boys one last time tomorrow morning before we all leave.

Plus, I feel good about my psychology final, so I'm in high spirits for once as I cross the street to the sidewalk that will lead me to my dorm building. Despite it being only around nine thirty on a Thursday night, the streets are relatively empty and a little quieter than usual, but that's fine with me.

I see my building, looming high in the night sky, and I breathe in the crisp, fresh air as I start to cross the alley that sits between my dorm and the building behind it. Maybe we can stay up tonight, put on a movie—*not* another *Twilight* movie, if I have any say in the matter—order some pizza or something to celebrate the end of the semester—

Someone steps out of the alley right in front of me, so quickly that I, being lost in my thoughts, almost bump into them. I mutter an apology under my breath, trying to step around them, until they grab my arm, and a wave of panic shoots through me as I look up into their face.

My breath catches in my throat.

There's something wild in his eyes I've never seen before, but it's when he smiles at me that a wave of terror really shoots through me. Because he smiles at me—that signature smirk of his—with a sinister mouthful of blood-covered teeth, including new, slightly extended, pointed canines.

"Tripp," I say, but he only pulls me closer to him, and I can practically feel the hunger radiating off of him.

He just continues to smile, as if I'm going to be his next meal, even as he says, "Hey, Lydia."

ACKNOWLEDGMENTS

This book was born in 2021 in my sophomore year dorm room, and was written and rewritten multiple times by the time I graduated college in May 2023. While I'd attempted to write a novel and so many short stories by that point, I fell in love with this story and these characters in a way unlike anything I'd written before. It's still so surreal to me that it's made it to this point, and I have a lot of people to thank for that.

First of all, thank you to my family, who's been there for every point of this journey and always been supportive of my writing. This story wouldn't have happened had I not chosen to major in creative writing and move into a Chicago dorm at 18, but it especially wouldn't have happened had I not been supported from when I was handwriting and illustrating stories about the Mario Brothers on wide-ruled paper at eight years old. Thank you, thank you, thank you.

Thank you to Abigail Wild, who helped make my dream of becoming a published author come true; my editors, Siri Mossblad and Brittany McMunn, for helping me make this story and the writing the best it could be; and the rest of the Wild Ink family for your enthusiasm and support.

Thank you to my college friends and roommates. Your guys' constant love and belief in me and my writing inspired so many scenes in this book and it truly wouldn't have evolved into what it is today without you bringing me out of my shell and listening to me rattle off plot ideas on the kitchen floor. You guys are the best.

Thank you to all my former classmates and my former professor Ann Hemenway for helping workshop the early version of this book in some of my classes, as well as my beta readers—your responses to this story and my writing helped drive me through the query trenches.

And last but not least, thank YOU (yes, you!) for reading. Every ounce of excitement, encouragement, and support I've received during this journey has meant more to me than I can possibly express.

ABOUT THE AUTHOR

Avery Timmons is an Illinois-based author holding a Bachelor of Arts in creative writing with a concentration in fiction from Columbia College Chicago. She has had numerous short stories and photographs published in literary magazines and anthologies. THICKER THAN WATER is her debut novel.

Regardless of genre, Avery loves to write about protagonists who are trying to figure out who they want to be and their place in the world. She often draws inspiration from the other things she loves besides books: music, theater, and the city of Chicago.

www.ingramcontent.com/pod-product-compliance
Lightning Source LLC
Chambersburg PA
CBHW031202310726
48969CB00001B/180